FORESTS
OF THE
NIGHT

ELLIOTT ARNOLD

FORESTS OF THE NIGHT

CHARLES SCRIBNER'S SONS
NEW YORK

FOR PETER BRUNSWICK

To Whom Some Of
This May Be Oddly
Familiar

FORESTS
OF THE
NIGHT

Prologue

✠ ✠ ✠

THE WINDOWS OF THE BASEMENT ROOM WERE JUST ABOVE THE level of the quiet, residential street and the rain falling on the German city and on the valley splashed against the opaque glass.

"Before I kill you, Helmut, you will tell me what you have said to the police president," Werner said. "You should still have enough loyalty to do that."

"Don't joke," Helmut said. "Don't talk about killing me."

"Do you believe I joke, Helmut?"

"Werner, we're friends. Of course you joke. But stop it."

"What have you been saying to Police President Eckardt?"

Outside there was a muffled rumble of thunder as though from a distant battlefield.

The basement was dressed as a library, a very luxurious library. The floor was covered with a carpet the color of burgundy wine. The walls were lined with books. There was a large desk with a green leather top. There were deep leather chairs. Three lamps gave off a soft and agreeable light.

There were fourteen men in the room. They were all quietly and expensively dressed. They were all in their middle twenties or early thirties except Werner Hausmann who was thirty-seven. Several of the men wore horn-rimmed glasses which made them appear even younger. Some smoked cigarettes, two or three puffed quietly on pipes. There were no cigar smokers. Among the men were three or four business executives, two attorneys, a doctor and a surgeon, a real estate developer. They were all regarded by associates as being very bright and it was considered they would go far.

Werner Hausmann, who was seated behind the desk, said, "Helmut, please tell me why you went so often to see Herr Eckardt."

"Two or three times, Werner. That's not so often, two or three times."

"Correct. You went to his office three times."

"That's not so often."

"In the beginning you did that. Then you stopped."

"There you are, Werner," Helmut said.

Hausmann picked up a piece of paper from his desk. "You met him after those three times in the Riemenschneider room at the Mainfränkisches Museum."

"By chance, Werner."

"Herr Eckardt had no previous reputation as an art lover. Nor had you." Werner Hausmann looked at the paper. "You also had a drink together at the Lämmle bar."

"For God's sake, Werner! People have a right to drink. There is no sin in that."

"No. You also by chance happened to find yourselves in the lobby of the Deutscher Hof at the same time. You chanced to encounter each other in the Kaisersaal at the Residenz. And by the sheerest coincidence you both happened to go at the same moment to the same font in the Marienkapelle." Hausmann raised his eyes. "In a church? Sacrilege."

Helmut Dietrich looked at his friends. They sat silently and listened to what was being said with the same attentiveness they had given to their professors in the classrooms of their universities not many years before.

2

"What is it you and Police President Eckardt have so much to talk about?" Hausmann asked.

"I'm a lawyer," Helmut said. "My work has crossed that of Eckardt's. If we happen to meet we have things in common to talk about."

"Of course," Hausmann said. He took a cigarette from a slim, gold case lying open on the desk and lit it with a gold lighter. He pushed the open case toward Helmut, who took a cigarette. Hausmann lit it for him.

"You don't practice criminal law, Helmut," Hausmann said.

Helmut, inhaling smoke, started to cough. Hausmann waited for him to finish.

"Helmut, you don't live here in Würzburg and you haven't been with us very long," Hausmann said. "How did you happen to join us?"

"I believe in what you stand for," Helmut said. "I believe in what the party stands for."

"Good. And you understand perfectly that we do nothing illegal. We are recognized as a legitimate political party with legitimate political goals that do not, as we define them publicly, in any way conflict with the Federal constitution. The police president has a file on everything I have said in open meetings, here in Würzburg and elsewhere in Germany. Herr Eckardt is a very busy man, Helmut. What was it he didn't know that you could have told him?"

Helmut Dietrich said nothing.

"Now, on the other hand, things have been said among us in private, because we trust each other," Hausmann said. "Things which at the present time are for our ears alone and not for the ears of the police president. Is that what you talked about with Herr Eckardt?"

When Helmut said nothing, Hausmann asked, "Do you believe in what we want to do?"

"Yes."

"What did you tell the police president? Before you die you should at the very least tell us that."

3

"Stop talking about my dying."

"What did you tell the police president?"

"We talked."

"About what?"

"Anything. Everything. It's hard to say exactly what."

"Is that all you have to say?"

"Yes."

"You are certain of that?"

"There is nothing else to say. Now let's stop all this nonsense."

"Anything done for the good of the party would meet with your approval, would it not?"

"Yes, of course. You know that."

Werner Hausmann stood up. The other men rose immediately. After a moment Helmut got up slowly from his chair.

Hausmann went to the door of the cellar library and opened it and held it open until all the men, including Helmut Dietrich, went out. He turned off the lights from a central switch and closed the door and locked it.

He went up into the street. The early spring night had closed in. It was still raining hard. The large drops splattered on the cobblestones. The air smelled fresh and clean from the rain.

One of the young men ran to a Mercedes parked in the street and opened a rear door. He climbed in. Helmut was guided to the car by another man, a little quickly perhaps, but perhaps not, considering the rainfall. He climbed in next to the first man and the man who took him there by the arm got in next to him.

Hausmann, hatless, since that was part of his image, walked unhurriedly to the car and sat down behind the wheel.

Other cars followed Hausmann's car and soon they were outside the city on a small, old country road. Nobody spoke.

"Where are we going?" Helmut asked.

Hausmann turned his head slightly to answer him. There was at that moment a flash of lightning that painted his profile in fire. "You will see, Helmut. It will come as a surprise."

"A surprise? What kind of a surprise?" Helmut looked at his friend on his right. "What kind of a surprise, Gerhard?" He turned to the left. "Hans?"

No one replied.

The rain streamed on the windshield. The wipers swung back and forth uselessly. Hausmann drove carefully and with skill.

They rode for about half an hour during which nothing was said and then they approached an old, walled town and there was another stroke of lightning that illuminated the window in the wall from which boiling pitch had once been poured down on invaders.

Hausmann slowed down. The streets of the ancient little town were empty in the downpour. Another bolt of lightning created a medieval scene and then left it in darkness and the thunder that followed was like a roll of drums.

Hausmann drove to the end of the town, abandoned now as though by pestilence, turned into a side stteet and drove up a slight incline. He stopped at a clearing below one part of the town wall. He turned off the car lights. The men got out into the rain.

One by one the other cars pulled up and were parked and one by one the headlights were extinguished. The young men gathered round.

"Helmut," Hausmann said.

"Yes, Werner."

"In the Führer's time they swore blood oaths on their daggers in the dark of night."

Helmut was silent.

"We know how foolish that would be today," Hausmann said. "It served a purpose then but it would be foolish today."

"Yes."

"But although we don't stand together at midnight and pledge our loyalties we do it in our hearts."

5

"Yes, Werner. I know that."

"We swear within ourselves. In our souls we swear the same things they did and because it is said privately within us it does not mean it has less force."

"Why are you telling me this, Werner?"

"You swore that oath."

"Yes."

"It's a pity, isn't it?"

"What is a pity? Why are you telling me this? Why are we here?"

"It is a pity, Helmut, that I am required to tell you anything at all," Hausmann said.

The cleared area was at that moment riven by two jagged streaks in the sky and in the terse, manic thrusts of light Helmut Dietrich saw a stake, the base of which was covered with tarpaulin. The night went black again so fast it seemed an illusion.

"The only thing is the party," Hausmann said. "Anything that is good for the party is good, and anything that is bad for the party is bad. It is not shouted. It is not paraded. But it is so. It is so just as though it were said in a stadium in Nuremberg to many thousands of people, to the world. That is our strength. We are still small. But we know the party is supreme."

Another flash of lightning seared Hausmann's face and then cast it back into the darkness.

"That is the power no one else in Germany possesses. We are not politicians although we shall achieve our ends by political means. We are dedicated, devoted, selfless men with a mission to perform—first for Germany and then for all mankind."

Werner Hausmann made a slight gesture and two men lifted Helmut under the arms and another man produced a flashlight and Helmut saw that what he had seen so briefly before, what he had thought was a trick of his eyes, was there.

"Werner," he said.

"In the end you are serving the party," Hausmann said.

6

"That is the final gift I give to you. In future others will hesitate before they betray me."

Helmut was led to the stake. He tried to pull away. "Werner!"

"No one will hear you, Helmut."

Helmut fought to get loose. The men who held him ignored him. They carried him to the stake.

"Werner!" Helmut screamed. "Someone! Help me! For the love of God!"

His words were lost as they left his mouth, lost in the wind, drowned in the rain, and he was taken to the stake and tied to it.

"Werner, for the love of God!" he cried out. "Are you mad?"

"You must feel a deep sense of satisfaction, Helmut, knowing that your final act in this world was to help the cause you believe in."

"Werner," Helmut said.

"Who knows, one day you may be a party hero. A martyr always makes a good hero. We will change the story of course. We will put it so that it was they who did this to you. You will go down in history."

From his elevation on the stake Helmut looked down and saw the tarpaulin pulled away and he saw the straw and the faggots as he had seen it only in films or in pictures in old books. He saw his friends pour liquid from cans on the straw and the faggots and then strike matches and despite the rain the straw took fire immediately and the wood caught on and in the yellow glare of the flames he saw his friends standing and watching.

"Werner!" he cried out. "Gerhard! Hans! Wilhelm!"

He called out the names of his friends and then the fire reached up to him and he screamed and he lived for a little while.

Police President Johannes Eckardt chewed on an artificial metal cigarette and looked closely at the charred body that had been fished out of the pool. It was unrecognizable. It might have been a man or a woman or a child or an animal.

He examined the blackened thing, soaked and dripping, and he looked again at the burned remains of the stake.

"Isn't this where they used to burn witches?" his laboratory specialist asked him.

"Yes." Eckardt looked toward the town where policemen were holding back curious people.

"I remember when I was a child," the expert said. "I used to live in this town. I remember my father telling me that in the old days they used to burn witches on the stake here and then dump them into that pool and if they survived it meant God had judged them not to be witches after all."

"Yes," the police president said. "That was what was done."

"But that was hundreds of years ago," the expert said.

Once more the police president bent down and inspected the lump that might have been anything.

"I guess this one was a witch all right," the laboratory specialist said.

The police president straightened. "Try to establish identification."

He went back to his car. He knew the order was unnecessary. Worse, he knew it was useless.

1

✠ ✠ ✠

IF HE HAD WANTED TO NOW BAUER COULD NOT HAVE CHANGED his mind. He could not have remained on the train.

The other passengers getting off were stampeding in the aisle, silent, grunting, wheezing, sweating, remnants of cigarettes dangling, cigars clamped by desperate teeth, all gripped by terror that the train would move on before they could climb down, bearing them to some strange, unwanted, fearful place, such as Kitzingen, the next stop, twenty-three kilometers away.

He was carried along as though caught in a hurtling of logs in a roiling strait, shoved, driven, elbowed. He could have passed out, he could have died; it would not have been discovered until he was disgorged from the carriage door and emptied upon the station platform.

Finally he was able to descend the three iron steps, gripping the railing with his free hand. Unaccountably unsmothered on the platform, he saw the conductor on the verge of apoplexy holding a thick, massive pocket watch in one hand, waving the other hand in frantic rage. The train from Frankfurt had been one minute and thirty-six seconds late in reaching Würzburg.

Bauer stepped to one side and drew in breath. He put down his small valise and let the others pass him by. Off the train, free now from the domination of the conductor, who gave his signal and who climbed back aboard, looking fiercely at his watch as though it were looking fiercely at him, the men and women still hurried.

It was German, Bauer thought. It was German and it made sense and it should have in no way surprised him. Moments such as these, spent in useless transit, between here and there, were wasted, unproductive, almost sinful and must be minimized.

Bauer wanted a cigarette. Why had he quit? Was another year or two or three or four worth it? Did he enjoy being alive that much? And what if it turned out in the end that they had all been wrong?

He raised his eyes and looked at the sign, which was in Gothic lettering, as had been all the station signs: **Würzburg**. Just the name.

He felt nothing of course. He had willed that he would feel nothing. He had no talent for feeling. That had abandoned him long before, with other things. It was like a limb unused, atrophied, no longer even with vestigial life. He could not, for instance, feel hatred for the Germans who rushed past him, not even for those who obviously were old enough to have been here, then. He had not felt it when he stepped off the plane at Frankfurt and touched German land for the first time since then; he had not felt it in the bus that took him from the airport to the railroad station in Frankfurt, surrounded for the first time since his childhood with Germans, German faces, German words.

But he had not known how it would be when he would arrive here, Würzburg. It was a much more complex name than Germany; deeper, with its own tendrils. And yet, he felt nothing. He took that as a kind of victory.

The last of the passengers passed him, still rushing toward that deadline they dared not violate. In passing, people glanced at him. First incuriously at his face, which was not a face that told them anything; then with perhaps a little more interest at his clothing, which said plainly that he was a foreigner, an alien; finally, almost with a sense of triumph at his shoes. Bauer understood all the looks, all the nuances, all the conclusions.

He was dressed, quite well dressed, as an American, which, legally at least, he now was. He had selected the clothing he had brought with him with the idea of being as inconspicuous as possible; he wanted no particular attention paid to him. But from the moment he had set foot in Germany he had realized how far he had drifted from his birthright. He was wearing a tweed jacket and gray flannel slacks. And the shoes. American shoes. American shoes as identifiable as such as though they carried American flags and played "The Star-Spangled Banner."

He looked down the now almost empty station and he saw at last the sign, **Würzburg**, without consciously, deliberately looking for it, and he felt something pass through him, not a feeling perhaps, just something; the affirmation that he was there, at last was there. He weathered that.

The platform, the station itself was new; well, new since the war. The old station had been totally destroyed. He had seen it being destroyed from a few thousand feet in the air and now, standing there in the summer closeness, he remembered the unbearable division of himself on that night, the part of him in the tail turret of the Liberator, the part of him in the flaming station that made a small part of the consummate hell.

It had taken him how long, a quarter of a century, to come down those few thousand feet?

He picked up his valise and walked slowly toward the station. The platform now was empty. There was on it a sense of vacuum, as though the atmosphere had been taken away by the hurrying passengers and nothing had been left behind. Or was it that the vacuum was in his own mind?

He reached the stairway and walked down to the tunnel that connected all the tracks. An arrow indicated the way out. He looked at the amusing, almost frivolous advertisements on the walls, restaurants, hotels, department stores, all produced with a charm and grace that was at the same time so typically and so atypically German. There was always in the dark depths an elf to be found.

He climbed a flight of stairs and found himself in the station that had replaced the old station and he discovered he was not quite prepared for it. The old station, as he remembered it from the times his parents had taken him there to greet or bid farewell to friends or relatives, had been a proper German station, such as most of the other stations he had seen between Frankfurt and here, heavy, Victorian, a secure, massive, reassuring structure, exactly right to welcome the new arrival, exactly right to speed him away.

It had been replaced by a matchbox of metal and glass, by a modern station restaurant, by little shops chiefly engaged in unloading gimcracks on tourists. It was noisy. It was crowded. There was a blending of voices that lay in the air like a bank of smoke. There were, among the good, stolid Franconian citizens, waiting placidly and patiently with their suitcases of dubious durability, a large smattering of long-haired hippies, knapsacks on their backs or at their feet, chattering with a unisexed animation, the new world people in their beards and hair and rigidly prescribed uniforms, their eccentricities, their manner and mannerisms, as inflexibly ordained, as minutely particularized, as immutable as those governed by the code of conduct laid down by the German General Staff.

After the first impact, he felt a sense of relief, and he found himself grinning. He had dreaded this moment. He had known the station was destroyed and yet it had not been destroyed in his mind and memory. It had remained there as one of the very close, intimate, unforgotten places, associated with special occasions of great excitement. What a marvelous release to find nothing left to remember. It was splendid, he thought, when ghosts attended to their own dissolution.

He started out of the station. He found himself facing the old remembered square, with the old remembered fountain, and that was wrong because surely the fountain must have been consumed in the flames along with all the rest. And something else was wrong; he strained to discover what it was.

Then he did. The old station level was a story above the ground. It delivered its travelers onto a terrace atop a grand staircase down to the street. That gave one an elevation to look across the square with its sparkling fountain, across the little park, to the buildings on the ring, to the foot of the Kaiserstrasse.

The present station was on street level. The fountain was there, water falling exactly as he had remembered it. There was something else different. What was it? He could see the fountain but he could not hear it. He frowned. Then he heard it again, the clang and the metallic clatter of a tram. He stared. It had been a long time ago. But he could remember it now without flaw. The fountain, the sound of the water falling, and what else? He heard the horns of taxis and of small private cars.

What else? The cobblestones were still there and then he remembered how there used to be the horse-drawn carriages gathered around the fountain. It came back to him now with the force of a blow, the ammonia smell of the horses, the smell of leather, the sounds of the horses' hooves striking the cobbles, the drivers waiting for fares, gathered round, talking, smoking. The creaking of the harnesses and in the winter the blankets on the seats and the gusts of vapor from the horses' mouths.

He breathed in deeply again. Then he looked beyond the square and he frowned. The hotels, the buildings were as he had remembered them. But that could not be. They had been destroyed. On that night they had been destroyed and he had watched, his eyes dry; bitter, proud, sad, triumphant, ripped apart inside, all at the same time. He was so young then, how old?—fifteen—sixteen? He had lied so much about his age then he could not now remember.

He shivered in the warm air. It was too much as it had been. The picture had been totally eliminated and yet in a

13

large part it was still there. It was as though it had never happened on that spring night in 1945 when men created an inferno and burned off the earth's face a city other men had created long before.

He could hear his father's bantering voice and the laughter of his mother that rose in the air like notes of music, the love in the greetings and farewells, their own departures and returns. The railroad station had always been the commencement of the freedom of summer. His father always had some trip, even if only a small one, planned for the end of school.

He picked up his bag and started walking past the stores that lined either side of the entrance to the station. Travel agencies. Sports shops. Magazines, newspapers, cigarettes, cigars. Advertisements for the opera and symphony and plays.

He saw a taxi. He raised his hand and went to the cab and got inside. The driver looked him over briefly, professionally, his eyes ending, as always, on the American shoes.

He got in and gave the driver the name of the hotel.

The driver nodded, faced front. He shifted gears and released the clutch and the car moved forward. His movements, Bauer noticed, were quick, purposeful, with military preciseness and a kind of panache. Not the lazy Würzburg way he seemed to remember.

The driver passed through the small park and entered upon the busy Kaiserstrasse. (After all these years, after the attenuated thousand-year Reich, the main thoroughfare again, everywhere, was the Kaiser's street. Had this for a time been Hitlerstrasse? In any event, the man with the spiked moustache had won his own back. Would the street and others like it, Bauer wondered, ever bear the name of someone who had not thundered?) He saw that it was crowded, as he remembered it always was, but that something new had been imposed upon it, it now was a one-way street.

He peered out of the window and he began to tremble. In this bright sunlight, in the noise and rumble of traffic, in the sounds of conversations, he felt he was on the periphery of a nightmare. Everything, everything, each shop, department store, restaurant, was as he had remembered it. That camera store. That food store. That sporting-goods house. That optical shop. That butcher, the wursts hanging in the window. It was all as before.

If this were not the illusion, he told himself, then the fire-storm, the holocaust, then that must have been the illusion.

The driver, pausing in the traffic, turned round again. His face was small, neat, composed. His eyes, under thin, blond brows, were sharp. Not sharp in a ferrety way, but acute and keen. He was about fifty, Bauer thought, and the package was tidy and neat and fresh.

The driver asked, "American?"

Bauer shook his head and the driver studied him for a moment longer and then turned back to his wheel.

To escape from the traumatic vision of the street: the shops, the shops that never should have been there, the shops that should have been other shops, different, altogether different, Bauer tried to imagine what the Deutscher Hof would now be like. It had been a lovely hotel before the destruction, and there had been a destruction, despite what his eyes kept denying, there had been a destruction, and he had chosen to stay there because it was the hotel where his father always had put up friends when they were too numerous to stay at the Bauer home.

. . . A banquet . . . huge, silver tureens, waiters in knee-pants and white silk stockings like waiters in an old painting, almost as many waiters as there were guests . . . what was the banquet for? . . . was it something for friends, or something given by his father in his capacity as city councilor? . . . he had been allowed to see just so much and the maid took him home . . . he had wanted to stay . . . one day, she told him, that one day he would be grown up and would not be taken away from something as magical as this . . . turning, trying not to cry at his disappointment, the last thing he saw was his mother, she was wearing a long, dark plum-colored dress, a glass of champagne in her hand, laughing at something being said to her by an officer in a white uniform

with blinding decorations . . . it must have been an official
dinner, with the uniform, but then his father had himself
fought in the army of the Kaiser and had once worn just such
a uniform with almost as many decorations so it could have
been a friend, an old army friend . . .

"I suppose the British and the Americans considered it
was necessary," the driver was saying, in English.

He had an accent, Bauer heard, but the English was excellent. "I beg your pardon."

"To have destroyed this beautiful city." The driver
hunched his shoulders. "Since the British and the Americans,
we always are assured, are humane, then they must have had
an excellent reason, not?"

"I wouldn't know," Bauer said.

Had there been a reason, a justifiable military reason, or
had it only been an act of terrorism? There had been a reason
for him, a reason so perfect it seemed contrived, a conclusion
too conveniently plotted, an unreasonably balanced *quid pro
quo*. But had there indeed been a reason in the prosecution
of the war, by then such a short time away from being ended?
They had at the time been told there was, and some important details were given, because even then, after all the
years, there were flying men who still nurtured principle, who
required that a target be militarily warrantable. But had these
reasons been valid? Had there really been any military reason
to destroy this city?

"It was a great personal shock to me," the driver said. "I
was not here at the time. I was away from Würzburg for a
long time. I was on the Eastern front. All the time we were
there we were told the Russians were animals but that the
British and the Americans were humane. And then to return
here and find what had been done by these humane people."

It was a nice point, Bauer thought. For someone who had
been in Hitler's army on the Eastern front to have found
himself susceptible to shock. It was a nice, typical German
set of values. He could see the driver after the war, with

16

friends, some of them from the SS, the uniform he had himself perhaps worn, some of them fresh from managing the gas chambers and ovens which now they swore never existed, he could see them cursing and wringing their hands over the damage done to their city by enemy monsters.

Bauer felt a sudden satisfaction.

They now were crossing Barbarossaplatz and Bauer saw that an underground pedestrian passage such as he remembered at Hyde Park Corner had been constructed there, with exits and entrances on all the little streets that spread out like spokes from Barbarossaplatz. Even now, at high noon, in the midst of the tourist season, this labyrinth was hardly necessary.

What local hunger did it ease? It must have been profound to have induced the thrifty Franconian burghers to build this *folie de grandeur*. Or was it just that there was so much money lying around?

The driver turned his car into Theaterstrasse. "You have been here before perhaps, mein Herr?" he asked.

"I was born here," Bauer said.

The driver turned to him quickly and then looked to the front again in time to swerve and avoid hitting a bicyclist and then he took another quick look at Bauer. He pulled the taxi over to the curb.

"Why are you stopping here?" Bauer asked. He looked around. He was suddenly closed in, as though he had said the wrong thing, as though he had removed from himself his cloak of protection, that having admitted his origin he now again was what he once had been. He would not have been surprised if the driver summoned the police.

How could it come back so swiftly, and with such total force? What was it about Germany and Germans?

"You said the Deutscher Hof, mein Herr," the driver said. He spoke now for the first time in German.

Bauer looked at him. Was the tone different? Was the driver too easy, patronizing? Or was it only the commitment of the German language, that German words always gave this impact to even the most ordinary statements.

He looked out the cab window. He was about to reply—in German?—that this was not the Deutscher Hof, that the driver had made a mistake, but he saw the sign. He glanced around more. He recognized the location.

"It is not as you remembered it," the driver said, still in German.

If the voice was easier, Bauer told himself, it was simply that the driver felt friendlier, felt less a strain talking his own language. It was only that, nothing more.

Bauer got out of the cab and looked at the hotel again. What had been a classic baroque building, cream and white, curved, with scrolls, ornate and elaborate, a building in its own setting, now was a bare, plain, unornamented structure, a kind of vertical motel. It did not even have a true entrance on the street. One had to walk through an arcade to get to the hotel door.

"The original went with everything else," the driver said.

Bauer paid him.

"There must have been a reason," the driver said. "I have been given to understand that the Americans are not a cruel people. Often I ask them why they set fire to this city. No one seems to have an answer."

"I have no answer either," Bauer said.

"But then you are not an American," the driver said.

"I am an American citizen now," Bauer said, wondering why he was bothering.

"Still," the driver said. He hunched his shoulders. "There are some Americans, native-born Americans, who don't even know about the holocaust."

Bauer picked up his valise.

"Mein Herr," the driver said.

Bauer turned and saw the driver extending a hand holding a card.

"Take my card," the driver said. "Call me if I can serve you. Perhaps you will want to make an excursion into the countryside."

Bauer took the card and went through the shopping arcade. He entered the hotel. The lobby was as barren as the outside of the building.

He walked past the angular, functional furniture to the desk and identified himself and told the clerk, a girl who looked fifteen and who might have been a year or so older, that he had booked. She looked at the large, open ledger and could not find his name.

"But I sent a cable," Bauer said.

"There is no record," she said.

"Do you have a room?"

"Yes."

"Then it does not matter, does it?"

"But if you booked your name should be here."

"Just give me any room," Bauer said.

The girl ran her finger up and down the page, became flustered and then frightened.

"Just give me any room," Bauer said again.

"But your name should be here," the girl said.

She was almost terrified now, at this man who was dressed as an American and who spoke German, Würzburg German, who had said he had made a reservation, and if this were so, then she could not give him any room other than the one that had been set aside for him, except she could not find that.

"It's just a mistake on the part of the cable company," Bauer said. "It doesn't matter at all." He felt weary.

"But you say you have reserved a room." The girl seemed almost at the point of tears.

"But if there is no record of that give me any room that is available."

"But if you made a reservation you have been assigned a room."

It was a long time since Bauer had encountered the kind of German efficiency that could work itself into chaos.

"I must call the manager," the girl said.

Bauer started to tell her there was no need for that, but by then she was on the telephone, and by then he realized that the rules had to be obeyed no matter the cost, that order and system must be maintained.

A small man of about Bauer's age, bald, wearing rimless glasses, dressed in a black morning jacket and striped trousers, came out of an office off the lobby.

The manager listened to the girl as she explained her dilemma and Bauer felt a chill go through him.

"It is simple," the manager said, speaking as though to a child. "For some reason, certainly not the fault of the hotel, the cablegram never was delivered here. Therefore, we will give Herr Bauer another room. Simply find out what his requirements are and then satisfy them."

He turned to Bauer. "I am sorry to have caused you any inconvenience, Herr Bauer, but the matter will be rectified immediately. I must just assure you that we are not responsible for the failure of the delivery of your cablegram."

He spoke in a careful, correct English, with British overtones.

Bauer looked at the opaque eyes, magnified behind the glasses, at the pink cheeks. Where had all the hair gone? Joachim, don't you recognize me?

The manager took out a card case, extracted the inevitable card, and presented it to Bauer. "Please call upon me personally, Herr Bauer," he said. "I am at your service."

Bauer accepted the card and glanced at it. Joachim Remers, Manager.

It was too much, too soon. He would do it later, when he was ready for it. If Joachim had not recognized him, then he too could plead the same excuse.

Remers bowed, a trained manager's bow, and started back for his office.

Bauer said, "Joachim."

The manager turned. "Herr Bauer?"

"Joachim," Bauer said, feeling his throat constricting. "Joachim, don't you recognize me?"

Remers walked back to him and looked at him closely.

"Peter," Bauer said. "Peter Bauer, Joachim."

Remers looked at him. He took off his glasses and wiped

them with a kerchief he removed from his breast pocket. He replaced the glasses. He gripped Bauer suddenly by the arms. Then he saw the girl at the desk looking at them curiously.

"Come to my office," Remers said.

He walked rapidly across the lobby and held open the door to his office. Bauer entered. Remers closed the door and turned to Bauer. Again he gripped his arms. "Peter," he said.

"You would not have recognized me?"

Remers shook his head. "No. I don't know. Perhaps. Peter . . ."

He stepped back and looked at Bauer and shook his head. "Peter, Peter, now that I look again, I can see the old Peter, something of the old Peter. Did you recognize me?"

"Yes."

"You had an advantage. You had the card with my name."

"Before that. Before you gave me the card."

"But I have changed so much. I have changed more than you have." He looked at Bauer again and touched his arm and said, "Sit down, Peter. I must sit down too. I must get used to this." He went behind his desk and sat down and Bauer took a chair.

"Peter, how long is it?"

"Thirty years, more or less."

"And you recognized me?"

"Yes."

"Even without my hair?"

"Where did your hair go? You had such a head of hair."

"I would like to know. My wife says I should wear a wig. I understand it is quite fashionable today."

"You had so much hair," Bauer said.

"Too much at one time." Remers opened a silver cigarette container on the desk and pushed it toward Bauer.

Bauer shook his head.

"And you let me go on talking to you in English," Remers said, taking out a cigarette.

"I was very proud of your English. Where did you learn that wonderful English?"

"I went to a special school. It is useful in my profession." Remers lit the cigarette and looked intently at Bauer. "I didn't know for a long time what had happened to you. It was just that one day you did not appear at school. Nobody told me why. Nobody told anybody anything. It was a long time before I understood. I went to your house once and asked your mother what happened to you. All she said was that you had gone away for a little while but she did not tell me where. It was such a long time before I understood. Peter, what brings you back to Würzburg after so long a time?"

Bauer very much wanted a cigarette. Why had he quit? "I came to find out about my mother."

Remers took a short puff on the cigarette and blew out the smoke immediately. "What about your mother?"

"I want to find out how she died," Bauer said.

Remers looked to one side and then to the other.

He's frightened, Bauer thought. My God in heaven, he's frightened. "Do you know anything about it, Joachim?"

Remers shook his head very quickly. Then he asked, "Peter, after all these years, why just now?"

Bauer sat back. "I always thought she had died naturally, I thought that all the time, unhappily, after what had happened to my father, but naturally, in her own home. Then, my aunt, Dorothea, you remember Aunt Dorle, we used to go there often on Saturdays after playing soccer and she would give us cookies and hot chocolate."

Remers nodded. "I remember."

"She was sent to Theresienstadt and she somehow survived and she went to America where I have been living. I saw her just before she died."

"What did she tell you?" Remers asked.

Bauer shook his head. "Nothing definite. She was afraid, even then. It stayed with her over the years. But just before she died she seemed to want to tell me something. She hinted at something. I tried to get her to tell me but she would not and she died."

Remers listened, the cigarette burning forgotten between his fingers. The pinkness was gone from his cheeks.

"Peter," he said at last. "Do you think that is wise?"

"I don't think wisdom enters into it," Bauer said. "It is simply that I must know how my mother died. That's all."

"Peter, none of you . . ." Remers felt the heat of the burning cigarette and he quickly mashed it out in an ashtray. "Peter, none of the Würzburg Jews has ever returned here. Oh, there are a few old ones in the sanitarium your father used to support. But none of the others has returned, not one that I know."

"It may be difficult," Bauer admitted.

"Peter, not one has returned."

"What has that got to do with anything?"

Remers lit another cigarette. "Peter, Würzburg is a conservative city, an old, very conservative city. It has never been exposed to fresh air. And then there was the fire bombing. Nobody has ever forgotten that. Even the children who were not born then have been told again and again about the firestorm. There is almost nobody in Würzburg who didn't lose some one, more than one, in that air raid."

"I still don't understand what that has to do with my trying to find out how my mother died," Bauer said, although he did.

Remers pulled on the cigarette and Bauer could see from the way he handled it that he was not very much used to smoking, that the cigarettes were probably kept out of courtesy for visitors.

"Peter, a small city such as Würzburg doesn't change. Things go along in more or less the same fashion. There are still some of the old people here. Many are in quite important posts. There is even still some of the old feeling." His voice trailed off.

Bauer leaned forward. "Joachim, are you warning me?"

Remers laughed and waved a hand. "No, of course not, Peter. What can you mean?"

"Then what exactly are you saying to me?"

Again Remers waved his hand. "It's just that it's often better to leave things as they are. Peter, why stir up trouble?"

"This is not the Third Reich," Bauer said.

Remers tensed so imperceptibly Bauer would not have caught it if he had not been watching for it. Remers jerked his head to the one side and then the other.

It's still here, Bauer thought. He had not at all imagined it. In this enchanting little city that looked as though it might have served to illustrate a child's fantasy, it was still there.

"Perhaps you should lower your voice a little," Remers was saying. He said it with a laugh to make it a joke. "You know the old saying, the walls have ears." He laughed again.

Bauer sat back in the chair. He felt a dull ache in the back of his neck. "Tell me about yourself, Joachim. You are married, you said. Would it be anyone I might have known? And how many children? There must be children, I know. And there is no need to lower our voices about all that."

Remers started talking and he didn't need the cigarettes any more and Bauer was pleased to see the color slowly return to the face of his old friend.

2

✠ ✠ ✠

BAUER TIPPED THE BELLBOY AND LOCKED THE DOOR BEHIND him. He did not know exactly why he did that.

He looked around. The room was of the new compact style with the modern, international low ceiling and had everything in it that an up-to-date hotel room should have: a bed, a dresser, an easy chair that appeared to be reasonably comfortable, another chair with a straight back, a small table. On the wall were several colored photographs of the country-side outside Würzburg.

The *Umgebung* of Würzburg. He hadn't seen or thought of that German word in a very long time. *Umgebung.* Translated freely the word meant "environs." But translated more exactly it meant "that which is given around a certain place." And what was given around Würzburg was good: rich vine-yards, farmland, hills; it was not for no reason the city was considered the end of the sentimental "Romantic Way"—or was it the beginning? In any case it lay in its own little valley where even the topography conspired to protect it. From harsh winds, and, as Joachim Remers had said, from fresh air.

The room, of course, was immaculate.

He sat down on the straight-backed chair. He realized he was shaking. He probably had been foolish to come to this hotel.

He must remind himself again that he was proof against feeling. He had rid himself of that. He had been helped by events, of course, but he had managed most of it himself. He had made that into personal law.

And, besides, how could this sterile, faceless, tasteless structure, with its garish arcade, with this room, this room which could be the archetypical second-rate room for every new second-rate hotel in the world—how could any of it bring back anything?

Air space was not a constant. Air space contained no memories. Air space was not cherubs and creamy colors and exotic designs and flowers and plants and old, rich, dark furniture and wallpaper of flock and chandeliers that gleamed with a hundred eyes.

And yet, and yet, if the sounds, if the sweet sounds of laughter and of love and of joy, the sounds of reunions, the coming together again of all the parts of the family body, if these sounds, emotions, were a constant, if they had lived, and they had lived, then perhaps they did still abide in these cold, savorless surroundings. Perhaps they had survived the calm, tidy, methodical genocide which had removed forever the makers of the sounds, and having endured, were there, waiting to reach ears that could hear.

He opened his bag. He took out a small, old photograph. It originally was a picture of a man and a woman burlesqueing the classic, old-fashioned pose, done as a lark, he had been told by his aunt, a kind of early camp. The man was standing stiffly, shoulders back, head up, a top hat held by its brim against his left breast. His right hand was resting on a leg-of-mutton shoulder.

That was almost all that was left of the woman who was his partner. The head, the face, almost all of the rest of her, had peeled away or had darkened into unrecognizability, so that almost nothing else was there.

There was no other photograph he had of his mother and father, no other photograph he had ever had, or could ever remember having seen, although he must have seen many, and the only vision he had of her was the image that drifted into his mind from time to time, always when his thoughts were elsewhere, far elsewhere. For when he tried purposefully to summon her features, her face obeyed only to the point of entering his mind in and out of focus, like a dream sequence on a cinema screen.

He closed his eyes and brought back the last time he had seen her; she had kissed him farewell, a light kiss on his cheek, she had been afraid to do more. "It won't be for very long, *Schatzi*," she had said. "It will not be very long before we will all be together again and until then you must be quite the little man."

He opened his eyes and he looked at the man in the picture, tall and slender, even in the contrived preposterousness of his pose unable to hide his natural elegance; his father, the Councilor Simon Bauer, a man with a reputation of being, as they said then, a ladies' man, a charmer to his fingertips. He had, Bauer remembered, on that same night of their parting, grasped his hand in the first man-to-man handshake he had ever offered him, and had said, smiling, with a voice that was perhaps somewhat hoarser than Bauer remembered it as ever having been, "Your mother is right, son. This is a temporary thing. They will soon see through this insane man and then all will be as before. But, meanwhile, perhaps this is wise."

Where were his two older brothers and his older sister at that time? He never quite knew. His brothers were probably away at school. And probably his being smuggled out of Germany was purposely kept from his sister. To protect her? To protect his brothers? It had in the end not protected them at all, nor his father with his famous Iron Cross he had won at Verdun.

. . . *The mountain climber, Axmann, Erwin Axmann, he remembered the first name suddenly, who joined the SS and* could not understand why . . . who used his black uniform and his prestige and his power and his skills to take Jews south across the Bavarian Alps into Switzerland . . .

. . . The journey had taken four days, five days, on trains, buses, on foot, there were several others, perhaps half a dozen in all . . . and Axmann, wearing his SS uniform where it was useful, dressing as a mountain climber when that better suited his book, shepherding them to safety . . .

. . . The night, perhaps it was the last night before he deposited them all across the border, Axmann lit his pipe and talked to him. "You are supposed to be a bright young lad, Peter. Your entire family is clever. Your father is wise. He pretends to be more interested in frivolous things but let me tell you, in the event you don't know, that he is one of the wisest men in Würzburg, and a man with a splendid war record as well. If there were many like him we would not be in this silly fix, headed for another disaster . . ."

. . . They were somewhere in the mountains then and it was cold and the stars were very bright and close and most of the other Jews were huddled in sleep still dulled from the shock of having to wrench themselves out of their lives and flee like hunted animals . . . it had hit Peter quite another way, as high adventure with this legendary master of mountains . . .

. . . "Yes, we are on a course of disaster, no matter what that little deformed monster Göbbels keeps telling us. Anyway, little Peter, when you get away from here and you have some time to sit down and think, you must ask yourself why is it that a perfectly intelligent man such as myself, a famous mountain climber, should have joined this perfectly stupid organization. It isn't even a decent police force. It's full of all kinds of silly bullshit, if you pardon me, like making vows to a dagger under a full moon, absolute childish bullshit . . ."

He remembered that certain moment when Axmann told them all that they had at last crossed the line, that they now

28

were safe in Switzerland; there was nothing on the land to tell them that, only the deep, hearty voice of the mountain climber, who at that moment possessed the infinite wisdom of God, to be able to look upon the snow and to be able to pronounce the verdict that there was Germany and here was Switzerland.

The last thing was Axmann clapping him on the back and telling him not to worry, that the Germans had too much sense to go along with all this much longer and that they would see through Göbbels before it was too late, with God's help. Only God had not helped very much after all, and even while Axmann was waving them on to their safety and turning round and going back again to his danger, even then the camps were being filled and the gas chambers were being filled and the smell of burning flesh sweetened the dimpled places in the land and German manufacturers, good, solid business-men, were importuning the government to allow them to demonstrate how their gas was more efficient than anybody else's gas (how had they known, upon whom had they experimented?). But perhaps they had never really tested it out at all, perhaps their gas was no better than anybody else's gas, perhaps they were just overselling their merchandise, just like any progressive, conscientious manufacturer, where his product was poison gas or children's toys.

He returned the photograph to the suitcase. He looked at his watch. He had listened to Remers for half an hour, and he had been sitting here in the room for perhaps another half hour and it was not yet one o'clock.

He had many things to do. He had to report to one of the American military establishments here. For some reason his chief in the Middle European section of the Department had insisted upon that. It was absolutely necessary for the American military to know of his presence. It had seemed absurd at the time, there in Washington, normal State Department cautiousness, and it still did. Despite Joachim's furtive trepidation. Joachim always was a nervous kid.

He stood up. He put his hand in his jacket pocket and took out a card. He looked at it. Manfred Reinhard. And a telephone number. And who was Manfred Reinhard? Manfred

Reinhard was the taxi driver. And where else but in Germany would taxi drivers carry cards? And cards which revealed nothing of their trade ("profession" he had called it himself) but merely their name and telephone number?

He tore up the card and dropped the pieces into the wastebasket.

He did not unpack. He did not know how long he would be in Würzburg. He might find out all he wanted to know in the next twenty-four hours.

It was more than that, naturally. Unpacking meant settling in, making himself at home, however briefly. And he could no longer make himself at home in this city in which he had been born.

3

✠ ✠ ✠

BAUER STEPPED OUT OF THE ELEVATOR INTO THE LOBBY TO SEE his friend standing in front of the desk talking to a heavy man wearing a dark suit and an air of authority. Remers raised his head and nodded, in a correct, grave manner.

He walked out of the hotel. He looked up and down the Theaterstrasse. It was so familiar, so known, so remembered, so as it should be, had been, and yet his reason told him it could not be.

Again he felt a kind of vertigo, a disorientation because of the overpowering orientation; again something within him suggested that perhaps the raid had never taken place, perhaps the war had never taken place. Perhaps he was not, after all, Peter Bauer, a man in his early forties, a man with a strange American wife to whom he was a stranger. Perhaps he was still the little Peter on the street on this summer afternoon, and that presently he would go home where someone would surely be waiting for him, his mother, perhaps, his father, one of his brothers, or his sister.

He looked across the street. Something else was pulling on him. What was it about that building? The one close to Barbarossaplatz?

He stood there. A short, fat man who perhaps was not looking where he was going stumbled into him, appraised him quickly as a foreigner, said something rude in guttural German, then nodded and put a smile on his face and mumbled something else intended as an apology.

Bauer walked slowly down the street and looked again at the building opposite, overlooking the *Platz*. What? What did he remember about it? It was almost as though he were lying on a psychiatrist's couch, with fingers of memory, probing, probing.

It could not be. Again the turning over of his insides. No, dear God in heaven, it could not be. It could not be that building. That building had been destroyed too when the entire inner city had been destroyed, and yet it was that building.

There, on the fourth floor, where the balcony was, had lived his parents' close friends, the Sterns. They were very wealthy and they were always having lunches and dinners and costume parties. And from that balcony he used to watch the annual summer parade honoring Saint Kilian, the Celtic apostle and patron of Franconia.

The Sterns. They had a little dog, a whippet, named Tasso.

The parade used to make its turning on the *Platz*, there, under that balcony, a place in the front row, to look down at the knights and monks, the clowns and the men with animal costumes, the bands, the noise, the crowds in the streets. And Marta, his aunt's maid, putting a pillow under his arms, resting on the iron railing, holding him by the back of his pants as he leaned forward.

Saint Kilian. How long had it been since he had thought of that name? He remembered now how shocked he was when he learned that the missionary, who had taught and had befriended the early Germans, was, in payment, slaughtered by them. And he had once known exactly how. What was it, had they beheaded him, or had they just smashed open his skull?

He started to walk away from the *Platz* up Theaterstrasse. This was a fantasy, a gothic dream, a witchery and he would live it for he had no choice, nor would have elected otherwise if he had. How often does one live out an enchantment in daylight on a crowded street?

He passed the *Bürgerspital*, which was old and mellowed, covered with a patina of time, an ersatz patina, it must be, and passed a toy shop, it was unchanged, he remembered dragging his mother there to show her a set of electric trains he had fallen in love with and how time passed and the trains were forgotten and then at the end of that semester when he had finished with good marks he had walked into the house and had found the trains and tracks, all laid out, running, signals blinking and his father flat on his face on the floor operating everything and telling him that he had bought the system for himself, not for Peter.

Nothing was changed. The collection of centuries they had never lived through was on all the buildings, in all the gothic-lettered signs.

He saw a strange building, a modern, angular, ascetic building, set well back from the street and he paused and tried to place it. Then he realized it was the Stadt Theater, built in the new modern style, quite different from the old one, and he was grateful for that, grateful for a brief respite of sanity.

But from there he could see the vaulted towers of the *Dom*, whose accretion of time had in some miraculous way been accomplished in the last decade or two.

And then, realizing now that from the start his aimlessness was not aimlessness at all, walking past buildings that were clusters of memories, of friends, of things having happened, he found himself walking toward that which he had resolved he would not seek out.

It was an easy promise to make to himself in his middle echelon office in the Department.

He walked and walked and he felt a new chill in the lovely sunny day, and then he was there and now that he was there he was bewildered, thrown almost into panic in being in another dimension entirely. He had walked through the streets of his boyhood, had passed one sight after the other, each sounding a pure note dead on key. But now, here, he was on the street where he had lived, and that was the place where he had been born, except it was not the place at all. What was there now was one of the bare, geometric buildings that seemed now to be infesting the earth everywhere.

Perhaps he was on the wrong street. He rushed to the corner to look at the sign. Annastrasse. It was the right street. He went back and looked at the building. It was the right number.

He looked up and down the street. All of the buildings were matchboxes, blocks, balconies, and many of the diligent *Hausfrauen* of Würzburg, unused to lazy amenities, had put the balconies to good, practical German use, hanging their wash there.

Of course. He drew breath. He had been so deluded, so mesmerized by what he had seen up to now that he was not entirely prepared for this. This neighborhood was almost on the outskirts of the city, but the fire raid had obviously spread even farther than he had imagined, even to here. Naturally the houses had to be rebuilt and since this was not the historic, ancient, inner, tourist part of Würzburg there had been no requirement to restore the past.

He smiled and, relaxed, started to walk away; how could one feel any emotion looking at an unremarkable, unclassifiable block of buildings, and then he turned and looked again, and his relief was ripped away, as his flesh might have been torn, and a force not to be denied flooded back the memories, the memories at this moment infinitely more dominating than what he actually was seeing, and in place of the matchbox and the laundry-beset balconies, he saw the rococo building, decorated, scrolled, fluted, where his family had occupied two apartments on the third floor, a wall broken through to make them one, where below them an uncle had lived with his wife and three children and on the floor above a cousin and his wife, with four children, all of whom had vanished into sickly smoke from a chimney above the kiln for humans.

He remembered with no relevance that the police president of Würzburg had lived in the building which his father had

34

owned, and that before it all began he and Councilor Bauer had been very good friends.

. . . *There were always costume parties. Councilor Bauer was one of the leading sponsors of the Mozart Festival and there were always dress balls to raise funds for the festival and the balls were always themed to an opera and he remembered one night when his mother and father had come to his bedroom to kiss him good night and he almost screamed in fright . . . the opera theme that year was Carmen, and his parents were dressed as wild gypsies, bandannas on their heads and knives in their belts . . . they were so upset at having frightened him that way they would not leave immediately, although they already were late, first they had to make him laugh and to accomplish that his mother had danced an imitation of the habanera, snapping her fingers and swinging her feet, and his father had sung the song, imitating a woman's voice . . .*

And now he started for school, as he had for so many years started for school, each journey filled with adventure, discovery. He used to take one of two routes, either through the back garden of the august Residenz or by way of the front of that stately building.

He found himself before the baroque palace, which once had been the official seat of the prince-bishops who had ruled there. He had always been told it was one of the largest and most beautiful in all Germany. He walked on, past the wrought-iron gate that was one of the local minor works of art. Who did anything like that anymore?

The school was not there. There were more of the apartment houses, turned out obviously on assembly lines, more balconies, more laundry hung out to dry. He started back. There was just one more place he must look for that day, the synagogue where his mother and father prayed, where he and his brothers were always dragged against their will.

It had always seemed painful to have to go to a place where

35

almost none of his school chums went. He could not then understand why there had to be this separation in one of the fundamentals of his life, why in school everything was the same, the teams, the classes, the after-school playing, but that here there was this severe, unalterable division. Most of his friends went to Catholic churches, Würzburg was a city of Catholic churches. It made him feel different and at that age, he remembered, difference was a disease.

The synagogue, he remembered, was in the old section of the new town and he walked through alleys of cobblestones, narrow passageways too narrow for cars to use, and nothing had changed there either but where the synagogue had been there was now an empty lot.

He looked at his watch. It was after three. He thought he would go back to the hotel and telephone the American authorities as he had been instructed to do.

On the way back to the Deutscher Hof he passed the local war memorial which immortalized for the city the heroes who had given their lives for the Fatherland in the First World War and he remembered that one of the first things the Nazis did, he was told, was to chisel out of the marble the names of Würzburg's dead sons who had happened also to be Jews.

He looked quickly at the listing of men whose name started with B. At the head of the group was a gash where once had been the name of Richard Bauer, *Leutnant* in the German Imperial Army. The gouge in the marble was jagged and broken. The force, the fervor, the passion used by whomever it was who had wielded the hammer and chisel had been so great it broke out a large chunk of the stone. It was probably the first name that was attacked, apparently there were no Jewish A's, and the craftsman, the undoer, the eliminator of history, must have been in full possession of his energy.

He looked over the rest of the memorial. The marble was scored here and there and there, gaping wounds that might have been made by the talons of a maddened bird or the claws of an angry bear.

His eyes went back to the top of the column of B's. His

Uncle Richard, who was, of course, only a memory to him, the legendary Uncle Richard who had fallen with a bullet in his face leading his men in a sally from a trench in France.

. . . Rainy days were miserable and it rained often in Würzburg . . . there was always his grandmother to visit . . . she had boxes of old photographs and that was a way to get through the rain . . . the photograph of a man in full-dress uniform of a German officer, spiked helmet, sword hilt held between two clasped hands, looking so warlike, so magnificent . . . gooseflesh always prickled his neck as he looked at this gorgeous bird of battle . . . once there was a rustle in the room and the faint sound of weeping and he looked up to see his grandmother standing over him, touching her eyes with a delicate lace kerchief . . .
". . . What might he have been if he had lived," his grandmother said . . .

What might he have been? Another candidate for a gas chamber? Would his record of having fought for his Kaiser and his country have meant anything to the new rulers? Had it in any way helped his father when his time came?

He spat on the memorial.

He started off, shuddering with an agitation he had vowed he would not suffer, and then his eye caught something else, something on the bottom of the memorial, set discreetly in one corner. He knelt and he saw that all the Jewish names had been restored, and since the reinstallation had been done by the methodical German mind, the name of *Leutnant* Richard Bauer again headed the list.

He straightened. His body hurt. He was aware of how futile, how stupid, how childish, had been his insult to these dead of another day; they had played no part in what had come later. He stepped away and his foot kicked over a dried wreath that had been long ago placed before the memorial. He stooped down and righted it, trying to make out what the faded words on the ribbon read, and unable to bring them

37

back from their months, years, of exposure to sun and snow and rain, touched them with his fingertips and went on.

He walked on, still shaken, despising himself for having allowed his emotions to take over. And then it struck him that once again the Jews had been segregated, that having been officially reestablished as having once lived and died, they still were not permitted to be mixed again in alphabetical anonymity with the comrades with whom they had lived and died, but were, for all time, confined in their own isolation, tagged on at the bottom of the monument, like a postscript.

4

✠ ✠ ✠

THE UNITED STATES ARMY HEADQUARTERS FOR THE AREA WAS located on the outskirts of Würzburg beyond the *Sportplatz* atop a winding hill that commenced its slow meandering on Rennweg to the left of the Residenz.

After Bauer identified himself at the gate and was waved through by the MP on duty there, an enormous, dazzling creature in burgundy ascot and white crash helmet, he settled back in the taxi, and although he knew from experience what next to expect and was quite prepared for it, he still could not escape a small and not altogether unpleasant jolt. He was, less than fifteen minutes from the heart of Würzburg, back in the United States.

He had seen enough foreign military establishments in Europe—American, British, French, even Russian—to know how every nationality made itself at home, but he never could quite get over how much more than anybody else the Americans, the least experienced in foreign occupation, were able wherever they found themselves to recreate their native land. And it always was the America not of the big cities, not of

39

New York or Chicago or Los Angeles, but the America of the small towns, of the midwest, of the south.

Outside the gate, just back there, was the heartland of Franconia, ancient Franconia, the city the Germans always described as their baroque jewel, the city that belonged more to the past with each finishing year; spires, like thistles in the air, the vast, moated *Festung*—against what could it now call itself a fortress? a platoon with machine guns could take it any day in the week—domes, palaces, cathedrals; a gothic, medieval smell, a life concept encased in every cobble, the compulsive drive backward in the duplication of what had been destroyed, the changing of nothing save the modern dwellings that had grown as fungi and would, without doubt, as quickly disappear.

And here, here, having crossed the magical line, having gone past the helmeted necromancer at the gate, was Macon, Georgia; Greenville, South Carolina; here was Kansas, Nebraska, Idaho. Here was the small, squat buildings, the PX, the commissary, the base theater, the barber shop, the Officers' Club, the Noncommissioned Officers' Club, the Enlisted Men's Club. Here were the children playing in the streets, the shouts, in American, midwestern-southern-western American.

They always were there, these outposts of America, like warts on the land; always there, stanchly, lastingly undigested and undigestible, cut off, protected from any kind of assimilation as though the base, the post, the camp were surrounded by invisible glass or by some new military plastic that was more than glass, that possessed in some alchemic way the power to prevent any kind of communication from the inside out or the outside in.

They came, these men, with their wives, their children, their habits, their life ways, first as proconsuls, conquerors in the land they had helped conquer, now as guests, as official friends, made by treaty and agreement, to be around and handy in the event of an attack from the former ally, now unofficial foe. They came and they stayed with the wives and the children and they left, all of them, intact, untouched, unaffected, untainted, and for what they saw and what they taught themselves during those years they might have all been encapsulated on the bed of the deepest ocean.

Now the taxi moved through streets that were named Madison and Jefferson, Jackson and Washington (so they would not during their tour forget their heritage, so the children would not forget, or would not come to think all streets had long, ugly, unpronounceable German names), and then the cab pulled to a stop in front of one of the larger buildings, a sign staked in the ground in front of which bore an alphabet-soup collection of letters, all of them informative to those learned in the esoteric code.

Captain Roy Atkins had said, when he had called, "You hurry round here, Mr. Bauer. Never mind it's this late in the day. You come by now and let me know what I can do for you."

Texan, Bauer had known immediately. He was getting good at that. As he had polished his own speech, he had taken interest in that of others. Texan, certainly, that was easy, but what part of Texas? With his European ear for the nuances of languages he had registered the subtle differences in Texas accents, as he had between the accent, say, of a man from Georgia and of that of a man from Mississippi or Alabama.

He paid the taxi driver and told him not to wait and entered the building.

She wore a dark, short skirt, a slate-colored sweater and boots that reached almost to her knees. She had loose, blonde hair that fell to her shoulders. She rapped lightly with her knuckles against the glass part of the door on which was painted, Captain Roy Atkins, and when she heard the growl from within she opened the door and entered the office.

"Mr. Bauer is here," she said. She spoke in English with only the smallest trace of German accent.

The American officer was seated behind his desk. The desk was uncluttered. It bore little more than a small sign, on which was carved, in gothic letters, **Captain Roy Atkins**, and two photographs, one of a smiling, freckle-faced woman, and the other of a pair of towheaded boys.

Captain Atkins looked at her for several seconds and then he asked without much interest, "Who the hell is he?"

"He called a little while ago, Captain," the woman said. "He said you asked him to come by today."

"If he says so, then I must have," Captain Atkins said.

"Shall I send him in?" the woman asked.

"Why not?"

"Do you want me to remain here while he is here, Captain?"

"Why would you want to do that?"

"Do you think you might want me to take down any notes?" she asked.

"I'll let you know," he said. "If I need you I'll let you know."

"I'll stay at my desk then until you know," the woman said. She started for the door.

"Marly," he said.

She turned. "Yes, Captain."

"Come here."

She walked back to the desk. "Yes, Captain?" Her voice was still cool, though perhaps not quite so cool.

He got up and walked round the desk. He put his hand on her shoulder. She did not move.

"What in the God damn hell has got into you?" he asked.

"Mr. Bauer is waiting," she said.

"Fuck Mr. Bauer. I asked you a question, Marly."

"I have asked you not to call me Marly," she said.

"You used to like it well enough. It used to tickle you. I remember you telling me nobody had ever called you that before. I remember what you were doing the first time you told me that."

"The gentleman is waiting, Captain."

He took her by her other shoulder and turned her gently to face him. He stared at her face. "Marly, for God's sake, what's happened to us, what's got into you?"

"I don't know."

"What's got into you?" he asked again.

"I don't know."

"It sure as hell hasn't been me, not lately."

"That's right."

"And that hasn't been my fault."

"No, it has not."

"Maybe that's what you need."

"Do you think so?"

"That's what you used to need. That's all you used to need. No matter what was wrong, with us or anything else, that always made everything right."

"That's quite true."

"Marly."

"Mr. Bauer is waiting."

His face went suddenly naked and she felt herself slipping.

"Marly," he said.

"I have asked you."

"You used to love it," he said. He removed one hand from her shoulder and opened and closed his fingers as though he were trying to grasp something and could not.

"Perhaps that's why I don't love it now," she said.

He dropped the other hand and his own shoulders sagged and unexpectedly, not so unexpectedly, not unexpectedly at all, she wanted to move even closer to him, to say the old things again, to again listen to the words that always were as touchstones of an incantation, that always erased, eliminated everything else and made for them their own, inviolable privacy.

To not do that, to not reach out for lost sorcery, she turned again and started for the door.

"Listen," he said.

She paused again.

"You know it isn't Peggy," he said. He said it slowly and patiently, as though speaking to a child, or as though it were a child speaking. "You know it isn't Peggy. It's the kids. You always knew that. You knew that for starters."

43

She held her lips together hard and then she said, "I'll send in Mr. Bauer and I'll wait outside at my desk in the event you need me for anything."

"God damn it, don't give me that fucking kraut cold-mouth," he said.

"Is that all, Captain?" she asked, and now, knowing even better than he knew, she wanted more than ever to run back to him, to touch him. And he was right. She had known all about it, everything, from the beginning.

When she stepped out of the office she saw the caller was standing. She had bade him take a seat but he was still standing, exactly where he had stood.

"Captain Atkins will see you now, Mr. Bauer," she said.

Even with her English Bauer thought he could say almost with certainty she was a native of Würzburg, certainly a Franconian, perhaps from nearby, from the *Umgebung*. Was she one of the things given around a certain place? He thought she was handsome and very German-looking and she made him feel a little nervous.

Typically German? He had read a book recently which had argued that there was no such a thing as a German "look," which had quoted observers of hundreds of years of the German scene. They had all seemed to agree that the Germans were a faceless people. The book suggested that the universal, pejorative concept of the German—bull-necked, red-faced, beer-swilling, pot-bellied, noisy, coarse, brutal—was a caricature largely created by the Germans themselves, in satirical writings, in magazines such as *Simplicissimus* and others like it. That the German face ranged from the idealized Nordic, even-featured blond (rare) to the swarthy, dark-skinned other extreme so precisely personified by the Leader who saw all Germans as being what he so obviously was not.

And that might all be true, Bauer thought. But he believed if he had seen this woman anywhere, just saw her, just watched her move, her facial expressions, just watched her speak, the way her lips went, without hearing the enunciation in whatever language, he would have known she was German, not Dutch, nor Swedish, nor Norwegian, but German. How? He did not know.

She opened the door and presented him with the impersonal smile that seemed to be the first lesson learned by secretaries everywhere and she stepped back to let him pass.

He looked across the small, neat, spartan room. He saw seated behind the desk a large young American officer almost running to fat, almost but not quite. A football player, he would guess, a few years back. Now struggling against the oncoming bulk of the former athlete.

The officer rose to his feet. There was, Bauer thought, a tension on his face. The officer held out his hand. Bauer could see a little crescent of sweat under his armpit.

"Mr. Bauer," the officer said. "Captain Roy Atkins here. Welcome to Würzburg."

5

✠ ✠ ✠

"BORN RIGHT HERE IN WÜRZBURG," CAPTAIN ATKINS SAID. "WELL, I'll be damned."

It was the third time he had remarked on that extraordinary fact and Bauer could no longer think of any appropriate response.

"And you're with the State Department," Captain Atkins said, also for the third time. "Well, I'll be damned."

Captain Atkins' voice, after two martinis, was a little loud. Despite the effective air conditioning in the Officers' Club there were tiny beads of sweat on his upper lip.

Bauer glanced at Captain Atkins' secretary, who had been identified to him as Mrs. Marliese Neubert. He had thereafter addressed her once or twice as Mrs. Neubert until Captain Atkins had assured him that she would prefer to be called Marliese.

"Everybody knows her as Marliese," Captain Atkins had said, looking at her. "Nobody calls her Mrs. Neubert. Anyway Mr. Neubert's not around any more."

Neither Marliese nor Bauer had said anything.

"Mr. Neubert's dead," Captain Atkins had explained.

At the moment, here in the club, Marliese was looking elsewhere, toying with the stem of her own martini glass with fingers Bauer saw were long and shapely. When Captain Atkins had insisted that Bauer go to the club and have a drink with him she had accompanied them without any specific invitation Bauer had heard.

"I'm not the kind of joker who asks questions, Pete," Captain Atkins said now. "I ain't about to start interrogating you, so it's none of my business what it is the State Department sent you over for."

"Thank you," Bauer said.

Captain Atkins leaned a little closer. Bauer could see little lines of tightness on either side of his mouth.

"I ain't asking any questions, Pete," Captain Atkins said in a low, sincere voice. "But I just want you to know that whatever it is, if I can do anything, you just call, you hear?"

"I'm not here officially," Bauer said.

"You got to do with Germany, haven't you, you told me that, didn't you?"

"Yes."

"This is Germany, ain't it?"

"But I'm not here officially. I'm here on personal business."

Captain Atkins waved a hand. "Oh, hell, I know all about that, Pete. I know this security shit. You crumble the cookies any way you like, right hand or left, big crumbs or little. But I repeat, Pete—repeat, Pete, how about that?—I say it again, you need anything, anything at all, you just holler, hear?"

"Thank you," Bauer said. He had the feeling that whatever it was Captain Atkins said to him he was really speaking to Marliese.

Again he looked, almost surreptitiously, at the woman. Then he asked himself why he was being so damned careful. Was it for his own protection, to prevent any kind of connection with her, to keep himself removed, so that if she had not already found him out she perhaps never would? Or was it because he had already come to the conclusion that she and the captain were lovers, and that there was under them a terrain of tenseness upon which he in no way wanted to intrude?

Captain Atkins sat back, his big hands resting on the table. He seemed to Bauer to be breathing a little hard for a man doing nothing but sitting and drinking martinis. Marliese took a cigarette from her pack and Captain Atkins immediately, automatically, picked up her man-size Zippo lighter with its military insigne and flicked it on. In front of Marliese was a large ashtray, stamped with the same insigne; the tray was filled with butts, all made by her.

"Would you have guessed that, Marly?" Captain Atkins asked on the sudden.

Although the question came from nowhere Marliese understood the code. "No, Roy, I would not have," she said.

"He don't hardly have an accent at all," Captain Atkins said to her. He turned to Bauer. "How old were you when you left here, Pete?"

Bauer resolutely kept his eyes away from her. "When I was a boy," he said. Would that now give him away?

"When you were a boy," Captain Atkins repeated.

Bauer looked at Marliese. She was gazing at him. Was it a contemplative look, he wondered?

"Your family leave Germany then?" Captain Atkins asked.

He really did not care, Bauer knew; he was asking questions because they were all there together and there wasn't much else to talk about and he was a courteous man with a sense of duty and responsibility to his guest from the Middle European Section of the State Department. He did not care in any way, and yet he was stripping Bauer, exposing him, and short of being rude there was nothing Bauer could do about it.

"No," he said. "My family did not leave Germany."

"You went away alone?" Captain Atkins asked. He twisted round and waved his hand at the bar. He turned back. "That normal, Pete? When you were growing up here?"

What the hell, Bauer thought. What difference did it make? "It was not normal, Captain," he said.

"Roy," Captain Atkins said. "Now you know we've gone past the mister and captain business."

"Roy. It was not normal at all, but those were not normal times. You see, Roy, I'm a Jew, and my parents had me smuggled out of the country to save my life."

48

Captain Atkins looked at him for a long time. Bauer wondered whether Marliese was looking at him as well.

"Well, I'll be damned," Captain Atkins said. "I'll be plain God damned. To save your life?"

"Yes."

"Isn't that spelling it out a little long, Pete?"

"No."

"Well, God damn me," Captain Atkins said. "Would you have guessed that, Marly? You were just as surprised as I was when we found out he was German. Would you have taken him for a Jew?"

"I don't know," she said. "I don't believe I have ever met a German Jew."

Now Bauer looked full upon her. Her face was without expression. Was there anything there, in her eyes, anything? Nothing. But why should it be otherwise? Of what possible interest could it be to her?

The waiter appeared with the fresh drinks. Bauer had scarcely touched his second drink but it was taken away and a new cocktail in a glass beading with cold was set in front of him.

"What happened to your family?" Captain Atkins asked.

"What happened to most German Jewish families," Bauer said. He felt embarrassed and uncomfortable and he wished he had the poise and wit to change the conversation to something else. Instead he felt compelled to go on. "That's why I've come here, as a matter of fact," he said. "I know my father was put to death in a concentration camp. I came here to find out how my mother died."

Captain Atkins took a long sip from his glass and put the glass down carefully. "Then it's the plain truth, it ain't a cover-up, you're here on personal business?"

"My business is very personal, Roy," Bauer said, wondering whether the friendship extended would now be withdrawn, perhaps even to the point of restoring the military rank and the last name.

After a moment, during which Marliese took out a fresh cigarette and lit it from the stub of the last one, Captain Atkins nodded his head slowly.

"How do you mean, Pete, how your mother died?" Then he did something that to Bauer was quite unexpected. He reached out and put his hand on Bauer's arm. "If it ain't too painful, Pete. Never any need to scrounge around an old attic if you don't have to."

"No, it's not painful," Bauer said. "But it probably isn't of any interest, except to me."

"I would like to hear," Marliese said.

Bauer looked at her again. She was sitting upright, her shoulders squared. It was funny, he thought; it was almost as though she were a defendant, listening to the details of a true bill brought against her.

"There isn't much," Bauer said, his eyes still on her. "It was just that all my life I had understood that my mother died a natural death and recently I was given to understand that she did not."

Captain Atkins nodded again. "And you want to know, Pete. Sure, you want to know. I can surely understand that. It's something a body'd have to find out, that's for God damn sure." He finished his drink in one swallow. "And yet, and yet . . ."

Marliese took a long pull on her cigarette and breathed out the smoke slowly and stared straight ahead.

"And yet what, Roy?" Bauer asked.

"What I mean is that I understand what you're doing and why, Pete, you got to believe that, and yet, what I mean, is that it's been so long, you know, so damned long ago."

"You mean I should just forget about it, let bygones be bygones," Bauer said. He tried to make it come out lightly.

"Now don't you get your back hair in a pucker, Pete," Captain Atkins said instantly, again with that odd sensitivity. "Nobody can forget anything like that. I couldn't, that's for damned sure." He raised his glass and saw that it was empty and without turning he lifted his arm and waved his hand at the bar.

"No more for me," Bauer said.

"Come on, Pete, come on," Captain Atkins said. "Got to have one for the road. Like I told you before, you ain't going

50

to find martinis like this anywhere else in this town. This boy whips up the best martinis in Germany, even if he is a kraut, excuse me, Marly."

It was always, Bauer thought, the index of quality at a military establishment, greater, more important, more revealing than any other statistic: the excellence of the martinis. And, of course, of the steaks. That had to come, too, in its time.

Again Bauer stole a glance at Marliese. She was still sitting stiffly erect, still staring at nothing. Her own glass, he saw, was empty. She had drunk along with Captain Atkins, drink for drink, and showed no sign of it. Unless the unnatural rigidness of her posture was not defensive at all, but simply a tactical position taken against the martinis, a German counteroffensive.

She had worked for the American military for a long time, Bauer guessed. She had picked up American ways. Even her speech, with its only faint German overtones, was the speech pattern of the Americans, the military Americans.

"It maybe wouldn't even be good for the community," Captain Atkins said in another elliptical foray.

"What do you mean, Roy, good for the community?" Bauer asked. "What has the community got to do with anything?"

The waiter appeared with the fresh drinks and Bauer, coming then to understand what the captain was saying, emptied his old one before the waiter got away with it.

"What I mean, Pete, if I understand you right, and I think I do, what you're saying is that maybe your mother just didn't die in bed, like."

"Yes," Bauer said. "That is exactly what I am saying."

"Well, what I mean, is that this is a nice little town, you know what I mean, nice people." Captain Atkins took the drink of a thirsty man. Then he stared morosely at the inroads he had made. "You know, they been trying to forget the past too. What I mean, hell, I've been here a coon's age and I got German friends, Marliese will back me up on that, her brother, Werner, for instance, one hell of a guy, one hell of a good guy. I find the Germans good people, it's hard to believe what they say about them, the way they were supposed to be then, but anyway, that's ancient history, you can't flog a dead horse forever, you know what I mean?"

"Yes," Bauer said. He wondered how soon he could leave, politely.

Captain Atkins raised his eyes from his glass and Bauer saw they were dilated and that while they apparently were focused upon him they were not looking at him at all.

"I mean, what the hell, everything gets itself exaggerated when you're fighting a war," Captain Atkins went on. "Par for the course. Look what them damned Commies are trying to promote about the boys in Vietnam, this Mylai crap. Who the hell can believe that propaganda? Anyway, that stuff is all over and done with here. All forgotten. The krauts are good folk. What good will it do to stir up old dog shit?"

Bauer knew that he should say nothing. He knew he should just let it run out and then excuse himself and get quietly away. He knew that Captain Atkins was full of martinis and that anyway he was not talking to him at all, that he was still talking through him, talking to Marliese across him, as though he were a bridge, an interpreter, something that kept them in the same orbit, as though without him there they would lose hold and career off on their own tangents. Except that they would not. They would fly off, all right, but condemned to a parallel course, endless, within sight and hearing, unable to speak or listen. How did he know all that? On what was he basing that? Was he just playing games to push everything away from himself, including himself?

He knew he should say nothing, that he was not even going to make a whisper up the hollow chimney, that he was only extending, prolonging something he wanted ended.

"Perhaps I should explain to you, Roy," he said. "Forty-three members of my family, forty-three relatives that I know of, including my father, my two brothers, and my sister—and perhaps my mother—were put to death by the Nazis. That is not propaganda, Captain. That happened. I can assure you that happened."

52

He did not look at Marliese.

Captain Atkins finished his drink. "Well, I can't argue with you, Pete," he said. "I wasn't here at the time."

With his drinking, Captain Atkins' voice, speech, seemed to grow softer, gentler, Bauer thought. It was the amiable, lenient speech he had occasionally heard from a sheriff or highway patrolman in the Deep South, courtesy to the point of mania, courtesy to that final eruption of hate and violence. And it was, it occurred to him now, in its way not unlike the kind of speech spoken right here, here in Würzburg, drawled and indolent.

It was interesting, he thought, that the first support for Hitler came from these people, the Franconians, the Bavarians, the ones with their charming lazy ways, their slurred-over speech, the happy, dancing, singing, fun Germans, celebrated, as they say, in song and story for their winsomeness, their marvelous childlike imagination, their fairy-tale land, their own unique *gemütlich* qualities. And that the ones who had most resisted the Leader, who in some ways resisted him to the end, were the dour, thorny northern Germans, the Prussians, the most totally unloved Germans of them all.

Now Captain Atkins looked at his watch and brought himself to his feet. "I got to go, Pete," he said. "We got a major going home on rotation and we're throwing him a kind of farewell party. I'd love to ask you but this is a sit-down affair and all the mouths've been counted."

"Thank you," Bauer said. "Thank you for the thought." He noticed Marliese made no move and that Captain Atkins seemed to have forgotten her.

"You going to be here over the weekend, buddy?" Captain Atkins asked.

"I don't know yet," Bauer said. He did not want to be left alone with her.

"Well, if you are, you sure got to come out and meet Peggo and the kids. I'll do you a barbecue. I tell you I make the best damned steak this side of San Antone."

"Thank you," Bauer said again.

Atkins stood there for a moment. He appeared to be in complete control. "Think about what I said, Pete. Maybe you'd be better off you just looked around the old home town, auld lang syne stuff, you know, old memories, that kind of thing. Make it easy on yourself."

He grinned suddenly, a wide, irresistible grin, and held out his hand. Bauer took it. The grip was firm and warm and not a bone-cruncher and the hand was not sweaty.

"Marliese, you look out for our visiting buddy, you hear?" Atkins said, looking at Marliese for the first time in a long time. "I know he was born here and all that but that was hell's own time ago and he's forgotten all about this pretty little town. You see he doesn't get lost on a dark street."

"Yes, Roy," Marliese said.

"There's no need," Bauer said.

"That's just what there sure as hell is, a need," Captain Atkins said. "That's what we're here for." He turned to the bar. "Put this on my tab, Fritzi, and anything else they may want here, up to and including the very fine steak dinners."

"Please," Bauer said.

Captain Atkins looked at him sternly. "This is an Army Officers' Club, Pete, and your money has no value here. Now you watch out for him, Marly, you hear?"

He waved a hand and left. He walked out of the room easily, steadily, lightly.

6

✠ ✠ ✠

BAUER TURNED TO HER. SHE WAS TAPPING A CIGARETTE OUT OF the packet. He picked up her lighter and held it out to her.

"You do not smoke?" she asked.

"No." He snapped shut the lid on the Zippo. He wanted to get away fast. The years were draining off, the years in England, North Africa, the United States, other places, the years and the things that had happened, all were sliding away, his American citizenship was sliding away, his career in the State Department, and what was left, naked, unadorned, were the basics, what had always been. He was no more than a German Jew, in Würzburg, sitting alone with an Aryan German woman.

How long the Leader's spell had lasted.

"Despite what the captain said, Frau Neubert," he said, carefully putting down the lighter, "you must not feel you must spend any more time with me."

He realized he had slipped automatically into German. He looked at her swiftly. She was holding the cigarette in front of her mouth without actually touching the filtered end to her lips and there was a faint smile there. Mocking? He could not say.

But it was as though with the departure of Captain Atkins they had both relaxed, had kicked off tight shoes, and were crinkling their toes. It should have made him feel more comfortable. It did not.

"It's my pleasure," she said. She drew tranquilly on the cigarette. "As I have said, I have never before seen a German Jew." Then she said, "Not that I would have known unless you had said so."

Was he to take that as a compliment? Well, it was, in a way, to his diligence.

"Not that I would have taken you as German at all," she said.

That, he thought, he could accept unequivocally as praise.

. . . *The school in Hampstead during the war when he worked to get the German out of his speech, the hours and hours and hours he had practiced the English accent, he had a talent for languages he supposed, as did most Europeans, especially European Jews . . . it was very difficult because he did not want just to be able to speak fluent English but wanted to speak an English no different from anyone else in London . . . having been forcibly separated from his own herd he wanted to lose himself in the new herd . . . he listened for hours to the BBC and imitated the voices of the announcers . . . he isolated his own linguistic habits and gradually eliminated them . . . and it had paid off . . . in the end he had achieved his goal . . . in England he was never taken for a German, nor a Jew . . . if there were any peculiarities now and then his accent was put down to some district of Britain, some local oddity of speech . . . and in the United States, at first, until he had again tempered his accent, he was taken for British . . .*

. . . He remembered his aunt and uncle with whom he first lived in London, who spoke with an accent despite the many years they had lived there, how they had at first thought he was wasting too much time on something they did not con-

*sider of prime importance, but how they had finally in some
way seen in it an application of purpose that was almost Tal-
mudic, and seen in that light, approved* . . .

"Well," he said, still in German, "now at last you set
eyes on a German Jew. You see the despised enemy of the
Fatherland."

He had no idea of why he said that. The drinks? It
sounded as stupid to him as it must have to her.

Her face was without expression.

"Excuse me for that, Frau Neubert," he said. "That was
an inane remark. I suppose when a tender place is touched,
one has a ridiculous reaction."

"Still tender?" she asked.

"It would seem so."

"After all these years?"

He shrugged. It was a normal shrug and yet it seemed to
him at that moment to be a characteristic Jewish gesture.
He felt something beginning to grab his belly, beginning to
squeeze.

"And after all that time in America?" she asked. "One
rarely thinks of Americans as being particularly sensitive."

"I am not an American, Frau Neubert," he said. "Except
by legal courtesy."

"Do you mind if we have another drink?" she asked.

"No. Not at all."

"You do not sound convincing."

"I just feel I'm imposing on you."

"Please just signal the bartender."

Bauer looked toward the bar. The German bartender, as
any professional, was waiting for that look and for the
raising of the hand. He nodded and set to work immediately.

Bauer picked up the Zippo and gripped it. "Is it true?"
he asked.

She was not on to his shorthand and she was with Atkins'. "Is what true?" she asked.

"That you have never seen a German Jew?" Stupid, stupid,
embarrassing question, and why was he obliged to ask?

57

"It's true, Herr Bauer," she said. "At least not that I know of. But having met you, one wonders. I may have often met others without being aware."

Again he felt that was a kind of tribute and he despised himself for it.

"And now that you know, what do you think?" he asked. "Do I look suddenly as though I had two heads?"

Why was he doing this? It was a kind of infantile masochism. Having at the start not wanted his secret—his secret? —revealed at all, now he wanted to wallow in it.

She cocked her head and studied him, the smoke curling up from her cigarette. Before she could say anything the bartender brought over the drinks. He took away the empty glasses and the ashtray and wiped the table and took a clean ashtray from a nearby table and set it in front of her.

"Thank you," she said to him in German.

He waggled his fingers and hurried away.

She picked up the glass and took a small sip and then as though remembering his question, she put down the glass and looked at him again. She looked at him intently, as though genuinely trying to ascertain whether he had one or two heads.

"No," she said at last. "You look in no way different from anyone else. No, that is not quite right either. What I wish to say is that you do not look Jewish, although I am not certain what that is. You do look foreign."

"Foreign? To you?" He did not feel at that moment foreign at all. He waited, anxiously, it seemed so important. He felt like a child who had asked a riddle and could not live another moment without the answer.

She took her time. "You look American, I suppose, and yet you do not look exactly American. But then my judgment has been formed here mostly, on the base." She paused and studied him again. "I probably would have judged you American if I had passed you on the street."

"An American Jew?" He had to wring it dry.

She shook her head slowly. "I don't know about that. I've

met American Jews on the base here, officers, enlisted men, but they were all so American that's all they were." She stopped and again tilted her head. The ash was growing long on her cigarette but she did not seem to notice it. "But after I heard you speak I would think no, you were not American, not British either. Perhaps Canadian."

She sat back, saw ash on the table, brushed it off with the side of her hand, picked up her drink and sipped some of it.

"Tell me about yourself," she said.

"I think not."

"And why?"

"It's an old tired story."

"Are you an American citizen now?"

"Yes."

"Does that make you happy?"

"It makes me neither happy nor unhappy." He finished off half his drink and felt the gin burn down. "Really, Frau Neubert, you must not waste this time with me. You must have something else you want to do."

"Do you have something else you want to do?"

"No. But that is not the point."

"Are you tired? You just arrived today."

"I am not tired. I want only not to impose myself upon you. I feel you are just obeying orders."

She took a fresh cigarette from the pack. "Roy gives no orders after four o'clock in the afternoon." She flicked on the lighter. "It must have been dreadful when you heard about your mother."

Councilor Simon Bauer, he told her, was a well-known philanthropist in Würzburg. The Bauers were all quite wealthy. The money came from a family clothing factory which had been in existence for many generations and by the time it had reached the hands of Simon Bauer it was able to run itself. Councilor Bauer had very little to do

59

with it. He paid his employees well, allowed his executives a free hand, and contented himself with living on his income, devoting himself to good living.

He was a veteran of the First World War and had won the Iron Cross, First Class, which made him a highly respected figure in Würzburg, even among those who were not by instinct admirers of Jews. This esteem was evidenced by the fact that he had been elected to the City Council, a great honor for any German. There was no talk then about his Jewish background. He was a war hero, a patron of the arts, a man who sponsored and personally supported many charities.

When Hitler had come to power his father had said, "Within twelve months they'll shoot this idiot. The German people can never put up with such a mountebank. He is utterly ridiculous and it will not be long before something dreadful happens to the poor fool."

They were seated on the terrace outside the club now. They had finished their drinks and although Bauer tried to pay he could not. The German bartender had just smiled and had said Captain Atkins would have his hide.

They had walked out. It was still light. They could see where the sun had fallen behind a ridge of hills covered by vineyards. The hills were soft lavender now, and there was a low, purple haze and it was quiet on the terrace behind the club.

It had seemed natural to talk. Perhaps it was partly because he was talking in German. But why was he going on this way? What was he trying to prove? And to whom? To her or to himself? Why was he dredging up these painful memories, spreading them out before her like a peddler showing his wares.

He knew the answer and it did not make him admire himself. He knew the need to demonstrate that his father was as German as any other German, more German than the Germans, that in all his deeds, his proud military record,

60

his social and charitable activities, he was the core of German life.

Why, he asked himself, knowing the answer to that one too and despising himself for it, why was he not talking about the father who went regularly to his synagogue, who put on his prayer shawl in the prescribed manner, and then read the hallowed words? Prayer shawl? Prayer shawl, hell! Even in his private thoughts he was an evasive weakling. *Tallith*, the beautiful, long, fringed silk *tallith*, which his father had inherited from his father and which had been destined to pass on to the eldest son.

"I remember that my family was so correct, so honorable in the strict German sense, that any experience with the police was unknown. It was just outside our experience. One day one of my father's brothers was arrested by the Gestapo. He was guilty of nothing—it was simply a routine Gestapo action against a Jew. But my father's reaction was characteristic. He didn't blame the Gestapo, he blamed my uncle. He felt that his brother had done something inexcusably shameful, that he had disgraced the family name by getting himself involved with the police. That had never happened in our family before. My father went to the police station to see what could be done. He had never been there before, despite his official position. He walked around as though he had entered another world. He was treated, I must say, with some semblance of respect—not because he was still, technically at least, a city councilor and not because of all the things he had done for Würzburg, but only because he had won the Iron Cross. In the end he was able to get my uncle released by paying a huge fine."

It was darkening now and he could not make out her face. All he could see clearly was the glow from her cigarette. She had not spoken for a long time.

"I think it was what happened to my uncle that made my father realize at last that something was happening to Germany, and that it was not going to end in the twelve months he had allotted it. My older brothers were married and so was my sister. I was very late, a last child. He made arrangements for me to be smuggled out of the country. And that was the last time I saw any of them—except the aunt who managed to keep herself alive in Theresienstadt and who eventually I brought over to the United States."

"What was it she said—about your mother?" Her voice emerged low from the twilight.

"Nothing, nothing actually." He told her how it was the night his aunt died. "When I spoke of my mother, her sister, there was something in her eyes I had never seen before. It was a terror, a guilt, the rejection of a long lie. . . . She started shaking her head and she took my hand and tried to say something. She couldn't. The words would not come. I begged her to tell me what it was about my mother and she kept shaking her head and she started to cry and she died. The tears kept running down her cheeks after she was dead."

He shifted his body on the hard, wooden, outdoor chair. He had been sitting in one position for a long time.

Nothing was said for a little while and the night came on them and then she asked, "What are you going to do now?"

"Try to find out," he said.

"Yes, I can understand that. But I mean now, tonight."

"I have no plans."

"Are you too tired to have dinner with me?"

"No."

"Will you take me to dinner?"

"Yes."

"But not here. Not unless you want the best steak in town."

He saw her stand up in the darkness and he got to his feet.

"I have a car here," she said.

They went back to the building where she worked. She pointed to a small German car. He opened the door for her and then went round and got in the other side.

"Where would you like to eat?" she asked.

"You choose," he said. "I'm a stranger here."

She took out a cigarette. He lit it for her.

"Did you never smoke?" she asked.

"Quite heavily once."

"And you gave it up? Were you afraid you would contract lung cancer or some other horrible disease?"

"Not particularly."

"Then why did you stop?"

"I suppose I did not want to belong to anything."

She turned her head. "Please?"

"Not even to a habit."

There was another military policeman at the gate, equally stupendous, equally resplendent. He glanced at the car and waved them on with a gesture that could have parted the waters of a sea.

She said nothing as she drove down the hill and then as they reached the Residenz she put her foot on the brake. "Would you mind," she said. "Would you mind if we did not have dinner?"

"No," Bauer said, for some reason unsurprised. "No, I wouldn't mind."

"I forgot," she said. "I promised my father I would visit him this evening."

"I quite understand."

"He is an old man. He would worry."

"I understand."

"I'll take you to your hotel."

"There is no need."

"It's nothing. It's almost on my way."

"I'd rather walk. Really, I'd like a little walk."

She had started the car and now she stopped it again. "You're sure? I can easily run you to the Deutscher Hof."

"I would like a little walk, I promise you."

She hesitated for a moment and then she nodded and he opened the door and got out.

He leaned down. "It was very pleasant," he said.

"Yes," she said. "Wasn't it?"

He shut the door and stood back and she drove off. He watched the little car until it turned a corner and disappeared.

He took a deep breath. There were people in the street

and there were automobiles moving around but it was quiet.

He started to walk. He was not accustomed to this much drinking. It had affected him and now it was wearing off and he seemed to hear all the words he had spoken to her. It was like meeting a stranger in a bar, someone you'll never see again. You talk and you drink and you talk some more. You talk the way you wouldn't talk to your best friend. Someone at a bar, and then you leave.

He found himself in front of the Stadt Theater again. He saw there was a performance that night of *Carmina Burana*. He frowned, slightly puzzled. That was a curious work to be presented to the good, stolid, God-fearing burghers of Würzburg, and their even more pious, self-righteous wives. Had the little baroque jewel become that advanced?

Then he smiled. Could it be? Impossible. Impossible even here. But it must be. For how many of them would know what the words meant? Could it be that it simply was that the words were in Latin and that the music sounded vaguely like Gregorian chants?

He walked over to the playbill in front of the theater. He saw that the words *cantiones profanae* which usually followed the title were not there.

It must be true. He walked away, feeling suddenly merry. They were sitting in there and if they were not dozing after their big German meals then they were as smug, some of them surely, as though they were in church. They were listening to the naughty songs as they might listen to the *Messiah*.

Ah, probably not at all. But it was fun to think that. The melody of the opening song came to him and he started to sing it. Passersby turned their heads and he realized where he was after all and he lowered his voice. The title came to him, *"Fortuna imperatrix mundi."* In English, as "Luck, Empress of the World," it might be the name of a Chinese restaurant, but in Latin it had a resounding tone, one that could pass muster in any church in the city.

He passed a small *Weinstube* and he entered. The room was full and heavy with smoke. He found an empty seat at a big table. He sat down. A man reading a newspaper attached to a hanging stick looked up and nodded. Bauer returned the courtesy.

The waitress handed him a menu but he did not need it. He ordered *Bauernwurst* and wine.

He wondered whether she really had promised her father she would see him and had just forgotten it. Not that it mattered. He was not disappointed. He was, in a way, relieved. It had been a long day. It had been a day many years long.

The waitress set the plate and wine and glass in front of him. *Bauernwurst*. When he was a child his father used to tell him that they named that just for him.

7

✠ ✠ ✠

MARLIESE CONTINUED ON THROUGH THE CITY, PAST THE STORE
windows bright with their night lighting, and turned right
at the ring near the Hauptbahnhof and drove on to an old
section of the city where squat, heavy, private homes still
managed to fend off the encroachment of the matchboxes.

She did not know why she had decided so abruptly not
to have dinner with him. She hadn't planned on that. She
had found herself almost surprised to hear herself make up
the lie about having to see her father.

Anyway, having made up the lie, she now would redress
her falsehood by fulfilling it. Her father would be glad to see
her. He was always glad to see her.

She drew up before one of the old mansions. She sat in
the car, finishing her cigarette. What was it that had made
her do what she had done? It didn't matter. As a point of
fact she didn't know why she had suggested dinner in the
first place.

She got out of the car and dropped the cigarette and
stamped on it. Her father did not like very much to see her

smoke at any time but he was outraged at the thought of her smoking in public. Werner, for some reason, even more so.

There were many things her father did not approve and did not understand. He did not understand at all, for instance, why she had continued to live in her own flat after her husband was killed. The family house was big and comfortable and empty and her father thought it made only good sense for her to move back. It made sense because she was now a woman alone and it made sense because of the money it would have saved.

She rang the bell. She had a key to the house but she preferred to ring the bell. A moment later the door was opened by Frau Koch and the old housekeeper's eyes in the wrinkles of fat on her face lit up when she saw Marliese.

Marliese went into the library. She stood on the threshold for a moment, looking across the room at the desiccated man slumped in the chair that seemed each year to get larger and larger and that by now was big enough for two of him.

Arthur Hausmann looked up from his newspaper. He removed his pince-nez. "Liesl, what a surprise," he said with pleasure. "Liesl, I'm so happy to see you." His voice was light and thin.

Perhaps that was the reason, she thought, just to see that happiness. She walked over to him and bent down and kissed his cheek. It was papery and the color of old parchment. "How are you, papa?" she asked.

"Tip-top, tip-top," he said. "Have you eaten?"

"Yes, no, not really, but I'm not hungry, papa."

He sighed. "You must eat more regularly, Liesl," he said.

"I eat enough, papa," she said.

"Have you been working? Did you just finish?"

"Yes, papa."

He folded his newspaper and looked up at her. "You know, Liesl, I really don't think it is correct for you to continue to work for the Americans. I could well understand it after Heinrich died. You had to do something so you wouldn't brood too much. But all that is past now. Have you considered giving up your job with the Americans and returning to your home here?"

Her eyes crinkled. "So that I could be on exhibition, papa?"

"Exhibition? What does that mean?"

"To be picked up by a good German widower who is looking around for a good German widow?"

"Really, Liesl," her father said. "Not that that would be such a bad idea. It isn't good for a woman to be alone. You're still young and you're beautiful and there would be any number of men who would seek your hand."

Seek her hand. Who but her father could put those old words together.

Seek her hand, he meant, when she rid herself of her American lover.

"In any case you might think about it," Hausmann said. "I have the feeling that it degrades us a little in the eyes of our friends."

"My working or my being a widow?" she asked.

"Your working, Liesl," he said, taking her seriously. "It was not your fault Heinrich was killed. That was an act of God."

She guessed in fact it was. If anything could be blamed on God, falling down the side of a mountain was surely it.

"I do wish you would consider it," Hausmann said.

She nodded and said she would as though he had not said the same thing in the same words every time she came to see him.

He opened his mouth to say something and then closed it. She straightened some magazines on a side table and sat down on a couch. The light was on the other side of him now and she had the sensation that it was shining right through him. Her father was in his late sixties and had always been a long, thin man, and through the years had seemed not to have aged as much as to have dried out.

She took out a cigarette and lit it.

"You smoke too much, Liesl," he said immediately. "You know how much your mother disliked your smoking. Even Heinrich used to say you smoked too much."

"He used to say that because he said it spoiled my wind for climbing mountains."

"And I'm sure it does."

"But I don't climb mountains, papa, and Heinrich never smoked and I'm alive and he's dead."

"Liesl," Hausmann said.

"And if I didn't smoke and I did like to climb mountains I might have fallen down with him and be just as dead as he is."

"Liesl," her father said again.

"I'm sorry, papa," she said.

"Now, Liesl, what has been happening to you?" he asked.

"Nothing much, papa. Oh, yes, today I met someone who was born here and who just came back today after twenty-five years."

"Is that so?"

"A Jew."

"Isn't that interesting," Hausmann said. He felt around at a small table next to his chair and found a packet of stubby, small cigars. "I haven't spoken to a German Jew in a long time."

He clipped the end of the cigar with a small gold instrument that dangled from a gold watch chain across his hollow belly. He lit the cigar carefully.

"What was your reaction to this Jew?" he asked when he had the cigar going to his satisfaction.

"I don't know," she said. "At first I didn't know he was a Jew."

"It's true," Hausmann said, puffing contentedly. "After all, they lived for many years in Germany and they are like chameleons. They take on the color and configuration of whatever their background happens to be. I have heard French Jews bear a strong resemblance to Frenchmen and that English Jews do so similarly."

"That must be true," she said. "This one lived for a long while in England and now lives in America. He was dressed as an American but he spoke more like an Englishman."

"Yes," he said. "They can trick you. They are quite clever, I must give them that. They are quick and they are clever. There used to be quite a few of them around here and they added interest. I must say, they added interest. Of course, all things considered, we're better off without them."

"It was almost as though one met a man from Mars only to find him to be quite ordinary. Even his appearance."

Hausmann pursed his lips judiciously, allowing smoke to escape. "The propaganda was too much that way in the old days," he said. "Herr Streicher used to give them all grossly exaggerated noses in *Der Stürmer*. I've known good Germans with noses as big as that of any Jew I ever saw. Where did you happen to meet this one?"

"At the base. He came to see Captain Atkins."

Hausmann leaned away from her and carefully broke off the ash on his cigar. There was a small silence in the room. There was a tacit understanding between them that she would not, unless it was absolutely necessary, ever mention that name.

Hausmann cleared his throat. "Tell me, Liesl," he said. "What part of Germany does he come from."

"I've already told you, papa," she said. "He was born here, in Würzburg."

"What is his name? It is quite possible that I might have known the family."

"Bauer. Peter Bauer." For a moment she imagined the name had had an effect on him but she saw she was mistaken, that it was only that he was still displeased that she had mentioned the other name. "Does that mean anything to you, papa?"

Hausmann moved his head slowly from side to side. "There were several Bauers here. There still are. Bauer is a German name as well as a Jewish one. What does this man do? How old is he? What does he look like?"

"So many questions, papa?" She was pleased that he was

still capable of evincing curiosity. "What does he look like? He is not bad-looking. He is dark, graying. His face is quite attractive, I suppose one must say. He's fairly tall. I think he must be in his early forties. He said he left Würzburg when he was a very small boy. He was smuggled out, he said, because his parents were afraid of what might happen to him. What does he do now? He is some kind of official in the American State Department."

Hausmann looked at the end of his cigar. "Did he speak of his parents? Did he mention his father and what his occupation was?"

"Yes, papa," she said, more and more pleased with his concentration and attentiveness. She had known there must have been some reason for her deciding not to have dinner with Bauer. "He said his father was a city councilor and that he had fought for Kaiser Wilhelm and had won an Iron Cross."

"What happened to him?"

"He said his father was put to death in Theresienstadt."

"And his mother?"

"That's why he's here. He said that he had always thought his mother died a natural death."

"What caused him to think otherwise?"

"Something an aunt seemed to hint as she was dying." She put out her cigarette. "He asked me to have dinner with him. Or rather I asked him to have dinner with me. We started out from the Officers' Club and on the way I suddenly did not want to eat with him. I don't know why."

"It would have been acceptable, Liesl," Hausmann said. "These days it is considered quite correct." He thought for a moment. "I don't know how I can make that statement since there are no Jews, German Jews that is, who live here now." He shrugged. "But with the new way of thinking I feel reasonably certain no one would have said anything if you had dined with him."

"Nobody would have known, I'm sure, papa," she said. "He has only one head."

Hausmann laughed loudly. "Only one head. That is quite

funny. The things you come out with these days, Liesl. Only one head." He shook his head, still laughing.

When she was gone Hausmann put through a call to his son, Werner. Werner's wife, Traude, answered and said her husband was speaking at a meeting in Schweinfurt.

"He's always speaking at some damned meeting somewhere," Hausmann said. "When do you expect him home?"

"He said he would not be late."

"Have him call me."

"Tonight, papa?"

"Of course tonight."

"Even if he is late?"

"You said he would not be."

"I never can tell, papa," Traude said, a little frightened, as would be any good German housewife, at the irritation in the voice of her father-in-law.

"Damn it, Traude, whenever my son gets home, tell him to telephone me. Can you understand that?"

"Yes, papa," she said.

He hung up and went back to his seat. He picked up the cigar. It was smoked down too much to be relit. He took another one. The doctor had told him no more than four a day and he had smoked his fourth. He lit the fifth and sat back and waited.

It was well after midnight when Werner Hausmann returned the call.

"Traude left a note that I must call you no matter when I returned home, papa. What is it? Are you ill? Do you need a doctor?"

"No, I am not ill," Hausmann said. "I have something important to tell you."

Werner breathed out hard. "Can it wait until morning, papa? I'm a little tired from all the talking I did." His voice rose slightly. "They stood up and cheered when I finished. You should come to one of the meetings. You would be proud of me."

"I have had enough meetings in my lifetime, Werner," Hausmann said. "No, it cannot wait until morning. You will listen to me now. Peter Bauer has returned to Würzburg."

"Peter Bauer," Werner repeated. "Who is Peter Bauer, papa, and why must I call you in the middle of the night to hear about him?"

Hausmann gripped the telephone. "Werner, does your speechmaking addle your mind? Does the name Bauer mean nothing to you? Are you so full of yourself that you have forgotten important matters I have told you? Is there no room anymore in your mind for anything except your damned politics?"

There was a moment's silence on the telephone. Werner Hausmann had not been spoken to that way by his father in many years.

"Werner," the old man rasped.

"Yes, papa."

"You are still there. Good! I thought perhaps you fell asleep."

Then Werner said, "Papa, Peter Bauer?"

"Yes, yes, Werner, Peter Bauer. So it comes to you at last."

"Peter Bauer," Werner repeated.

"The son of Councilor Simon Bauer. The son of Hedwig Bauer."

"My God," Werner said quietly.

"Yes, finally it gets through that thick skull."

"Papa," Werner said. "Perhaps it is not altogether important. After all isn't it natural that he should one day want to visit the city where he was born? It's entirely natural."

"He came here from America to find out how his mother died," Hausmann said. "And I know you will consider that perfectly natural as well."

Werner was silent and then he asked, "How do you know all this, papa?"

"From Liesl, from your sister. She was here tonight. She told me he reported his arrival to the American military authorities." Even at this moment he could not bring himself to pronounce the name of Captain Roy Atkins.

"Is he in the American Army?"

"He has a post in the American State Department. He apparently is important enough to have to notify the American authorities of his presence here."

"What else did Liesl tell you?"

"They went to the Officers' Club with—with the man she works for. They were alone after—after the man she works for left. He told her a great deal, Bauer did. About his family. About how he always thought his mother died in an ordinary way and now he does not."

"Let me think for a moment," Werner said.

"Yes, perhaps that is what you should do," Hausmann said. "If it is not too late and you are not tired from all that brilliant talking." After a few moments, Hausmann asked, "Are you still there?"

"Yes, papa."

"Then for God's sake say something."

"Papa, perhaps you are making too much of this," Werner said soothingly. "After all, what can he find out now? That his mother died in a certain way? And beyond that, what? Perhaps not even that much. So much time has passed, papa. Records have vanished. The firestorm saw to that. People are dead. Memories have faded."

"Werner, you are a dumb ass," Hausmann said very slowly.

"Papa!"

"A damn fool."

"Papa, please."

"None of your precious followers can hear me. You're worse than a fool, Werner. You're an idiot."

"Papa, please don't excite yourself."

"Unless you are behaving so stupidly to keep me from being alarmed. Is that it?"

74

Werner breathed out hard. "Yes, papa," he admitted. "You know what Dr. Kruger has said."

"Then don't. I am not entirely senile yet and the devil with what Felix Kruger says. He was an old woman when he was six years old."

"All right, papa."

"You may be clever but you don't know everything."

"I never pretended I did, papa."

"We must cope with this."

"Yes, papa."

"And don't try to treat me as a foolish old man and tell me there's nothing to worry about."

"No, papa."

" 'No, papa, yes, papa'! Is that all you can say?"

"I will take care of this matter."

"What will you do?"

"I will arrange to meet Bauer, first of all."

"Meet him? Now that's the intelligent thing to do! And what will you do after that, Werner? Bring him here and introduce him to me? You're still talking brilliantly, son, absolutely brilliantly."

"Papa."

"Now listen to me very carefully. He must have no connection with this family, do you understand, no connection at all."

"He already has a connection with this family."

"Liesl? Her name is Neubert not Hausmann. That tells him nothing."

"Papa, I am not going to just wait for this man to do something. That is not my way. I am going to make it a point to meet him."

"To what purpose?"

"If I am to deal with him I should know something of him. Besides, papa, it is an opportunity for me. He's a rare species, almost nonexistent in Germany now, totally extinct here. I might learn something that could be useful to me, while he is still around."

75

Presently Hausmann said, "Well, perhaps you are right."

"The worst thing is to be in the dark."

"All right. And you can be clever when you keep your wits about you."

"I'll speak to Liesl tomorrow. Bauer undoubtedly told her many things she neglected to repeat to you. Since she doesn't know anything she wouldn't be able to assess what is important and what is not."

"You can think straight when you want to."

"I came by that honestly enough, papa."

"Never mind that."

"And I'll speak to my friends. We can make a plan of action and formulate our tactics."

"I will assume you will know exactly how little to tell them."

"Naturally, papa."

"Hmm. Well, that may not be a bad idea. Perhaps you finally can get some practical use out of that so-called brain trust of yours."

"I will call a meeting of my council tomorrow."

"Werner."

"Yes, papa."

"You must be very clever. Whatever is done, you must be very, very clever. Remember this man is an official of the United States government. The American military authorities have been notified formally that he is here in Würzburg."

"I will not forget, papa. You know what my philosophy is."

"I have heard it often enough. Werner, just one thing more."

"Yes, papa."

"Werner, I'm an old man. There is little that can be done to me any more and before too long there will be nothing that can be done. But you, you have your life and your career ahead of you. What I am trying to say, Werner, is that through no fault of your own you have more at stake here than I have."

"Get some sleep, papa," Werner said. "I will take care of this business. I promise you."

Hausmann hung up. He stood motionless by the telephone for a little while and then he walked slowly back to his chair. He sat down heavily. He was exhausted. But his son's assurances made him feel a little better. Werner had a good head on him and perhaps his way of thought was a good way. A great many persons seemed to be thinking so.

And yet he had by this time worked out his own private relationship with God, not at all unusual in an old man who was soon to be ready to start finding out new things, if there were new things to be found out, and being a devout Catholic, he believed with all his soul there were. He had an understanding with God and being not only an old man and a true Catholic but a Catholic old man who was a German he also held the conviction that in one way or another in the end the books were always balanced. It would be disorderly to think otherwise.

8

✠ ✠ ✠

EMERGING FROM THE HOTEL ARCADE, BAUER SAW THE DAY WAS
gray and there was a hint of rain. He saw, leaning against
his car, the taxi driver who had brought him from the station the day before.

"Did you just throw away the card I gave you yesterday?"
the driver asked.

"Yes," Bauer said. "As a matter of fact, I did."

"So many people do. And cards are so expensive to print."

"And why did you guess I had done that?"

"I saw you at the American military base yesterday. You
didn't call for me to take you there."

"I'm sorry," Bauer said.

"Well, perhaps we can make up for it today. Do you happen to want a taxi, mein Herr?"

"Yes, it so happens I do. Do you always follow up your
fares this way?"

The driver shrugged. "Business isn't very good at this hour
of the day. A hotel—a tourist—that's the best chance."

He opened the door of the cab and then stiffened. He

touched his cap in a kind of salute. "Where may I take you, mein Herr?"

"Do you know where the old Jewish cemetery is?" Did he imagine he saw a flicker in the driver's eyes?

"Yes."

"I want to go there. I'll want you to wait there for a short while and then take me back. Can you manage that?"

"Yes."

Bauer entered the cab and the driver shut the door and got behind the wheel. At the first traffic pause he asked, "Have you been there before?"

"Yes," Bauer said. He knew exactly where the driver was headed and could have saved him time and effort. He preferred to allow the man to grope in his clumsy German way.

"Not many people go there these days," the driver said.

"I would not think so."

"In a way it's a forgotten place."

"It must be."

The driver turned left on Ludwigstrasse. "Do you have some old acquaintance buried there?"

He was really lunging, Bauer thought. "Several."

"Is that true?"

"My family," Bauer said. "Generations of my family."

The driver glanced at him briefly. "I would not have guessed you were of the Jewish faith."

The Jewish faith . . . "Why is that?" Bauer asked.

The driver hunched his shoulders. "One has a memory of . . . of those of the Jewish faith. But then it's been so many years since I've had anything to do with one of our own Jews. Of course there have been many among the American officers and soldiers."

"Many?"

"Perhaps one is just conscious of them. But I used to think that the United States Army deliberately sent them here, to Germany. As a kind of revenge. Or perhaps it was that the American Jews asked to be assigned to Germany. For their own reasons. As a point of interest the last time I

79

went to this cemetery was to take two American Jewish officers there."

"How did you know they were Jews?"

"They told me. They made it a point to tell me."

They entered Berlinerplatz. The driver was silent.

"You need not feel embarrassed," Bauer said at last. "I will lay out your problem, and I will agree in advance it is a formidable one. Here you are, a former German Army officer. Correct?"

"Correct."

"It was the army, was it not? Not, by chance, the SS?"

"*Wehrmacht*," the driver said.

"Of course. Then you had a proper military rank and not one of those linguistic consortiums such as *Unterstürmführer* or *Oberstürmbannführer*."

"I was a major," the driver said.

"By the way, Major," Bauer said. "Were the SS officers always addressed by their full titles? I never had the opportunity to find out myself."

"I had very little to do with the SS."

"Naturally. Well, let us continue. Despite your previous eminence as a field-grade officer you now make your living driving this cab with only memories to sustain you."

"You are being sarcastic, mein Herr, but I will assure you I do not suffocate myself in the past."

"Only mildly sarcastic, Major. But there are things which you cannot entirely forget."

"Granted."

"All right. Now here am I. On the one hand I am officially an American and a potential source of income for you. Correct?"

"Correct."

"On the other hand, unfortunately, I am a Jew, and moreover a native, German Jew. That has by tradition to trigger a certain reaction in you, particularly the part of you which remains forever an officer in the German Army. Am I still on the right course?"

Presently the driver nodded again, more slowly this time.

"So what do we do to resolve this dilemma?" Bauer asked. "One, we arrange it so that this would be our last journey together. That would be the simplest solution, except that you would suffer financially. Second, we could pretend the situation does not exist, that I am, in fact, what I appear to be, an American tourist. That would be a small conceit and I am certain we could both sustain it. Or, third and last, we can face up to the reality of the matter, and somehow live with that. That would require a certain humility on your part, true. But I too have a sense of humiliation about the entire circumstance, past and present, so we would be about even there."

Both men lapsed into silence. The day seemed to be growing darker. This German grayness seemed to Bauer to be particularly dreary, drearier than grayness in Paris or London or anywhere else.

Passing now through the outskirts of the city he tried to recall his last visit to the cemetery. All he could remember now was his abhorrence. For a reason he did not yet fully understand, and which he knew he should, since surely it was one clue to what he was, even as a child he had loathed the various religious ceremonials of death and burial. The entire concept had always seemed barbaric to him, something more fitting for a New Guinea aborigine, whether practiced as he remembered it from his childhood in Germany or as he had witnessed it in other countries since. All religions, he felt, were equally offensive in their atavism. He had always hated the whole rite in synagogue or church. He felt even more strongly about people finding it necessary to visit graves attempting to communicate with the dead; the sick, imperative need to stand or kneel before a stone and believe they in some way were reaching to whatever lay buried below.

He closed his eyes and his mind, dwelling as it had on death, made a small shift in gears.

. . . Below the Dom looked like the cap of a mushroom . . . he had never before seen Würzburg from the air and

it appeared now not unlike the miniature of the medieval city of Würzburg that was in a glass case in the museum in the Festung . . . he remembered the uncanny effect in the museum of looking through the binoculars on the chains into the glass case and now he looked through glasses and it was another kind of eeriness . . . here, now, in the Liberator, looking down, everything was exactly as he had remembered it and the new angle made no difference at all . . .

. . . the command came over the intercom . . . he pushed the button, releasing the flares . . . now what he had seen until then only in the light of the night came out boldly, garishly, as though it were some monstrous fête . . . now the city was lighted from the sky as though ordered so by some supernatural force, and now what he had seen and recognized because his memories filled in what he could not truly see, he could see in weird detail, the outlines of streets and houses and buildings and churches and spires and domes weaving drunkenly in the drifting flares, casting wildly staggering shadows . . . and he had the feeling he could even make out his house on Annastrasse . . . he could not but he had the feeling he could . . .

"We are here, mein Herr," the driver said.

Bauer opened his eyes. He looked out of the car window. A faint drizzle had started. The entrance to the cemetery had not changed, and he also now remembered the last time he had been there. A second cousin had died.

The driver got out and opened the door and Bauer stepped out. He looked more closely at the former major, the short journey of that morning having given them some small intimacy they had not possessed when they had started.

He rather liked what he saw, and he thought surely that was odd. One doesn't usually find German ex-army officers attractive, nobody does, but especially not a German Jew. Was it because of the more or less menial work the major now was doing, a subjective kind of grace that existed largely in the eye of the beholder? He decided not. There had been a comedown for this man but not so dramatic a comedown to create around him any romantic aura. He was no former Russian grand duke now nobly holding life at bay by working as a doorman.

The former major had a good face and a good stance and Bauer would guess he had been a very good officer.

"I only glanced at your name before I threw the card away, Major," Bauer said. "Could you tell it to me again?"

The driver raised his head and once again took on something of a military deportment. "Manfred Reinhard, at your service, mein Herr."

There was the faintly mocking tone in his voice but now it did not bother Bauer. "Yes, I remember now. My name is Peter Bauer."

Reinhard rubbed his chin. "Why does that name sound familiar to me?"

"It is not an uncommon name, Major," Bauer said.

"There was a well-known man by that name in the old days. A Jew. He was even a city councilor."

"He was my father."

"Is that a fact? He was a famous man."

"Yes. He was put to death in Theresienstadt," Bauer said.

He was instantly ashamed of having said that. It was, he knew, childish and pointless and misdirected at the wrong man and surely at a wrong time. Without saying more he entered the cemetery grounds.

He walked along a gravel path bordered by grass cropped neatly. He felt the wetness in the air.

He saw the caretaker's cottage, a small, gray building, only a little darker than the day. He entered. An old man was squatting on a stool behind a counter. He was smoking a pipe with a stem so truncated the bowl seemed almost to touch his mouth. He had a stubble of a beard and he wore a black cap that lent his lined face a kind of official status. The room smelled of stale tobacco.

He gave Bauer a quick, professional survey, removed the pipe from his mouth, and said, in English, "Good morning."

"Good morning," Bauer said in German.

The man's eyes opened a little more. He looked, Bauer thought, like a character in *Waiting for Godot*.

"I am in charge here," the man said, now speaking in German. "What can I do for the gentleman?"

"I want to go to the section where the Bauer family is buried," Bauer said.

"Bauer? Bauer?" The old man shoved the pipe back into his mouth, reached below the counter, brought up a large, old, black book. He set the book on the counter and took out of his pocket a pair of steel-rimmed glasses. He set the glasses on his nose, looked again at Bauer, the glasses enlarging the rheum in his eyes, and then he opened the book. He ran a finger down the list of names, found what he wanted, nodded, closed the book, returned it to its place, and came up with another book. He opened it and Bauer saw it contained numbered plans for different parts of the cemetery. The old man poked around until he found what he wanted, nodded again, closed the book, put it down on the shelf, took off his glasses, and came round the counter.

"I will take the gentleman there," he said.

"There is no need for that," Bauer said. "Just tell me where it is."

"I will take the gentleman," the old man repeated.

They stepped outside. The caretaker took a keyring out of his pocket, selected a key, and locked the door to the little house.

What was there inside to steal, Bauer wondered.

The old man started down one of the paths. The drizzle had stopped and now there was nothing more than a gray, heavy misting, and as the old man pattered on ahead Bauer thought he looked now more like one of the gravediggers in *Hamlet*. He thought he could hear the old man mumbling to himself but he could not be sure.

He looked around. He was surprised to find everything well kept. He had not known what he would find but he

84

had not in any case anticipated this kind of consideration. The graves were cared for and, astonishing him more than anything, the stones were intact. He had read somewhere that the gravestones in Jewish cemeteries had been removed by the Nazis to make paving blocks.

He came upon a stone larger than any of the others and much newer. He paused and read the gothic script:

IN MEMORIAM TO OUR JEWISH CITIZENS WHO WERE PUT TO DEATH IN CONCENTRATION CAMPS

He began to shake again and he detested himself for feeling and for showing his feelings and then he heard a sanctimonious voice at his side and smelled the acrid odor of very cheap tobacco.

"It is our memorial to our fellow citizens," the old man said, talking around the pipe, the words blurring. "It is our way of trying to make up a little for what those swine did."

Bauer looked at him. He was standing, his feet apart, his hands clasped behind his back.

"It is an example, mein Herr, of how generous this community has been, to collect money from the good people of Würzburg, and to build this memorial to the poor Jews. You would never believe how hard everybody worked to collect the money."

Bauer said nothing. He wanted to move on but it was as though he were rooted, as though he were drugged by the pipe smoke, held immobile by the slow, monotonous voice.

"It was such a terrible thing those swine did," the old man said. "It was something none of us knew about at the time. It was only afterward we found out what the swine did. Then we thought it fitting that we honor the poor dead."

Keep talking, Bauer thought, his hands clenching painfully at his sides, the shaking gone now. Keep talking, all the banalities, all the comforting clichés, all the satisfied self-love. And how much of the damned money that was spent on this piece of stone was not in one way or another originally extracted from those same Jews?

"We loved our Jewish citizens," the old man continued, in

85

what now had taken on the form and rote of well-worn patter, the speech of a museum guide. "We had nothing to do with the National Socialist swine, you understand. It was a fine thing that was done here for the poor Jews and we all were happy to do it."

At any moment, Bauer thought, when the voice ran down he would hear, "This is a recording. . . ."

He started on again and the old man, who was about to philosophize further, hurried after him and then passed him so that he could lead the way. They walked through the grave-yard, the old man turning now right and now left, and then he trotted ahead, peered down, and then straightened, removing his pipe and his cap as well.

"Here is what you seek, gentleman," he said in appropriate, sepulchral tones. "I will leave you. One does not want the presence of a stranger at a time such as this. You can see the lodge from here so you will not get lost on your return."

The old man put on his cap, touched the beak in the manner of touching a forelock, and shuffled away. The tobacco smoke lay in the thick, absorbent air. Bauer looked down at that piece of German earth where members of his family, going back to the grandparents of his parents, lay buried.

He stood there, reminding himself of his lifetime of feelings about cemeteries and gravemarkers and the disease of necrophilia, reminding himself that he was there for a purpose and not for any reason of sentimentality.

He walked slowly into this, his own private piece of the cemetery. He was, he was suddenly and intensely aware at that moment, the last of the line.

He, Peter Bauer, expatriate, ex-destroyer, ex-R.A.F. flyer, was the final one of them all, the terminus, the last station. And that was the way it was going to have to end and he wanted on the sudden to apologize to someone, most of all to his father, who was nowhere around.

He paused before a stone that bore the name of his uncle, Richard, the hussar, the one whose photograph had so often enthralled him in his grandmother's house.

86

He looked at the weather-softened name and dates for a time and then he moved on, slowly. He began to feel a pounding in his chest. It was getting to him, despite every barrier he had set against it. The given names on the stones (the "Christian" names? Christian?) were almost all unfamiliar to him; most of them had lived and died and had been buried before he was born. But he felt a burden, a dull weight; the burgeoning of the Bauer family, a tree of death.

He made himself continue on until he came at last upon a portion of virgin, untilled earth, covered with weeds. There were no graves here. There were no stones. This was that small morsel of Germany his parents had marked out for themselves and which they unexpectedly were prevented from ever claiming.

He looked at the undisturbed ground which no hand had ever touched, at the patch of shoddy weeds still wet from the rain, and he felt an oncoming of an agitation greater than any he had ever before experienced. He felt a chill creep into his bones, he felt his muscles contracting in short, violent, wrenching spasms. He fell to his knees because he could no longer stand. He tasted the salt from his tears and he reached out and touched the soggy, unoccupied, unused earth.

Presently he brought himself to his feet. His body felt as though it had been pummeled. He was cold and tired and he rubbed the palms of his hands together and he felt more a Jew than he had ever before felt, standing there on a ragged piece of land which had been earmarked for a special purpose and which now grew its own weeds for its own mourning.

He started back at last.

Well, he had made the first move.

This, the fact that his mother's body was not there proved nothing, in reality. It was too much to think that if she had died naturally the authorities then would have had the kindness to permit a normal burial for a Jew. It would have been a small miracle to have found her there, to have his question answered; but then, he thought, leaving his ancestors, miracles, especially small, gentle, bite-sized miracles were not entirely unknown. A tiny, quite unrealistic part of him had hoped against all hope he might have so been favored.

He walked in the drizzle that started again along the clean paths and reached the lodge and entered it. The old man, reading a local paper now, folded the paper, put it down, and stood. Bauer gave him a few marks. The old man removed his cap again and bowed.

"Thank you, gentleman," he said. "You appreciate how we watch over these souls."

9

✠ ✠ ✠

BAUER WALKED BACK TO THE TAXI. REINHARD WAS LEANING against the fender, puffing on a cigarette. He threw away the cigarette and opened the door for his fare.

Bauer got in and Reinhard started back. Bauer very badly wanted a cigarette and considered asking the major for one.

He was almost at the point of so doing when Reinhard pulled up to the curb. He got out and went round and opened the rear door. "Come on, my friend, we'll have a cup of coffee. You look as though you could use one."

After a moment Bauer got out of the cab and he followed the driver into a small *Gasthaus*. Reinhard selected a table and gestured for Bauer to sit down. A waitress shambled up and Reinhard ordered two coffees, curtly, at the same time drawing off the gloves he used for driving. He was army now. The waitress, catching the old, unmistakable sound, seeing a remembered gesture, curtseyed and hurried off.

"Well, my friend, you look as though you've been pulled through a wringer," Reinhard said.

"It shows that much," Bauer said.

"You Jews never were much good at hiding your emotions."

"We try. Sometimes we try very hard."

The girl brought the coffees, surely breaking all records. She curtseyed again and backed away.

Bauer wrapped both hands around the cup, grateful for the warmth. He drank some of the coffee. He saw Reinhard contemplating him.

Reinhard poured cream into his coffee, carefully measured out a spoonful of sugar, stirred it in. His movements, Bauer saw, were economical, precise. He might have been a laboratory worker mixing chemicals.

"And what did you think of Würzburg's pride?" Reinhard asked after tasting the coffee and finding it good.

"Please?"

"The cemetery. The sop to the local conscience."

"Is that what it is?"

"Didn't you see the memorial?"

"Yes."

"And did it impress you? Did it indicate to you that the people here were sincerely atoning for old sins?"

"I'm not certain what my feelings were at that moment."

"Did the phony old geezer give you that spiel about how the people of Würzburg collected money out of the goodness of their hearts? Out of their love for their martyred Jewish friends and neighbors?"

"He did."

"Bullshit."

"How is that?" Bauer drank some more coffee, thankful to listen to anything that would help him manage his own feelings.

"The Americans were responsible for that," Reinhard said.

Bauer heard now that Reinhard's enunciation was more clipped, almost staccato, and saw that in the set of his head there was a kind of finality that accepted no contradiction.

"How did they do that?" Bauer asked, feeling better with each moment.

"When the Americans first occupied Würzburg there were

quite a few Jewish officers. Almost the first thing they did was put Germans to work restoring the cemetery."

"Ah," Bauer said.

"Nothing had ever been done to damage it, you understand." Reinhard took out his cigarettes and offered the pack to Bauer.

Bauer shook his head. There was, he realized, a new and subtle development in their relationship. The major had had his own reasons for wanting the coffee, for wanting to remove himself from the confines of the taxi. He was full of himself now. And he could never have managed this behind his wheel.

All he lacked, Bauer thought, was a monocle.

"Nothing of what you might term as 'desecration," Reinhard said. "Nothing serious, anyway. Vandalisms. Small boys. But the cemetery had been abandoned and had gone back to weed. Terrible shape. Unfit for human habitation." Reinhard chuckled at his own humor "Well, anyway, the American Jews put it to rights."

"I see," Bauer said. He was much calmer now. Things were sorting themselves out. It was curious, he thought, how disturbing was a challenge to old convictions, even when the challenge was a positive one.

"But that wasn't the end of it," Reinhard said. "No, not at all. When our good town fathers saw how important that cemetery was to the conquerors they conceived the notion of putting up that monument. They worked it out by the slow grinding of their brains that the Americans would like that and that was a time, Herr Bauer, when it was valuable to do things the Americans liked."

"I understand," Bauer said. He finished his coffee.

Reinhard snapped his fingers. The waitress, as though waiting with held breath for the favor of just such a signal, rushed up. Reinhard pointed to both cups. The girl scooped up the cups and saucers and ran away.

"Odd thing," Reinhard said in the manner of a field-grade officer explaining some tactical problem. "We Germans are able to practice self-delusion to a degree that leaves everybody else out of the running. I'm told the Egyptians have this quality today. That they believe that simply saying something will be done does it, as though the words themselves do it. Fantasizing. But they couldn't hold a candle to us."

"How, exactly?" Bauer asked. He was wondering now why Reinhard was going to all this bother and he thought perhaps it was something just a little beyond the satisfaction of his own ego and he thought that could not be so at all, since Reinhard was a German, very much a German, and everybody knew Germans never did things like that.

"Well, they collected all this money. Regular campaign. Door-to-door business. It wasn't all that money but in those days, right after the end of the war, times were hard here. And they put up that piece of stone as the local expiation of the genocide."

The girl returned with the fresh coffee. Reinhard favored her with a brief smile and she rejoiced as though he had handed her a purse of silver.

The major—Bauer no longer could think of him as the former major—went through his ritual of adding cream and sugar. He tasted, approved.

"Perhaps there was some small scrap of conscience involved," Reinhard said. "Certainly there was a sense of guilt. But the motivation almost entirely was to please the Americans. The people here reckoned their few marks made a sensible investment."

"I'm sure it did," Bauer said.

"Yes, it did. The Jewish officers and men—and some of the non-Jewish ones as well—were as pleased as they could be. They felt they had made a vital contribution to the cause of reforming the horrible Germans. But you see, my friend, and this is where the dishonesty comes in, the Germans could not leave it at that. You see, what was done as an intelligent ploy has in the passing of years become something else altogether. Now that the Americans are no longer here as an army of occupation, now that there no longer is any requirement to butter up the boys who won the war, the Würzburgers have come to a totally different attitude about that monument. Now most of them really believe it was erected by them out of the compassion of their hearts. The sane, reasonable original motivation has been forgotten, wiped out."

"You sound cynical, Major," Bauer said, thinking how healthy that was.

Reinhard waved his cigarette. "Not at all. Just realistic. One has to face up to truth. Else nothing is learned, nothing even remembered. One of our national tragedies, we never can admit a simple truth. We never can admit we did indescribable things to other human beings. Just as we have always believed we can never be whipped honestly, that if we lose there must be some other reason."

"And how have you worked all this out, Major?" Bauer asked. "For yourself?"

"Herr Bauer, I am a German who has no apologies to make to anyone for anything."

"You are a fortunate man," Bauer said.

Reinhard regarded him for a moment and then continued. "I was a professional soldier. I did what I believed to be my duty. Believed it then, believe it now. When it was all over and I was at loose ends I used to visit one officers' organization or another. Couldn't stomach it. Not for long. Damned self-pity. How we could have won the war if Hitler had left the generals alone. Bullshit. With what we had lined up against us we'd have lost anyway. What the hell, my friend, one gets knocked down, one picks himself up off his ass and carries on. I wasn't much good for anything. Officer without army is absolutely useless, I assure you. In time I took a job driving a cab. Later on bought my own. Not a bad life. Now and again I meet interesting people, foreign chaps such as yourself."

Bauer said, "Foreigners, like me?"

Reinhard chuckled. "Knew you'd make a grab for that, my friend. Well, Herr Bauer, what the hell, just what is it that makes a man? I suppose what you're born with, your ancestry, heredity, blood, whatever the devil you want to call it, has something to do with it. But the older I get the more I believe it's experience that shapes most of the man and your experience has not been with this city or very much with this country, I would imagine. Whatever you are, my friend, you're certainly not a Würzburger, and probably not even much of a German."

"Yes," Bauer said. "That is what they said in the old days."

"Bullshit, Bauer," Reinhard said. "Don't go Jewish on me. I've been trying to talk to you as one man to another."

"You're quite right, Major," Bauer said, wanting to call him Reinhard, without any prefix, unable to do so. "I'm sorry."

After a moment Reinhard said, "I suppose you must be considered a man of the world."

"Or a man without a country."

Reinhard nodded. "I envy your experiences and what you have seen of the world, Herr Bauer. But I also am German enough to believe one should not be without connections. Do you have connections?"

"No," Bauer said.

10

✠ ✠ ✠

BOCKSBEUTEL—BUCK'S BAG, BUCK'S SACK, BUCK'S BALL. BAUER
had almost forgotten that word. Probably the first "dirty"
word learned by every boy in Würzburg. And one any boy
could say with straight face in front of his parents because
while the origin in the hoary past was from some ancient
Franconian with his humor and his own sense of imagery, it
now was simply the proper and accepted name for the little
wine bottle.

Bocksbeutel. And how long had it taken for each boy who
relished saying the word, how long had it taken for him to
discover that a buck, a ram, had not one but two balls? And
that they hung in width as well as depth, and not flat like the
round bottom of the bottle under its long neck?

He looked now at the huge man whose head almost grazed
the low ceiling beams, whose hand, big as a ham, gripped the
slender bottle neck, the man himself as big and broad and
massive as Bauer had remembered him. And surely that was
extraordinary. Bauer had not seen Erwin Axmann from that
night he had deposited him across the border into Switzerland
and Bauer had been only about twelve then and everybody

who was grown up looked big. But he had always remembered Axmann as a tremendous man, powerful as a bear, a man who could crawl up the face of mountains with others hanging on a rope beneath him like the tail of a kite.

Axmann held out the bottle as though it were a chalice, and he hunched over, a man who had learned to lower his head going through doorways. He filled the small room. The room was not so small. Axmann just filled it.

"I should have done much more, Peter," he said, his voice by now weathered into a growl. "Much, much, more. Looking back now I see what a damned fool I was. My only excuse is that even at the time I thought I was a damned fool. But I didn't do enough."

"You did enough, Herr Axmann," Bauer said.

Axmann removed the cork from the *Bocksbeutel* with his teeth. He picked up a glass and filled it to the brim and handed it to Bauer without spilling a drop. He filled a glass for himself, as full. He moved with the control of a man who had spent his life training his body to serve him.

And how old was he? Bauer asked himself. Seventy, at least, perhaps more, and the hair which Bauer had remembered as being black now was white, but thick as a shock, and the face, even then leathered by sun and wind, now was like hide, and the bright, clear, blue eyes seemed as hard as agates.

The cottage was on a hill above a vineyard across the Main. It was isolated and compact and this room, with its beams and darkened fireplace and smell of pipe tobacco, was taut and spruce as a captain's cabin.

Axmann wore an old-fashioned moustache that swooped down, white as his hair; the rest of his face was shaved clean and there were none of the little nicks that clot the chins and jawlines of old men and there were no small patches where the razor had failed to clear.

He wore a gray loden suit with dark green lapels, and knickers, long, thick socks, and heavy shoes.

"*Prosit*, Peter," he said, extending the glass with one hand, the other still clutching the bottle neck. "Welcome to my house."

"*Prosit,*" Bauer said.

The men drank the wine. Axmann smacked his lips and wiped his moustache with the back of the hand holding the bottle.

"You should have come back a few years ago, Peter," Axmann said. "I would have had a wife around to greet you." He drank more wine. "I'm the only damned widower I know. With the rest of them it was the other way round."

He walked to the mantel, a tree trunk split down the middle and rubbed and smoothed and varnished on top, and put down the glass and bottle and dug his fingers into a tobacco jar. He took out coarse tobacco and filled the bowl of a curved, long-stemmed pipe.

"It's a little lonely around here without her," Axmann said. "But then there you are. If anyone's got to be lonely I'm just as pleased it's me. The SS? I should never have been fooled into joining that stupid organization."

"Was it stupid?" Bauer asked. He had already posed his question and it had been deposited in Axmann's mind, a sum, and soon would be refunded, and perhaps with interest.

"It was stupid," Axmann said vehemently. He took the lighted match away from the pipe bowl and waved it in the air. "It was damned stupid." He finished with the match and the bowl and he took a pull or two. He tossed the match into the open hearth and retrieved his wine glass and sat down.

"It is so funny," he said. "As the years pass, the SS—the whole damned Hitler government—has come to have a reputation for efficiency. And the SS is supposed to have been the most efficient of all. What rubbish! Believe me when I tell you most of the SS were country bumpkins who pretended they had sense—just like me."

"They seemed to find out what they wanted to," Bauer said.

Axmann waved that away with his pipe. "There was always order in Germany. Everything is always written down somewhere or other, lists of everything and everybody. Any damned idiot could put his fingers on what he wanted. Drink, drink, Peter. That's *Stein.*"

Bauer drank of the wine and looked at the man and smelled the tobacco, why did it smell so good and why had the tobacco of the old man at the cemetery sickened him and it probably was the same tobacco?

"Why did you join, Herr Axmann?" he asked.

"That's a good question, Peter," Axmann said. He drank some wine and pulled on his pipe. "I suppose we all were in some kind of hypnotic state. That man Hitler after all was quite a talker. You know the feelings we Germans have about Germany. And Germany was on its ass when he came along and soon the world began to look at us with respect again." Axmann got up and refilled the glasses. "What happened to you, Peter? I remember the night I dumped you across the Swiss border."

"I went to England."

"Your aunt and uncle," Axmann said.

"How did you know about them?"

"Your uncle used to be in the wine business here. He went to London, sometime in the early twenties."

Bauer knew that he should know better than to be surprised. But what a small town, what a small, closely knit town, in those days the Jews and the non-Jews all part of the fabric.

"You were too young for the war," Axmann said.

"I was in the war."

Axmann tamped down the ash with his thumb. "Of course, this no longer was your homeland, not after what they did to all of you. But it's not so easy for me, Peter," Axmann went on. "You come along out of the blue and ask me why I joined the SS and I try to fumble through some kind of decent answer and you are kind enough to let it go at that. But it's not so easy, I can tell you, when one of my sons starts cross-examining me."

"Your sons? Asking you questions?"

"One after the other as they grew up. They look at me and they ask me why I joined the Party, why in the name of God I joined the SS of all things. They don't get excited. They just want to know. And I sweat, Peter, I sweat. When they were

98

younger and their mother was alive she used to tell them to mind their manners, that children didn't question their elders, but they weren't buying any of that. They wanted to know. And I had to sweat blood to put out something that satisfied them."

"What you did, Herr Axmann," Bauer said. "The people you guided to safety, the lives you saved. That should be answer enough."

Axmann nodded. "Thank the good Lord for that. It was, Peter. It still is. That small thing I did, that's all that saves me from the contempt of my own children. Can you believe that?"

Bauer leaned forward again. "Contempt? It's as strong as that?"

Axmann snorted. "Strong? That's not the word for it, Peter. Why didn't I resist? Why didn't I stand up to Hitler? My God in heaven, was anybody standing up to Hitler then?" He paused. "I tell a lie, Peter. I tell my children I joined the SS just so I could use the uniform to save what Jews I could."

"That's not much of a lie, Herr Axmann," Bauer said.

"Perhaps not, perhaps not." Axmann stood up and paced back and forth. He paused for a moment in front of a glass cabinet which contained many of his trophies for mountain climbing, skiing. "Perhaps it's not a very big lie, perhaps I won't get punished too much for it."

Bauer said nothing as the huge man looked into the cabinet. His own eyes wandered round the room. It struck him that there was no sign of hunting, no heads stuck on the walls. Nothing but a few old prints, photographs, a long decorative pipe with a striped tassle that never was meant to be smoked and apparently never was, and over the mantel a large, dulled photograph of a woman with blonde hair done in the old style.

"You asked me a question, Peter," Axmann said. "A very important question, the question that brought you all the way over from America, and we have been talking about other things and meanwhile I have been trying to put my poor mind to work. My mind never was very much and it seems to be

99

less and less these days. I am trying to remember. What I remember is that your mother, Frau Bauer, arranged with me for me to take her away on a certain night, to Switzerland, to the same place I took you. It was all arranged. I went to your house, on schedule, at exactly the appointed time."

"And she was not there?" Bauer asked.

"Oh, she was there all right," Axmann waved the pipe again. "But she had some excuse for not going that night. I can't remember what the excuse was. I remembered I begged her, everything had been arranged, all along the line, I had friends helping, you understand, but she wouldn't go. She said she had something to do first and that I should come back the next night. I warned her that every minute was dangerous but she wouldn't change her mind."

"And the next night," Bauer said. "You went back?"

Axmann shook his head.

"Why not, Herr Axmann?" Bauer asked. "Why didn't you go back?"

Axmann held up his hands. "There was no need. During the next day I heard that she had been arrested by the Gestapo."

Bauer carefully set his empty wine glass on a small table. "Did you see her, after that?" he asked.

Again Axmann shook his head. "Whoever had denounced her—and I never found out who he was, or what he denounced her for—was very clever. He had arranged for her to be picked up by the Gestapo from another *Gau*. He knew that perhaps because of your father, his war history, his reputation, that she might get some special treatment from the local Gestapo."

"My father had not."

"True. But he was already dead and some of the local people had had time to think about that. And she was a woman." Axmann tamped the pipe again and relit it. "I made a few inquiries, Peter, but I couldn't go too far. I couldn't ask too many questions. I was under a little suspicion myself by then. There were some of my colleagues who had a very good idea that I was smuggling out Jews and I had to be careful."

"Did you know where they took her?"

"No."

"Did you know when she was put to death."

"No."

Presently Bauer stood up. "Thank you, Herr Axmann."

"For what? For nothing. Have some more wine."

"No, thank you."

"I'm sorry I can't help you more. So many years have passed. It all seems as though it never happened."

"Yes," Bauer said. "It always seems to work out just that way."

"And yet it seems to lie on the mind like a fog, like a fog in the valley below. It will be a long time before it is altogether out of the German mind." He walked Bauer to the door. "I wish I could have helped you more. It seems to be the way I do everything, less than I would wish."

"You have helped me, Herr Axmann," Bauer said. "I never thanked you for what you did for me then. Or what you were prepared to do for my mother."

Axmann waved the pipe. "You were good people. Your father was always fair to me. Once, because of an accident on a climb, they would not renew my license. They said it was my fault. One of the other climbers had been killed. Councilor Bauer investigated and then certified I was in no way responsible, my clients had disobeyed my instructions. He saw to it my license was restored. It was the difference between making a living for my family or seeing them starve. You owe me no thanks, Peter."

Axmann opened the door. The day had cleared. They could see below the river and on the other side the buildings, the churches higher than any of the others.

"How long will you stay here, Peter?" Axmann asked.

"I don't know. Until I find out everything, I suppose."

"Come back again. Come and have dinner with me. If you can stand the terrible cooking of an old man."

"I will, Herr Axmann."

"You must find out everything?"

"Yes."

"I suppose so. And yet perhaps it is best to let sleeping dogs lie."

Bauer looked up at Axmann. The old man was staring down into the valley.

"Since I arrived here more than one person has said that to me," Bauer said. "Am I being warned against anything in particular?"

"Oh, I wouldn't call it a warning, not exactly."

"What would you call it, Herr Axmann?"

"It wasn't a warning, not exactly."

"What was it, Herr Axmann?"

The big man looked around as though to make sure they were alone; Bauer remembered Joachim Remers doing the same thing, more than once.

"It wasn't a warning, Peter," Axmann said again. "It's just that there are people around here who don't want to be reminded about those days."

Bauer nodded. "I can appreciate that."

He held out his hand. Axmann gripped it. Bauer felt his hand lost.

Axmann held on to the hand. "Peter," he said.

"Yes, Herr Axmann."

"I have said there are people here who do not like to be reminded of those days."

"Yes, Herr Axmann."

"But there are also some who never stop reminding themselves." Axmann seemed suddenly to realize he was still gripping Bauer's hand. He released it.

"I understand," Bauer said.

"Silly people," Axmann said. "All of them too young. Not too young for their silly meetings and speeches, you understand, I don't mean that. They're old enough for that nonsense. But too young to have known anything about those old days firsthand."

Bauer nodded.

Then Axmann spat and made a wide gesture with his hand as though he were sweeping clear a shelf, a table. "Ah, the devil with those fucking mothers' pricks!" He looked at Bauer and at that moment seemed to have lost twenty years. His face was young and hard and tight. "Don't listen to me, Peter," he said. "I'm an old man with the best behind him. You do what you have to do. You find out what you need to know, you'll never sleep peacefully otherwise."

"Thank you," Bauer said.

Axmann clenched a fist that looked like a piece of rock. "That was the mistake that was made in those days. Everybody was too damned frightened. And then it was too late." He opened his hand and put it on Bauer's shoulder. "Come back, Peter, come back, there is still much to talk about. I'll ask around. Maybe somebody else knows something."

"Is that wise, Herr Axmann?"

Bauer felt his shoulder being crushed under Axmann's fingers.

"Fuck being wise, Peter! What do you say to that?"

"I'll be back, Herr Axmann."

"I'll keep thinking. Something may come to me. Come back. The meal won't be that bad, I promise you."

"I'm sure not," Bauer said.

"And there's always plenty of wine, Peter, the best. Whatever the devil shit this part of Germany produces, it also produces the best wine."

Axmann removed his hand from Bauer's shoulder and Bauer felt that he had lost a friend.

He started down the path to the road where the taxi was waiting. He heard Axmann call out. He turned to see the big man lumbering toward him.

"You've remembered something else," Bauer said.

Axmann scratched his head. "Yes and no. I'm not sure. But there is something trying to say something to the inside of my head. Just give me a moment, Peter, and perhaps it will come to me."

"Shall we return to the house?" Bauer asked.

"It may be nothing. And a taxi is expensive these days. Just let me think. I'm not used to it nowadays and I've almost forgotten how." Axmann frowned and then he said, "I seem to remember something about a painting. What your mother told me. She had to dispose of a painting before she would leave. Does that mean anything to you?"

"My father collected paintings," Bauer said.

"This was something special. Something your father believed was special. Something he loved very much. Your mother wanted to save it."

"He had so many paintings," Bauer said.

"Ah, God in heaven, this head of mine." Axmann rapped his skull with his knuckles. "The man who did the painting in the Residenz. The naked women and the tits. The ceiling man. The Italian."

"Tiepolo," Bauer said.

Axmann slapped him on the back. "That's the name! That's the name! Did the councilor have one of his paintings?"

"I think so," Bauer said with rising excitement. "Yes, I know he did."

"Did he love it?"

"I believe so. I believe it was the painting he had over the fireplace."

"Well, then that's it. Your mother said it was your father's favorite painting and she had made some arrangement with someone to store it so the Nazis wouldn't confiscate it. Confiscate! Steal it, is the word! Your mother wanted to save that one picture because of what your father thought of it. You see, she believed she was coming back. She believed with all her heart she was coming back."

For a moment Bauer was unable to say anything. Then he asked, "Did she tell you who she was leaving the painting with?"

Axmann bit his lips and scratched his head. "If she did, I don't remember now. Once again I do too little."

"No, Herr Axmann. You have been a great help to me."

"Too little, Peter, too little."

Bauer went down the rest of the path. Reinhard opened the door of the taxi. Bauer turned and looked back at the great, white-haired man, now outlined against the afternoon sky, a statue, heroic size.

Bauer held up his hand. Axmann took the pipe from his mouth and waved it, like a plume, in the air.

"Back to the hotel, Herr Bauer?" Reinhard asked.

"Yes."

"That old man. He used to be famous. I remember," Reinhard said, starting down the hill.

"That's the way many of them were in those old days," Bauer said. "Famous."

He sat back in the seat and smelled through the open windows through the fresh drizzle the grapes ripening on the vines, the smell gentle and pure, fragile, as the wine itself. It was such a tender wine, he thought, and in such a strange place.

He tried to remember the painting. Tiepolo. He wasn't much in fashion these days. Naked women and tits. Bauer tried to think back. The picture over the mantel. It was a scene in Venice. Venice of the Renaissance, the High Renaissance. There were men in armor, Moors, courtiers, and the women. The opulent, tall women with their queenly manner and their glowing, pink skin. And their bosoms were bare, their nipples painted so they were jewels, precious stones displayed with all the rest of the precious stones they wore.

"Major Reinhard," Bauer said.

"Yes, Herr Bauer."

"While we're up here, before you take me back to the hotel, I want to go to the Marienberg. I want to go to the Mainfränkisches Museum."

"You disappoint me, Herr Bauer," Reinhard said.

"And why do I do that, Major?"

"I've been trying to figure out just what you're doing here. And now you're behaving like a tourist, after all."

11

✠ ✠ ✠

HE STOOD FOR A LONG TIME BEFORE THE ADAM AND EVE.

He hadn't remembered the power in the work of Tilman Riemenschneider, or perhaps it was only that he had been too young then to absorb it. The statues, large as life, had once stood in front of the main entrance to the Marienkapelle in the marketplace down below and across the Main, until it was realized that time and weather were eroding the work of the gothic genius, and the sandstone figures were brought into the protection of the museum.

What was it in the faces? They cast a spell, as did all of the faces of that simple man who worked mostly in wood and who had his own vision, as stainless and innocent as that of a child.

The faces held him. He looked at them and his eyes were unable to let go. He wanted to move on but he could not.

. . . All his life, his father said, Til Riemenschneider remained faithful to his gothic ideal . . . "Decoration means very little to him, perhaps nothing at all," Simon Bauer said to his son . . . "He is concerned only with people, with their faces and their hands and the clothing they wear. He is concerned with emotion and the conveying of emotion . . ."

. . . "They look so sad," the boy Peter said. "All of them look so sad."

. . . "Yes," Councilor Bauer said, "They are melancholy and they are grave and when you have lived a little longer and you look at these statues again you will find that that simple man will say many things to you . . ."

What did they say to him now, faces worn by the years? He wanted to lower his eyes and try to know but he could not.

He heard heavy footsteps. It released him. He turned and saw a cleaning woman with a pail of water and a rag. She was red-faced and fat but she had good legs and that was undoubtedly the reason she wore a short skirt.

A cleaning woman, a *German* cleaning woman, in a museum, in a mini skirt?

She greeted him in a fruity voice and went to a window, swung it open, climbed on the ledge, and started to wash the outside of the glass.

Bauer turned to the carving of the Virgin and Child. The wood was darkened from the years but in some way the face of the Mother took on even more from that. It was a haunted face. She knew, even then, Riemenschneider was saying, was saying across almost five hundred years. She knew, from the beginning. And how had he managed to convey the possession of that terrible knowledge, that unendurable prescience, how, in this personal shorthand, this little cut here, this little scraping there, so bare, so uncluttered, how had he managed to put it into the obsessed face?

Bauer made himself look away, to the carvings of the Apostles, with their quality of brooding, the wood blackened, shadowed too, the scars of the years, of what had happened, of what had happened then and what had happened since.

He brought his eyes back again to the Virgin and his hand rose, almost by itself, and the tips of his fingers touched the wood.

"It is not allowed!" a man's voice said.

The words were in German. The words, as they had been spoken, could only be in German.

Bauer turned. He saw a guard standing by the open window where the woman was cleaning. From where he stood, Bauer saw, he had himself a good view when he looked up.

Now the guard pointed to a sign on the wall. It stated, in German officialese, that anyone who touched any of the statues would be severely dealt with by the police.

Bauer wondered whether to be an American or a German.

"I'm sorry," he said, in German. "I didn't see that sign."

The guard, mollified, glanced upward, to show the cleaning woman the power of his authority and to also enjoy what he saw, and then he walked slowly over to Bauer. He stood at his side and contemplated the statue with him.

"It is beautiful, not?" the guard asked.

"Almost unbearable," Bauer said.

The guard nodded. "It affects many people that way. They want to touch. For some reason they want to touch. That is why it has to be forbidden. If everyone were to touch—" The guard shrugged.

"It's extraordinary," Bauer said. "They are all extraordinary."

"They tell me they were better before," the guard said. "Of course I am not old enough to remember."

"Before what?" Bauer asked.

"The raid. During the war. That's why they're so dark."

"Please," Bauer said.

"They were scorched. Can't you see. They're burned."

"I hadn't known it was that," Bauer said after a little while. "I thought it was a natural darkening of the wood, from the passing of time."

"The passing of time—hell!" the guard said. "It was those damned Americans and Britishers. They should have been put in front of a firing squad. Every damned one of them."

The guard touched his cap and wandered back to the window and the woman, in a manner of gracious accommodation, spread her legs just a little bit wider.

Bauer started out of the room. He glanced back at the wooden statues. They all had a relationship, the Virgin and the Child and the Apostles and Peter Bauer.

The assistant director was a tallish man with a pink, bald head surrounded by a small cloud of hair, fuzzy as sugar candy. His face was pink and his skull was pink and the hand he held out to Bauer was pink and soft with shining finger-nails.

"Herr Bauer, Herr Bauer, what an incredible surprise, what an exquisite pleasure. In my wildest dreams it never occurred to me that I would have the honor again to meet a member of your distinguished family." His voice was as soft and as pink as everything else.

Of course he did not, Bauer thought.

"How you are all missed," Herr Phleps said. "Such a distinguished family, such a distinguished family, and what those swine did to you." He put out his other hand and clasped Bauer's hand with both hands. "Our good city misses you all."

Bauer disengaged his hand.

"Your father, the councilor, was such an eminent gentle-man, so illustrious. He was held in such esteem, such esteem. I don't believe that in the history of our beautiful city has a layman contributed so much to the development and the sus-tenance of the arts."

And the sad thing, Bauer thought, the saddest thing of all was that this man believed he was saying comforting things, things Councilor Bauer's son would want to hear. The simple horror was that Herr Ludwig Phleps was sincere.

He smiled and the smile Herr Phleps gave him in return established the fact that the director had pronounced correct condolences and that Bauer had appreciated them.

"Yes," Bauer agreed. Who was he to change German mentality at this point in time? "Yes, I have been given to understand my father was a patron of the arts. In a way that is why I am here today, Herr Phleps."

The director threw up his hands as though he had held a basketball in them. " 'A patron of the arts'! That is an understatement, Herr Bauer, a positive understatement. There are many patrons of the arts but Councilor Bauer was quite something else. He was a luminary of the arts."

Herr Phleps sighed and took out an enormous cambric handkerchief and mopped the top of his head.

"You must be a very busy man," Bauer said. "I don't want to take too much of your time."

Herr Phleps waved the kerchief as though it were a flag of surrender. "The Tiepolo, ah, the Tiepolo." Herr Phleps restored the kerchief to his breast pocket so that only a third of it hung out. He crossed his arms behind his back and made inquiries of the ceiling. "Yes, Herr Bauer, I do seem to remember your father owned a Tiepolo. He had such a splendid collection, so many things of beauty. They would grace this museum."

"Have you any idea what happened to the Tiepolo, Herr Phleps?" Bauer asked.

Herr Phleps released his hands, brought them round, raised them, dropped them. "It is my recollection that all was lost, all was lost, in that horrible phosphorus raid." Herr Phleps shuddered delicately. "I shall never forget that night. The way the balls of phosphorus ran along the streets," Herr Phleps said. "Nothing could extinguish them, nothing. Building after building, thousands, thousands of people."

"But wherever I look, Würzburg is exactly as I remember it to be," Bauer said.

Herr Phleps chuckled. "It is exactly as you remember it, Herr Bauer. Except for those disgusting new apartment buildings."

"Except for those," Bauer agreed.

"It has been called a miracle. It was a miracle, Herr Bauer. And, if I may say so, without seeming to boast, it was a miracle that could be accomplished only by Germans." Herr Phleps regarded him roguishly for a moment, holding back the secret. Then he popped out the word. "Photographs. Photographs, Herr Bauer. No one else but Germans would have thought of photographs."

Herr Phleps sat down at his desk and arched his fingers. "You would not have believed what happened to your birthplace, Herr Bauer. To say that Würzburg was destroyed somehow does not adequately convey what happened here. Other cities have been destroyed. Perhaps the word has lost its meaning. Here, on that night more than four thousand buildings disappeared. They simply vanished, Herr Bauer, as though they had never existed. And to what purpose, Herr Bauer, can you tell me that?"

"I cannot," Bauer said.

`"And so, you want to know what was done about it. I will tell you. A committee was formed. I had the honor of serving on that committee. And we discussed how to recreate Würzburg. Not just clear up the mess but recreate the city we all had known and loved. Well, what we did was gather photographs, we gathered them from everywhere, here in Würzburg, elsewhere in Germany—our city has always been loved and so many visitors took photographs of it then, just as they do today. We found photographs in art books, travel guides, studies of the baroque cities of Germany. Someone even turned up a motion picture travelogue in Berlin. We stopped almost every frame on that reel and enlarged it."

Herr Phleps paused for effect.

"And from all those sources, Herr Bauer, the buildings were restored, exactly as they had been, *exactly*. The structures, all the churches, were copied to the last detail, were aged, scarred, by a specially developed process made to look weathered. If we found in a photograph there was a big scratch—we made that scratch over again. If a brick were missing—it was left out." He paused again. "There you have it, Herr Bauer. And now that you know, don't you agree that only we Germans could have made this miracle?"

"It is really extraordinary," Bauer agreed.

"You should be proud of your countrymen, Herr Bauer. Councilor Bauer would have been proud. He would have been in the forefront in the reconstruction. We were struck a low blow, yes, but we did not complain. We pulled ourselves up by our bootstraps and we remade our beloved city into the baroque jewel it always has been. I tell you, your father would have been proud."

"I believe he would," Bauer said, rising. "And I am most grateful to you for taking the time to tell me about it."

"A pleasure, Herr Bauer, you must believe that, an honor and a pleasure." Herr Phleps floated to his feet. "For the son of Councilor Bauer . . ." He fluttered fingers.

"And that is all you can tell me about the Tiepolo?"

"Alas, unfortunately, yes." Herr Phleps' eyes fell. "I'm afraid that lovely canvas has been lost forever. Without question it died—and I say 'died' advisedly, Herr Bauer, works of art have life—in the holocaust, along with everything else."

"Thank you again, Herr Phleps. It was kind of you to see me."

"Such a distinguished father. His absence is the city's loss, the city's loss."

"I'm sure it is," Bauer said.

Herr Phleps walked round the desk and escorted Bauer to the door. Bauer smelled a faint aroma of pink cologne.

"Remember, Herr Bauer, you are a member of the aristocracy," Herr Phleps said. "Never forget that. Aristocracy!"

Outside the rain had stopped. Bauer saw a bride and groom emerge from an arched tunnel and start across the cobblestones. The bride wore a white lace dress and the man was in morning coat and striped trousers and gray ascot.

Bauer looked at them bemused. Was there in this venerable pile a place for marriages? Or was this a premarital or postmarital sacrament, a tribalistic genuflection, a hieratic pilgrimage, so that something very German could rub off on the union?

He watched the bride, broad and blinding as a bed sheet, clutching a small bouquet in a large hand, as she stepped delicately over the wet stones in white shoes that seemed too small for her feet. Her liege lord was a foot shorter than she and at least fifty pounds lighter and she rested daintily on his arm as he led her to a car that looked smaller than she was. They slipped in and drove away.

Bauer looked down the vaulted port from which they had appeared. It was empty and dark and filled with a gloom that had taken centuries to collect. Above the port were three figures, symbols to protect the citadel. The head of one of the figures was missing, decapitated perhaps by the swinging of a mighty Teutonic sword.

Bauer walked to the parapet and looked across the moat and down at the city of Würzburg, half submerged in a bath of murk and mist. Only the church spires wholly ignored the vaporous pool.

The river, crossed by three bridges, the old one in the middle, the other two at suitable and respectable distances from the saints, was high from the rain and the lock on the near side unleashed a torrential wash. On the other side a white, windowed riverboat was disgorging its passengers. (RIVER CRUISES ALONG THE ROMANTIC MAIN — RESTAURANT ON BOARD — EVENING CRUISES WITH DANCING — PLEASURE CRUISES AS PER ARRANGEMENT)

Arrangement with whom? And for what unique German pleasures? A miniature gas chamber? A model oven? A cross-section of a group grave, reconstructed from photographs, exact to the last detail, aged by a special process?

The passengers, who during the daylight hours had had without doubt to settle for the less recondite German pleasures of food and beer and the ineffable romance of looking at the factoried shoreline of the Main, crossed the gangway and then as though ferried by Charon were slowly, gradually absorbed into the blurred shadows until they were no more.

. . . *The initial, perhaps the most important part of the mission was accomplished in the briefing room, before the*

113

raid . . . that was where the British had an edge, there were so many refugees in London, and by no means all of them Jews, there were Polish refugees and German Catholics and political escapees from Austria and Czechoslovakia and they all had memories and they were all in their own way experts, they knew their own city, their own town, their own village, their own countryside, there was scarcely a part of the occupied continent from which someone or other had not fled, and they could give priceless information to the military forces they believed were fighting, along with other reasons, for their right to return to their homes . . .

. . . The aerial photograph of Würzburg . . . a large plan put together by sections of smaller photographs . . . is this the railroad station, he was asked, or something camouflaged to look like the railroad station, or is this the real railroad station camouflaged to look like something else . . . ? are these trees, is this a church, is this a factory . . . ?

. . . If the V-2's were not stopped, someone had proclaimed—was it Churchill?—then every German city with a population of one hundred thousand or more would be destroyed . . . first Dresden and then came the turn of Würzburg . . .

. . . Wooden roofs in Würzburg . . . wooden roofs made to order for fire bombing . . . Hitler had no one who could be so minutely factual about British towns and villages . . .

At that moment Bauer remembered that when he was in school all the students were taught—for what reason?—how to defend themselves against sulphur bombs. Water, it had been shown frighteningly by the teacher, was utterly ineffective. Sand had to be used, he had shouted, sand, sand, and he had demonstrated.

Bauer could smell the stink of that sulphur.

Wasn't that supposed to be the smell of hell?

Was that how the city had smelled that night?

114

Dresden had been obliterated by then and now it was to be Würzburg. And by this time the city where he had been born had been officially declared *Judenrein*. Every Jew who had not escaped, every Jew who had not committed suicide, every Jew who had not been clever enough to be safely dead —(his mother, his mother—he had been informed by underground sources she was dead, nothing more)—had been taken to Theresienstadt to make their patriotic contribution to the Final Solution.

Not one hand was raised to help.

Not true. Erwin Axmann had raised a hand. And how many others? Were there others? It would be pleasant to believe there had been others.

He put his hand on the moist, cold stone of the wall and leaned forward. Standing there on the eminence of the *Festung Marienberg* one could almost imagine one was in a low-flying airplane, a B-24, for example, the British called them Liberators.

Words pebbled in his mind, rattling there, clicking, clacking, ricocheting round and round like manic billiard balls: Pathfinder, Guide, Master Bomber, Market Leader . . .

"Marker Two, tally-ho . . ."

How many years had it been since he thought of all that?

He felt ice creeping into him.

Lying on his belly in his flying suit in the freezing airplane he saw what his eyes did not accept, what his mind would not take in.

There was an explanation for it, he was told later, a scientific explanation, and he was enough German to grant as rational anything science could explain, but he had not believed it then nor could he make himself believe it afterward.

The suction of the oxygen made a circular sweep, a swathe of fire like an acetylene torch turned upside down, an acetylene torch big enough to encompass a city, deep red and white inside and brown and yellow outside, and the smoke somehow more terrifying than even the flame.

The city broke open and exploded and buildings melted and vanished as though an earthquake had released maddened fire confined until then from that moment when time had begun.

"We've created hell," someone said over the intercom.

. . . We've created hell . . .

. . . It was a creation flying men said they had never before seen, not in a wartime of bombing . . . the great flame made of all the smaller flames and as he looked down, each street was etched in fire, clean and clear and illuminated in brilliance, the smoke drifting away and leaving, as though made of transparent glass and lighted from beneath, the plan view of the city, so familiar, so known . . .

. . . "God Almighty," someone whispered through his earphones.

. . . God Almighty . . . ? was this a time to summon God . . . ?

. . . The plane banked and he stared at the sea of flames and now the heat rising from below could be felt against the plane and the plane no longer was freezing and he wanted to remove his sheeplined flying suit and he could feel the sweat running down his back and between his toes . . .

. . . Now the light was so bright he could read numbers on other planes and see men in cockpits and then the pilot banked again and the inside of the plane was lighted by the burning city in dark, red tones of sunset, and outside in the night the sky glared in scarlet and white and dirty gray . . .

. . . And the plane kept circling as though the pilot were trapped, forced by a power to continue to gaze down on what had been done, and now there were other voices on the intercom and the pilot still circled and circled and the plane got hotter and minutes passed before the pilot finally could wrest himself from what was holding him in thrall and turn homeward . . .

. . . There was a violent shudder by the airplane and a gripping, as though the dying city were trying to hold it back, keep it there, as though the airplane and the city were now bound, inextricably joined, and the one could not be without

116

the other . . . the plane reared like a wild animal and tore itself free . . .

. . . And what had he thought . . . ? no one had seen it as just another raid, not the most experienced . . . they had all been told by those empowered to tell, required to tell, that Würzburg was an important factory city, which it was not and which it had never been and never would be, but they were told that because the RAF pilots were not to think, the navigators and the bombardiers were not to think they were destroying cities of no military value simply to break the morale of civilians . . .

. . . That was something only the enemy did . . .

. . . What did the Würzburg Jew think . . . ? for the pilot it was not his first raid nor if he were permitted to live would it be his last . . . and he could when the first appalling impact was tempered remember the destruction of places in Britain, his home perhaps, his own personal deaths . . .

. . . But this was where Peter Bauer was born and no matter what had happened, no matter how one tried, one can never disown a birthplace, one can never disown a birthright . . . lying there in the tail turret, fighting back a sickness, he made himself see his father being pushed into the gas chamber at Theresienstadt, or was his father still enough of his own man to enter under his own power . . . ? even that was not enough for what was yet before his eyes and he made himself see other faces, his brothers and sister and their children, and his uncles and aunts and cousins and friends, and finally all the Jews, all the rest of the Jews who had been solved finally and for all time.

. . . He raised his head in the narrow, cramped, cold-again shell and he asked God to help him, the stern, just implacable God of the Jews, the severe God to Whom Jews have turned eternally.

. . . Give me knowledge that it is right, he implored, cleanse me, please, dear God, give me to know that that which has been done had to be done and was right and appropriate and condigned . . .

. . . but by then looking back at the burnt offering of

117

what had been a city on this earth, seeing this immolation, a Dante with a vision of hell spread out not in the imagination but before eyes, he was vouchsafed to know there was no right and no wrong . . .

He learned later the flames could be seen for half an hour after the planes had turned for home but he was not to know that, was never to know. He never remembered returning to the base in England. Everything had left him, consciousness, sight, the ability to hear. The return was a blackout.

He was told later that he had been debriefed on landing and had given reasonable and as it turned out quite creditable assessment of damage done during the period of his flyover but he never could remember that. Afterward he had gone to his quarters and had gone to bed, but he never remembered that either.

When he woke in the daylight it was his next moment of awareness after having begged the help of God.

And was that the sign of His compassion? Those merciful hours of nothingness?

He looked down at the city now. The darkness was crawling up its feet like a growth.

He heard a discreet cough. He smelled the cigarette smoke and turned to see Major Reinhard standing next to him.

"How long have you been here?" Bauer asked.

"About ten minutes, Herr Bauer. You have been standing here a much longer time."

"Yes," Bauer said.

"Shall we go?" Major Reinhard asked.

Bauer nodded and they started for where the taxi was parked.

They drove down behind the fortress. On the grounds Bauer could see two boys armed with homemade bows and arrows playing Indians among the trees. One of the boys made contact and the victim fell over into satisfactory death.

They drove onto the quay and across the Old Bridge. The formidable faces of the saints were softened in the dusk.

Bauer remembered asking his father once why there were no statues of Jewish saints. There were no Jewish saints, the councilor had said, Jews did not believe in sanctifying anybody but God Himself, and that included the Jew Jesus Christ. But there must have been great Jews, Peter had insisted. What about Moses, for instance? For some reason, Simon Bauer had said, the Würzburgers never considered it necessary to erect a statue to Moses. As a point of fact, his father had added, to his knowledge that need had not been felt anywhere in Germany.

Reinhard drove down the ramp onto Domstrasse. Bauer leaned forward.

"Could you drop me off here, Major? I think I'd like to walk back to the hotel." When Reinhard drew up to the curb, Bauer asked, "What do I owe you for the day?"

Reinhard turned his head. "Are you going to use me tomorrow?"

"Yes."

"Then let me put you on a daily basis. It will be cheaper for you. You can settle with me when you're ready to leave Würzburg."

"Is that what you prefer? I don't want you to lose money on me."

"It makes me feel a little more important that way. I feel less like a taxi driver and more like a private chauffeur."

The distant mocking smile was there again and Bauer grinned.

"Is that a step upward?"

"Difference between a whore and a mistress," Reinhard said. He reached into his pocket and took out his business card. "Try to hold on to this one, Herr Bauer. They don't print them for nothing for me."

Bauer got out of the cab. On the sudden, he asked, "Have a drink with me, Major."

12

✠ ✠ ✠

THE GASTHAUS WAS LIKE ALL THE OTHERS, LOW-CEILINGED,
smoky, filled, babbling. They sat down at a bare wooden
table and Bauer ordered a bottle of wine after looking at
Reinhard and gaining his assent, and then he looked round
the room and was surprised to see how many elderly women
were there, alone or with other women, as old, and most of
them drinking beer out of huge steins he would have thought
too heavy for their withered hands to lift.

They all were dressed most primly in somber clothes, gray,
black, dark green, and while a few of them wore hats that
resembled flower pots, most of them wore men's Tyrolean
hats complete with brush but left uncreased in the crowns.

He looked at the faces of the women closest to him. They
were bleak, glazed, locked-in, as though imprisoned not by
their own memories, experiences, not even by what they had
heard or read or learned, but a special form of taxonomic
inheritance ordained for them generations before they were
conceived. Their eyes saw nothing and their ears were deaf-
ened and their faces were stony and removed, and the thin

lips were knife slashes save for those regularly spaced moments when they parted and had introduced between them a careful, miniscule measure of the beer.

Bauer had a conceit at that moment that with their granite faces and iron eyes and the black hats with the undented tops they looked like Navajo Indians, feathers included.

He smiled at that vagary and then he stopped smiling because he sensed something else, he could almost smell the Jew-hatred that lay behind the faces, a stale miasma that was also part of the inheritance, that filled them as the air they breathed; it was the air they breathed. What one of these creatures would have during the terror raised a hand, one finger, an eyelid?

But did he sense something else as well? An unease? A disquiet that nearly was fear? A fear of what? When had they been safer and richer and more secure? Was it that stability itself that frightened them?

More probably it was not there at all but instead something within him, that was part of his own patrimony also prescribed a thousand years before he was born.

He was aware that the waitress had brought the wine and had filled the glasses and that Reinhard was silently contemplating him.

"Was it something that might amuse me too?" Reinhard asked.

"Please?" Bauer felt the room closing in.

"You were smiling."

"Nothing. It was nothing."

Reinhard picked up his glass and waited. Bauer raised his and they both drank of the wine.

Reinhard lit a cigarette. "I have been curious as to what you are doing here, Herr Bauer."

"I expect that you have," Bauer said.

"Despite the obligatory visit to the museum with its gloomy Riemenschneiders I somehow have the impression you are not a simple tourist."

"You would like to know."

"As your driver, not at all, that would be presumptuous. As one sharing a bottle of wine . . ." The major shrugged.

Presently Bauer told him.

Reinhard drank more of the wine. He made an appreciative face. "No matter how much I drink of this *Stein* it seems to taste better to me all the time."

"And now will you tell me I would be wiser if I let sleeping dogs lie?" Bauer asked. "If I did not stir up muddy waters? If I did not remind some people of that which they do not want to be reminded?"

"You have been told that?"

"Often. You would be amazed, Major, at how often in less than two days."

"By the old mountain climber on the hill?"

"By him. By others. Even by the American military."

"They should all know," Reinhard said.

Bauer emptied his glass. "And now, Major, it's your turn."

"You should not gulp down that wine, Herr Bauer," Reinhard said reproachfully. "It is to be savored. Don't you ever read the local travel literature? Franconian wine is liquid gold and is to be drunk slowly as though each drop was the last drop left in this world."

"I apologize," Bauer said. "And I will get hold of this informative travel literature."

"I am not changing the subject, Herr Bauer," Reinhard said, pouring more wine into Bauer's glass. "But I also am not presenting you with any warning of my own."

"And why not?" Bauer asked. "Why are you different from the others?"

Reinhard did not reply.

"I'm sorry, Major," Bauer said after a moment. He leaned back against the slats of his chair. "Sharing a bottle of wine doesn't stake that kind of claim."

"Don't be an ass, Herr Bauer," Reinhard said quietly. "It isn't that. It isn't that at all. It is simply that I am an old soldier and long ago I came to believe that when a man reaches the age of reason he has the right, God-given, to

122

stumble around wherever he pleases, even, if it suits his book, when he finds himself in the middle of a minefield."

There was a sudden loud braying, a shattering sound, and Bauer jerked his head to see one of the beer-drinking women, a wizened ancient, her face upturned, her mouth opening and closing like that of a dying fish, her skinny little body convulsed with her laughter.

Opposite the stricken woman was a female companion, a bulky, formidable heirloom, who had apparently said whatever had been said to trigger the hysteria, and who now had disengaged, her face under its black, domed fedora again encased, and forever finished, seamed and veined as Carrara marble, her eyes looking inward, all of her totally detached from the paroxysm she had produced. There was, Bauer thought, nothing of her alive, except for the faint, slow fall and rise of a mountainous breast.

What had she said to bring about this madness, Bauer wondered? Had she perhaps disclosed that a mutual friend had cancer?

The laughing woman's head went back more and more as her neck muscles weakened in her joy and her own hat, one of the flower pots, tumbled off and fell to the floor, disclosing a skull meanly covered by thin, dyed hair.

Bauer picked up the hat and held it out to the woman who did not ignore him but who simply was unable to do more than laugh. He placed it on the table.

He listened to the lunatic screeching in disbelief and then he realized he was the only person in the room paying it any attention. No one else was looking at the woman; not an eye was raised from a newspaper, not a head was turned. Even Major Reinhard seemed at the moment engaged with his own thoughts.

The laughter didn't diminish. It seemed to Bauer to be building to something else, something higher, more blaring, more maniac, a new dimension of insanity and he wanted to cup his ears. He stood up.

"Forgive me," he said to Reinhard. "Forgive me but I must leave now."

He summoned the waitress and asked for the reckoning and paid it and then rushed out of the place. As the outside door closed behind him he could still hear the woman's shriek.

13

✠ ✠ ✠

"ADOLF HITLER SIMPLY WOULD BE OUT OF STYLE TODAY," Werner Hausmann said.

He was sprawled indolently on the banquette, his long legs extended. Bauer noticed that the busy waiters stepped carefully over his polished shoes and that not one of them, not so much as by a glance, suggested he pull them in.

"Too old-fashioned, you understand, Herr Bauer, too old-fashioned," Hausmann said. "Oh, yes, he was quite effective in his own time, when radio was just coming in, but today, on television—all those exaggerated gestures, all that shouting—" Hausmann shuddered. "He would be ludicrous."

"Do you believe that?" Bauer asked. He found himself fascinated and he made no excuses to himself.

"Believe me, my dear man, today Herr Hitler's behavior would set back the cause of German nationalism for half a century."

"I was under the impression that he managed to accomplish that in his own period," Bauer said.

Hausmann raised his head slightly. His eyes were clear and well set apart and magnificently blue and were, Bauer thought at that moment, possibly the coldest eyes he had ever seen.

The two men were seated in the bar of the Deutscher Hof and had been there for almost an hour. When Bauer had returned to the hotel after leaving Major Reinhard the desk clerk told him Herr Remers wanted to see him. She picked up the telephone and Remers bounded out of his office. He appeared more breathless than that short journey should warrant.

He took Bauer by the arm and led him away from the desk to a neutral point in the middle of the lobby. "I was not aware that you knew Werner Hausmann," Remers said with no preamble.

"I don't," Bauer said.

"But you must, Peter. He is in the bar waiting to see you."

"Who is Werner Hausmann?" Bauer asked.

Remers looked rapidly to the right and to the left. The lobby walls had ears too, Bauer saw.

Remers moved a little closer so he could lower his voice. "He is an architect."

"What does he want with me?" Bauer asked. "I have no intention of settling in Würzburg."

"He said that if his name was unfamiliar to you to tell you that he is the brother of Frau Marliese Neubert who is employed at the American army base."

"Oh, yes," Bauer said. He started for the bar.

"Peter."

Bauer turned.

Remers looked at him anxiously. "Since you arrived here yesterday, Peter, I have thought so much about you, about the old days."

"Yes, Joachim," Bauer said. "They keep coming back."

"Such fun we used to have."

Bauer nodded.

"The things we did, Peter."

"We must have a good talk about them, Joachim," Bauer said, starting off again.

"Peter," Remers said, putting his hand on Bauer's coat

126

sleeve. "Peter, just a little while ago, a few minutes ago, as a matter of fact, I was thinking about when we were in school."

"Yes, old friend," Bauer said.

"Peter," Remers said, still clutching the sleeve. "Peter, do you remember a biology teacher we once had, a man named Otto Beck?"

Bauer thought for a moment. "Vaguely. Why?"

"He has been in my mind for the last thirty minutes. At first I could not remember his name but then when I saw you now it came to me."

Remers pulled away his hand and walked rapidly back to his office. Bauer, puzzled, stared after him, and then went on to the bar.

Otto Beck? What was he supposed to remember about him?

He sighed. Remers, his old school chum, apparently had become something of a fiddle-faddler.

The bar was crowded. The maître came up to him immediately, breaking off a conversation he was having with someone.

"Herr Bauer," he said. "Herr Hausmann has been waiting for you."

The voice of the professionally composed, professionally impassable major domo had undertones of respect Bauer had not detected before. They could not be, he knew, for him.

"Herr Hausmann has been here for thirty minutes," the maître said, leading him hurriedly away. His voice now had the faintest suggestion of reproach.

That, Bauer was certain, was for him.

The maître guided him to a banquette and upon reaching there he straightened and then to Bauer's astonishment he jerked his head forward in the short, neck-snapping bow, the archetypical German gesture, the gesture only a German can properly deliver, the lightning-quick genuflection normally accompanied by a simultaneous clicking of heels.

The supreme commander of the bar and dining room, Bauer observed with interest, was addressing himself to the

127

youngish, rather elegant man at the banquette as might an orderly reporting to a general.

Were architects held in such esteem, Bauer wondered.

The maître introduced Bauer.

No, Bauer decided, it could not be described exactly as that. What the maître accomplished was to identify Bauer to the man and in some subtle and also uniquely German way at the same time to suggest this was not a meeting of equals.

Without seeming to do anything the young man dismissed the maître and stood up and held out his hand.

He was, Bauer judged, as he grasped the hand, in his middle thirties, and he saw the family resemblance.

Hausmann was dressed, he saw, in a most un-German fashion. His suit, body-shaped with a flaring skirt and modish broad lapels was much nearer Savile Row than it was to Kaiserstrasse. The shirt, with broad stripes and a long, loose pointed collar was pure Turnbull & Asser. The tie was probably the widest in town. The slim, gleaming shoes could have come from no other place than a bespoke shop on Jermyn Street.

And yet, Bauer sensed at the same time, there was nothing of the fop about Hausmann. He wore his clothes with the style and the indifference of a Regency rake.

Bauer would not have been in the least surprised if, instead of the extended cuffs with their heavy gold links, Hausmann's shirtsleeves had ended in lace.

Hausmann said he was drinking Scotch and soda which also did not surprise Bauer. He was aware that when a German was a genuine Anglophile he pursued that passion with German thoroughness. Bauer said he would have the same.

Hausmann offered him a cigarette from a slim gold case which Bauer would make a small bet originated on Duke Street. He knew he would have won his bet when he saw the gold Dunhill lighter Hausmann took out of his pocket.

"What is it I can do for you, Herr Hausmann?" Bauer asked.

128

"When my sister told me of you, I wanted to meet you," Hausmann said.

"And why was that?" Bauer asked.

"One rarely has the opportunity to meet a German Jew," Hausmann said. "Much less a Jew from Würzburg." He smiled a smile that only by a shade missed being convincingly artless.

"And now shall I stand up like a trained bear and do a little dance?" Bauer asked.

"Oh, come now, Herr Bauer, your race is nothing for you to be ashamed of," Hausmann said.

Bauer knew better than to start defending himself on that tired terrain. "Well," he said, "now that you have had yourself a good look, what comes next?"

Hausmann appeared delighted that Bauer had not gone for the hook. "I thought we might have a little chat."

"I know nothing about architecture," Bauer said.

Hausmann's grin now was a frankly happy one. "You know of my profession," he said. "I am also by way of being an amateur politician."

And gazing into the pleasant, boyish face Bauer did not have to ask what streak of politician. It all fell into place, Remers, the maître, all of it, and at that moment too he remembered who Otto Beck was. Otto Beck was the teacher who had joined the Nazi party very early on and who had managed long before it was fashionable to do so to indicate what, if he had the choice, he would do with Jews.

And why had he not placed that name instantly, he asked himself? Otto Beck, who was partly hunchbacked and who had a deformed, shortened leg, had been one of the frightening specters of his childhood. Was it because of Remers' odd manner? Except that he comprehended now what it was Remers had tried to tell him. He had underestimated his old friend. The obtuseness was on his side, not Remers'.

Bauer looked at Hausmann, at the cheerful, winning, attractive features, and he was grateful he now was an American citizen, and he felt a scorn for himself for having to remind himself of that fact at this moment.

Now the eyes lost their coldness, leaving only the memory of a cobra, and they crinkled at the edges. "That is quite amusing, Herr Bauer," Hausmann said. "But fortunately, whatever mistakes Herr Hitler made, German nationalism has too much viability to be cut down for too long."

Bauer had listened to him now for almost an hour and he could not now remember precisely how or when it was during that hour that they had come round to discussing Adolf Hitler. It must have been a perfectly natural course, a casual drifting, because Bauer could not recall that moment when the name first was thrust between them. And yet it was a name almost nobody mentioned in Germany these days. But there they were, speaking it aloud, unconcerned about who might overhear, just as though there never was the endemic, unspoken agreement to pretend the man had never existed.

"But you must understand, Herr Bauer," Hausmann said with great earnestness, "that while we are strongly nationalistic we are not neo-Nazis, which we are sometimes called."

"I must admit," Bauer said, "that I have heard that description."

"You see, my dear man, many of the ideas generally attributed to Hitler, existed long before him, have been a part of the German ethos for hundreds and hundreds of years, some of them from the very beginnings. There were so many different ideas, philosophies, some of them disparate, in conflict with each other, a whole jumble of ideas, and what Hitler managed was to hold all of them together by the leader principle. But you must understand that these concepts existed before him and continue to exist even though he no longer is here."

"Is he missed?" Bauer asked, deadpan, and rather pleased with himself under the circumstances that he could manage that. Perhaps it was just the third Scotch.

Hausmann considered the question seriously. "No, Herr Bauer, as a point of fact Hitler is not held in very high repute among us today."

" 'Us'? Does that mean Germany or just the members of your party?"

"I cannot speak for all Germany, not quite yet," Hausmann said.

Bauer heard this said calmly and without any suggestion of rhetoric. "Why do you downgrade him?"

Hausmann smiled. "That should be quite obvious, my dear man. Hitler in the end turned out to be a coward."

Bauer was beginning to feel he was in some kind of singular German Wonderland.

"He ordered everyone to fight to the end," Hausmann said, something new creeping into his beautifully controlled voice. "To the very end, to the last bullet, the last building, the last street, the last human being—scorched earth and death. And then he took the easy way out for himself. It would have been a hell of a lot better for the pages of history if he had had the courage to remain alive and face up to the people who defeated him."

Now Hausmann's eyes were dilated and his jaw muscles bulged and whitened the skin on his cheeks.

At that moment, Bauer thought, Hausmann seemed slightly mad, the kind of madness that had already proved so irresistible in Germany, and he again felt a little crawling on his flesh.

But then, he reminded himself, Hausmann had had a number of whiskies too. And, after all, Scotch was not an indigenous German drink.

Hausmann lit another cigarette and in the first deep inhalation located and repossessed his cool. "As it was, my dear fellow, he left us a mess to clean up," he said quietly, letting the music back into his voice. "And I don't mean the rubble that was in the streets. I mean the stigma that he attached to the word 'German.' " He said in a very low voice, "There is no question. One must accept the truth. We Germans are a people disliked everywhere in the world."

Bauer was most conscious of the fact that the plural pronoun and the noun that followed were not intended to include him.

The waiter appeared with fresh drinks which Bauer did not remember either of them ordering. The man started to pick up the ashtray and tidy the table but Hausmann waved him away.

Now that he had been formally blackballed from the club, Bauer felt he might make comment as an informed outsider. "Well, if that's true," he said, trying to project a certain impartiality, "you can't deny it's a condition you've all worked very hard for."

Hausmann considered that. Then he said, "You know, Herr Bauer, it has often occurred to me that in some ways we Germans are very much like you Jews."

"Now that's a fascinating observation," Bauer said.

"It's true, it's true, Herr Bauer," Hausmann said with intensity. "Look at it. Both the German and the Jew have always been disliked. And why? We are both efficient, clever, far superior to others. And now that you Jews have your own country the similarity is even more pronounced."

"Yes," Bauer said. "That is a favorite thesis of the Russians."

"It's quite true. Look at the Israeli army. Magnificent! Magnificent! As good, for its size, as anything we Germans have ever put on the field. Why, that entire little country has taught us something. Like Israel, just like Israel, we Germans must have a contempt for world opinion. We must learn from them that when something has to be done force is all that counts."

"I would not have considered that was something Germans had to learn," Bauer said.

Hausmann smiled and then he reached across the table and patted Bauer on the arm. "Very amusing, my good friend. But in point of fact I am talking about Germany of today, not a quarter of a century ago. The Israelis are probably the finest fighters in the world today and we could do far worse than to learn from them."

"Then you must regret, Herr Hausmann, that these Jewish qualities were not appreciated by Hitler and utilized by him."

Hausmann in the act of raising his glass to his lips lowered it without taking a drink. "You try to be sarcastic, Herr Bauer, but the fact is that given the chance the Jews would have made the finest Nazis of all."

"You have interesting philosophies, Herr Hausmann," Bauer said. Who manufactured this Looking Glass? Zeiss? Leitz?

"I have always believed that," Hausmann said. He drank some of his whisky. "The Jews would have been Hitler's stoutest supporters, with money, with their newspapers. And why not? He stood for exactly what they stood for. Anti-communism, middle-class bourgeois stolidity, order. The German Jews could have written Hitler's book. Except for the one thing." Hausmann shrugged. "The *Führer* wasn't wise. He traded off the Jews for street gangs. And before very long he had to destroy those same street gangs, only by then, with all the exaggeration, he had lost the respect of the world as well."

"Exaggeration?" Bauer repeated.

"You know, Herr Bauer, the gross aggrandizement about the numbers of Jews done away with."

"I thought the figure was fairly permanently fixed," Bauer said. But it wasn't, was it? He remembered Captain Roy Atkins.

"Oh, come now, my dear fellow, you surely don't believe those monstrous numbers," Hausmann said.

He leaned forward, his hand clenched round the cigarette lighter. His eyes glared and his voice, in which Bauer had heard almost constantly the subtle music of the trained speaker, now rose and became almost metallic.

"We all know what must be said for propaganda purposes during a war," Hausmann went on, hitting the banquette with the bottom of the lighter. "Six million Jews? Ridiculous! Insane!"

Bauer glanced round the room. He wondered, as he had wondered earlier in the little *Gasthaus*, why nobody in the room seemed in the slightest to be aware of the noise Hausmann was making, at the thumping on the table. Even the waiter knew it was not a summons for him.

133

But Hausmann caught himself immediately. When he replied to Bauer he had himself again in hand. "Of course I don't know the exact figures, my dear man," he said, easily. "Nobody ever will, naturally. But I would make a very good estimate that it never was more than one million. Yes, one million at the very most, probably much less."

"And what happened to the others?" Bauer asked.

"They got away. Just as you did."

Bauer considered this and he wondered if this one day was to be the official German history.

"I will be perfectly frank with you, Herr Bauer," Hausmann said, putting down the lighter and picking up his drink. "There was in Germany then an uneasy feeling about the Jews. And the Nuremberg laws were acceptable to most Germans, no doubt about that. The majority of Germans did think Jews had a bigger place in business, the arts, education, than their numbers warranted, and they believed these laws would set that right. But no German, outside of a few Party fanatics, could believe seriously in what came to be called the Final Solution." Hausmann leaned forward confidentially. "Let me tell you something, Herr Bauer. When the first gas chambers were made they were built to look like ambulances, and the railway stations at the death camps—those camps that existed, and they were far fewer, believe me, than has been charged—they were constructed to look normal and quite harmless. The gas chambers themselves were made to look like rest rooms and showers. And do you know why?"

Bauer said nothing.

"Do you know why, Herr Bauer?" Hausmann asked.

Bauer made himself say, "No, why?"

"To fool the people to be executed? Would you say that?"

"I wouldn't know," Bauer said. He heard the thickness in his own voice. He told himself he must not be sick. That would without question be considered here to be a very Jewish act.

"Who cared about fooling them?" Hausmann demanded to know. "They were to be dead shortly in any case." He

134

shook his head slowly and sadly at all the misguided people in the world. "No, it was to fool the ordinary German, the man in the street, who might become curious and enquire as to what it was all about. You see, my dear man, we Germans are not at all like the Russians. The czars could turn their cossacks on Jews and the Russians would watch happily. But we Germans are too softhearted for that sort of thing. The places of execution had to be thoroughly disguised so nobody would know what was going on. When Germans say today they did not know—they are telling the simple truth."

It was the new history, Bauer knew, and it would be believed, first by the Germans and then in time by everybody else, because it was so much more reasonable.

He heard Hausmann say in a brand new voice, a voice filled with affection, "Liesl, you're here, I've been wondering what was keeping you."

Bauer looked up quickly and then rose to his feet. Hausmann, he saw, before he turned around, was half out of his own seat and was leaning across the banquette, kissing his sister's hand.

"Frau Neubert," Bauer said. He could not at that moment, he knew, manage a hand kiss. He wondered if ever he could. He thought not.

"I asked Liesl to join us, Herr Bauer," Hausmann said. "I knew you wouldn't mind."

"A pleasure," Bauer said.

"Sit down, sit down, *Liebchen*," Hausmann said. He made room for his sister next to him. "Waiter, waiter!" He snapped his fingers and when the waiter landed on cue from somewhere, he said, "A martini for my sister. Very dry. Very, very dry." He looked at Marliese as the waiter flew away. "Such bad American habits you have picked up. How are you, my Liesl?"

"I'm very well, Werner."

She had her hair done up on top of her head this time and she gazed at her brother with what Bauer could describe as adoration.

"We have been having a good talk. Herr Bauer and I," Hausmann said. "It has been very interesting. We have been examining the old days."

She looked at Bauer. "I wouldn't have thought Herr Bauer would have wanted to be reminded too much of that."

"Not at all, not at all!" Hausmann said.

The waiter was back with the drink and he set it down before Marliese and he and Hausmann waited for her to take the first sip and to see her nod her approval.

"Excellent," Hausmann said. "Tell Erich he again escapes being shot at dawn."

The waiter grinned and fled and as though there had been no interruption, Hausmann said, "Not in the slightest. Herr Bauer has enjoyed every word of our discussion, is that not so, my dear man?"

"I have found it illuminating," Bauer said.

"There, Liesl, you have heard him yourself. He has found it illuminating. As for me, I have found it most refreshing. The opinion of a foreigner is always most valuable. Just one or two things more, and then it will all have been said," Hausmann said.

Marliese put her hand gently on her brother's hand. "Oh, Werner, please don't let's go on with that."

He looked at her with what Bauer would have taken as part of the same affection. She removed her hand instantly and lowered her eyes.

"What I just want to say to you, Herr Bauer," Hausmann said, "is that you must remember one very important thing. Toward the end of the war Germany was being very heavily bombed. German sensitivity was dulled because of fear for their lives. The value of the human life became nil. Death, death no longer was connected with anything, not with personal guilt, not with innocence. Death was a simple, automatic fact, a machine, a machine that operated dispassionately, disinterestedly, without prejudice, against everyone, German and Jew. The gas chambers, Herr Bauer, worked as impersonally as the bombing planes."

Again Marliese reached over and covered her brother's

136

hand. "Please, Werner, I do not want to hear about that."

After a moment Hausmann raised her hand to his lips and kissed the back of it. "As always, you are right, little Liesl. And you should not. You had enough of it firsthand." He said to Bauer, "Perhaps you can persuade her one time to tell you about the firestorm. She was only a very little girl then but she has never forgotten it."

Hausmann looked at his watch. "God in heaven! How late it is. It just proves that when one is interested the time flies. I am very sorry, but I must leave you both."

"Werner, I just got here," Marliese said.

"I know, I know, *Liebchen*, but I have a very important appointment and I am already late. You will excuse me, Herr Bauer. I hope we shall have the opportunity to again exchange ideas."

"I would like that very much," Bauer said.

"And you are my guests here."

"This is my hotel, Herr Hausmann."

"That is not exactly correct, my dear man. It is my hotel." He smiled with great charm. "You see, I designed it."

"My congratulations," Bauer said. "It's most attractive." He considered the remark not unworthy of a French diplomat or a Madison Avenue executive.

Hausmann plainly esteemed Bauer's good taste and thanked him for it. He bade them both farewell.

"A final word, Herr Bauer. People have charged Germans always with brutality. But it is war that brutalizes people. Lidice? Oradour-sur-Glane? Those towns symbolize to the world the purest essence of German cruelty. Perhaps it will come to pass one day that Mylai will occupy that same exquisite status in the history of your self-righteous Americans."

Bauer wanted to answer that. He wanted very much to answer that one. But Hausmann, as would any good actor, having delivered his curtain line, walked immediately off the stage.

14

✠ ✠ ✠

BAUER ROLLED A PIECE OF BREAD LIKE A WORRY BEAD BETWEEN
his thumb and forefinger and looked out the picture window
of the restaurant across the quay and across the river to the
floodlit *Festung*. He felt good. He felt comfortable and relaxed and she had done that for him and he was grateful to
her.

"We play gin," he said. "Mostly we play gin."

"Gin? But that is something to drink. What I am drinking
now."

"It is also a card game and we play it all the time. Yes, I
would have to say I am married, legally married."

He looked on the quay. Two lovers were walking slowly by,
holding hands. Bauer was very glad he had accepted her invitation and that he was where he was.

"If you take me to dinner tonight I promise you that I
won't run out on you this time," she had said in the Deutscher Hof after her brother had sailed out, leaving people
and things fluttering in his wake. The maître at his station by
the door after having received something from Hausmann
remained stiff for several moments as though he had with-
stood a tornado.

"I must apologize for last evening," she had said. "It was quite rude of me."

Regretfully he took his eyes away from the phenomenon of the maître. "Not at all."

"The strange part of it is that I still don't know why I did that."

"You had promised to see your father. It was perfectly understandable."

"I had not. I just made that up. You must have known that."

Why was she bothering to tell him all this? The eternal German necessity to be truthful in small things? "I just took you at your word," he had said, stealing a glance at the maître who by then appeared to have recovered his wits. "There's no need to reproach yourself for anything."

"It was unlike me," she had said. "I'm not normally rude."

How important it was, Bauer had thought, as the waiter, still unasked, brought new drinks, how important it was for Germans to establish the fact they were not rude, that they were civilized human beings in possession of civilized manners. It was a driving compulsion as though incivility was inexcusable under any circumstances, particularly after it had been shown.

"You will take me out to dinner tonight?" she had asked again.

He was tired and he thought he had had enough of the Hausmanns for one evening and he would have in any case preferred a quiet meal alone and an early night but, and he had smiled wryly to himself, he was too German to be rude.

As they walked to the restaurant he wondered again why she wanted to spend the evening with him and, remembering some of the things her brother had said, and what her brother represented, he had the sudden suspicion that perhaps he was under a family surveillance but he decided that kind of fancy led straight to paranoia and whatever else Würzburg was going to do to him he would not allow it to do that.

He had allowed her to choose the place they would dine and he hoped against hope that it would not be full of *lederhosen* and fat waitresses carrying three or four liter-sized steins of beer in each hand, he could do without things *gemütlich* at the moment, but he realized that probably was asking too much, and then he was pleasantly taken aback when she led him to the quay and to a lovely, un-German restaurant that specialized, it turned out, in Dalmatian food. Why Croatian cuisine in Würzburg? He did not want to ask. He did not want to know. The reason undoubtedly would be German and irritating. He was just happy to be there.

"Why is it called gin?" she asked now.

"I don't know. But we play it all the time, my wife and I. We play for points. I'm thousands and thousands of points behind."

"Why does she beat you so much?"

"She's a much better player than I am. When she is not playing gin with me she is playing it somewhere else with one of her women friends. All her women friends play gin. They are almost professional. I have tried to pay my wife and break off the game but she always says she'd rather just keep the score and settle some other time."

"Why did you marry her, Peter?"

He shrugged. "I don't know that either. I don't know whether in fact I married her."

"Please?"

"Oh, we're married all right. But I mean I don't really know whether it was that I married Lucille. Lucille, specifically. You see," he said, seeing the puzzlement on her face and thinking at that moment that it was a most exciting face, "you see, I've often thought that it just happened to have been the time for me to get married, and she was there. You would be surprised, Liesl, how many men, especially in the United States, get married because it happens to be that time."

She made an effort to comprehend. "Do you have children?"

"No time. We do nothing but play gin."

She giggled. It was a delightful, spritely sound. "Is she an American woman, Peter?"

140

"Very much so. And for many generations. In the event I might forget that she reminds me of it often." He looked at her and grinned. "Are you wondering why she married a refugee German Jew?"

She took a sip of her martini. "Yes, Peter, as a matter of fact, I was wondering just that."

"Bless you for not denying it," he said. "Well, I've never figured that out myself. I think it was because she thought at the time it was the chic thing to do. You know, like having the token Negro at a dinner party."

"Where do you live?" she asked.

"In Washington. We have a little apartment."

He looked again at the *Festung* in its evening dress. The massive fortress did more than overlook the city; it dominated it and not just physically. It seemed to have life and to look into the eye and heart and soul of everyone below, to miss nothing, to escape nothing.

He turned to her again and it seemed quite normal for him to be there with this handsome woman and the fact she was German did not for some reason at this point trouble him and he was pleased with the way she sipped her drink and smoked her cigarette and was inquisitive about his life.

"This is such an attractive place, Liesl," he said. "Thank you for bringing me here."

Somewhere along the line they'd got to a first name basis, and, on his part, on a diminutive first name basis. When? He could not remember and it didn't seem to matter. Perhaps it was the influence of Captain Atkins who had willed it so.

She looked at him steadily for a moment. "My brother is an extraordinary man, Peter. Brilliant. I love him very much. But he is a powerhouse. He comes on very strong. I thought perhaps you needed a restorative. A quiet place with a pretty view." She took a long, slow pull on her cigarette and exhaled as slowly. "I also believed that after an hour or so of Werner you might appreciate a little to get away for a while from Germany. Now, I want to hear more about your marriage."

He thought she must be an extraordinary woman and he wanted to tell her so but he did not know how to do it. He

141

had no way with women. "There's very little more to say about it."

"Is she pretty? You haven't said that."

"Yes, I think one would call her pretty."

"Describe her to me."

He shrugged. "She's tallish, American kind of tallish, and she has a very good face."

"And she plays gin, this game."

"She plays gin and she does interior decorating."

"Is she good at that?"

"I'm told she's very good."

"But not to your taste."

"Why are you interested in all this?"

"I'm interested and I also am selfish."

"I cannot imagine why you're interested but in what way are you selfish?"

"I often want to talk about Heinrich. Almost everyone I know has heard everything I have to say about him many times and are fed up and everybody else doesn't give a damn. I want to have some credit with you so I can talk about my husband." She put out her cigarette. "I'm hungry, Peter. Could we order some food?"

The dinner arrived flaming on swords with great flourish by a costumed waiter, but despite that it was very good and there was a sound wine to go with it, Yugoslavian wine it turned out, and the coffee afterward was strong and bitter and the German brandy, which he had never before drunk, or didn't remember if he had, was superb.

She lit a cigarette with the coffee and he wished very much then that he could have a cigar but he knew that would open the door and he forebore.

They strolled along the quay. Behind them the riverboat had just landed. There were voices behind them but as they walked they lost them and it was still.

"Tell me about Heinrich," he said.

"I haven't asked you about your mother," she said. "How

awful of me, I'd forgotten about that. Did you find anything new?"

Had he? "No, nothing very much. Tell me about Heinrich. Unless this is not the time." She had told him she was a widow. Or had he just imagined that?

"You are being kind."

"Do you mind if I smoke?"

He looked again at her in surprise. "I haven't so far, why would you ask?"

"But this is in the open," she said. "Werner disapproves entirely of women smoking but he gets absolutely livid when he sees a woman walking down the street with a cigarette in her mouth. He says it is not German."

"We're in a strategic position here," he said in a stage whisper. "If we see him coming you can slip the fag to me."

"But he must have already noticed that you don't smoke," she said in the same conspiratorial voice. "He would never believe it was yours."

"He would, Liesl, he would. He could never believe that his sister was not one hundred percent German."

After the briefest moment she asked, "Are you being sarcastic about my brother, Peter?"

How abruptly the game had ended, he thought, hearing the ice cracking under his feet. "No, not in the least, I promise you."

She took her cigarettes from her bag. "He saved my life when I was a child. At least it was what I always told myself, that he saved my life. I didn't need that to love him but if I had had that need it would have been that."

"Werner saved your life?" He took the Zippo from her hand and lit her cigarette.

"Heinrich. I suppose Werner saved my life a thousand times in one way or another, especially after Heinrich was killed, but I am speaking this time about my husband." She turned to the river. "It was during the fire bombing here. I was just a little girl, as Werner told you. It happened I was spending the night with another little girl at her house. I remember her name, Hilde. Hilde Engel. We were asleep when the bombers came over and I remember there was so much screaming and crying and then Hilde and I were somehow in the street and people were running around sobbing and shrieking and there were some people with suitcases and there was one woman who was singing and jumping up and down and she opened her suitcase and took out things and tried to give them away and nobody would take anything, all everybody wanted to do was get away, nobody would take anything from her. And Hilde and I didn't know which way to go and then Heinrich came along, he wasn't much older than I was, just a few years, he just by chance came along, and for some reason he took my hand and kept running, dragging me after him, and I tried to hold on to Hilde but I couldn't, she just all of a sudden wasn't there and then I fell and my ankle twisted and I couldn't run any more and Heinrich picked me up and carried me. The whole street caught fire. I always told him he saved my life."

"He probably did," Bauer said. He thought how totally she had taken herself away from him, what a space there now was between them, a space far greater than the distance between a bombing plane and a running child.

"He did," she said. "Hilde was burned to death. Her whole family was burned to death. Werner used to say that I didn't belong on that street and that's why I didn't get caught in the flames. But it wasn't that at all. It was Heinrich." She smiled. "He always denied it. He was that way. It embarrassed him when anyone would say he had done something like that, even when he was a boy. He used to tell the story in a different way. He used to tell everybody that the first time in his life that he saw me I was in my nightgown."

Bauer knew he would have liked this man.

She threw the cigarette into the water. It made a little arching, falling star that vanished.

"What did Heinrich do?" Bauer asked, from across the long distance.

"He was an architect. He was a partner in the firm that

engaged Werner when Werner finished school." She stared at the water. "It was such a little mountain."

Bauer said nothing.

"He was an architect and they said that he was a very good architect, old-fashioned, he hated all the modern designs, he thought the railroad station they built to replace the old one was hideous. He could hardly bring himself even to look at the new apartment houses."

Yes, he thought, he would like this man very much.

"It was silly," she said. "It was not even an important mountain."

"How did it happen?"

"It was the thing he loved most. Next to me, he would always say. He would say that but in a certain way it was ahead of me but I didn't mind that. He climbed many of the big ones in Switzerland, he was very good and he was careful. And the one that killed him was such a small one, just a little thing in the Bavarian Alps, hardly more than a hill. How did it happen? Nobody ever knew. Such a stupid little mountain. But he was a big man and he fell down hard."

Somewhere a clock tolled eleven.

"I didn't mean to go on this long about it," she said, still not looking at him. "I really didn't, Peter. I should be quite over it by now. I am quite over it. It's just that once in a while I like to bring it back, bring him back. It does something good for me. But really, I'm quite over it now."

"When did all this happen?" he asked.

"Almost three years ago. Just about that, three years ago. It will be three years this winter."

"Did you have children?"

She shook her head. "No. We tried, of course. I mean we made love because of the way we felt about each other but we made love to have children too. Heinrich wanted children, many children, a big family. But we just didn't have any. It was something he always blamed himself for. It never crossed his mind to think it might be me. I've since been obliged to find out otherwise."

Presently she asked, still watching the water pass her by, "Aren't you interested in how I found out, Peter?"

He could have no communion with this woman who once had fled from a burning street in a burning city but she could not know that. "It's not my business," he said.

She hit her fist on the quay wall. "Oh, don't be so God damned polite!" She turned on him and for a moment he thought she would strike him.

He should have been shocked by her vehemence. He was not. He should have backed away but he did not. He knew about being alone in a crowded life. He knew about the need to tell even if it has to be there is no one to tell but one's self. He knew what happened inside when there were others there and they would not listen, no longer listen, never listen. He could tell her all about that.

He wanted to touch her, to calm her, to assure her that it was all right, that he understood and that it was all right and to please lean, to lean as hard as she had to lean.

But was it all right? And if it were all right, what was it? And what did he understand? And who was he to privilege himself as a strength?

He was too far away in a four-engined bomber and no matter how they stretched their arms their fingers could never touch.

"That was outrageous of me, Peter," she said. "You must say that you forgive me."

"It was nothing."

"I never shout that way. I never act that way. Please say that you forgive me."

"It was nothing, Liesl. For a moment you took me into your heart. It was only that."

"How extraordinary of you to say that, Peter," she said after a moment. "No German would ever think to put it that way."

"No," he said. "We Jews have a little language of our own."

"I didn't mean that either," she said quickly. "I don't even think of you as a Jew."

146

"Is that intended as a compliment?"

"Oh, go to hell, you son of a bitch," she said, and her face broke into a sudden grin and he could see now there had been tears in her eyes. "You are a silly son of a bitch."

"Good," he said. "Now I don't feel so lonesome."

The grin broadened and he thought at that moment she looked enchanting and he thought how nice it would be if everything were simple and there were not so many things else.

They started walking along the quay and then they went off the quay into a side street.

"After Heinrich was killed my father waited what he considered a decent interval and then he started urging me to get married again. He considers it immoral for a German woman my age not to be married," she said. "And to be working. And for foreigners."

They were alone in a narrow, twisting street and their heels made sounds on the cobbles and the echoes fell back from the walls of the buildings that bracketed them.

"Only that is not what he really considers immoral," she said. "You must have gathered that Roy Atkins and I have been having what is generally described as an affair." She gave a short laugh. "It's funny. Roy has managed to father three children—one of them, in point of fact, since I started sleeping with him. And since Roy is not a man to bother with any precautions, he believes that to be the woman's problem, it turns out I'm the barren ground. It wasn't Heinrich at all."

At the entrance to the building where she lived, a small, old-fashioned apartment house, selected, Bauer knew without having to ask, by Heinrich Neubert, she held out her hand.

"Good night, Peter."

He took the hand.

"I'm beholden to you," she said.

"In no way."

Her hand tightened on his. "You are a silly son of a bitch, aren't you?"

He waited until she unlocked the door and entered and closed it behind her and then he started back to his hotel.

The street was empty for several blocks and his only company was his footfalls; curtains were drawn and shutters were closed; dwellers had cocooned themselves for the night, isolating themselves from the street, the city, the world, and, if favored, in sleep, ultimately from even themselves.

Then he entered upon a larger thoroughfare and there were still live people there and they walked and they laughed and they talked and he heard the German spoken as they passed and the words and the language were seemly and he was filled with peace and he felt at home, so much so he did not experience any sense of wonderment that that benediction should be bestowed upon him in, of all places, Germany, in, of all places, the city of Würzburg, which he had helped once to put to death.

15

✠ ✠ ✠

ERWIN AXMANN WAVED HIS PIPESTEM AS THOUGH IT HAD power. He roared, "Get the hell out of here, you damned hoodlums! What the devil do you think this is, the Third Reich?"

Werner Hausmann smiled politely and recrossed his legs. "You would know more about that, Herr Axmann, than any of us. Now, please, sir, I ask you again, what exactly was it that Peter Bauer wanted to know?"

Axmann, backed against the cold stone fireplace in his cottage like a beleaguered bear, looked at the young men seated in his room. There were a dozen of them. He had answered the bell in the early evening thinking a neighbor was calling for a chat and when he had opened the door they had walked in without a word, unangrily but in no way to be denied.

They had seated themselves immediately and they now sat upright, not stiffly but alertly, and in their beautifully tailored suits and shining shoes, with their cleanly shaved faces and neat haircuts, neither too long nor too short, in their bright manner and youthful attentiveness they might have been members of a board of directors in meeting, an attractive, fresh, modern board. Some of them, coming directly from their offices, carried attaché cases which they set down carefully at their feet.

Hausmann had waited, with quiet, seignorial courtesy, as befit the chairman of the board, for the others to find their places before he sat down, first asking Axmann's leave.

"I just left him a little while ago," Hausmann was saying now. "He is a charming man, charming. We had a most interesting hour or so and exchanged ideas. Breath of fresh air, Herr Axmann."

"That's your affair and not mine," Axmann said. "Now you and your gang get the hell out of my house."

"I know why Bauer is in Würzburg, of course," Hausmann said.

"Then why do you bother me? What right do you have to force your way into my house?"

"We didn't force our way in, Herr Axmann," Hausmann said in his gentlest voice. "We rang the bell and you opened the door. Not like the old days, is it? Swinging axes, kicking down doors. The SS never bothered to ring a bell, did it?"

"You damned swine, I'm going to call the police!" Axmann started for the telephone.

Before he took three steps one of the young men reached down and pulled the telephone wire out of the box on the wall.

Axmann stopped dead. The young man resumed his posture of interest and his pleasant, observant smile.

Axmann started for the front door. Well before he reached there two of the young men stood up and blocked it.

And it was done without orders, Axmann saw. Each of them had known what to do and had done it on his own and with celerity and almost a kind of grace and with no signal from Hausmann.

I'm too old for this, he told himself.

"Now, Herr Axmann, you must understand I find Bauer's mission commendable," Hausmann said.

Axmann realized too that Hausmann had never taken his

eyes from him, not even to see whether what had had to be done was being done.

I'm too old and too tired for this.

"I have no quarrel with a man who wants to find out the circumstances of his mother's death," Hausmann said. "After all, Herr Axmann, how many mothers does one have in one's life? All I want to know from you is why he came here."

Axmann backed up to the hearth again. "Why the devil do I have to answer you about anything? Now I tell you swine again, get out of here."

"Come now, my dear Herr Axmann," Hausmann said. "This should make you feel good. This should bring back old memories. After all you were an officer in an organization that practically invented this kind of thing, in Germany at least. What dreadfully cruel people you were then." He took a cigarette from his gold case and lit it. "Don't you find it amusing, Herr Axmann, that a former SS officer should find himself at the short end of this kind of interview?"

There were restrained chuckles in the room.

They were, it was borne upon Axmann, the only sounds any of the others had made since they had invaded his home. They said nothing, it was clear, while the chairman spoke.

"That was a long time ago, Herr Hausmann," Axmann said.

"You know who I am?" Hausmann asked, not surprised.

Axmann leaned his big head forward. "I know you and I know these swine who follow you and your politeness and your fancy clothes don't fool me, it's only your kind of uniform."

"You would know more about those things too than we would," Hausmann said.

There was, Axmann saw, not the slightest reaction from any of them. They remained silent, watchful, almost deferential. He might have been talking in a language they did not comprehend. He might have been some uncommon creature they were interested only to observe.

"For the last time," he said, "get out of my house."

Hausmann flicked his cigarette ash on the floor and for a

reason he did not understand that struck Axmann as the most ominous sign of all.

"And for the last time, Oberstürmbannführer Axmann," Hausmann said. "Why did Peter Bauer come here?"

16

✠ ✠ ✠

THE NEXT MORNING WAS BRIGHT AND SUNNY. WHEN BAUER LEFT the hotel he found Major Reinhard waiting for him. Although he had not ordered him to be there it pleased Bauer to see him. It lent his course another degree of steadiness.

He saw that today Reinhard had tucked his trousers into leather gaiters, giving him more the accepted appearance of a chauffeur. It was probably very childish, Bauer knew, but he liked that too; it was another handhold.

He raised his brows and cocked his head to indicate his observation, comprehension, and approbation. Major Reinhard, somewhat sheepish, broke into a grin.

"I was going to visit a hospital and old peoples' home this morning," Bauer said. "It is why I didn't call you. I was going to walk."

Reinhard opened the taxi door. "You're paying me by the day, Herr Bauer. It would be unprincipled of you not to allow me to give you your full money's worth."

Bauer gave him the name of the hospital and got into the car.

"What do you know about Werner Hausmann?" Bauer asked, as they drove off.

"Well, well, well," Reinhard said.

"Translate, Major."

"The first 'well' is surprise. The second 'well' is no surprise. The third is in the event anything happened to the first two."

"I have received all three safely. What about Hausmann?"

"Up and coming architect. Built some of the new stores. A few apartments. None of them to my taste, but there you are."

"What else?"

"Politician. Labels himself conservative. Consensus is he'll go far, maybe very far. Quite a few people are happy at that prospect."

"Carry on, Major."

"Very cosy speaker. Confidential type. Low key. No screaming, you understand?"

"Yes," Bauer said.

"Very modern, like his buildings. He's a stylish mug. Father used to be a big lawyer around here. Retired now. There's also a sister. Good-looker. She works at the American military base. Works for an American captain there. General gossip is that she's sleeping with her boss."

"I've met her."

"Well," Major Reinhard said.

"Is that the fourth well of the series?"

"That's a new one, Herr Bauer. Totally unrelated to the others. Sorry what I said about her having an affair with this American. Just that's what people say. Probably just that, gossip, no truth to it at all."

"Probably," Bauer said.

"You do get around, Herr Bauer," Reinhard said as he pulled up to the hospital. "And with the very best people."

Bauer stepped out of the car.

"This is the original building," Reinhard said, joining him. "By some miracle it escaped the fire raid."

Was it a miracle? It was such a small thing and he had made such a point of it to the wing commander. He had

154

pointed out on the enlarged plan how the hospital was almost on the edge of the town, at the opposite side from the railroad station, in what then was almost isolation. He had spoken of Sister Angelica and Father Stolz although he could not be sure they were still there or if the hospital were still a hospital. The wing commander was a harassed man but he seemed to understand and had promised they would try to avoid the hospital, all the hospitals, but Bauer had never known.

"Do you know this place?" Reinhard asked.

"Yes," Bauer said. "My father supported it."

He remained there for a moment, unable to enter.

. . . The hospital was always Christmas because although he went there occasionally with his father at other times of the year the big visit was Christmas and the nuns who served as sisters were in their brightest smiles and there was a tree on each floor at the nurses' station and everybody gathered around the tree on his floor and those patients who were confined to beds because of illness or age were wheeled out so they too could see the lighted trees . . .

. . . Sister Angelica, whose face was illuminated by some private, ancient glow, no brighter than that of a taper, but unflickering, who, even to the small boy Peter lived in a world that was not this world, pushed the big cart, it was a stretcher on wheels actually, what the people were moved to the operating room on, but at these times piled high with presents provided by Simon Bauer and his friends, his Jewish friends and his Christian friends . . . and the presents were not just any old kind of presents, impersonal gifts unasked for, brightly wrapped things to be handed to the old and the poor and the ill, no, Simon Bauer and Sister Angelica and Father Stolz had long ago worked out their scheme . . . for weeks before the holidays Sister Angelica and the other sisters and Father Stolz and the junior priests, in the most casual way, managed to find out what most of the patients would want most if they had their choice, and sometimes, to Peter, whom his father kept informed, they seemed strange wishes, an old man with a terminal illness, wanted, he had disclosed shyly to Father Stolz, a wrist watch so that in bed in the ending hours he could mark them for himself, an old woman wanted a doll such as she had when she was a small girl . . . one woman wanted a music box with dancing figures that turned round and round and round, an old man wanted a harmonica, a boy with infantile paralysis wanted more than anything in the world to own a pair of ice skates . . . each request, desire, dream was noted, with the name of the patient and when possible each request was filled . . . the commonest exception was when the patients died before the holiday time came round . . .

. . . And one Christmas, it must have been the last Christmas before he was whisked away in the night by Erwin Axmann, Peter remembered his father had procured for Sister Angelica a small crucifix which had been blessed by the Pope . . . she accepted it, Peter always remembered, with a kind of sadness which he understood later to be an expression of consecration . . . it was another part of his growing up . . .

Bauer felt his heart pounding as he went across a little plaza and entered the building.

. . . "Why are the people here, Papa?" . . . he was very young . . . "Because they are sick and they are old . . ." "Why do old people have to go to a hospital, don't they have any family . . . ?" "Some of them do and some of them don't . . ." "If they have a family why doesn't their family take care of them . . . ?" "Sometimes they cannot afford to, sometimes they don't have enough room or someone who can watch and take care of the old person, and some families are just too busy to have old, bedridden persons around . . ." "I'd never let you or mama have to go to a place like this . . ."

There was a young woman, not a nun, or not dressed as a nun, seated at a desk and Bauer went to her and told her he had returned to Würzburg after being away a long time and that he wondered whether any of the older nuns were still there. The woman relayed the message on the telephone and a few moments later a brisk, cheerful young man appeared. He introduced himself as Herr Schultz, the assistant administrator.

"The hospital no longer is administered by the Catholic order which administered it formerly," Herr Schultz said, "but there still are a few of the nuns here. Come, Herr Bauer, and we'll try to see what we can find."

He followed Schultz as he had many times followed his father, each small step like a light drumbeat, he remembered that old picture of a mountain lake, and that one, a pastoral scene, trees around a pond.

They stepped through a door and were in an inner courtyard he remembered clearly. In the courtyard, in the sunlight and the warmth, were patients, elderly people seated around, some on benches, some in the chairs in which they had been wheeled. Nothing had changed, nothing.

He saw two nuns with folded arms walking slowly toward them and as they drew closer he saw that one was very old and when they came to where Bauer and Herr Schultz were standing the old nun said tranquilly, "Now, there is the little Peter."

Bauer felt his blood turn to ice. He looked at the face, framed as in a medieval painting by the white starched coif, the face as unlined as that of a child, the skin so pale, so gossamer, as to be almost transparent.

"Sister Angelica," he said.

Herr Schultz and the younger nun had left them and they were alone.

"You have not been here in a long time, Peter," Sister Angelica said.

She started to walk and he followed at her side as, as a child, he had followed at her side.

"I've been away, Sister Angelica," he said.

157

"So many people have gone away. I haven't seen your father in a long time."

"He has gone away," Bauer said.

Sister Angelica unfolded her arms and pointed to a window on the third floor of one of the buildings. "That is where your sister had her appendix removed. How is Emmy?"

"She's very well, Sister," Bauer said.

"And your mother?"

"She is well."

She touched the tip of a finger, small, frangible as milk glass, the fingernail trimmed in a neat arc, to a crucifix that hung from her neck on a gold chain.

"It was so dear of Councilor Bauer to get this for me from the Holy Father. Councilor Bauer is such a thoughtful man. It would be so nice if he could find time to visit here the way he used to." She sighed, a suspiration so faint it almost was without existence. "But the councilor is such an important man and must have so many things to occupy his mind I suppose he just forgets."

"He has not forgotten, Sister Angelica," Bauer said.

She smiled as imperceptibly as she had breathed. "I am happy to hear that, Peter. I have prayed that he does not forget us."

"He has not forgotten, Sister, I promise you."

The younger nun now rejoined them and Bauer understood that he must leave, that she was so old—how old?—she must be very nearly a hundred now and the skin as pure and sweet and virginal as that of an infant and the sea-blue eyes which today had never quite looked at him, and that the younger sister must think he had tired her, and she was wrong. Nothing of this life could tire Sister Angelica, not then, as he had remembered her, and surely not now.

"Good-by, Sister Angelica," he said.

"Good-by, Peter," she said, resting her arm on that of the younger nun. "It was thoughtful of you to pay us this visit. You must come again when you have the time."

"I will, Sister."

"Tell the councilor we miss him."

"I shall, Sister."

"And remember me to the rest of your family, please."

Bauer nodded.

"Emmy has recovered, has she not? She is well now?"

"Yes, Sister."

"I am happy to hear that. She was so frightened. I told her it was nothing, these days. But she was so frightened."

Sister Angelica's farewell smile seemed lent to her. The younger nun dipped her head in curtsey to Bauer and led her away.

Bauer looked around and found an unoccupied bench and sat down and closed his eyes. He opened them to see Herr Schultz walking rapidly toward him.

"I have another surprise for you, Herr Bauer," Herr Schultz said in his liveliest manner.

Bauer shook his head.

"I checked the records," Herr Schultz said. "There are several of the old priests here." He nodded rapidly. "Still here."

"I must go," Bauer said, rising.

· "There is Father Schirmann and Father Buchner," Herr Schultz said, talking right through him. "Both of them remember your father well."

"I really must go," Bauer said. The hospital had come to be a prison.

Herr Schultz was not to be gainsaid. "And there is Father Wagner and Father Stolz, Father Stolz remembers you," he said with arm-raising triumph, as though he had pulled the ultimate rabbit out of the hat.

Bauer tapped gently on the door.

"Come in," the voice said. It had rusted with age and had come through a closed door but it was enough to make new ice in Bauer's veins.

He entered the room. It was small, furnished as austerely as a monk's cell. The old man wearing the vestment of a priest sat in a straight-backed chair. His face was shrunk in its size from whatever it had been. On the wall almost directly behind him was an old German wooden crucifix.

"God's greetings, Peter," the priest said. "Little Peter."

Bauer took the priest's hand and pressed it against his cheek. When he was able to, he asked, "How are you, Father?"

"I could not be any better, little Peter. Except that God has decreed I must live through all these years to give me time enough to atone for all my sins." The priest chuckled.

Bauer swung a chair around and sat down, leaning on the back. "Have you been here the entire time, Father?"

"Except for the time I spent in Theresienstadt."

Bauer's hands closed on the sides of the chair.

Father Stolz shook his head. "No, Peter. It was afterward. I didn't see any of them, my son."

Presently Bauer said, "But you became chaplain there."

"I was a prisoner."

"You, Father?" Bauer asked in surprise.

The priest nodded. "An enemy of the state. That's what I was called," he said proudly.

"What was your offense?"

"A gross one. I delivered sermons."

Bauer nodded. He understood. He could almost hear the sermons. And he thought Councilor Bauer would be pleased to know he had not been wrong in his love for his old friend.

"It's what a priest is supposed to do, is he not, little Peter?" Stolz's voice took on timbre.

Bauer held his lips together tight. It was the old voice, the voice he never forgot, the voice he would have known in the longest distance in the darkest night.

"It is a priest's duty, his sacred duty, to keep his parishioners in sight of the word and justice and morality of God."

And how many did that? Bauer wondered. Possibly more than one knew.

"They let me alone at first because we are a Catholic city and it was still something here to be a priest, despite what Hitler and Himmler and the rest of them kept saying. They did not like what I said and I was given a hint now and again, not exactly a warning, perhaps, but just a little hint, but outside of that they let me alone."

Father Stolz subsided. He was breathing hard. His words were taxing him but he would not stop and Bauer knew better than to try. The priest was a small man, always thin, always frail, and always with his power, and the power was there now.

"And then what happened, Father?" Bauer asked in a whisper.

The priest fixed his eyes on him. They were eyes newly minted.

"I don't remember when it started or why or how but slowly I began to feel that something terrible was going to happen to us here in our city. I felt it in my soul and it writhed there like a serpent and I wrestled with myself and finally I was made to know that I must speak out." His fingers curled like claws on the square ends of the chair arms. "I told them there would be a punishment by God for the evil of Nazism, that God would strike and that His blow would be a Godlike blow."

The priest leaned forward and the years were stripped away from his face, not in layers, not by degree, but at once, and his features were as new as his eyes and his voice buried the years.

"I said God would strike and there would be fire and death and destruction and pestilence. I saw it, I saw it in a vision, and I knew I was given this vision by the Lord and that He meant for me to reveal it. And the fire raid came, the holocaust, just as I had said it would, just as I had foretold again and again from my pulpit. And then I watched one night as my city was destroyed in flames sent down from above, just as I had seen in my vision, in punishment for the evil it had created and condoned and ignored and abetted."

Father Stolz leaned back in his chair and raised his head and turned it and looked upon the crucifix on the wall and at that moment Bauer thought the face belonged to El Greco.

The priest lowered his head. "They hated me," he said.

"They hated you?" Bauer asked. "For warning them?"

161

"My parishioners hated me and people who had never before known of me hated me."

"But why?" Bauer asked.

The priest lifted his eyes. "Because I had predicted the fire-storm, my son, they blamed me for it."

"But that is insane," Bauer said, knowing it was not insane at all.

"Perhaps without intending to do so, the Gestapo did me a service taking me to a concentration camp," Father Stolz said. "The people here might have burned me at a stake."

The words were said quietly but they were the words of melodrama and yet, Bauer, knowing the people of Germany, of this part of Germany, of this marked part of Germany, knew there was in them no melodrama at all.

"I shall never forget the night of that bombing," Father Stolz said. "It is many years ago but in that memory there has been no passing of years."

Bauer closed his eyes.

Father Stolz said, "It was an act of man, the size of an act of God."

Father Stolz stared at him and Bauer wondered whether the priest was staring into his soul.

Bauer pushed himself slowly to his feet. He rested his weight on his hands on the top of the back of the chair.

"May I come to see you again, Father?"

"You must come again, little Peter. You have not as yet told me what has brought you back to Würzburg."

The narrow edge of the chair back cut into the palms of Bauer's hands. "When you were in Theresienstadt, Father, there were none of them there?"

"No, my son, as I have told you."

"None of them? No one?"

"No."

"You would have known, Father?"

"I believe I would have known."

Bauer leaned forward, holding on to the chair as though it were the only thing that saved him from falling into an abyss without bottom. "Was my mother sent there, Father?"

"That is what brings you here."

"Father," Bauer cried out. "What happened to my mother?"

The priest gazed at him. "I don't know, my son."

"I must find out," Bauer said.

"Yes, I suppose you must."

"Do you know anything?"

"No."

"Nothing?"

"Nothing at all. She just disappeared from the city."

The words hung in the air as tiny puffs of smoke and then were not there.

Bauer breathed out heavily and straightened. His hands ached. He looked at them. The palms were marked in red lines from the chair in a kind of private stigmata.

The priest looked at him with compassion. "You will find out and then you will hate just a little more."

"Good-by, Father," Bauer said.

"God bless you, little Peter."

When Bauer emerged from the hospital he saw Major Reinhard was in his usual position, leaning against the front fender of his car, this time looking at a newspaper.

He held the paper out to Bauer.

NOTED MOUNTAIN CLIMBER FOUND BURNED TO DEATH IN MYSTERIOUS FIRE

Charred Body of Erwin Axmann Found in Ruins of His House

17

✠ ✠ ✠

THE ROAD LEADING TO AXMANN'S COTTAGE WAS NOT AS UNCLUT-
tered as it had been the day before. Curious people had
walked or had driven up and the cars were parked on both
sides and there were scores of persons standing around. As
Reinhard drove closer to where the cottage had been Bauer
could see police cars.

They reached a police barricade and a uniformed officer
told them this was as far as they could go. Bauer got out of
the taxi and walked the rest of the way. He was stopped by
another man in uniform and went past him by the simple
device of looking official and ignoring the policeman's opening questions.

The cottage, he saw, walking up the dirt path, had been
almost totally destroyed. All that was left standing were the
stone fireplace and the chimney. There were black tendrils
still rising and in the air was a stale, smoldering smell.

A dozen-odd men, most of them in police or firemen's uniforms, were rummaging about, asking each other questions,
nodding gravely, putting down notes.

One of the men not in uniform, a strapping man in a dark,

rumpled suit, chewing on something, detached himself and strode over to Bauer.

He glanced at him briefly. "Who are you?" he asked in English. "What are you doing here?"

He asked the questions in a courteous growl and Bauer realized immediately he was accustomed to getting answers. He was aware at the same time that what the man had in his mouth was an artificial cigarette.

"My name is Peter Bauer," he said in German. "I am an old friend of Herr Axmann. I visited him only yesterday."

"How did you get past the police barrier?" the man asked, shifting to German with no change of expression.

He was, Bauer would judge, somewhere in his forties. He had thick, sandy brows over penetrating gray eyes.

"I walked past," Bauer said.

He saw the man look over his shoulder to see which policeman had been guilty of negligence.

"Someone tried to stop me," Bauer said. "I walked past him. But he tried to stop me."

"Grieb," the man said, not raising his voice.

The police officer who had tried to block Bauer ran up the dirt path on the double. He came to a halt, saluted, went into a brace in one unbroken movement.

"Herr Police President," he said. He had not bothered to look at Bauer.

"You are relieved from duty."

"*Jawohl*, Herr Police President."

"Tell Pfister to replace you."

"*Jawohl*, Herr Police President."

"You will return to headquarters."

"*Jawohl*, Herr Police President."

The policeman saluted again and walked rapidly down the path, still not having turned his eyes on Bauer.

"I am Police President Eckardt," the man said, working on the fake cigarette.

"So I gathered," Bauer said.

"Some of the people who live around here said that a foreigner visited Axmann yesterday. You aren't a foreigner."

"I was born here, once upon a time," Bauer said. "What started the fire?"

Eckardt removed the gadget from his mouth and inspected it as though he thought he might discover something about it he had not known before. "I'm not going to say to you, 'I ask the questions around here,' " he said. "We can do without that, can't we?"

"I hope so, Herr Police President."

"So instead I will simply ask you why you suspect something." Eckardt puffed on his fake cigarette.

"Do you always have this number of officers around every time a farmhouse burns down?"

Eckardt removed his hat and ran his fingers through straw-colored hair that was somewhat longer than Bauer would have expected from a ranking German police official.

"It was a very slow morning, Herr Bauer," Eckardt said, letting a slight breeze cool his face. "Very little else happening in our sleepy little community. The men like to get a little fresh air into their lungs now and again. What makes you suspicious?"

"I am not suspicious," Bauer said. "As I have told you, Herr Axmann was an old friend, an old family friend. I had not seen him in years. Naturally I have a personal interest in this."

"Naturally."

Eckardt turned his face from the breeze and cast a glance at Bauer. It was an incurious, cursory brush, and Bauer felt he had been briefly under a microscope.

"He was an old man," Eckardt said. "He was a chronic pipe smoker. It is more than probable that his reactions, his sight, something, hearing, were not as sharp as they once were. Accidents do happen, Herr Bauer."

"Herr Police President," Bauer said slowly, "I spent a few hours with Herr Axmann yesterday. There was nothing wrong with his eyes or his ears or anything else."

Looking at the burned area where the cottage had been, Eckardt said, "Look at them poking around up there, like

166

children. One never gets over one's childhood fascination with fire—and the results of fire."

"And as far as starting a fire with burning tobacco that might fall out of a pipe . . ."

"What do you suggest, Herr Bauer?" Eckardt asked with interest, turning to him.

"I suggest that Erwin Axmann was an outdoors man all his life, and that being careless with matches or a pipe or anything like that is entirely out of character."

"Then you do suspect something."

"I know only that Herr Axmann talked at length with me yesterday and that we drank some wine and that he walked me halfway down this path when I left. His memory was excellent. There was nothing in any way senile about him, if that's what you have in the back of your mind. Beyond that, I know nothing."

Eckardt considered that, denied it. "There is something you know, Herr Bauer." He removed the contrivance from his mouth with his first and second fingers as though it were genuine. "We are such weaklings, Herr Bauer," he said, lowering his voice. "Here I am trying to stop smoking and instead of doing it intelligently, as an adult, I have to resort to something like this. A pacifier such as one would shove into the mouth of a puling infant. There is indeed something you know and I am delighted you saw fit to come up here. You save me the trouble of having to trace you down—and even perhaps discovering that you had departed."

"What is it I know?" Bauer asked.

It was an odd feeling, being interrogated by a German police official. It was a situation he had never before experienced, of course, and Herr Eckardt was the absolute substance of civility, and yet it soothed Bauer to remind himself that he was an American citizen and possessed the right to hold up his blue passport as a shield.

He looked up to where the chimney stood as a gaunt marker, a larger than life gravestone as befitted the dead man and the Viking funeral.

"Why you came here yesterday to see Herr Axmann," Eckardt said unhurriedly.

"My family knew him in the old days."

"It was just a sentimental visit?" Eckardt removed the artificial cigarette and shoved it into his breast pocket and looked at his watch. "Is that what has brought you back to Würzburg, Herr Bauer? More nostalgia?"

"How do you know that I have just arrived here, Herr Police President?"

"Please, Herr Bauer." Eckardt waited and then he said, "You have not answered me. Why are you here in Würzburg?"

"Am I required to answer you, Herr Police President?"

"Only if you respect normal amenities, as I try to do."

"I came here to find out how my mother died."

Eckardt nodded. "Those Bauers, the Jewish Bauers. Then you have already told me a small lie, Herr Bauer. You did not pay a visit to Axmann for sentimental reasons alone. You had some definite questions to ask him."

"It can't hurt him now," Bauer said. "As a point of fact, the way people in Germany profess to think now, it may make him a local treasure, something they can boast about to tourists."

"Did Axmann smuggle you out of Germany?"

"Yes."

"And he was supposed to have got your mother out as well?"

"I didn't know that until I saw him."

"And was he able to tell you why your mother didn't leave on schedule?"

"It had something to do with a painting."

"The Tiepolo."

Bauer looked at Eckardt with increased attention. "Why do you bother to question me, Herr Police President?"

Eckardt took his hand out of his coat pocket and waved it and then jammed it into the pocket again, to keep it away, Bauer suspected, from the little artificial cigarette.

"This is such a small place," Eckardt said. "One always

hears when something out of the ordinary occurs, such as the visit of a former Würzburger Jew, the son of a former city councilor."

"What else do you know, Herr Eckardt?" Bauer asked. "Perhaps you also know the name of the person my mother was going to entrust with the painting."

"I have no idea, Herr Bauer."

Bauer turned to the smoking debris. "Where is the body?"

"There was very little body."

"Were there any marks on him?"

"There was very little body, Herr Bauer, and what there was was burned almost beyond recognition."

"How were you able to identify it? Is it at all possible it was not Axmann?"

Eckardt shook his head. "Oddly enough, the least burned part was his face. Probably he tried to shield it from the flames."

"Where was he found?"

"Near the fireplace."

"And you were able to identify him positively?"

"The face was identifiable. We were able even to see a scar on his right cheek. It was badly burned just there but we could make it out. Probably an old dueling scar."

"Axmann had no dueling scar or any other kind of scar on his cheek."

"He had one when we found him. Right here." Eckardt ran a finger down the side of his cheek, from the ear almost to his mouth.

"Could it have been freshly made?"

Eckardt looked at his watch. "Ten minutes," he said with satisfaction. "That's getting better." He fished out the metal tube and put it into his mouth.

"I'll have a stop watch next time," Bauer said. "Could it have been a fresh scar?"

"Wherever it is you live now, Herr Bauer, are you by chance a police officer there?" Eckardt asked.

Bauer shook his head. "No, Herr Police President, I am not a policeman."

"I cannot tell how fresh or how old the scar might have been. That side of his face was scorched too much. It could have been there for years."

"It was not. It was not there yesterday."

"Then it was new. He must have gashed himself in some way."

"Or was slashed."

Eckardt looked at him in open astonishment. "Why would anybody want to do that? This is Germany, after all, not the United States."

"I have no idea who might want to do that, Herr Eckardt. I would like to attend the services. I am staying at the Deutscher Hof."

"Have you found out anything more about the painting, Herr Bauer?"

"No."

"It is too bad Herr Phleps could not have been more helpful."

Bauer grinned. "Actually, Herr Police President, this is quite comforting."

"Please?"

"Everybody keeps insisting things have changed in Germany. That's a little hard to adjust to. It's pleasant to know that some things remain constant."

"Don't take too much comfort, Herr Bauer," Eckardt said. "In the old days you would not have allowed yourself the privilege of making that remark."

"I suppose not," Bauer said. "If you find out anything I would appreciate your letting me know."

"Before you go, Herr Bauer," Eckardt said. This again was his casual voice which by now had come to put Bauer on guard. "It's just a stray thought, but do you suppose this tragic business here could have any connection with your visit to Axmann?"

"How could it?" Bauer asked, and yet he felt a slight chill. "In what way?"

Eckardt shrugged. "I don't know. The idea just occurred to me."

170

"I would not know, Herr Police President," Bauer said.

Eckardt looked around, at the nearby cottages, at the people still gathered on the other side of the police barrier. "People around here are pretty close-mouthed. They're not apt to offer much information. That's the way they are by nature and of course the older ones have certain memories."

"They told you a foreigner had visited Axmann."

"That's exactly the point. Because they believed you were a foreigner. That makes you an exception to the rule, beyond the pale, so to speak. But there could have been a gang up here last night and nobody would breathe a word."

"That's your specialty," Bauer said.

"Of course. But let me put this to you. If there is the slightest chance that there is some connection between your calling on Axmann and this"—he waved his hand toward the burned down house—"then I might suggest, Herr Bauer, that in your interest you consider terminating this investigation of yours."

Again Bauer smiled. "Is that an order, Herr Police President?"

Eckardt's gray eyes turned full on him. "I have no authority to give such an order, Herr Bauer, and you know that as well as I do. I just do not want any trouble in this city and I will do everything that is in my power to prevent it. This may be a perfectly innocent fire, an accident happening to an old man. It almost certainly is no more than that. But what I am trying to present to you, Herr Peter Bauer, is that if there is one chance in a million that this was deliberate murder and arson there also just might be another chance in another million that it involves you. When I happened to meet Phleps in a restaurant at lunch today and he told me about you, I told him to say nothing to anyone about the questions you raised about the Tiepolo."

"Just like that," Bauer said harshly.

"I'm trying to protect you, you idiot!" Eckardt's voice grated in sudden anger. Then he said, "I beg your pardon."

Bauer nodded. "Do you have anything specific in mind, or anybody?"

Eckardt ignored that and gestured toward the ruined cottage. "This is a messy business. And with a foreigner and a Jew and an emigrated Würzburg Jew whose family was destroyed by the Nazis—it could be filthy. And we have many visitors here at this time of the year and before long we're going to have our annual carnival. As a favor to me, Herr Bauer, please stop going around asking disagreeable questions."

"So I have already been advised."

"There you are!" Eckardt said heartily. "Now, why don't you visit some of the scenes of your childhood, have yourself a look at some of our famous attractions you have undoubtedly forgotten, and then go back to wherever the devil you came from?"

"I will consider it," Bauer said.

The wind had risen and was stirring the leaves in the trees and was blowing around ashes and the smell of the fire was stronger.

"I will appreciate that, Herr Bauer. Werner Hausmann is curious company for you to seek out."

The acrid smoke burned in Bauer's nostrils. "I did not seek him out, Herr Police President," he said slowly and distinctly. He felt suddenly very tired and just a little bit afraid. "Is there anything else about my private life you would like to know?"

"I'm not in the least interested in your private life," Eckardt said.

He turned abruptly and went back to the cottage and Bauer walked slowly down the path. The new police officer on duty looked at him with open hostility and he looked closely as though to make certain he would recognize him again.

Soon, riding down in the car, the sour, biting smell was gone and the smell of the grapes was there again and below the Main moved slowly in the sunlight and the city itself on the far side looked like a colored photograph of itself. There were hikers in the hills with rucksacks on their backs

172

and a blonde girl in some kind of peasant dress sat on a stile and waved as he passed.

He sat back in the cab. It had to be an accident. It was incredible to think otherwise.

That sudden flare of naked anger. That side of the police president. Well, Bauer could not fault him for that. He was a good policeman and it was the tourist season. But how had he known about Hausmann? Who was the one being watched, Hausmann or him?

18

✠ ✠ ✠

IT WAS A LITTLE MORE THAN HALF A MILE FROM WHERE CAP-
tain Roy Atkins lived to the building where he worked and
every once in a while he walked. It was healthful to exercise
and he had very little of that these days. He was running just
a little bit to fat, well, not exactly fat, but to beef. He was
about twenty-five pounds heavier than when he played football in Texas and that extra meat worried him.

He considered walking on this warm Saturday morning but
he realized that in this weather he'd be sweating by the time
he got there and he had just taken a shower and had put on
some German cologne and had sprayed on deodorant and
there was no sense wasting any of that.

He didn't need the walk. Just thinking of her gave him the
sweats. After all this time she turned him on the way she had
from the beginning. He wondered if she'd show today. She
always used to, no questions asked, her pants as hot as his
were, hotter if Peggy had been at him the night before, but
she'd stood him up a time or two lately. Good excuses, but he
could remember when there never were any excuses.

He got into the Pontiac station wagon and put the key into

the switch and then he remembered Peggy would need the car that morning to go to the commissary.

God damn! If he could only get that gold leaf he could afford a second car, at least a motor scooter.

He got out of the car and started walking. Slowly, taking it easy, still feeling the sweat start to collect in the small of his back.

He wondered whether she'd show. She wasn't supposed to be there Saturdays but in the beginning he used to ask her if she'd mind, there was paper work to clear up, but she knew exactly what he meant. She knew but she liked him to ask her that way, as though there really were some work to be done and what they did on the couch just happened to happen, unexpected, unplanned. After a while there never was any question why she came there but he would still always ask her if she'd mind, there was paper work to be cleared up.

Hell, he didn't know what she was getting so damned ornery about. She should know better. She should know that a married man with three kids, a career man in the army, a lifer, didn't just dump his wife. Even though there had been only two kids when they started. Why had that bugged her so much when Peggo got pregnant?

He wondered just how much Peggy knew. She knew, of course. Everybody knew, he supposed. The base was that small and it was hard for anybody to keep secrets. But he wondered how much, just how much, Peggo knew.

Well, it didn't matter. He did his own homework and it wasn't his fault if Peggy didn't turn him on any more. He wondered whether any wife turned on any man after ten years and three kids.

He reached the building where he worked and he looked into the parking lot and he did not see Marliese's little German car. Maybe she wasn't going to show up. Of course she was going to show. Just a little late, that's all, maybe some trouble with the car. But maybe the kraut wasn't going to show up and he felt lousy at that thought and then he got mad.

He went into the building and unlocked the door to his office and sat down at the desk. Maybe it was good she was going to be a little late. Give him some time to cool off after the walk.

He looked at his watch. It was well after ten. Maybe she was going to give him another standup.

He sat there making himself think about other things and he looked at his watch again and it was almost ten thirty and he thought if she wasn't there pretty soon it was going to fuck up his meeting Peggo at the club for lunch, and he thought that if that happened Peggo would just have to wait, she'd be with somebody she knew and she could have a blast or two and he'd have an excuse and she'd buy it, and he heard footsteps coming down the hall and he hadn't realized how relieved he was going to be, how relieved he was, how much afraid he had been that she wouldn't show.

She entered the office. She was wearing a pants suit and her hair was falling on her shoulders, the way he liked it, because sometimes when she got on top of him it fell on his face and it made it even better, more exciting. He sat in the chair for a moment, not jumping instantly to his feet. That was to show her that he was a man, that he was an officer, that he was her boss, and that she was a kraut. That made up a little bit for her being so God damned late.

Then he got up. "Hello, Marly," he said.

"Good morning, Roy," she said.

She looked smart, he thought, despite that coolness in her voice. He'd take care of that. She'd be singing another tune before long. She looked smart but he preferred her in a dress. She had great legs and small ankles, not like most of the kraut women with their piano legs.

"What is it that you want me to do today?" she asked.

She always asked that, but it seemed to him she was asking it for real this time, only that couldn't be, he was just pissed off because she had kept him waiting and he was reading all the wrong things into what she said.

He walked over to her and helped her take off the jacket of the pants suit and he held his arms around her, around the

176

white silk shirt with its built-in silk tie, and he wondered how a woman could do that to him for so long, there had been a lot of popsies in his life, but nothing like this.

"You know what I want you to do today," he said.

Sometimes he invented some work or other, something that took only a little while, to save her face, or perhaps to save his own, but the way things had been with them lately he wanted to nail this down, and besides there wasn't all that time, Peggo was going to be waiting on him.

She slipped out from under his arms in some way he didn't expect or understand except that now he wasn't holding her and she had moved half across the room.

"Just that?"

He began to get mad again. "Just that."

"And you're that certain?"

"Marly, we didn't just meet yesterday."

"No," she said. Then she asked, "Do you remember when it was we met?"

"Of course I do. Like it really was yesterday."

"When was it?"

"The New Year's party at the club. You came with some kraut, a lawyer, or something. What the hell are you asking me about that for? The New Year's party the year before. You testing me, or something?"

"No. It was just so long ago I'd almost forgotten myself."

"It was in your car, that same night, and it was as cold as a witch's tit and you said you'd never done it in a car before and I could believe that, that runty car like to have broke my back, and we got back in the club and nobody had noticed we were gone, not Peggo, not the kraut lawyer, nobody."

He walked over to her and put his arms around her again. "I'll never forget that night, hon, and none of the other times afterward."

He tightened his arms around her and it was like squeezing a clothing dummy.

"Marly," he said, walking back to his desk. "I was married when I met you. You knew I was married when you fucked with me in the front seat of your car. I'm still married."

He sat down. He felt better behind the desk. It reminded him he was her boss.

She took out a cigarette and lit it and sat down on the couch, crossing her legs.

It struck him that most German girls never crossed their legs. They usually sat with their knees pressed together as though trying to protect it.

"Why are you acting so funny lately," he said, not really as a question.

"I've got a right to act funny," she said calmly. "Even krauts have that right."

"What the hell does that mean?"

"I don't know what that means."

"Then why did you say it? You always say things you don't know about?"

"No more than you do, no more often. Why do you say things you don't know about?"

She stood up and walked to the window and looked out into the summer day. "I'm quite sure, Roy, that every woman who ever was involved with a married man has felt the way I've felt lately, has said what I've said. It's all so damned, what do you call it, corny. It's all so damned corny. But it ought to be something more than this. My God, how awful that sounds! And yet there's no other way to say it. It ought to be more than this."

"More than what?"

"I mean, and I know exactly what I mean this time, I mean that after all this time and the way we've exposed ourselves to each other and I don't mean our bodies, I mean ourselves, the way we are when it goes off right and it usually goes off right, I mean that it ought to add up to something more or at least something different, instead of you just ordering me up here on a Saturday morning to get—what did you call it once?—to get your ashes hauled."

"That what's bothering you?" He laughed loudly. "Hell, probably any girl'd feel sore about a stupid crack like that. I don't remember saying it but if you say I did I must have and

178

I'm sorry, Marly, I'm sorry. That's just an expression we used to use as kids and maybe it just slipped out. I'm real sorry about that."

He stood up and started toward her.

"That's not what's bothering me," she said. "What's bothering me is that it's such a lovely day and there are so many things we could be doing, so many places we could go to."

"You'd like that?" He put his arms around her again, this time cupping her breasts. "You'd like that better than this?"

"No, not better than this."

"There you are," he said, fingering her nipples, it always drove her wild.

"After this," she said. "Roy, could we go somewhere after we make love? Could we go for a drive or a walk or a drink or for lunch or anything?"

"You know I can't, hon," he said, rubbing the nipples harder, once she got started she couldn't have them rubbed too hard, it really blew her mind.

"You have to meet your wife?" she asked.

"What's that got to do with anything, hon," he said soothingly. "We're here now, what's it got to do with anything I got to do afterward?"

She started to pull away but he rubbed her some more and he could feel the nipples getting hard now and he pinched them a little, she could go on giving him this shit but he knew her and he knew her body like a book, Christ, he should, he'd gone through that book a time or two, and he could feel the nipples getting rigid now, her kind of hard on, and he knew he had it made, not that he'd ever doubted it, not from the moment he'd heard her footsteps, but now he had it in his hands and she could rattle on all she liked but she was hooked. He unbuttoned her shirt, unfolding the looped ascot.

"You bastard," she said.

He grinned. He knew what she meant when she said that. She always said it when she was coming after having said she wasn't going to be able to make it any more, that she had come all she could come, that she was empty and finished and dry, and then, if it turned out right, as it did now and again and she knew she was going to come again, that's when she said it, and what it meant was that he was able to do that to her, that he had that power over her. But she had never said it before, before she'd even made it once.

"You fucking bastard," she said.

She put out her cigarette in the ashtray on the desk. She unclasped his belt and opened the top button on his pants and unzipped his fly and slipped her hand inside.

"There you are, baby," he said. "Now why the hell did you want to waste all this time when that was waiting for you?"

She led him to the couch. She sat down facing him and she pulled down first his pants and then his jockey shorts and in a little while Roy Atkins was the happiest person in Würzburg, maybe in all of Germany, maybe in the whole world, and in a very little while after that so was she.

19

✠ ✠ ✠

IT MIGHT HAVE BEEN A RELIGIOUS CEREMONY CONDUCTED BY high priests, perhaps latter-day Mayans. The men were bent over the sacrificial brazier inspecting the glowing charcoal, impervious to the smoke, searching all their arcane knowledge and experience to determine whether this was yet the moment the gods had decreed for the hieratic immolation.

The high priest, Captain Roy Atkins, as befit his exalted rank, was clad in the ritual garments that proclaimed his status: floppy white chef's hat and flowing apron on which was printed a number of phrases which plainly were intended to appear to the innocent to be nothing more than simple humor but which without doubt had a deeper, more subtle meaning to the initiate.

One of the assistant priests said at last, "Not enough ash, Roy."

The first words had been spoken.

Captain Atkins responded sonorously, "That is what I think too."

Bauer noted that in making this corroborative pronouncement Captain Atkins in his present sacerdotal capacity had with congruous solemnity eschewed the contraction.

The light, pleasant smoke from the round grill rose in the summer air, the incense of this imported religion which was winning converts everywhere. Grills and charcoal were on special display in the local stores, Bauer had seen, and German butchers were learning to hack their meat in slightly different ways to make them suitable for consecration.

The present sacrifice, a steak as big as a small suitcase, remained on a wooden platter awaiting its summons to immortality, for the moment ignored, dripping blood as silently and as steadily as had its precursor, the human heart.

The men gathered round the grill did not move. They continued to stare at the somber coals awaiting a sign no demotic creature could ever hope to see. They could have been painted, Bauer thought, by Rembrandt.

He had been to many of these barbecues in the backyards of Virginia and Maryland and they never ceased to fill him with wonder. He had in his work witnessed far-reaching decisions by military men and by officials in the Department in which he now served made with less brain-wracking and soul-searching than it took them to decide upon that precise moment to put a steak over charcoal.

Seated comfortably on a reclining chair in the yard behind the building in which the Atkins lived, made very welcome in the open, free-handed American military way by Atkins and his fellow officers and their wives, a half-consumed martini in his hand, the sun on him but not oppressively so, the day warm and clear and sweet, the remembered hills all around him, Bauer felt himself a stranger in his own land. The aliens belonged there far more than he did.

The men were almost all in crew cut, some cut so short it was impossible to tell the color of their hair. They were in slacks, Levis, sport shirts; the shirts hung outside their pants. Three or four of them wore western boots.

The women were in slacks or shorts. Two or three of them wore wide-brimmed western hats. There were no children.

Bauer wondered about that. What had happened to the

children? Obviously they were not eligible to attend a sacrament of this consequence, but where were they? The army had made provision for that, he was certain.

He looked at the faces around him. There were marks on some of them of too much drinking, of too much eating, of a kind of frustration, of some dissastisfaction, perhaps, perhaps even a measure of bitterness. But in the context of the world, in the context of what he himself had seen and experienced, the faces seemed to him to be untouched. They seemed to him to be just passing through, using up their time, moving with some invisible protection on all sides, living, working, acting, believing, enjoying, suffering, but all within the narrow framework of the limited shelter presented to them as their national inheritance.

He remembered Major Reinhard asking him as he drove him up to the base, "How have you found the Americans, Herr Bauer? Of course we see them as they are here, the military, the tourists, but how are they when they are at home, living in their own surroundings?"

He had thought for a moment. "I don't know. I hate to make generalities." A lie. He was always making generalities about the Germans. "I think perhaps not too much has happened to them."

"You are saying then that you believe they are shallow?"

"No, Major, I'm not saying that. Shallowness implies to me an unrealized potential, a fraction of the possible, superficiality when there is an area for something more. I don't think that quite applies. One has to judge—and God knows, who has the right to judge?—within a frame of reference. By their standards, based on their national experience, they lead quite full and satisfying lives, or they think they do, which is possibly the same thing. It isn't their fault that they look upon the business of living with eyes that are different, say, than the eyes of a refugee German Jew whose family was put to death in a manner that would have been considered barbaric a thousand years ago. And in what was believed, especially by the Germans themselves, to be the most civilized country in the world."

183

"Are you happy living among them?" Reinhard had asked.

"I think so," Bauer had replied. "Happier than I should be here."

"Yes," Reinhard had said. "And isn't that a disgrace?"

A little later on, Bauer had said, "I once heard a high-ranking military officer in Washington say that perhaps there should have been some bombing in the United States during World War II, that Americans should have been hurt in some way, so that the war wasn't something thousands of miles away. And I remembered as he said that how Germany itself had not been hurt very much during the First World War, how all the fighting had taken place on foreign soil, so that after that war, even though Germany was defeated, very few Germans, apart from the soldiers themselves, had ever really experienced what war was like, had ever really tasted the true measure of war. That perhaps is why their reservations were limited when Hitler led them to his war."

"Are you suggesting, Herr Bauer, that having managed to come through the Second World War unscathed the Americans might become the new Germans of this world? Is that what Vietnam is all about?"

"I wouldn't know, Major. That's not for me to say. The Americans have given me their citizenship but I still feel I am a guest in their country. But there is one thing that works against that theory."

"What is that?"

"The majority of Americans, I believe, are inherently decent."

They were passing through the gate at the base and the MP gave them directions to reach Atkins' quarters.

"You are suggesting of course that we Germans are not," Reinhard had said.

"But then, Major, I'm prejudiced."

Now, watching them, listening to the casual chatter and kidding all around him, Americans never seemed happier than when they were ribbing someone, Bauer felt he could say for certain that they were not, in his mind at least, in any way the new Germans, Vietnam and anything else to the contrary. But they were, he thought, the new Americans, and that was not yet a completely definable breed.

He looked at Atkins' wife, Peggy, and saw that at that moment she was gazing at Marliese. He had been a little surprised to find Marliese there, after what she had told him, and he had thought at first that the Atkinses had one of those American marriages and that the wife didn't care. He did not believe that for very long. He believed now that Peggy Atkins cared very much and he saw she was trying to treat Marliese the same as any of the other guests and that she was doing a very good job of that, almost good enough.

He rather like Peggy Atkins and had liked the way she had greeted him and bade him welcome. He felt sorry for her but that again was not his affair.

"What do you think?" Captain Atkins asked, again peering into the bed of coals.

The acolytes inspected.

"About ready," Major Johnson said.

"I agree," one of the other men said.

"Peggo," Atkins said.

"Yes, Roy?"

"I'm going to put on the steak," Atkins said.

Peggy Atkins nodded.

Bauer knew that she understood from that earnest fiat that she now was on notice to have everything else ready at that moment when the steak was ready, the salad, hot rolls, whatever.

Atkins lifted high the platter on which rested the steak. It was unnecessary for him to hold it before each member of the congregation to look at, smell, perhaps even to touch. Most of them had already done that.

He gripped the steak between enormous tongs and laid it gently on the grill. There was an instantaneous sizzling. Atkins smiled. Everyone relaxed. The omen was favorable.

Bauer was watching Marliese to try to divine how this American tribal custom struck her. She was taking it calmly, he saw; she'd been on the base for a long time. He happened then to catch sight of Atkins; Atkins too was looking at

Marliese and Bauer was astonished to read on his face the pride and the possessiveness. What he was saying in his silence was that he had hunted down this dangerous animal just for her, that he had killed it with his two hands and he now was providing his woman with food.

Bauer saw Atkins look at his watch. That was a signal for the other men grouped around the fire with him to inspect their watches. It was an essential part of the liturgy, Bauer knew. There was a mathematical formula that had to do with the thickness of the steak, the heat from the coals, the distance of the grill from the coals, and other variables, including climate, temperature, and altitude.

Bauer sipped some of his fresh drink. Martinis were fragile things, he realized as he had realized before, and must be taken at the flood.

He sensed a stillness again. He looked up. Captain Atkins, using the tongs, lifted the steak and turned it over. He was immediately handed a fresh drink by his wife. Bauer saw Marliese was alone and he joined her.

"Do you wonder why I'm here?" she asked.

"I haven't got round to you yet," Bauer said. "I'm still wondering why I'm here."

"Roy said that Peggy asked him to ask me because she thought I would make you feel more at home."

"I'm very glad you're here," Bauer said.

"I dislike polite words."

"How can I convince you impolitely?"

"Why is that?"

He shrugged and finished his drink. "You do make me feel more at home."

"Thank you, Peter."

"What I don't know is, if that's good."

She started to say something but said something else. "It's the moment. Hold your breath."

Atkins was just finishing looking at his watch. He picked up the steak with the tongs and deposited it on the wooden carving board. He picked up a large knife and honed it, wield-

186

ing the blade with expertise. He brought the edge to concert pitch and then surveyed the smoking meat now with the eye of a surgeon. He came to a decision at last. He held the steak down with a large two-tined fork and made an incision. The men bent down and looked. They raised their heads and nodded as one.

Captain Atkins sliced rapidly, professionally. Peggy, aided by a couple of the other wives, added mounds of German potato salad, cole slaw, and hot rolls.

Bauer, when he and Marliese were served, cut into his portion and took a bite. It was, he was in no way surprised to discover, the greatest steak he had ever eaten.

"How is it, Pete?" Atkins sang over.

The captain, Bauer comprehended, was again communicating with Marliese.

"Marvelous," he said truthfully.

"Great steak, Pete," Atkins said. "We get the greatest steak in the commissary here."

"And you've cooked it to perfection," Bauer said, without the slightest exaggeration.

Atkins grinned with becoming modesty. "Well, yeah, that's got something to do with it, I guess, but you got to have the meat to start with and there's nothing like that good old American beef."

"I agree," Bauer said, feeling like some type of new electronic equipment through which sound signals could be passed. He suspected if he stopped chewing he would feel vibrations. He looked up to see Peggy Atkins.

"Would you like something to drink, Marliese?" Peggy asked.

"Thank you, Peggy."

"Beer or wine, I forget which you take."

"Wine please."

"Mr. Bauer?"

"I'll have wine too, Mrs. Atkins."

Peggy kept her eyes on Marliese as she addressed Bauer and he thought he saw in her face the strength of her own pioneer ancestors; that was what the faces of those early American women must have owned. And they too must have seen the ghosts in the night.

Peggy went away and Bauer turned back to Marliese. She was gazing past him now, looking directly at Atkins. And there was something very unpleasant in her and in the set of her mouth. She looked cold and hard and old in a way that had nothing to do with her years or what she had endured, and she looked somehow very German. Her face was the young face of those old faces of the women in the *Gasthaus*, and amid these nattering, martini-drinking American women who sounded like noisy birds, growing louder and hoarser with each drink, she seemed at that moment to have been thrust out onto another plane, as though in a collage, from another time and another place, an anachronism of Teutonic *diablerie*, her expression congealing bale that was a thousand years old.

He was repelled by what he saw and was held by it.

He looked to Atkins, to see whether the casting of this ancient evil German spell was having its intended effect on him, whether he was shriveling under the force of the malevolence, and what he saw now interested him even more. For Atkins was at that moment vulnerable and he was wearing his weakness as a sign and this defenselessness was his protection, the only protection that could have served him, shielding him as might a cross. He had passed, Bauer saw with wonderment, through a sea change, a purification helped perhaps by alcohol, and was not at this moment in his life a clumsy, insentient lout flaunting a mistress before wife and friends, but instead a man helpless and yielded in his feeling, open wide before anyone who bothered to see.

Then Atkins recovered, and so quickly Bauer looked back at Marliese, and her own face now was freed of its fiends and was ordinary and he blinked his eyes and wondered whether he had seen what he had seen or whether, a victim of his own private demons, he had imagined all of it.

Peggy Atkins returned with two glasses of wine.

188

"This steak is delicious," Bauer said, because he had nothing else to say, knowing that nothing he or anybody could say would alter the expression on her own face. He had not imagined. She too had seen her husband a few moments earlier.

"Yes," Peggy said. "It always is." She clasped her hands and turned to her husband. "What are you holding up for, Roy? You have other guests and the rolls mustn't get cold." She started to giggle. "Don't you think that's funny, Roy, I mean about letting the rolls get cold?"

Atkins hastily applied himself to slicing the rest of the steak, a man released, and the knife glinted in the sun. Peggy remained standing in front of Marliese and Bauer, her hands still clasped.

"You see the point of the joke, don't you, Mr. Bauer?" she asked in a very pleasant voice. "You see, my husband, Roy, is always telling me to be sure to have the rolls ready so the steak won't get cold. So I just turned it around and told him to hurry up with the steak so the rolls wouldn't get cold. Don't you think that's funny, Mr. Bauer?"

"Yes," Bauer said, smiling, trying hard to swallow a very tender piece of meat. "I do."

"It was stupid of me to come here," Marliese said, after Peggy left them.

She had not, he saw, touched her own food. He said nothing.

"Peggy Atkins always gets peculiar after she's had a few drinks," she said.

"You'd better eat something first," Bauer said.

"First?"

"Before you leave."

"Am I leaving?"

"Aren't you?"

She nodded. "I hope Roy doesn't get funny. He's had a lot to drink."

"He'll get funny all right if you leave all that steak," Bauer said. "That would really be hitting below the belt."

"I can't eat any of it."

"Believe me, Liesl," he said, "he'll accept any rejection but that."

"I couldn't. I think I'd choke."

"You try, and then I'll leave with you."

Right after he said that he wondered why he had thought that might be any kind of inducement but he saw that she looked at him with a sudden, almost overwhelming gratefulness, the eyes of a very little girl presented with an unexpected gift.

He tried to remember the face he had seen earlier but he could not.

20

✠ ✠ ✠

BAUER DROVE SLOWLY DOWN THE HILL TOWARD THE CITY. SHE had handed him the keys when they left and had got into the passenger side without a word and had said nothing afterward.

It was still early afternoon. There was the feeling of Sunday. The domes and spires made their familiar profile. He glanced at her. She was curled up in the seat, staring out the window.

Bauer turned his eyes ahead. He could still see Atkins' face when he said he had another appointment and had to leave and Marliese saying she would take him back to the city because she was going that way, she had to visit her father who was not well. Atkins had nodded, in control but still assailable, Peggy's eyes on him assessing his disappointment, and Bauer had felt the sadness at the eternal snare, and he was relieved, as he always was at times like these, that he was incapable of such involvement, that it had all been burned out, cauterized, long before.

"I don't suppose you're free for a few hours," she said.

She was not looking at him and he had his chance to lie. "I'm free."

"Would you like to take a little drive into the country?"

"Yes."

"You're sure?"

"I'm sure."

"You're not doing it just because of the hell I went through back there?"

"Did you go through hell?"

She lit a cigarette and opened the window and shook her head to loosen her hair.

She had lapsed into German in almost tired relief and he had followed, and he thought again that when she shifted languages there was a change in her, a refocusing. She became somehow younger and gentler and that surprised him because he had never considered German a gentle language.

They passed the side of the Residenz and soon were riding through the grounds of the university.

He looked at the buildings in the sprawled-out complex. Some were as he had remembered them; others, rebuilt after the bombing, were of another style entirely.

He looked at the students strolling along the tree-lined streets.

"When I was a child, more than anything else I wanted to go here," he said. "And do you know why? Not because the university is so famous and so good, not because Roentgen discovered the X-ray here, nothing as sensible as that. No, Liesl, I wanted to go here because there used to be six Jewish fraternities here and three of them were dueling societies."

She looked at him in astonishment. "Really?"

He chuckled. "It surprises you that Jews could duel?"

"I suppose that's not being very kind. I'm quite ignorant about some things, Peter. You know that."

"Not at all. Just improperly educated. The only bloodthirsty Jews you ever heard about were the Jews who were supposed to drink the blood of good Christian German babies."

192

"I'd heard of that," she said. "I never believed it."

"Then you must help convince the others," he said gravely. "In any case there were these bloodthirsty young men. Dueling was against the law, but the Jews violated the law with the same indifference shown by the German fraternities. And the Jews wore small caps and ribbons across their chests, just like their German counterparts. The dueling took place in the basement of the fraternity houses, except for the duels of honor, which were always conducted somewhere in the forest." He glanced at her; she was staring at him. "Yes, Liesl, Jewish honor, defended with a Jewish sword. It's a fascinating concept, isn't it."

"Yes," she said. "I suppose it must be."

"And that's what I wanted most, to come here, to join a dueling society, and to manage to get a scar on my cheek. I thought it would be so marvelous, to go through life with a dueling scar on my cheek." He was silent as they drove out of the university grounds. "Your brother is quite right, Liesl," he said. "Given half the chance, the Jews would always be more German than the Germans."

Presently they were outside the city and she told him what direction to take. The hills rose on both sides of the road and at the feet of the hills there was already the evening's lavender mist. In the distance he could see several small towns, each with its spire piercing the sky, sharp, everlasting points to prick God into remembering their presence, each of the towns sprinkled with haze as though dusted with bluish talcum.

The road began to climb and then they were on a flat elevation and they passed a wine garden and he looked at her and she nodded and he pulled in. He found a table almost at the edge of the terrace and she excused herself. He sat down and saw that the river was below them again and that here it almost doubled on itself, coiled and lit darkly in the shades of the valley.

When the waitress appeared he ordered a bottle of wine and he looked again at the valley. There were not many persons on the terrace and those who were there were in accord with the day, even the children, and when they spoke it was in low tones. It was quiet and it was still a feeling of Sunday.

He rose as Marliese returned. "What a lovely place."

"Yes, isn't it?"

"Have you been here often?"

"Not lately," she said, sitting down.

He lit her cigarette. "I've ordered wine."

"It's very good here."

"The greatest in the world?"

She smiled. "No, just very good. It comes from that little vineyard over there. I feel filled with peace, Peter. Thank you for leaving the base with me. Thank you for bringing me here." She drew on her cigarette and breathed out the smoke. "Do you wonder why I went there?"

"No," he said.

"I can't not do anything he asks. Not for very long."

The waitress brought the wine in the *Bocksbeutel* and so sure was she of what she was serving she simply poured the wine equally into both glasses without going through the ceremony of pouring a little for him to taste first. They sipped the delicate distillation which traveled so badly and which was filled with its own charms when it was drunk here close to where it was born.

Below them, on different sides of the Main, Bauer could make out three different towns, all of them medieval in appearance, all of them walled, all of them in the same kind of red stone or brick, all dominated by their church spires. The low-lying haze gave them the illusion of floating.

"It could be an illustration out of Grimm's," he said.

She nodded. "It's very pretty." She lit a fresh cigarette from the stub of the old. "It's like a sickness. He has to parade me in front of his wife and all his friends."

He said nothing. He wanted no part of this but he knew it would not go away.

"And I'm as sick as he is because I allow him to do it," she said. "And everybody is so damned sorry for Peggy. Poor Peggy. They've made one word of it by now. Poorpeggy. Everybody says that Roy gives her such a damned bad time and right now I'm to blame. I'm not the only one, you know. I think I'm the only one at the moment but I'm not sure of that either."

He drank his wine and watched the darkness rise in the valley and he looked at the red-colored towns that might have been put together from things out of a child's toy box and he wished he were alone and was not being encroached upon. He'd walked away from all this long ago.

"Did you hear her little joke?" Marliese asked. "Everybody heard her. Everybody thinking, Poor Peggy and that damned kraut swine. Why don't you ask me some questions? Are you that uninterested?"

He felt himself again being drawn in, against all his instincts, against all his desires. "Do you love him that much?" he asked, not wanting to know, not wanting to be part of it in any way, hoping something would happen to distract, something huge and gothic, a thunderclap by Thor. But nothing like that ever happened when it should and Thor held his peace and the night remained quiet.

"I did not at first," she said. "I did not at all. I just wanted to get him into bed. It seemed a hell of a long time since Heinrich was killed and at that time there hadn't been anybody else. I'd got bored with playing with myself, I guess. The law of diminishing returns became operable with me quite early on. And then Roy came along and I guess it was exactly the right moment. I thought he'd be marvelous in bed and I set about to find out." She waited a moment and then asked, "Aren't you going to ask me whether I was disappointed or not?"

"You'll tell me," he said.

"Well, damn it, he was. Is. Absolutely marvelous. He healed everything. No, he didn't heal anything at all, but he just made it stop hurting so much, about Heinrich. Or if it didn't really stop hurting I didn't feel it so much. I had something else to feel good about and get hurt about."

"Hurt?" He looked at her profile. It was comely and he felt himself bit by bit being drawn in.

"The nights I knew Roy was with his wife, thinking of

195

him making love with her, producing another child with her. That hurt and that wasn't bad. What do doctors call it, counterirritant? I was able to walk down a new street with new aches." She finished her wine and held out the glass and he refilled it. "Then, inevitably, I came to hate him."

"That's a strong word," he said, thinking then that perhaps with Germans, especially Franconian Germans, it might not be too strong a word, that there was something barbaric here in all this calm and stillness and beauty and that if the venom did not lie closest to the surface of all of them it was carried in the deepest part.

He remembered the incredible expression on her face when she looked at Atkins at that moment of the cookout. No, hate was not too strong a word at all.

"I know," she said. "But it's the word. I've come to hate everything about him, including the gallant Peggy, including the three brats. The way he looks, the way he cuts his hair, the little habits of speech, the way he sweats half the time."

"Except the way he makes love," Bauer heard himself saying and it was at that moment that he knew that he too was going to make love to her and at that same moment he knew she had known that before he had.

She nodded slowly. "And that, God help me, is better than ever. I must really be sick. I hate him and he puts his hand on me and I go into jelly."

What was it, he thought, was it being German?

"Is that being German?" she asked.

He looked at her. She was beautiful at that moment, more so than at any time since he had met her. Was he being German too to think that just then? Or Jewish? Or was it just his new unaccountable prescience that soon he would share a bed with her?

"I've tried to reason it out," she said. "It sounds crazy but can it have anything to do with the fact that I'm German and he's the conqueror?"

She took out another cigarette. He flicked the Zippo. Her eyes were troubled and frightened.

"It sounds absolutely mad," she said. "Cheap, bite-size psychiatry. But it's all so impossible and it's there."

He didn't want to hear any more about Roy Atkins and her; he had not wanted to before but now it was for different reasons and that irritated him more than anything else. He was glad that he was not going to remain in Würzburg very long.

"You're just a healthy woman trying to beat those diminishing returns," he said, saying it to make a joke, hoping she would smile and agree and then drop the business.

"I am that," she said. "I am that way. I'm very much that way. But that isn't it, or at least not all of it. Since I've known Roy there have been other men and it was always good but never that good."

"Were they also American conquerors?"

She laughed. It was clear and unanticipated and it was filled with the wine and the air and the sun and the hills and the river below and several persons at other tables turned and glanced at her, ready to be annoyed, as good Germans, and instead smiled in response.

"No, Peter," she said, still laughing, putting her hand on his. "They were also-rans, like me, like all the rest of us here, losers. Well, you've been patient beyond all call of duty and that's enough of that nonsense. I'm sorry I had to dump all that garbage onto you but there you are."

"Archaeologists consider garbage one of their most valuable sources of information into man's past."

"Well, then, perhaps that applies to my past—past, present, and, I'm afraid, the future as well. But the devil with that now. How do you like this wine?"

"You asked me that."

"I'm changing the subject. It may take a moment or two to manage but I'm changing the subject. From Captain Roy Atkins, U.S.A., all-American stud, to this marvelous bottle, the ram's ball. I love that. I wonder who called it that first."

He picked up the bottle. "You know, Liesl, you see this bottle everywhere in the States. But not from Germany. The people in Chile grow something they call Chilean Rhine

197

wine and they put it in little bottles shaped exactly like this and that's what you see everywhere. The funny thing is that when most Americans see this over here they think you're copying the Chileans."

"But that's monstrous," she said. "The little ram's ball belongs to us. We should sue or at least declare war. I must tell you again, Peter, you were very kind to indulge me today. I would have driven out here alone if you hadn't. I would have gone alone and if I were lucky I would have found some American, some tourist, someone in the army, and I'd pick him up."

"Why an American?"

"One doesn't find Germans alone on Sunday looking for a girl, not out here in the country. They're all with their wives and children. Look around you. Would you like to know what I would do with him?"

"No."

She giggled. She was just a little pootled, as the British would say.

"Where shall we go now?"

"I'm easy," he said in English.

"You sound so damned British," she said. "How can a German from America sound so damned British?"

This time she got behind the wheel and she drove back to the main road and then she took another road and after a while they entered a small walled town. She parked the car and they started to walk again, past the old tower with its slitted pitch window and then they were on cobblestones along an old wall and they came at last to a clearing overlooking a black pool.

"This is something special," she said. "Do you mind my being a girl guide? They used to burn witches here. They'd set up a stake right here and when the witch was good and flaming they'd dump her into that pool down there and if she survived the people took that as God's judgment that she wasn't a witch after all."

198

"That was quite a burden to lay on God."

"Well, that's all for today," she said brightly. "And the reason I brought you to this town was not just to show you this fascinating place but because there is a really splendid country inn here and if all that marvelous American steak hasn't turned you off food for the next week we could have a bite to eat. How does that sound?"

"Very good." And now he understood how it was happening, was going to happen, and he wanted it very much and he didn't want it at all.

She slipped her arm under his. "Wouldn't it be fun if you thought I was a witch."

"I suspect you are," he said.

"Then you could burn me and throw me into the water and see whether or not God agrees with you."

"Nobody believes in witches any more," he said. "Not even God."

"I don't know." She walked up to the edge of the clearing and looked down into the pool. "They found a charred body in that pool a few months ago. It was charred so badly they never were able to find out who it was. Somebody had thought it was a witch. And it seems God agreed."

21

✠ ✠ ✠

THE INN WAS A FORMER MONASTERY. IT WAS DARK AND WOODY inside. There were several small rooms. There were hunting prints on the walls, good ones. The proprietor greeted Marliese warmly. He was introduced to Bauer as Herr Geyer. He was pleasantly stout and he was dressed in flannel slacks, corduroy jacket, and open-necked shirt.

Herr Geyer seated them at a small corner table and a few moments later a waitress put a bottle of wine and a wurst plate in front of them and then brought over a thick loaf of bread.

Bauer looked around. "It's very attractive. It's amazing how uncrowded it is. In the middle of the tourist season."

"You'll find no tourists here."

"How does he keep going?"

"This little town is the center of a wine industry."

"Every little town around here is the center of a wine industry."

"This one especially. The monks used to press wine in the cellar here. The wine buyers make this their headquarters. Herr Geyer much prefers them to tourists. He says the tourists may have more money but that they always insist on beer instead of wine."

"You seem to know him quite well."

"I do," she said.

He picked up a piece of wurst and put it on some bread and offered it to her.

"Don't be so damned careful," she said.

"It isn't any of my business."

"Don't be so damned careful," she said again, leaning toward him, ignoring the food. "Don't think being curious, normal, human, curious, is the same as being involved. We are not involved and you can ask me anything you like and if I feel like answering I will." She took the bread and meat. "People talk to each other, Peter. It's no sin. And in answer to what you were thinking, no, I have never been here with Roy. And yes, I have been here with other men."

"I wasn't thinking that," he said.

"And why were you not? Aren't you even a little bit inquisitive about my personal life? Just as a woman you've been spending a few hours with? You can't be that disinterested, Peter. You wouldn't be here."

He shifted uncomfortably.

She pointed to the plate and switched to English. "Have some of that wurst. It's the greatest in the world. No disrespect to your American food but when you want wurst there's nothing like good old German wurst. Right?"

He laughed at how accurately she mimicked Atkins' accent. He ate some of the wurst and drank a little wine. "I was surprised at him today."

"That he threw me at his wife?"

"That, at first. Not later."

"I thought we weren't going to talk about him any more. What surprised you later?"

"You think you're trapped, Liesl? He's trapped worse than you are."

She lit a cigarette and raised her face in what he had come to recognize as a gesture of hers, a thrusting of the chin, but a very small, almost unnoticeable thrusting. "It's just so awful," she said. "Two people disgusted with each other and neither one knowing quite how to let go."

"I don't think Captain Atkins wants to let go at all."

Her mouth tightened and he remembered that other expression on her face.

"No, of course not," she said. "Not the way he has it set up, his adoring wife and his three towheaded kids and his cushy berth here in Germany and soon he'll be a major, which seems to be something very important to him, he can buy a scooter then or something, and he's having the best of both worlds, the marvelous way the army watches over all of them like an old nanny and the romantic German economy as well, and all of that with a good-looking German mistress with a very developed libido. My God, Pete, you ain't hardly likely to find that anywhere nohow."

She peered at him and her face suddenly was very tired. "But that's just it, Peter. Down deep he wants to let go because down deep Roy Atkins is a very moral Southern Baptist man, and down deep he knows what he is doing is sinful, and all the other little tarts, well, he dropped them, didn't he, and he felt very good about that, righteous, until the next one, and then he dropped her too and he had all that good Baptist virtue all over again, but this little tart has been sharing a couch with him for almost two years now and he's getting laid now better than when we started, which means better than he ever has in his life and he wants to hold on and he wants to let go." She jabbed her cigarette into an ashtray. "Jesus Christ, Peter, the whole damned world stinks with guilt!"

After a while she picked up a knife and dug it into a cheese pot and spread the cheese thickly over a piece of bread. "Here, try this, specialty of the house."

"It is very good," he said.

She held the knife in her hand and her eyes went away and looked at something that was not there and he remembered again what had come upon her as she gazed at Atkins earlier that day, what there was inside her always, lying muddied in the blood, cold, coiled, always waiting, always ready, and he wondered at his being there, how it had transpired that he was here with her in this unlikely place where once monks had trodden grapes and in the wrung-out juice had found divinities.

He wondered why he was there and what it was that held him there against everything and how he did not want to be there and why he could not have left. And he found himself slipping, one layer under the other, into a weird suffusion of surrealism, trapped by her and her voice and where they were and what was outside in the night.

"And I will not make it easy for him," she said, an incarnation—Stheno? Euryale? Medusa?—and opposed to all truth dazzlingly beautiful. "He would like me to make the stand now, to let him off the hook, part of him would anyway, but I will not make it that easy for him because I loathe him. And he can have me any time he wants, any way he wants, that is my tot."

Herr Geyer, puffing contentedly on a cigar, wandered over, a plump piece of smiling salvation in his converted demesne, and coming back from a long way away, Bauer blessed him.

"Is everything in order, my friends?" Herr Geyer asked, giving forth in every way every solid boniface virtue.

Bauer nodded.

"I see that you are eating the spread," Herr Geyer said, emitting a cloud of smoke that miraculously cleared the air.

"It's marvelous," Bauer said.

"Just don't ask me for the ingredients. People are always trying to find that out."

"Something passed from generation to generation," Bauer said. "Well, I can understand that."

"Not at all." Herr Geyer chuckled. "It is just something put together quite recently by my wife. By accident. We happened to have some things left over in the kitchen—different cheeses, other things—and she's a very thrifty German wife and she just couldn't see them go to waste. She just mixed them all up." He shook his head. "It was so successful from the start, and then when we ran out we had the devil's own time trying to remember what went into it. It took us weeks to get it exactly the same way again."

Laughing quietly, leaving behind a smoke screen, Herr Geyer strolled away to greet some newcomers who had just entered.

"That's very funny," Bauer said.

"I don't think it's true. I think it actually has been in his family for all those generations. But he prefers to tell it this way."

"Inverted snobbery?"

"You can call it that. Yes, I suppose that's exactly what it is."

"I hope this place never gets spoiled. It's a lovely kind of Germany."

"The rooms are lovely too," she said. "Would you like to see one?"

There was a new timbre in her voice, the slightest richening, so slight almost to pass without detection.

"Yes," he said. "I would, very much."

The room, up a flight of stairs and down a corridor lined with caricatures of monks well jollied by their handiwork, or was it footwork, was large and furnished in country style with an offhanded luxury.

"You're not surprised," she said.

"No, Liesl."

"But you don't object?"

"No."

"Well, that's something. Are you going to kiss me? We must start somewhere."

"Do you mind leaving on a small light?" she asked. "I like to see too."

She was a golden girl, he saw, and she was magnificent, and she started to laugh.

"What's funny?" he asked.

204

"I'm not laughing at you, Peter. Oh, I suppose I am. It's just that I've never been with a circumcised man before."

"I guess it would be a rare configuration around here."

"Let me see him. It's not funny, really, not once you get used to it, not funny at all. He's rather adorable. He looks quite jaunty with that little hat. It does look like a hat, like a fireman's hat."

"It has been so described before, in familiarity."

"In what other way? Really, he's not funny at all and he is adorable. He seems so very proud. Is it true that that desensitizes him so that he lasts longer or is that just an old wives' tale? Those old wives! Always gossiping about everything."

"I wouldn't know. I have no basis of comparison."

"I might," she said. "I just might. Just a little. Let us see, Peter. Let us see now. Those old wives. Oh, that's delicious, Peter, that's delicious, that's really delicious, oh, treasure, treasure, he is a love, he's just a love, working so hard under that cute hat, oh, treasure, he's just that, treasure, just, just delicious."

She lay there afterward, her long body a little damp, the furies for the moment subsided, her breasts rising and falling just a little faster still, and he felt completed and whole and full of himself and tender and very close to her.

He turned out the light. She had seen all she wanted to see. A new light fell into the room from the German night outside the window.

He leaned over and kissed her.

"She's so silly," she said sleepily.

"Who?"

"Old pushface, whatever her name is, your silly wife."

"Lucille?"

"Preferring that silly game. What was it? Scotch?"

"Gin."

"Gin. So silly, so very silly."

He filled his lungs with the invisible German things that filled the room. Along the long way he had come finally to understand why they were there and why she had arranged for them to do what had been done and what she had tried with her might and her main to rid herself of, knowing beforehand she could not, not rid, but perhaps diminish a little, just a little, if only for a little time.

He felt very good. Had he exorcised some ghosts of his own and were they his own and had he exorcised them?

He thought, smiling wryly to himself, that the Nazis would have screamed that that just proved them right, they always maintained it was the perverted sex dream of every male German Jew to make love to a blonde Aryan goddess.

She snored gently.

22

✠ ✠ ✠

IN HIS HOTEL ROOM THE NEXT MORNING HE SHOWERED AND
shaved and dressed and sat down and recomposed himself.
Well, there was very little to keep him in Würzburg now.
The details? Who exactly had arranged for his mother's
arrest? Who would remember that now and who, remembering, would tell him? And what purpose would it serve?
Only to make him hate more, as Father Stolz had promised,
and he did not want to hate, not anywhere, not even here.

Had Marliese done that for him?

They had slept through the night as healthy animals, spent
by the day in the open and the walking and the wine and
from the demands they had made on each other. They had
been wakened—she had not forgotten anything, she must be
a superb secretary—quite early, she had to go home and
change and get to the office, and they had returned in the
lightening morning to the city. She drove and smoked.

They rode with each other as acquaintances, chatting spo-
radically and aimlessly, he might have been a hitchhiker she
had given a lift, and she had dropped him off cheerily at his
hotel, a cigarette in her mouth, looking at her watch. They

had said good-by. Not, so long; not, see you again; not, when will I see you. Just good-by, casual, unweighted, a finality.

For there was nothing more for them to do for each other or with each other and there would be no reprise. They had the luck to pass by each other when it happened to suit their books and they had served each other and then went on. It had had a clinical genesis and now was sealed with surgeon's suture. He knew he could never see her again if he wanted to, which he did not, could not send flowers, a note, anything, because in the double frame of reference of time and need the two persons who had spent the night with each other no longer existed.

There was still a thing or two he wanted to do before he left Würzburg. He looked at his little engagement pad. He saw he was to have dinner that evening with Remers, to meet his wife and family. He telephoned Major Reinhard and told him he did not believe he would need him that day. He consulted a timetable; he saw there was a late afternoon train that would get him to Frankfurt in time to catch a sleeper to Paris where he planned to spend a few days. He thought he probably would make that train the following day. He would settle with Reinhard then.

He left the hotel. The day was clear and not too warm, as kind as it had been when he had seen it born earlier on. He walked to Barbárossaplatz and along with the rest of the orderly German pedestrians went through the underpass although there was no need for that. He walked down the Juliuspromenade and noted that a small Italian enclave had been established in this Franconian stronghold: Città Bavaria it was called, with some small inexactitude in locale, and it consisted of a cinema which presented Italian-made films, a small coffee shop filled with chromium machinery, and, as he could see by pressing against the glass door, a discothèque in the basement.

He walked into Schönbornstrasse and then turned left into Herzogenstrasse and presently, as certain as a homing pigeon, reached his goal.

He stood there for several moments and looked at the

window. The sign was in the inevitable gothic and it read "Hans Vogel, Photographer" and in the show window were samples of Herr Vogel's work, photographs of some of the most valuable citizens of Würzburg, and again it was all as he had remembered it from the last time he was there.

He opened the door to the shop now, hearing the bell ring, the same kind of bell. He could almost hear their voices as they left him to go shopping, his mother making him promise to smile, making Herr Vogel promise to make him smile.

"Can I do something for you, gentleman?" a timid voice inquired.

He turned to see the small man, bent over now, the Kaiser moustache white and drooping now, the eyes not so bright and covered with spectacles thick as glass bottoms.

"Herr Vogel?" Bauer again felt the turmoil.

There was a hesitancy. "I am Vogel," the old man said. "Can I do something for you, gentleman?"

"Herr Vogel," Bauer said. "I am Peter Bauer."

Vogel peered at him, confused.

"My father was Councilor Bauer," Bauer said.

Vogel removed his glasses and wiped them and replaced them and looked more closely at Bauer.

Bauer shook his head. "You wouldn't recognize me, Herr Vogel. The last time you saw me I was a small boy and my mother and father brought me here for you to make a photograph of me for my grandmother's birthday."

The old man was nodding now, something was nodding him, and something very close to a terror was enveloping him. He backed away from Bauer very slowly and his lips twitched and his hands opened and closed as though of their own will.

"It can not be," he said. "It must not be."

He stared at Bauer as he might stare at an apparition and then the fear left him and he sat down very carefully in a chair, emptied.

"Yes, Herr Simon Bauer, the city councilor," he said. "Yes, your mother, Frau Bauer, Frau Hedwig Bauer." He removed his spectacles again and his face was unguarded as well as spent. "She always laughed. She always smelled so

209

lovely. When she was here I could always smell her cologne even when I went into the darkroom with all the chemicals there."

He spoke in a voice drained of everything but its words. He put back the glasses and peered at Bauer. "Why did you bring this all back to me? I have spent more than twenty-five years trying to forget those days and here in one instant a stranger walks into my shop and brings it back."

"I'm sorry, Herr Vogel," Bauer said.

Herr Vogel waved his hand, the fingertips darkened by fixative. "It is not your fault. The fault is there are no defenses. One tries but in the end there always are no defenses. There simply are no defenses." He stood up and held out his hand and Bauer took it. "You have been away?" the old man asked, in a conversational tone of voice, having summoned from some unsuspected source a new and different defense, or perhaps just retreating to a new line.

He still had not addressed Bauer by name. Perhaps, Bauer thought, that was the new outpost for his stand.

"Yes, Herr Vogel, I have been away."

"What brings you to me? Do you want another photograph taken? I am not busy at the moment."

"No, not that," Bauer said. "What I came for, Herr Vogel, was this: You took many photographs of all my family. I wondered whether by any chance you still had any of them in your files, or if not the photographs, perhaps negatives."

Vogel shook his head. "Everything was destroyed. There was a bombing here and a great fire."

"Was nothing salvaged?"

Vogel made himself speak with an effort. "There were some old filing cases in the basement. They were badly burned. I think there might be some photographs in there that might not have been destroyed. Perhaps some negatives. I don't know."

"Is it possible," Bauer asked, "that there might be a picture of my mother or father?"

"Anything is possible!" Vogel said in sudden anger. "I have never looked." He sat down again. "I have never been able to bring myself to open those files. I rebuilt my shop and I had it designed as closely as possible to the way it was. But those files have remained untouched. I have told myself again and again that one day I must do something about them. But they are still there, a graveyard." He removed his glasses again. "They are a conscience and I have not wanted to be confronted. I did nothing. We knew what was happening, we all knew, but I did nothing."

"Nobody did," Bauer said.

"I am not responsible before God for anyone except myself and all I will be able to say to Him, if indeed He will have anything to do with me, is that I knew what was going on, I watched it go on, and I did not raise a finger."

"What could you have done?"

"Nothing. Except justify my privilege of being a German, a Catholic, and a human being."

"They would have killed you."

"I could have faced Him more easily that way."

"It may be sufficient that you think it, Herr Vogel," Bauer said.

"I doubt that very much," the old man said.

"Herr Vogel," Bauer said presently. "Could we have a look at those files?"

Vogel looked up, startled. "No, of course not. I've told you. I am unable."

"Perhaps I could look at them alone," Bauer said.

The photographer considered that. Then he said in a low voice, "That would be another lapse. Another avoidance."

He went to the front door and locked it. He hung a sign, "Closed," on the door and then walked past Bauer through a curtain that was exactly like the curtain Bauer remembered, into the back room, where there were the same chairs and the same plant arrangements.

Vogel opened a door leading to the cellar. He hesitated for a moment and then he pressed the switch to turn on the cellar light and started down, gesturing for Bauer to follow.

The cellar was airless and musty and in the staleness Bauer imagined he could still smell the fire and he knew that was nonsense and he thought of Axmann and the little cottage on the hill.

He looked around. There were still black patches on the wall where the flames had touched. In one corner were three filing cases made of steel, the outsides scorched. "It was because they were here in the cellar," Vogel said. "That is how they escaped as much as they did."

They walked across the basement floor, raising small tufts of dust, and Vogel looked closely at the files and then he tugged vainly at one drawer. Bauer asked him to let him do it. Vogel kept pulling more and more frantically. He could not budge the drawer.

"Please, Herr Vogel," Bauer said.

Vogel kept jerking and tears began to run down his cheeks and finally he stopped, breathing hard, and he laid his head against the file and he wept.

Bauer waited and then he moved the old man away gently and he turned the file around so that it faced the light and he rocked it back and forth and then pulled on the drawer and pulled again and felt it give and then pulled it again and it came out with a screeching sound that was like a cry of pain.

Inside the drawer were photographs, darkened, some of them black, and attached to each was the negative. Bauer's fingers began to tremble. He came to "Bamberger" and he went on. Then to "Bangerskis." He saw "Barco," "Bartels," "Bassewitz." Many of the negatives had been softened by the heat and were now glued to the photographs. One picture broke into crumbs in his hand. There was a section where a dozen or more photographs and negatives had melted and then had hardened into shapelessness and he looked farther and he came at last to his own name.

The first picture became dust as he tried to extract it. He went more slowly, his heart beating hard. He came to a photograph which disintegrated as he tried, so carefully, to lift it out. A small piece remained intact in his fingers. It was the hand of a woman, and on the finger he saw a ring with a square-cut stone that prodded an old memory.

He started to extract the negative and then he paused until he could control the shaking in his own hand. He lifted out the dry, gray plastic, working as slowly and as carefully as an antiquary in a dig separating a delicate shard. The opaque oblong was seared around the edges, an unevenly circled umbra. Within the jagged whorl was the figure of a woman with a parasol, wearing a large hat, the outlines of which made him start shaking again.

"Do you think you could make a print of this, Herr Vogel?" he asked.

The old man took the negative from him in what appeared to be too brisk a manner, to show too little care for its brittleness, its age, its long incarceration. But as Vogel held the negative up to the light and scrutinized it professionally from all angles, Bauer relaxed. His was the amateur's concern. Vogel, automatically released by the unmysterious demands of his trade from his own memories, from the conviction of his own iniquities, was his own man again.

"I think so," Vogel said in a perfectly natural way. "Yes, I think I can."

All tremors gone, he trotted rapidly up the cellar steps and went into his darkroom. As Bauer watched he carefully put the negative into the enlarger. He turned out the light and the infrared safety lamp instantly turned the room into the workshop of a sorcerer.

Vogel switched on the enlarger light. The outlines of the negative showed blurred on the test sheet, as the outlines of a summoned spirit might in the beginning appear to the invoking medium. The old man, a master now working at his craft, adjusted the distance until the image was focused sharply. He studied the result, satisfying some demand of experience, snapped off the enlarger light, and in the faint red light appearing like some gnome of necromancy fingered boxes on the shelf until he found what he sought, by black magic, surely, since he could not read anything in that darkness, took out a box, opened it, took out a sheet of sensitized paper, returned the box to its place, and then inserted the paper into the frame under the lens of the enlarger.

Again he switched on the enlarger light and allowed it to remain on until the infallible timer in his mind bade him turn it off. He removed the exposed sheet and carried it to the developing tank.

Bauer looked over the old man's shoulder as he slipped the sheet into the tank and moved it slowly back and forth. For a moment nothing happened, nothing could be seen in the dull red obscurity, and then a reflection emerged on the paper as though it were at that moment being born, the photograph of a young woman, laughing at some inner joy, one hand resting on the top of the handle of a parasol, the other raised, in greeting or in farewell.

The scorched edges of the negative had in the print come out white so that his mother appeared to be resting on a billowing cloud.

In the total absorption now of his profession, unaware of Bauer's presence, Vogel removed the photograph at that instant it called for removal and dropped it into the fixative. He slid it around in that tank and when he again was content the inexorable rules had been followed he took it out, turned on the normal light and studied it, humming tonelessly now, and then put it, face down, on the dryer.

Ignoring Bauer he did one or two trivial chores, and then returned to the dryer at just the time when the photograph, dried, was disengaging itself. He pulled it off, looked at it again, nodded, uninterested in the subject, pursing his lips with satisfaction at a job again done competently, having created the image originally, and having done so again now.

He handed the picture to Bauer and he capered out.

Bauer followed slowly. He took a seat in the studio and looked again at the picture. He might have remained there for some time; he was incapable of moving.

Vogel bounded in again, carrying a brown envelope inside of which was a cardboard stiffener. He took the photograph from Bauer and slipped it into the envelope, closed the flap, and spread open the two metal stays.

"That will be five marks," Vogel said.

Bauer stood up. He took out the money and gave it to

214

the old man. They walked to the front door. Bauer wanted to say something. He felt he should say something.

"It's a lovely day," Vogel said.

"Yes," Bauer said. "Isn't it?"

He shook Vogel's hand and from the very bright light in the photographer's eyes he knew he must say no more. When he left he heard the bell tinkle behind him.

23

✠ ✠ ✠

WHEN BAUER ENTERED THE DEUTSCHER HOF, CARRYING THE
envelope with the photograph, together with some gifts for
Remers' wife and children, he saw the lobby was unusually
crowded, and that the people were not quite the caliber of
the hotel's prosperous clientele. They were elderly and rather
poorly dressed and plainly not at ease. As he was collecting
his key he heard Remers' voice.

"Peter, Peter, thank goodness you're here. You can't imagine what it's been like." He whipped out his kerchief and
mopped his bald head. "These people, Peter, really it's been
quite extraordinary."

"I see them," Bauer said. "What are they here for?"

"You."

"Me?" Bauer looked around the room in astonishment.
"What for?"

"It's my fault. The information I sent to the newspaper
about you."

"What information? What newspaper?"

Bauer looked around the lobby again. Some of the people, sensing he was the one they had come to see, looked

back hopefully. One or two started to get up from their chairs.

"Joachim, what is this?" Bauer asked, bewildered.

Remers grabbed the packages from Bauer's hands and gave them to a bellboy to take to Bauer's room and then he took Bauer's arm and shunted him into his office. He picked up a Würzburg newspaper from his desk and held it out to him.

"I didn't think you would mind, Peter," he said, nervous and apologetic. "The directors approve when I show initiative. But I never imagined anything like those people out there. My goodness, if any of the directors walked into the hotel now—" His entire body shook.

Bauer saw on the front page of the paper a story which disclosed the arrival at the Deutscher Hof of Peter Bauer, son of the late, lamented Councilor Simon Bauer, the famous Würzburg philanthropist and patron of the arts. Herr Peter Bauer, the account went on, spent the war years in Great Britain, and then went to the United States and became a citizen of that country. For the last eleven years, it continued, Herr Bauer has been associated with the United States Department of State, and at the present time, due to his innate skill and the intelligence one would expect from a member of the well-known Bauer family of Würzburg, Herr Bauer now occupied one of the highest desks in the Middle European department, where he dealt exclusively with German affairs. And so on, and so on. The facts were as Bauer had related them to Remers and were, allowing for journalistic hyperbole and understandable local pride, more or less true.

Bauer looked up. Remers was peering at him, wringing his hands, waiting to be sentenced.

"I really didn't think you would mind, Peter," he said again. "The directors always like very much to see this kind of publicity. It goes down on my record."

"What has this got to do with those people outside?" Bauer asked.

"They all read this and now they want you to clear them."

217

"Clear them of what?"

"You've got to handle this right away, Peter," Remers said, worrying his hands. "I just can't have people like that sitting around in my hotel."

"Joachim," Bauer said. "Please start from the beginning. What is this all about?"

"These people have come to see you, to be cleared."

"So you said. Cleared of what? And why by me?"

"They have personal problems. Some of them have trouble getting work. Some of them have difficulty in collecting their pensions. Some of them think they should be getting larger pensions."

"But why?"

Remers shrugged. "They are suspected by the authorities of having had some Nazi associations in the past."

Bauer put the newspaper on the desk.

"Then let them sweat!"

"They may not all have been Nazis. They want an affidavit, Peter, clearing them."

"From me? Joachim, this is a very bad joke."

"You've got to do something."

"Look, Joachim, I don't know these people, I don't know anything about their past, and I don't have any authority to clear them—if I wanted to. And if they stink to the German authorities, then they stink to me too."

Remers mopped his brow again. "I've tried to tell them you're not here officially. But you're with the State Department and your father was one of the most prominent Jews here in the old days. They think you can help them."

"Let them ask my father." Bauer started for the door.

"Peter, please," Remers pleaded.

Bauer was suddenly seized with outrage. "Why the hell should I do anything to help Nazis? You must be mad."

Remers ran to him and grabbed his arm. "Peter, you must get rid of them."

"Get rid of them yourself. You brought them here."

Remers shook his head helplessly. "They won't listen to me, Peter. They'll just sit there. They won't move. Peter, if

218

any of the directors walked in now and saw that riffraff in my lobby it would cost me my job."

Bauer remained silent.

"Please, Peter," Remers said. "We are friends."

After a minute, Bauer said, "All right, Joachim. What would you like me to do?"

"Sit down at my desk. Listen to each of them. I'll tell them they can have only a few minutes with you. Then just scribble on a piece of paper and sign it and give it to them."

"And what shall I scribble?"

"Whatever it is they need." Remers dropped his hand. "Peter, these people are frightened."

"The hell with them!" Bauer said harshly. "The hell with them and the hell with their damned fear!" He started again for the door.

"Peter, I know what you think about them," Remers said quietly. "I know what you must think about them. But they are old and they are frightened."

Bauer turned and looked at Remers. His friend was standing quite erect and his head was raised and he seemed taller and there was something on his face Bauer had never seen before.

"They probably know as well as you do that whatever you give them won't help much," Remers said. "They probably want the piece of paper more for themselves than for the authorities. Perhaps they will die a little easier if they have something they can leave behind in their family Bibles."

Bauer nodded slowly. He walked past Remers, patting him on the arm, and sat down at the desk.

Remers hurried out of the room and returned a few moments later with a very small, very old woman. He held her by the arm and led her to the desk.

"This is Herr Bauer," he said to her.

Bauer thought his voice was extraordinarily gentle and he was happy he had had the instinct to choose Remers for a friend those long years ago.

"Herr Bauer," Remers said, sitting the woman down carefully. "This is Frau Brunner. She has somehow mislaid a clearance she once received from an American officer and it sometimes causes her delays when she goes to collect her pension. Perhaps you can help her. There, Frau Brunner, Herr Bauer will listen to you."

He left the room.

Frau Brunner was dressed in black, black hat, black dress, black gloves, all so old they had a patina. She was without many teeth and her face was as lined as an etching.

"They laugh at me," she said in an old, indignant voice. "They give me my money, certainly, they have to, that's the law, but they laugh at me when I tell them each time how an American captain wrote down that I had nothing to do with those Nazis in the old days. He did too, and I never had!"

She stopped talking as suddenly as she had started and she left her mouth open and Bauer thought it was like looking into the hungry craw of a large baby bird.

"And you would like me to write down the same thing for you?" Bauer asked.

Frau Brunner closed her mouth and nodded her head.

Bauer saw that Remers had provided him with a large note pad. His old friend, he considered, must go far. "What is your full name?" he asked.

"Frau Eva Brunner," she said. "It is just that I have worked hard all my life and I don't like to be laughed at."

"No," Bauer said. "Nobody does."

He thought for a moment and then wrote, "I have questioned Frau Eva Brunner and I will certify that she has no record of any past experience with the National Socialists." He signed his name, wondering in passing, what his chief in the Department would say about this, and passed the paper on to her.

She opened her reticule and took out a tiny pair of spectacles in gold-rimmed metal, small enough to be spectacles for a child. She adjusted them and read what he had written.

He watched anxiously, hoping he had found the right words, asking himself why it was mattering to him. He saw her start to blush.

She lowered the paper and removed her glasses.

"Is that all right?" he asked.

She reached quickly across the desk and took his hand and he realized she was going to kiss it. He withdrew it hastily and stood up.

"There are others," he said, trying to be as gentle as Remers, knowing he did not quite make it.

Frau Brunner rose to her feet. "Thank you, Herr Bauer. God's greetings."

"God's greetings," he said.

She left and Remers brought in an old man, and then another old man, this one almost deaf so that Bauer had to shout, then an old woman, and then two sisters. To each of these Bauer gave a document absolving them of Nazi past. With each client he found himself feeling a little more euphoric. Was this what power did to a man? It had to be the strangest experience in his life.

He greeted another old woman who stood before him for several moments, peering at him from vague eyes.

She shook her head at last. "I would not have recognized you," she said. Her voice was thin and distant. "I would not have recognized the little Peter." She giggled like a baby. "But there are so many things I don't recognize these days."

He leaned over the desk. "How do you know me?"

The woman cocked her head. "You don't look like the councilor and you don't look like your mother." She held up both hands. "Oh, your mother was so happy you were safe. In that bad place where I saw her all she could say was that no matter what happened at least little Peter was safe."

Bauer walked slowly around the desk. "Who are you?"

"You would not remember."

"Tell me who you are. Please tell me."

"Your Aunt Dorle, you remember her?"

"Yes. Please, who are you?"

"I worked for her for many years."

He leaned back against the desk. "Marta."

"You do remember me?" Her face brightened.

"Marta." He took her in his arms and held her.

"You do remember me," she said again, very pleased.

"Marta. Barbarossaplatz where the parade made the turning and you held me so I wouldn't fall over the railing."

She sat down, smoothing out her dress daintily. "I don't remember that. But then I forget so many things now."

"You put a little velvet pillow under my arms to make me more comfortable. And the great parade, the knights and the crusaders and the monks and the big floats."

She nodded vigorously, her eyes bright and clear now. "Now I remember. It was the velvet pillow. That made me remember. It was a blue pillow and it had flowers on it."

"Yes," he said. "Yes." He looked at the old woman and then he turned away because he could not for a moment look at her any more. "Yes, Marta, the pillow was blue and it had little yellow flowers on it."

"You were such a little boy," she said. "You've grown so big."

He walked round the desk and stood with his back to her until he recovered himself. He turned and sat down.

"Where did you see my mother, Marta?" he asked.

"In that bad place."

"What bad place?"

"It's so hard to remember."

"Please try to remember, Marta."

"They beat me because I tried to take her some butter and fresh eggs." The spark was gone from her eyes now and they again were vague and her voice was faint.

"Try to remember, Marta," Bauer said, leaning on the desk, clasping his hands tightly to keep them still.

She frowned and puckered her mouth. "It's so hard. There was no need to beat me like that."

"Where was it, Marta?"

"Oh, it was that bad place. It always had such a funny smell. It was the smoke from the chimneys. You could smell it from far away. I never smelled anything like that before. It was so sweet, as though they were making candy."

"How did it happen she was taken there?" Bauer whispered.

"I don't remember." She frowned again and bit her lips

and shook her head. "I remember your Aunt Dorle told me your mother was going to go away, that was after the councilor, after the councilor had happen to him what happened, that your mother was going to be with you and the relatives in London. And then all of a sudden she was in that bad place. I never smelled anything like that. It was a sweet smell but it wasn't nice."

"Who arranged to have my mother arrested, Marta?"

The old woman shook her head.

The door opened and Remers stuck in his head. "Will you be long, Peter? There still are a few more."

"In just one moment, Joachim."

"If one of the directors—"

"I won't be much longer, Joachim." When the door was closed Bauer said, "Marta, think, try to think, who denounced my mother? What was his name? What reason did he have?"

She looked bewildered and then a little frightened. "I don't remember, little Peter."

"That's all right, Marta," he said soothingly.

He reached over and stroked her hand. She looked at him with a shy smile.

"Do you know anything about a painting?" he asked.

She smiled and nodded. "There were always so many paintings. Your Aunt Dorle had paintings. Your Aunt Dorle is dead now too, isn't she?"

"Yes, Marta."

"But she didn't die in the bad place."

"No, Marta. She went to America after the war."

"I know," Marta said dreamily. "She wrote to me from America and wanted me to go there and be with her but I was too old. But she wrote. She wanted me to go there."

"About the painting, Marta," he said.

"Whenever we visited your house on Annastrasse I saw paintings there. The councilor loved paintings."

"A special painting, Marta. A painting by an Italian artist named Tiepolo."

Marta frowned and began to slip away again. "I don't know anything about that."

"What else can you remember about my mother, Marta?"
The old woman came back quickly. "She always used to laugh so much but when I saw her in the bad place she didn't laugh. There was no need for them to beat me. Your family was always good to me and all I wanted to do was to give Frau Bauer some butter and fresh eggs."

"How long was she there?"

"I don't know. They beat me on the head and told me it was a good thing I was a German or else I'd be put in there with your mother. I can't remember anything else. Could you give me a piece of paper that says I'm a good woman?"

The door opened again. "Really, Peter," Remers said.

"We're through," Bauer said.

He wrote on the note pad and signed it and got up and walked round the desk and gave it to her. She folded it without reading it and put it into her purse. He helped her to her feet and she took his hand and kissed it. He did not take the hand away.

He held her hand against his cheek. "Thank you, Marta," he said.

"Your family was always good to me. But those people shouldn't have beat me on the head."

"No, Marta. Are you all right now? Do you need money? I have money. Do you need any?"

"Oh, no," she said. "I live in a very nice house and they are nice to me. I don't need anything, little Peter. Except this paper you gave to me."

"You're sure, *Liebling?* Just a little money to put in the bank? A little nest egg in case you need it?"

"Oh, I have money in the bank, little Peter. I have saved up all the money I can ever spend. I just wanted this paper."

"Bless you, Marta. Bless you, and thank you."

"God's greetings, little Peter."

"God's greetings, Marta."

Again the door opened and Remers looked in, exasperated. "Peter!"

Bauer held the hand of the old woman and conducted her to the door. He watched her walk across the lobby.

"Herr Bauer, this is Herr Alois Volkmar," Remers said. "Herr Volkmar, I am sure Herr Bauer will be able to help you."

"We'll see," Herr Volkmar said.

He was one of the better dressed of the petitioners, a heavy man whose neck ran over his collar.

"Such a damned nuisance," he said.

Bauer started back for the desk. Volkmar pushed ahead of him so that he was at the desk when Bauer got there. Volkmar put a briefcase on the desk and opened it and took out a batch of papers.

"Such a damned nuisance," Volkmar said again.

"What can I do for you?" Bauer asked.

"Always red tape," Volkmar said. He had as yet not bothered to look at Bauer. "I'm a busy man, Herr Bauer, why was I kept waiting so long out there?"

"I have no idea." Bauer sat down. "What is it I can do for you?"

Volkmar slapped the batch of papers down on the desk before Bauer. "First read those. And you have to start at the beginning and read all of them so you'll know what it's all about. Such a nuisance. What the devil does it matter?" He sat down. His thighs strained the seams of his pants. He put his pudgy hands on his knees. He glared at Bauer. "Everybody had to join the Party, not? How did you earn a living if you did not? All of this damned nonsense, all of these damned questions—what did you do then, what did you do! And all of them in it just as deep as I was only today they're sitting on the other side of the desk and they're asking questions as though butter wouldn't melt in their mouths, the damned hypocrites! I did what I did because it had to be done, the same way they did, the bastards! You ran away from here, Bauer, so you don't know how it was then. Well, I'll tell you how it was. You joined the Party or you starved and I was damned if I was going to starve. Especially when all the rest of them were getting fat and rich."

Bauer stood up and walked slowly to the door.

"Where the devil are you going, Bauer?" Volkmar demanded. "You haven't read those papers. Damn it to hell, I've been sitting out in that damned lobby for more than two hours. Where are you going, Bauer? Bauer, where the devil are you going?"

Bauer opened the door.

"Come back here, you damned Jew!" Volkmar shouted. "Come back here! God damn it, you people started all of this!"

Bauer walked into the lobby.

Remers rushed up to him. "What's wrong, Peter?" he asked.

Bauer walked past him without answering.

"Peter," Remers said. "There are still two more people."

Volkmar appeared at the door to Remers' office. "The Jew never looked at my papers," he shouted. "Stop that Jew!"

"Oh, my God," Remers said. He took Bauer by the elbow and hurried him out of the lobby. "Oh, God."

"Stop that Jew!" Volkmar bellowed.

Bauer found himself in the street and he tried to breathe. He knew he had to breathe and he tried to do it. He heard Remers call after him but he did not hear what Remers said. He walked down Theaterstrasse and he tried to breathe and he knew there was something he wanted to do, had to do, but he did not know exactly what it was. He turned into another street and then into another. He bumped into someone and said something in apology and continued on.

It was several minutes, perhaps more than several minutes, perhaps closer to half an hour or even an hour before he realized why he was walking, what he was walking to, what he was seeking, knowing at the same time it would not be there, was not there, had not been there for a very long time. He wanted to say a prayer for his mother. He wanted to say a formal prayer in a formal place. He had not been in a synagogue in all the years of his manhood but he wanted to go into one now and speak some words and he knew there was no place to go, and he could not stop walking and looking, knowing there was no place.

He saw he was in front of a church. He went inside. It was dark and cool. He stood just inside the door and felt the cool air on his face. He walked farther into the church. It was empty and cool and dark and he thought he might find some small place where he could say some words.

He saw a sign:

> IT IS FORBIDDEN TO TAKE
> PHOTOGRAPHS. THIS IS A
> HOUSE OF GOD AND NOT A
> MUSEUM.

The sign, he noted, was in English, for the American tourists, not for Germans, the Germans did not need to be reminded this was not a museum but was in fact a house of God. But was this so? Was God still alive in Germany? Or had He, during the purification, been consigned elsewhere, with the others?

He looked around for some small quiet place. He saw marble statues everywhere and busts, all provided with gothic descriptions, and relics and paintings. He saw ahead of him the rows of pews facing an altar that seemed very far away. He wanted only to sit down and bow his head and say some words, what words he did not as yet know.

He walked toward the high-backed benches in the dim light and the feeling of the cool, quiet air, and he saw something gleaming above his head. He looked up. He saw the golden pipes of the organ probing like giant fingers at the vaulted ceiling and he saw that two of the pipes had been constructed horizontally and ended in large, shining brass bells, pointing toward the altar like the twin mouths of polished cannon.

Why? What for? Self-destruct for Doomsday? A defense against the last Judgment? Or was it merely for recalcitrant parishioners? Or was it the guard set on the Figure drooping in His pain lest in an act of final revulsion He abandon them all to make the city free of its last Jew?

He turned and rushed out of the church, startling an old lady who had just entered and who was dipping her fingers in the font, who turned and watched him flee, the holy water dripping unheeded from her fingers on her dress and shoe.

He started back for the hotel. He would have to wait to say the words or perhaps he would never say them or perhaps there were no words to be said. She had brought butter and fresh eggs and for reward had got beaten on the head so that forever thereafter nothing was wholly clear to her and what words could be said after that?

He smelled something sweet and he saw he was passing a confectioner's shop. The window was filled with bonbons. A mother and a little boy were coming out of the store and the mother dipped into a small paper bag and took out a chocolate and gave it to the child and the child put it into his mouth and Bauer started to run.

He ran for the hotel. He felt it coming on. He prayed that it would not catch him before he reached his room. He realized he was running the wrong way, away from the hotel, and he turned and people looked at him, the tall, thinnish man in the American clothes and the American shoes, the beset face, and he felt it coming, closer, closer, and he asked that it hold off, that it be held off, if he could only get away from that sweet smell, and he saw the hotel and turned into the arcade and ran across the lobby and he bit his lips and he asked that it stay away, just for another few moments, and he waited, sealing his mouth, until the elevator door opened and he rushed inside and waited and when it stopped he rushed down the corridor and opened his door and ran into the bathroom and raised the toilet seat and bent over it and vomited.

It came out, a monstrous, stinking, tidal wave of slime, of what he had been told and what he had seen and what he remembered and what he imagined, and he crouched there, heaving, until there was nothing more to heave, still heaving, dry, wrenching spasms that tore him apart, that burned his throat, that scraped him like sandpaper, and finally he stood up, gasping, coughing, and he flushed down what he had been made to remember and what he had re-membered without having been made to remember, and he stood there, trying again to breathe, breathing fast and hard and deep, not feeling any air, and when he was able at last he lurched out of the room to the bed and fell upon it.

His belly was corrugated, ridged and tight with pain; it felt as though it had been punched and the punching had not stopped. He doubled up, his knees against his chest, in the first, the original position, and he retched again, drily, the sandpaper lacerating again, there was nothing to come up, and he remained there, half awake, half unconscious, sometimes fully the one, sometimes the other. He heard the telephone.

He raised his arm to look at his watch. It was a leaden effort. He propped his wrist with his other hand. The telephone rang again. It was after seven. He picked up the telephone.

"Bauer," he said.

"I'm ready, Peter," Joachim Remers said.

"Joachim." Bauer tried to sit up. He could not command his body.

"We must hurry, Peter," Remers said. "Peter, I'm sorry about Volkmar. I had no idea. You must realize that."

"Joachim," Bauer tried again. He could not be paralyzed. He must be able to move.

"Peter, we must hurry," Remers said in his voice that was not very different from the voice of the boy Bauer knew. "Tilly is making a pork roast and it must be served at a definite moment and she is keeping the children awake so they can meet you. They're all dressed up and waiting and we really must hurry."

"I'll be right down," Bauer said.

Dinner was pleasant and soothing and Frau Tilly Remers was a love who was ready to burst into tears when Bauer refused third helpings, until Remers explained to her that that was how inhospitable Americans were, even Americans of German origin, after which she subsided.

Bauer returned to the hotel and when he got into bed he fell immediately into the sleep of the dead.

24

✠ ✠ ✠

HIS MOTHER WAS SITTING ON A SLED, A CHILD'S SLED, COVERED
with a furry blanket, and the sled was being pulled by Erwin
Axmann and she was wearing a fur coat that was drawn up
around her throat and she was wearing a fur hat like a cos-
sack's hat and it was tilted on her head and Axmann was
pulling the sled up a hill and she was laughing the way
people laugh when they're being pulled in sleds and he
could see the vapor from her laughter in the clear, cold air.
Axmann's face was grim as he pulled the sled with one hand
and took giant steps up the hill and the countryside was
funny because where Axmann walked pulling the sled there
was snow and ice and Axmann was dressed for the cold too
but behind them the sun was blazing and everything was
green and looked hot and as the sled moved up the hill the
snow and ice behind it disappeared and the ground was green
and hot.

He was somewhere there, watching, very close, because he
could see their faces clearly and he knew it was himself, he
never doubted it was himself, and he tried to make himself
known to them, so they could hear him and see him, so he

230

could be with them in helping Axmann pull the sled, but he could make no sound.

Then Axmann slipped on the ice and fell down and something happened with his leg because he could not stand up again and his mother threw off her blanket and got out of the sled and she tried to pick him up but he was a very big man and she could not lift him.

And Peter, wherever he was, from whatever place he was watching, tried to get over there to help, but he could not bring himself any closer and he called out again, he thought he called out, but there was no sound.

His mother tried to pull Axmann to the sled and Axmann helped her by pushing himself and they got to the sled and it took a long time with his mother tugging and Axmann pushing, but they managed to get him into the sled and then his mother picked up the rope and tried to pull the sled but she could not. She leaned against it and Peter could plainly see the strain in her face, the face that was exactly the face that had come out in the photograph. He must be very close to her to see her so clearly and he called out again but the sounds he made, if he made sounds, did not reach her.

He opened his eyes and he knew the phone had been ringing for some time and he lifted the receiver. Would he have caught up with the sled? Would he ever have caught up with the sled?

He looked at his watch. It was not yet eight o'clock. "Bauer here," he said. His voice sounded thick.

"Police President Eckardt. I would like to see you."

"For what reason?"

"I don't make social calls, Herr Bauer."

"You will please tell me first what this is about."

There was a brief pause. "Your driver, Reinhard, is dead. Now shall I come up or will you come down here?"

Once again seated in Remers' office behind Remers' desk, Bauer watched as Eckardt paced up and down. He was as carelessly dressed as he was when Bauer first had seen him at the ruins of Axmann's cottage. His suit jacket seemed almost too small for him and Bauer could see it stretch tight as the police official turned and moved his arms. There was something lacking; Bauer could not think what it was.

"His wife, widow, informed me he was driving for you," Eckardt said.

"That's correct," Bauer said.

"That you had hired him by the day, as a private chauffeur, so to speak."

"That's right, Herr Police President. How did it happen? How did he die?"

"That from time to time you two would stop somewhere and have a drink together and a talk."

"Was there anything wrong in that, Herr Eckardt? Now when do you intend to tell me how Major Reinhard died?"

Eckardt paused in his marching and surveyed Bauer with distaste. "He was found burned to death—in his car."

After a moment, Bauer said, "You say that in an odd way, Herr Police President. It was an accident."

"It was intended to appear to be so," Eckardt said. He continued to gaze upon Bauer with aversion.

"Intended," Bauer said. "All right, Herr Eckardt."

"The car was just a few meters off the road, between Randersacker and Theilheim. It was head-on a large boulder. We were to believe that he ran off the road for some reason. That he crashed into the boulder and caught fire and somehow could not extricate himself."

"But you obviously do not believe that," Bauer said.

Eckardt began his pacing again. He reached into his jacket pocket and took out something and began to work it between his hands.

Bauer looked more closely. He saw that the police official was counting off beads, and he remembered now what it was that he had missed, the little artificial cigarette.

Eckardt looked down at the beads in his hands. "Greek," he said. "They're supposed to help."

"All right, Herr Police President. Will you please tell me

why you do not believe Major Reinhard died accidentally."

Eckardt counted off beads. They looked small and very fragile between his burly fingers. "I don't believe it at all," he said. "As a matter of fact I don't think it was intended that I believe it, not entirely anyway. I know that in any case you were not intended to believe it."

Bauer felt a cold air on his neck. "What are you getting at, Herr Police President?"

"I don't know," Eckardt dropped the bead chain into his pocket and faced Bauer. He clasped his hands behind his back. His face turned cold and hard and professional. "Fire, Herr Bauer," he snapped. "Does that suggest anything to you?"

"Erwin Axmann."

"Yes, Erwin Axmann."

Eckardt leaned forward slightly and Bauer felt he was leaning on him.

"And you believe there may be a connection between the two deaths?" Bauer began to smell the German thing again, the thing that was always in the air.

"I don't know!" It came out as a small explosion. Then Eckardt said more quietly, "What is it that we do know? We know that two persons, two persons who presumably were strangers to each other, two persons leading peaceful and uneventful lives, have died violently by fire within a few days of each other. And what is the one thing these two persons had in common? Just think. They both were involved to a greater or lesser degree with you. Now you tell me, Herr Bauer, does that suggest anything to you?"

Despite himself, despite everything he had reminded himself of in the last few days, Bauer shuddered between his shoulders and he tried to hide that by making a movement with his hand but he saw he was not hiding anything from Eckardt.

"You would know better about anything like that than I would, Herr Police President." He was relieved that the words came out evenly.

Eckardt was silent for a little while. His hand went into

233

the bead pocket but came out empty. "Oh, I may, one day I may. But there is one thing that I am certain of now, Herr Bauer. One thing I don't need for the future to tell me."

"And that is?"

"That you at best are hard luck."

"At best."

"I won't go any deeper because at the moment I don't have the facts and I may never have the facts. I have told you before, Herr Bauer, that this is a very closed-mouth community. What I would like to persuade you to do, however, is leave. Leave. As soon as possible. Today, for example."

Bauer nodded. "I plan to leave this afternoon, Herr Eckardt."

"It comforts me to know that we are in accord," Eckardt said.

"I owe Major Reinhard some money."

"Add up what it is and leave it in an envelope at the desk here. I will see that Frau Reinhard receives it."

"Is there anything I can do?" Bauer asked.

"It will satisfy me fully if you do not miss that train."

"You will be satisfied," Bauer said.

"Very good." Eckardt started to leave. "By the way, Herr Bauer, the services for Axmann take place this morning. I'm going there. I'll give you a lift if you like."

25

✠ ✠ ✠

CAPTAIN ROY ATKINS LOOKED UP AS MARLIESE ENTERED THE office with the Tuesday morning collection of twixes. She placed them on the desk directly in front of him and started out of the office.

"Marly," he said.

"Yes, Captain?" She turned with a secretary smile.

"What the hell is eating your ass this morning? And don't tell me I have cables to answer. I know that I have cables to answer."

"Roy, let's not start anything this morning again," she said. "Not until I've had some coffee."

"Bring some coffee in here. I'll have some with you."

"I already have mine on my desk. Is there anything else?"

"Yes, there sure as hell is," he said. "I want to know what's bugging you. Anybody's got a right to be pissed off around here it's me not you. I haven't been tearing around getting myself laid."

"My coffee's getting cold."

"Fuck your coffee! I'm your boss and I'm asking you a question, you God damned kraut!" He got up swiftly and went to her. "I didn't mean that, Marly. It's just you get my balls in such a bind I don't know what I'm saying half the time." He put his arms around her. "I'm sorry, honey."

He tried to kiss her but she slipped away from him and walked to the window. She folded her arms and stared out.

"He told me that he made propaganda broadcasts during the war," she said.

"Who? What are you talking about?"

"He told me he broadcast to German troops from Beirut. He told me that's what he did during the war."

He looked at her for a moment and then went to the desk and picked up the cable on top of the pile. It was the answer from Washington to his routine query on Bauer. It was concise and impersonal.

"He even made up a rather sweet little story," she said. "He told me he managed to dig up a German priest in Lebanon and that he persuaded him to broadcast Sunday church services for the benefit of SS troops who were not permitted to have them. I thought that was rather touching. Particularly since he is a Jew."

Atkins sat down and read the cable again. "They give him high marks."

"Why wouldn't they? He's one of them."

"Well, maybe it ain't our place to pass judgment."

She turned to him. She asked slowly, "Are you defending him?"

"No."

"Then what is it you're doing?"

He stood up. "Look, Marly, the love I got for that Jew bastard is smaller than flea shit, one hell of a whole lot smaller."

"Yes," she said. "That's what you've given me to believe."

"What I'm saying, all I'm saying, is that it ain't neither your place nor mine to lay down judgment."

She looked at him with interest. "You are defending him, Roy."

His big hands knuckled the desk. He shook his head. "I'm only trying to be fair and it sure as hell ain't easy. I'm only saying that he told us how he left here, why he left here. He didn't leave any love behind. He didn't leave much of anything behind."

"Do you believe that?"

He saw there was something very close to amusement on her face and he wondered why he had ever believed he knew that face. "I believe some of it," he said. "And just some of it is pretty lousy."

"You must discuss this with my brother."

How, he wondered, had he ever kidded himself that he had crossed the gap? Whatever had made him think they were even remotely on the same beam? They were shouting at each other from across the tops of mountains and something very dark and very dirty lay between.

"I have talked to Werner," he said. "And I've listened to what he says."

"But obviously you do not believe him. What you are saying is that my brother is a liar."

He hit the desk with his fist. "I'm not saying anything of the kind! For Christ sake, don't twist my words around!"

"How could I do that?" she asked. "We are talking in your language."

"I believe your brother," he said in what he knew was desperation, knew was useless, and he knew it was all over and that what they were talking about was not Bauer, not really Bauer, not Bauer the way they were talking, that it was something else, something Bauer was mixed up in all right, but something else. "I believe Werner up to a point," he said. "That's all you can believe anybody is up to a point because nobody knows everything about everything and nobody knows anything straight, all the way straight. Everybody's got an angle. Your brother's got an angle and Bauer's got an angle. We all got angles. I think maybe this Nazi-Jew business has been exaggerated but I sure as hell don't buy that it was made up out of whole cloth the way your brother swears it was. I think some of it happened and Bauer thinks all of it happened, is all I'm saying."

"Is that all?"

"No, that isn't all! That's not all of it at all!"

"What else is there?"

"What there really is is that you don't know really know what happened back then." He picked up the cable. "All you got to go on is this."

"What more is there to know?" she asked coolly. "He was one of the flyers who destroyed this city. It says so right there. What else is there to know?"

"Oh, shit, men put on a uniform in a war they have to do things. They hardly ever are pretty things."

"They have to obey orders? Is that what you're saying?"

"You're damned right."

"They hanged Germans for that," she said.

He stared at her.

"I'd better get back to work, Roy," she said.

"What the hell you so mad about?" he asked. "What Bauer did or because he's a Jew—or because you let him crawl into your pants?"

She looked at him for several moments, appraisingly.

"You're weak," she said. She said it in an informative way, as though telling him his tie was crooked. "You are all weak. Look at how you have treated us."

26

✠ ✠ ✠

POLICE PRESIDENT ECKARDT BROUGHT BAUER BACK TO THE
hotel after the prayers were said for the soul of Erwin Axmann. Bauer thanked him and again assured him he would
be out of Würzburg that afternoon.

He went into the hotel and settled his account and was
handed a letter which had arrived in the morning's post. He
glanced at the envelope. The letter, written in unfamiliar,
awkward Germanic hand, had been addressed to another
hotel in Würzburg and had been forwarded.

He slipped it into his pocket and he worked out what he
owed Major Reinhard. He doubled the amount and put the
money in a hotel envelope. He had to add a note. What
could he say? He put down a few words of condolence and
sealed the envelope and gave it to the desk clerk, telling her
Herr Eckardt would have it picked up.

He asked the girl to ring Herr Remers and ask if he could
see him for a moment. Remers appeared at his office door
immediately and led Bauer in.

Bauer sat down. "I'm leaving this afternoon, Joachim."

"I know. You said so last night. I'm sorry to see you go,
Peter."

It was pleasant to hear that although he knew that Remers did not entirely mean it. Not with the two deaths and the police and the petitioners in the lobby. Remers' life would be more peaceful when he was gone.

"The train doesn't leave until late this afternoon," Bauer said. "Would you mind if I stayed in the room past check-out time?"

"Of course not!" Remers said heartily. "What a question!"

"If you've booked the room I can get out sooner."

Remers shook his head. "Not at all, Peter, not at all. You stay as long as you like."

Bauer stood up. "I enjoyed myself very much last night, Joachim," he said. He had.

"We enjoyed having you. Tilly says you're a fascinating man."

"Yes. She's a fine woman, Joachim, and your children are lovely."

"They are a nice little family," Remers said.

"You've done so well, Joachim, in all things," Bauer said.

Remers beamed. "One does the best one can with what one has, Peter."

"Yes." There was nothing more to say. After everything and after all the years there was nothing more to say. He held out his hand. "Good-by, Joachim."

Remers gripped his hand. "I'll probably see you before you go."

"Yes."

Remers walked him to the door. "Peter, will you come back here again?"

"I think not."

"God's greetings, Peter."

"God's greetings."

In his room Bauer packed his few things. He looked at the photograph of his mother. That was a plus. He supposed finding out for sure what had happened to her must be

240

reckoned a plus. That was what he had come for so it must be a plus.

He looked around. He'd packed everything. He looked at his watch. He had plenty of time. He probably should have something to eat. He was not hungry. Was there anything he wanted to shop for? He had no desire to go out into the streets. He sat down.

Why had he doubled the money for Reinhard? Was it because of fondness for the former *Wehrmacht* officer or was it just a sentimentality because he was dead? Or was it the feeling, the feeling he did not want to recognize, the feeling that Eckardt might be right, that the death was in some way related to him? And that he also was connected with the death of Erwin Axmann. And if that were so, if that suspicion were hiding anywhere down deep, then he should be frightened and perhaps that was why he was frightened and why he had felt it comforting—Eckardt's own word—to be close to the police official all morning and why he had not wanted to see him drive away and why he was so restless now for the time to pass, for it to come to the moment when he could board the train and get away from whatever it was, if it were anything.

He looked at his watch again. The hands seemed glued to the face.

Could he be in danger? It seemed ridiculous. It was a cliché to point it out, even to himself, that these were not the old days, that this was a new Germany, and whether or not it was altogether a brand new Germany, as the Germans proclaimed, it was definitely not the old Germany.

He wondered whether he had locked the door. Or did it lock automatically? He went to the door and double-locked it. He returned to the chair and sat down. He felt foolish.

The smell of fear.

What was the smell of fear and what was the smell of Germany and were they related and were they for him the same thing? Would a Jew always smell fear in Germany? Was that something that now had been made an inseparable part of the blood memory as though it had been there forever?

What was the smell of fear? It must be many things and they could not all be bad, some of them must be quite pleasant, like the smell of chocolate candy coming from a smokestack, the kind of smell one would pause for and breathe in deeply in Switzerland, for instance.

Did people get accustomed to smells? After a while, did the sweet smell from chimneys, in Germany or Switzerland or any place else, become ordinary so that people ignored them, more, did not smell them at all, they were part of the ordinary smell of the landscape, of living?

What he smelled now was the open ossuary of his mind.

He stood up. The room was closing in again. Perhaps he would take a walk. He looked at his watch again. Time seemed to have stopped dead in Würzburg.

He picked up his jacket. He saw the envelope sticking out of the pocket. He took it out. There was no return address. The other hotel had evidently held on to it until someone happened to read the newspaper story and saw where he was staying.

He opened the envelope. The writing sprawled on a slant. He looked at the bottom of the sheet. The letter was signed Axmann.

"Dear Bauer, after you left the name came to me, the name of the person your mother was sending the painting to. It was Arthur Hausmann. He is still alive, I think. Anyway his name is in the telephone book. I seem to remember something about him being engaged to your mother, before she met your father. It was a pleasure to see you again, Peter. Come back to Würzburg one day and we will climb a little mountain together, God willing. God's greetings."

27

✠ ✠ ✠

WERNER HAUSMANN HAD A FASTIDIOUS NATURE AND THE GEN-
eral appearance of the convention hall in the new hotel
suited him. It was large enough to hold three hundred persons—a respectable figure in Würzburg—it was quiet and
subdued in its decor, and it had, of course, excellent, modern
acoustics. What pleased him most of all was that it was in
every way opposite to a beer hall.

The people sitting before him, listening to him, and they
filled all of the three hundred chairs and there were more
standing on the sides and in the back, were precisely the type
he wanted to speak to. There were good, solid men, smoking
small, expensive cigars, there was quite a number of young
men, all of them neatly dressed, and there was a scattering of
women, mostly of middle age. All in all, an audience made
up of ladies and gentlemen, most of them old enough to have
some personal memories, but not old enough to have been
very deeply involved, or at least not inflexibly involved, together with young people who were much too young then
but who wanted to know. And to come to know in a way

that would be palatable today. It had, in fact, to be presented palatably to every one in the room.

As always, it gratified him that almost no one there could ever have been caught in a beer hall. If it were going to be done, he was wise enough and sensitive enough to know, it had to be done decently, and with decent people.

"I do not make an all-out blanket condemnation of the recent German past," he said in his unexcited, musical voice. "There is no one who can force me to do that. Ladies and gentlemen, I know and you know there were some things of value in the concept of National Socialism. These elements existed in our Fatherland before National Socialism was created and, thank God, they have survived Hitler's death. Many of us today believe in these ideas because they are fundamentally German ideas."

His listeners nodded soberly. Even the younger persons displayed grave agreement. And this too pleased him. He would have been annoyed by any less seemly reaction.

He could see to the end of the room, even in the subdued lighting. And although there were many smokers, the ventilating system kept the hall clear of smoke. It might have been a religious meeting. No uniforms, no flags, no political symbols of any kind.

"National Socialism ruled for about twelve years," he went on. "The history of our Fatherland goes back more than one thousand years. The ideals of our people, the dreams, the hopes, the national purposes, go back often to the beginning, and because these are our heritages, they still belong to us, and because some of them were adopted by the National Socialists does not make them wrong."

He paused and heard low, courteous murmurings of assent. He did not permit himself any expression of response. He felt strongly that he was reaching these people and that they were hearing what they wanted to hear. He had somehow to reach out and find in them, for them, a sense of dissatisfaction. And that was not nearly as easy as it was when the Leader started out. For today Germany was the most prosperous country in Europe, perhaps in the world. There

244

could be no economic dissatisfaction. Everybody in the room was evidence of that. And it was not for nothing that the new hotel had provided itself with a large parking lot, the first hotel in Würzburg to feel the need for that. And tonight that area was filled with cars, and most of them new cars.

He had thought a great deal about all that in the lonely hours every leader must spend in making preparation for the day of his leadership. There was no one hungry in Germany and the mark was the soundest money in the world but there was something lacking and he needed only to reason out what it was. He had been given his clue when he read somewhere that Germany was an economy in search of a government. He had first thought that a typical, superficial, modern wisecrack. But he had thought more on it.

And it was true. The government was too low-profile. This was the natural pendulum swing from the last Reich, when the profile was vertical, and, according to the Leader, reached beyond the skies.

No one wanted that again, surely. No one would put up with it. But it also was true there was in Germany a kind of emotional vacuum.

There were some young radicals who prided themselves on the fact they felt no patriotism, who proclaimed that love of country was outmoded, that they were part of the whole world of young people, that their country was the earth.

That might be true for them, he had finally come to conclude. If that satisfied them, well and good. They would be dealt with in good time. But most Germans had to have something to believe in, something Adolf Hitler had supplied in his time, something that was not being supplied today. It was not enough for these people sitting in front of him to have good jobs and good pay and fine automobiles and television sets and every other luxury a human being could desire. No, they had within them something, an energy, a faith, a creed, that had to be deposited somewhere, on something. And that was what he intended, little by little, to provide.

"Of course," he said, in the manner of a professor addressing a seminar, "while we must not just condemn National Socialism out of hand, we must also not make the opposite mistake of looking back with nostalgia at what many of our elders still consider the most glorious days in the history of our country."

There were not too many now who still thought that, he knew. But for those few who did it was a kind of throwaway piece of sentimentality.

"There are times for expansion and growth and there are times to meditate and reflect," he said philosophically. "We had for a short period a development of power probably greater than at any time in our history. And then followed a period of despair and discouragement when our government collapsed during the final days of the war." He paused for a moment to allow them to remember. "Now we must live in a quieter period. We must live in a period of contemplation. And we must discover in this contemplation a sense of new dedication to our Fatherland."

There was a shuffling of feet, the loudest response in the room of the evening, still decently muted, and he could see many persons turn and look at each other and nod.

He was surprised to see his sister enter the convention hall. He had often attempted to get her interested in politics, particularly after her husband had been killed but he had never succeeded. He was pleased to see her now. It seemed everything was going so well. He wished only that she had come earlier so she could have heard all his remarks.

"We must be grateful to the National Socialists still among us for many of the values of our country today," he said, catching Marliese's eye as she slipped to the rear of the auditorium. "It was the discipline they learned from the National Socialists that prevented Germany from being torn apart after the war—broken into pieces internally as it had been externally—and then handed piece by piece to the Reds. Although those people who followed Hitler in the sincere belief they were acting in the best interests of their country have been hounded and jailed and persecuted, although they were discharged from their jobs and in many instances from

246

their professional posts, although in some extreme cases they even were driven from their homes and towns and cities and forced to go elsewhere, assume another name perhaps, although all this has happened, these people continued to be law-abiding citizens, to accept their fate, to go back to work. Discipline. The discipline our fathers learned during the Third Reich."

The audience broke into applause now, controlled and steady. He looked with pleasure at his sister and was delighted to see that she too was clapping her hands.

"Now what is it that we want to do today?" he asked. "We do not want to re-create the past. That is ended. For better or worse those times are gone. We do not want to overthrow our state but merely to improve it. We must see to it that decent Germans obtain important positions."

There was instantly a new atmosphere in the room as though he had struck a tuning fork and they were responding to the vibrations. Decent Germans. The code name for the old-line Nazis and those who followed them, however secretly and differently today.

"We accept the rules of the democratic game," he said to his increasingly inspired audience. "But we want to make this game a little better by giving more authority to the people in positions of authority."

He paused again. The older heads were nodding vigorously now. Authority.

"Our enemy is anything and everything that divides German from German," he said, allowing for the first time some ringing in his voice. "We are not trying to give comfort to the old National Socialists. They have done their jobs. Nevertheless, while accepting the fact that many of the tenets of National Socialism are to be respected, we have no sympathy for political persecution. We are against a police state. We are for justice. We cannot have dictatorship."

The response to that was just a little slow, but the applause came at last.

"There is just one thing more I wish to say, my good friends. When the war ended, we were a country that had been leveled to the ground. Our industrial plant was demolished, and another country, perhaps, would have been forced by circumstances to become a rural, pastoral, agricultural country, as some influential persons among the victors desired us to do.

"But all this destruction proved a blessing in disguise. America poured four billions of dollars into making Germany again self-sustaining and being the kind of people we are we used this money well and built new factories on top of the ruins of the old. The result, my friends? Today West Germany has the most modern plant in Europe. Our exports are booming. Our standard of living is higher than any of our neighbors. It might be said, my very good friends, that despite our temporary agonies, Adolf Hitler won his war."

There was a taut, almost shocked silence and then a burst of applause, and Hausmann was interested to see that for the first time many of the men and women rose to their feet as they clapped. The old name, used intelligently, still had magic.

He waited, his head lowered chastely, for the applause to subside and for the people to resume their seats. When the auditorium once again was quiet he raised sincere eyes and spoke in a sincere voice.

"But along with this economic success we have had a spiritual malaise, a national feeling of guilt. We have gone to the length of expunging the years of the Third Reich from our biographies, from our histories—even from our minds. This must not continue. We must think of the good and the bad but we must think. We cannot simply turn our minds away and pretend those years never existed. They did exist, for better or worse, and every one of us in Germany has to one degree or another been shaped, affected, modified by the Third Reich. We would be quite different people today if it were not for those years.

"So I say to you, my good friends, do not be afraid to face the truth. Try to lose that sense of guilt that has been imposed upon us for having done nothing more than love our country —for having wanted to defend it against its enemies. Be

248

proud of the past, not just the twelve years of the Third Reich, but the whole past of our country. Be proud of the German past and be proud of today and have strength and courage and faith—faith more than all else—for the future. I thank you."

The room sprang to its feet in an explosion of applause and cheers. Men and women pushed down the aisles to congratulate him, to become part of him. Many of the women were misty-eyed and not a few under their high-crowned Tyrolean hats were weeping openly. Some women and some stolid men as well reached up to touch his hand or some part of his clothing.

He looked over the heads of the people, making appropriate, modest answers to the spate of emotion he had released, and he saw his sister still waiting and when he was able at last, he made his way through the last of the people, shaking hands, allowing himself to be touched, to where she was standing.

He clasped her in his arms. He was a little drunk on his own words and how his listeners had received them. He felt filled with power. He felt nothing was beyond him.

"What an unexpected pleasure, Liesl," he said. "To know that you finally are becoming interested in my politics."

"I did not come here about politics," she said.

28

✠ ✠ ✠

SURELY THE HOUSE MEANT SOMETHING. SURELY IT WAS MORE
than now and what he felt now. It was not that the house was
familiar, not in the sense he could actually remember having
been there, and yet he knew that sometime back he must
have been there, that was what he was feeling, not just what
he had learned.

How long was it he had been standing in this fresh, soft
German evening, in this old, comfortable German neighborhood? How long had he stood gazing across the street at the
dwelling of Arthur Hausmann?

It was a solid, sturdy, middle-class house, a house that was
substantial and not too stylish, not stylish at all, style was bad
taste. It was not splendid. It took quiet satisfaction in the
similarly substantial brick blocks on either side of it. It was
the home of a reasonably wealthy German who did not want
to make any issue of his wealth or success.

How long had he been standing there?

His first instinct upon reading Axmann's letter was not to
move, to stay behind his double-locked door until train time,

and then to get away, to get out, to leave it all behind, all the things he hated and loved and remembered and wanted to forget, to get out, to get away, out of Würzburg and out of Germany.

There must be more than one Hausmann, he thought. It did not have to be her father, Werner Hausmann's father. It was not an uncommon name. It could be anybody.

He stared at the telephone book in the room for a long time before he brought himself to pick it up and open it. There was more than one Hausmann. There were three. There was an A. Hausmann, listed as a butcher. There was Arthur Hausmann. There was Werner Hausmann.

He sat there and resolved he would remain until it was time to go to the railroad station and he had telephoned down and had asked the bell captain to have a taxi for him at that time and that proved he was not going to leave the room, and the room got too small and he started to smother, the air was turned off, and he rushed out and went to the river in the summer afternoon and he sucked in the river air and he walked along the quay and he told himself he would have to get back to the hotel pretty soon now, it was getting close to train time and the taxi would be waiting and he walked and then it was dark and he was there, where he knew he was going to be, there on the street with the little curve in it and the houses with low lights on inside now and the stillness and the occasional passers-by who spoke in low voices in this prosperous German residential area and who glanced at him incuriously and then went on.

He started across the street. He did not know what time it was. It did not matter. He did not trust time any more, not time here, not time in Germany. Time moved or didn't move, to suit itself, a life of its own, and he didn't trust it.

He walked up to the front door and he did not hesitate. He rang the bell without delay, as though he had an appointment there and this was the moment of the appointment.

An elderly woman, the maid, answered his ring, and then excused herself and went away while he waited calmly in the foyer and then she returned and nodded and led him into a room where a small, fragile man was seated in a leather chair.

The old man looked up. "Sit down, Herr Bauer. I have been expecting you."

In the yellow light from the lamp in the library Arthur Hausmann's face appeared embalmed. Old-fashioned reading glasses hung from his neck on a black silk ribbon. Although the night was not cold there was a rug on his lap.

"Can I offer you something, Herr Bauer?" Hausmann asked. "A drink of some kind?"

"No, thank you."

Hausmann nodded. "You may leave, Frau Koch," he said to the maid.

When they were alone, Hausmann folded his hands on his lap and waited silently.

He was not going to say anything first, Bauer knew. He was passed, the way Father Stolz was passed, his body alone lent for a little more time, and he had gone too far to start anything for anyone.

"Do you know why I am here?" Bauer asked.

"Of course," Hausmann said placidly. "I have said I expected you."

"I almost did not come."

Hausmann shook his head slowly. "You could not have avoided it. It is the same for both of us. I have been expecting you for many years. It might be said you have kept me alive."

Bauer said nothing.

"From time to time I thought perhaps I would die before you finally got here," Hausmann said. "But I knew I could not. We have had our own appointment in Samarra and the appointment had to be kept."

Hausmann looked at him directly for the first time. His eyes were alive in his face, but that was almost all. It was as though his body had been sustained for this, for this alone.

"Tell me," Bauer said. "Tell me what happened."

"Certainly."

"My mother entrusted you with the painting. I know that much."

"The painting, yes. The Tiepolo. I cannot return it to you. I do not have it."

"I am not interested in the painting," Bauer said.

Hausmann nodded. "Of course not. But it was not because of the painting. For a long time I believed it was because of the painting because I wanted the painting very much and I had wanted it for a long time. But it was not because of the painting."

"What was not because of the painting, Herr Hausmann?"

Hausmann picked up a small cigar he had allowed to expire in the ashtray and he considered relighting it and decided against it.

"What was not because of the painting?" Bauer asked.

"It was simple to think that at first. Greed. Pure greed. I told that to myself. Although perhaps love of a beautiful painting is a special kind of greed that is just a little bit less distasteful."

"Please, Herr Hausmann, tell me what happened." Bauer wondered why he felt nothing; he felt nothing and he felt nothing against this frail old person. He now was about to have the last door opened to him and he should have felt something but he felt nothing.

"That goes back a very long way. That would take a very long time."

"From the night my mother went to you, the night she was supposed to leave Germany and did not."

"Your mother came to me. It was fitting that she should do so. We knew each other very well." Hausmann closed his eyes. "We knew each other very well."

His hands lay on the rug on his lap like pieces of yellowed celluloid, the hands of a large doll, not quite life-size, hollow and empty. If he breathed on them, Bauer thought, they would float away.

Hausmann sat up a little straighter. "She told me she was going to be smuggled out of Germany, to Switzerland. I asked her who was going to perform this dangerous act but she told

253

me she was sworn to secrecy. It was not correct that your mother should not have trust in me. We had been friends for a long time."

Bauer remained silent but he felt something quickening within him. He could after all feel.

"She asked me if I would keep the Tiepolo for her," Hausmann said. "It had been your father's favorite painting. She thought that one day when things were different she would return to Würzburg and she wanted to know the Tiepolo was safe."

Some color had risen in Hausmann's face and he looked less breakable.

"What was it?" he asked, of himself. "I cannot say. You see, I loved your mother. At one time we had been betrothed. It was before she met your father. She broke off the engagement. It was a scandal. It was a very difficult time for me. Everybody was kind, of course. There were even those who said I was fortunate, that being married to a Jewess was not quite correct. But despite all that I was embarrassed to a degree I cannot explain. To this day I remember the feeling, that everybody, on the street, in homes where I visited, was laughing at me because your mother had discarded me."

"Yes, it must have been hell," Bauer said.

Hausmann looked at him closely. "It was hell," he said. "It was just that, Herr Bauer, hell." He pulled the rug a little higher as though hell, as he remembered it, was cold. "I married soon afterward and my marriage was not a bad marriage but for many years afterward when I met your mother, at the opera, at the theater, at a dinner, I still felt people were whispering to each other that there was Hedwig Bauer and there was Arthur Hausmann and that one time they had been in love and that she had jilted him." He breathed out, a tiny wisp of air. "Was that it? Was that it, Herr Bauer? I asked myself that question for such a long time. I didn't want to think it, but I thought it, that in the end she was being made to pay for her cavalier treatment of me."

"And all the other Jews being made to pay for that too? Your vanity came high, Herr Hausmann."

254

"I didn't think of any other Jew. Only the one Jew."

"And you felt satisfaction."

"No."

"You should have."

After a while Hausmann continued. "She gave the painting to me. I promised I would hide it for her. She thanked me. She left."

Go, Bauer told himself. Just get up and go. "And then?"

"And then I called the Gestapo."

After a very long moment Bauer let out a cry and he jumped up and grabbed the lapels of Hausmann's coat and he lifted him from the seat and held him close enough to get the stale cigar smell from his mouth and to feel the distant beating of his heart.

The old man made no resistance. He looked at Bauer, his eyes only inches away. "You may well want to kill me," he said.

He was very light. It was as though Bauer were holding an old suit of clothes stuffed perhaps with nothing more than rags.

"It would not take very much, Herr Bauer."

Bauer lowered him carefully, almost with a tenderness.

"There is nothing inside, yes?" Hausmann said. "There has not been for many years."

Bauer rearranged the blanket on Hausmann's lap. He sat down. His hands hurt with the ache of an arthritic. "What happened next?"

"I tried for so long to work it out to my own satisfaction," Hausmann said. "I am a trained lawyer and my mind works logically. For so long I have asked myself was it greed or the sense of having been rejected? For so long I have wanted to know was it the painting or was it that I could not forgive her."

"What happened?"

"I have even wondered whether it was a mixture of both."

"Finish! For the love of God, finish."

Hausmann looked at him pityingly. "Patience, Herr Bauer. I have had to learn patience and so must you. You see, you have brought me the answer. All these long years I could not find it and tonight you have brought it to me. You see, Herr Bauer, I know now that it was more than either of those two things, that it was in fact neither of them. I know now that it was just that I was still in love with your mother. It was quite simple but I did not know that until tonight."

"God in heaven," Bauer whispered.

"Yes, perhaps He is."

"And the end of it?"

"I realize tonight that if she had asked me I would have left with her. Isn't that incredible? I know now I would have given up everything—my marriage, my practice, my position—to have gone with her. I believe I have known that all along, from the start, but I have not been able to admit it until you gave me that wisdom tonight. You see, Herr Bauer, that is why I telephoned the Gestapo. Because after all those years of having lost her, after all that happened to both of us, I still was in her power."

Bauer waited. "Please finish."

"There is nothing more. The Gestapo went to your house. They arrested your mother. They took her to Theresienstadt."

"And there she remained."

"And there she remained."

"And there she was put to death."

"And there she was put to death."

"And you stayed here with the painting she gave you because she trusted you as a friend and because you once had loved each other, and you did nothing."

"I had already done, Herr Bauer. After what I had done there was nothing more that could be done. And nothing could be undone. Not then."

"Do you know how long she was there before she died?"

"Such information was not made public."

After a moment Bauer rose to his feet. "This must have been painful for you. Thank you for telling me what you have."

"It is I who thank you," Hausmann said. His voice sounded tired but somehow curiously victorious. "I have unburdened myself. And I have done you no service. I have laid upon you what for all these years has lain upon me." He looked up. His eyes were sharp. "You see, Herr Bauer, one is conditioned and one may not escape that conditioning. There can be no expiation man can make to man and yet one is still victim to one's weakness. Even at my age one lightens the load."

Bauer said, "I can see myself out."

"Just one more thing. Are you not interested to know the ultimate fate of the Tiepolo?"

"No."

"But you must know. It is the final knot on the string."

Bauer waited.

"It was less than a week later when men came to my door and demanded that I give them the painting. They had action commandos in those days collecting art for the important men, Göring, Göbbels, even Hitler. It was fashionable to show an appreciation of art. Even that little Tiepolo. And in this small, obscure city. They heard about it and they tracked it down and they came here and collected it."

"I'm sure my mother would have been annoyed to have known that."

"Yes. I am certain she would."

Bauer started for the door.

"Herr Bauer."

He paused and turned his head. He was startled at what he saw. He knew he should not have been, that he should have expected exactly that, but the intensity of what he now beheld startled him.

He saw in Hausmann's face the German arrogance of total victory. The body was a frail shell and the skin of the face looked as though it had no more depth than tissue paper but the eyes were animal bright, fox bright, and very sharp and very clear and were filled with success and the mouth was turned up in shrewd and satisfied appreciation of that success.

"I would not have believed it," Hausmann said with exquisite exultation, having in the end won at last. His voice was pure and powerful. "You have given me succor."

"I am happy to hear that," Bauer said.

257

He left the house. The night was quiet. Now almost all the lights in the other homes had been extinguished. He started for the hotel. He did not feel anything after the blow on the back of his head, not the cloak that was thrown over him, not the arms that lifted him into the automobile, not the low voices nor the motion of the car as it was driven unhurriedly away.

29

✠ ✠ ✠

THE BROKEN STAINED-GLASS WINDOW CAME TO A POINT stabbing the dark sky, a point on which a star rested as an ornament. In the night the colors of the glass were somber and here and there the broken leading went off at angles like small, tentative branches of a growing tree.

One half of the church was gone; one whole wall, part of the ceiling where the wall had stood was open to the darkness. The destroyed wall had been shored with lumber and earth part of the way up to where the sloping ceiling had been.

The rear of the church was a mangled clutter of what had been pews, holy fonts, doors, statues. There were no craters as from a bomb. The destruction was that of fire.

All of this Bauer saw bit by bit in murky chiaroscuro as he opened his eyes, feeling at the same time a dull pain in his head, realizing when he tried to touch his head that his arms were bound and that he was bound to the chair on which he was seated.

He tried to bring his eyes and his senses into focus and he heard Werner Hausmann ask in his polished, cultivated baritone, "It's a mess, isn't it, Herr Bauer?"

Bauer turned his eyes away from the burned-out church, which he had been positioned to see when he regained consciousness, and looked toward the voice, feeling new pain when he twisted his head. He saw in the spotty lighting Hausmann sprawled on a chair. Near him were a dozen or more young men, seated circumspectly, straight in their chairs, as though at a business meeting.

They were all just under or just over thirty years of age and they could have been British as easily as Germans, or French or any other upper middle-class European. They were bright-looking, serious young men who might have been rising computer experts or young insurance executives.

The lighting came, he saw as his eyes became accustomed to it, from a number of carbide lamps scattered around the devastated church. One of the lamps hung from the partly broken crossbeam of the life-size crucifix. The image of Christ had been removed and the crucifix looked bare and abandoned in the bluish lantern light.

"We thought you might be interested to see at first hand the kind of present you gave to us, Herr Bauer," Hausmann said placidly. "Most of our native city has been rebuilt so that until now you perhaps have not obtained a correct impression. This little church has been left unrepaired from the night of the firestorm. A sort of memorial, one might say. One would have hardly dared to hope one would have had the honor to bring here a person who helped create this memorial."

How had they found that out?

Hausmann uncrossed and recrossed his legs. His shoes gleamed in the uneven spectral lighting.

"This was probably one of the most lightly damaged of places, Herr Bauer. In most instances there was nothing left, nothing but holes in the ground, many of them filled with human bodies, or what had been human bodies."

Bauer tried to pull his hands free. He tried to pull away from the chair. "Hausmann, you muddle-assed bastard!"

"Why was Würzburg bombed?" one of the young men asked.

260

"This is my colleague, Herr Gerhard Ullrich," Hausmann said, in the clublike manner of introducing one gentleman to another.

Bauer looked at Ullrich. One of the lamps was on the floor, not far away from him, and his face was lighted on a slant from below. He was a skinny man, with bony, intense features. He wore horn-rimmed glasses and the shadow from his long, thin nose made a distorted, living triangle on the cheek away from the lamp.

"Would you care to answer Herr Ulrich?" Hausmann inquired.

"Go to hell," Bauer said. "Untie these damned ropes."

"Answer him," Hausmann said.

"Bombing Würzburg was an act of war."

He didn't know why he answered. He didn't know why he didn't shout out. Was it because he was frightened? Or was it because he knew it would mean nothing, and because he couldn't give them that?

Ullrich corrected him almost pedantically, a teacher setting straight a misinformed pupil. "An act of atrocity," he said. He had a high-pitched voice, the other kind of German voice, the voice opposed to the deep, velarized German voice. "There was nothing in Würzburg to justify bombing, even by the barbarous British and Americans, nothing, no industry of any kind, nothing of military value. It was intended to stampede the people into ending the war."

Having finished his brief, explanatory peroration, Ullrich sat back and the elements of his face changed in the changed light and he became someone else.

"Then it had a military purpose," Bauer said.

"Don't be tricky, Herr Bauer," Hausmann said. "You people are known to be tricky. Don't be tricky."

Bauer felt the thing moving in him again.

"I'm not being anything, Hausmann," he said. "I don't have to be anything. I don't have to make answer to you or anybody else. This isn't a court of law. I am not on trial."

"Perhaps not," Hausmann agreed. "But only technically not."

"I'm sure you know this, Herr Hausmann," Bauer said, hoping it wasn't in his voice, wondering which was the greater fear, the fear or the fear to reveal that fear. "I'm sure that you know it but perhaps the others do not. I am an American citizen."

The old cliché. And yet.

"Oh, yes," Hausmann assured him. "That is quite well known to all of us."

"I am also an official of the State Department," Bauer said, knowing from having to say that the extent of his fear.

"Yes, we are aware of that as well," Hausmann said with a smile. "You are a long way from home."

Ullrich leaned forward again. "Admit that bombing Würzburg was an act of terror."

"Fuck off," Bauer said, without looking at him. "Hausmann, stop being a bigger bloody idiot than you are. Take off these damned ropes and let me out of here." He again tried to pull himself free.

"Answer him," Hausmann said tranquilly.

Bauer turned his eyes to Ullrich. Behind Ullrich's thick glasses was nothing but an intense, intellectual interest, nothing more personal than that. He looked at some of the other faces. They were all as totally impersonal. For some reason that intensified his fear.

He said, "Würzburg was the last link in a chain that was built, link by link, when the Stukas first dive-bombed people in Poland."

He was surprised to see one of the young men, a fresh-faced youth with apple cheeks and blue, untroubled eyes, was putting down what he was saying on a yellow, legal-size pad, and he could see from the short, jerky movements of the young man's hand that he was putting down the words in shorthand, his head bent down, his forehead puckered in concentration, a bit of his tongue sticking out of the corner of his mouth as might a child's.

"May I ask Herr Bauer a question?" another of the young men asked civilly.

"Of course, Hans," Hausmann said. To Bauer he pointed out, "We are democratic."

"If Herr Ullrich's analysis is incorrect, as you suggest, Herr Bauer, could you tell me for exactly what military reason Würzburg was bombed?"

Hans was an intelligent-looking youth with fine, fair hair. He too had a pencil and paper. He might have been a newspaper reporter.

"I have no idea," Bauer said. Why were the words being put down? Who was going to read them afterward? After what? He felt it coiling inside of him.

"But you did participate in the bombing, Herr Bauer," Hans said.

"Würzburg was scheduled for bombing," Bauer said, feeling more and more the inverse insanity, the quiet interrogation. "I had no voice in that decision."

Was he copping a plea? Would it help? Where was their anger? He would have felt less disoriented with anger.

"Of course you could not have," Hausmann said easily. "What was your rank, Herr Bauer?"

"Leading aircraftsman."

"I am unfamiliar with that designation but I would guess the rank was not very high," Hausmann said.

"The lowest," Bauer said. Another copout?

"There, you see, Hans, Herr Bauer could have had absolutely nothing to do with the decision to bomb our city. Our city and his city. That decision was made on an exalted, policy level. Correct, Herr Bauer?"

"Yes." Was it only that or did it have to do with Arthur Hausmann too?

"Additionally, you must have been very young," Hausmann said. "How old were you then?"

"Sixteen," Bauer said, not sensing the trap.

"Sixteen," Hausmann said, nodding slowly. "Sixteen. You were quite young."

"Yes," Bauer said, wondering why Hausmann seemed to be suggesting an out, an excuse, extenuating circumstances. Per-

263

haps he was blowing things out of proportion. Perhaps his peril was not as great as his belly was telling him.

"Sixteen," Hausmann said again. "Herr Bauer was only sixteen at the time." He said softly, "I didn't know the RAF accepted men of that tender age."

Now Bauer knew and his stomach knotted.

"Did they draft sixteen-year-olds in Britain?" Ullrich asked, and his voice was as silky as Hausmann's.

"No," Bauer said. It was too late.

"Then how did it happen they drafted you, Herr Bauer?" Hans asked, looking up from his note pad.

"They did not draft me." It was much too late and the trap had been set in front of him and he had not seen it.

"You are saying then that you volunteered?" Hausmann asked.

"Yes."

"You must also have lied about your age," Hausmann said.

"Yes."

"You volunteered and you lied about your age to make it possible for you to destroy a part of Germany," Hausmann said.

"Yes."

"That part where you were born."

"Yes."

Hausmann sat back. None of the men reacted. None of them showed a sign of anything. They might have just heard the outcome of a sporting event in which they had no interest.

What was it in this detachment that terrified him more than anything else?

He strained at the ropes. He couldn't move. He couldn't feel his arms. He couldn't feel his legs. The numbness. The ropes. Or fear?

The church was utterly still. He was suddenly aware of the fact that he had heard nothing outside the building, no traffic, no sound of any kind. Where was this church?

It would do no good to yell out. They'd anticipated all of that. And they could stop that soon enough.

"Well, gentlemen, I believe we have all the necessary facts

264

in hand," Hausmann said genially, taking out his cigarette case for the first time, as though he had disciplined himself not to smoke during the trial but that now he might since the testimony was taken and the verdict was in.

He tapped the cigarette on the back of his hand and lit it. Several of the others lit cigarettes and three or four of the young men took out pipes and pouches of tobacco. Everybody was pleasantly relaxed.

The lighters and matches were struck, making bright pinpoints in the shadowed circumfusion of light. Smoke drifted up and vanished.

"We all have to go to work tomorrow," Hausmann said, having drawn with appreciation on his cigarette. "We mustn't make this too late a night."

Two of the young men rose immediately and went over to Bauer and untied his bonds and got behind him and lifted him to his feet. His legs were paralyzed and he would have fallen had they not held him.

"You would have been wiser, Herr Bauer, to have listened to Herr Eckardt, after the first time," Hausmann said. "And you would have been even wiser if you had stayed away from my father."

He appeared to be on the point of saying more, and then he stopped.

His sister, Bauer asked himself. Was that also one of the counts in his indictment?

Hausmann looked at the men. "Kurt, you will be the first," he said. "You appear to have more difficulty than the others in this."

The young man with the apple cheeks, who had by then collected his tongue into his mouth, put down his pencil and pad with the shorthand hen-tracks and walked slowly to Bauer.

When he got close enough Bauer saw his eyes were not untroubled.

"Very well, Kurt," Hausmann said.

Kurt gazed at Bauer.

"Hausmann, for God's sake," Bauer said.

265

"Kurt," Hausmann said without raising his voice.

"Hausmann!" Bauer called out.

"Kurt, how many members of your family perished in the firestorm?" Ullrich asked.

The young man shivered and he brought his knee up hard into Bauer's groin. Bauer gasped and he would have doubled up if the hands had not held him immobile.

"There, Kurt, that was not too bad, was it?" Hausmann asked affably.

Kurt held his lips between his teeth.

"Try it again, Kurt," Hausmann said.

"Hausmann, you son of a bitch! Stop this!" Bauer said, his voice hoarse with the pain.

"You do not even remember your parents, Kurt," Ullrich said. "You were too young when they were burned to death."

Kurt stared into Bauer's eyes as though asking for something, his permission perhaps, and then he kneed him again, with more force than before.

Bauer gagged and felt the vomit surge into his throat.

"That's excellent, Kurt," Hausmann said. He now had put his feet up on another chair and he was leaned back in his ease, his cigarette smoking between his fingers. He smiled pleasantly at Bauer. "We don't believe in this kind of violence, Herr Bauer, not at all, not in the slightest. We deplore it. We are not hooligans. We are civilized, educated men who believe in law and order." He held up a hand and sighed. "Unfortunately that is not always true of those who are not in sympathy with our goals. And if there is a confrontation, you must agree we need at the very least to know how to protect ourselves."

"Albert," Ullrich said.

One of the youngest of the men, a studious-looking youth, puffing a curved briar pipe, walked to Bauer and dug his heel into Bauer's shin. Bauer let out a cry of pain.

Albert turned and looked at Ullrich, as would a student who had just written an equation on a blackboard.

"Too high," Ullrich said. "Closer to the instep for full effect."

Albert tried again. Again Bauer cried out.

"That's better, Albert," Ullrich said. "But you must practice on your dummy so that you can achieve the greatest result the first time. No," he said quickly as Albert prepared to give Bauer a third stomp. "Not again, Albert. We must preserve Herr Bauer until everyone has had the opportunity to avail themselves of him."

"Stop this, Hausmann," Bauer said. "Hausmann, you insane bastard."

"Hans," Hausmann said.

That young man put down his pencil and pad and went to Bauer and punched him in the jaw and Bauer tasted blood in his mouth.

"Good," Ullrich said.

Another youth was summoned and he buried his fist in Bauer's belly and by now Bauer could make no sound of hurt.

"Too low," Ullrich said patiently. "You must hit precisely on the solar plexus. Try again."

The youth, who was large, with thick, meaty hands, tried again.

"Much better," Ullrich said.

Another man hit Bauer on the side of his head with a small, padded cosh and Ullrich warned him not to strike too hard lest he cause death. Another young man punched Bauer in the mouth. Another man, a mellowed meerschaum between his lips, punched him in the kidney. Another stomped on his instep and another kicked him in the groin and another in the shin again and from time to time Ullrich made corrections. Bauer thought Kurt was ordered around for seconds but he could not be sure.

He was not sure of very much of anything by then. He thought the beating and the kicking and the punching had stopped, although it might simply be that he was beyond feeling, and then something was tied across his mouth and then he was being carried and then he was being lifted and a rope was tied around his chest and his wrists were tied to something and his body felt very heavy, with all the pain he could feel the heaviness, and his wrists hurt and he didn't know why that should be since he could not remember anyone hitting him there, although he wasn't sure about that either.

"Take off his shoes," he heard someone say from very far away.

"Why, Kurt, why do you ask that?" he heard Hausmann ask in the distance.

"It looks wrong with his shoes on," he heard Kurt say.

He saw the lamps were being extinguished, sensed it, he could not see very well, perhaps the lights were not being put out, perhaps it was that he was seeing less and less, and then everything was dark, or he was blind, and then everything was quiet, or he was now deaf.

In the passing time the moon rose and illuminated the church in which the young men were no longer and the pale light lay as a shroud on the figure tied to the cross, but he didn't know that, he was beyond knowing anything.

30

✠ ✠ ✠

THE WEATHER REMAINED CLEAR AND ALL THE LITTLE GIRLS
formed a ring in the grassy field in the lovely afternoon and
played a game in which another little girl inside the ring tried
to escape and could not unless she was fast asleep or clever or
very strong.

Fräulein Schneider, who was still a Fräulein at the age of
forty-three, sat under the shade of a tree and watched the
little girls play and nodded with approbation as each child
beat in vain against the arms and the bodies of her captors,
and found the climax of her pleasure at that moment of frustration when the small prisoner dissolved into tears. It was for
Fräulein Schneider the perfect application of that unique
German word, *Schadenfreude*, which meant joy in the hurt to
others.

She frowned now when little Marie Lenz, having been
trapped for several minutes, having been unable to get
through, having burst into tears, now ran away from the
group, still weeping. Fräulein Schneider hauled herself to her
feet. She was a large woman with a horsey face. She walked
over to the girls and reformed them and picked out a new

girl to be the prey and then, the game resumed, her charges laughing and shouting once more, she went to where Marie Lenz had taken herself.

There was a little stream that ran at one end of the field and Marie was standing at the edge of the water. She was a small child and there were dried tears on her cheeks. She did not look up as the teacher approached.

"Come back to the game, Marie."

"Please, Fräulein Schneider," Marie said, her eyes filling with tears.

"What will you do?"

"I'll just stay here and be quiet, I promise. Please, Fräulein Schneider."

"I know what you will do, Marie," Fräulein Schneider said in her grimmest voice. "You will stay here alone and have your fantasies. I have never known a child who makes up things the way you do. And the lies you tell! Really, I don't understand it at all. You come from such an excellent family."

Marie said nothing. She could never explain to Fräulein Schneider that sometimes she had to fib, because the things she thought about, birds, little animals, dogs, horses, flowers, even the things most grownups didn't like, like caterpillars, were sometimes so private she simply could not reveal them.

Fräulein Schneider gave forth a sigh that was close to a whinney. She had remembered in time that Marie's father was one of the wealthiest men in Würzburg and that her mother was undoubtedly a social leader. "I will allow you to stay here, Marie. But you must promise me not to have your silly daydreams."

"I promise, Fräulein Schneider."

The teacher waited a moment and then asked, "And what else, Marie?"

"Thank you, Fräulein Schneider."

Fräulein Schneider patted her on the cheek and then went back to the shade of the tree.

For a little while Marie did nothing. Despite her promise to Fräulein Schneider, which she intended solemnly to keep, she was basically a truthful child, she could not entirely control her imagination, and looking up she saw in a cloud formation a chariot and horses, and to keep her promise to the teacher she looked away and thought about what she wanted for her eleventh birthday, less than two weeks away.

Not far away she saw the ruins of the church. She had been told about that church. All the children had been told about that church by Fräulein Schneider. It had caught fire from a stray bomb during the terrible fire attack on the city.

She walked to the church. The sun was striking the stained-glass window. She wondered how the church had looked before it burned. She went inside.

She walked slowly toward what remained of the altar. The power in a church, even in a burned-out church, was greater than the power of any schoolteacher, she knew. If she asked help from this superior power it might prevent Fräulein Schneider from sending out a bad report to her father. It might do more.

She knelt in front of the crucifix and crossed herself and prayed.

"Dear Lord Jesus, please help me to be a good girl and not imagine things and not tell lies and not make Fräulein Schneider angry," she prayed. "Please, dear Lord Jesus, don't let Fräulein Schneider send a bad report to daddy. And please, dear Lord Jesus, if you have time and if it's possible, please make daddy buy me a doll house for my birthday."

She crossed herself again and she saw something wet fall on the floor in front of her. She looked closer and saw that the wet spot was red and there was a little pool of wet red and some of it had dried and caked around the edge and turned brown. She backed away and looked up. The figure on the cross was hanging in the normal way although he was not dressed the way she was used to seeing the Lord Jesus. But he was hanging there in the proper way, arms stretched out, his head on one side almost resting on his shoulder. He had a bandage across his mouth but the bandage didn't stop the blood from collecting on his lip and dripping from there to the floor.

She rose very slowly and she crossed herself again and

backed carefully out of the church and just as she was leaving she heard a sound from the figure on the cross, a low sound, not words exactly, but something, and she was filled with happiness she had never before known and she smiled back radiantly at the figure because she knew he had heard her prayer.

When she emerged from the church she saw that the game had ended and that Fräulein Schneider was looking around, probably for her. She called out joyfully and ran to the teacher and the other girls.

"Where have you been, Marie?" Fräulein Schneider demanded, gripping her by the arm.

Not even the teacher's strong hand could make her forget the experience she had just undergone. "I was in the church, Fräulein Schneider."

"You know that church is in dangerous condition and that you are forbidden to go in there," Fräulein Schneider said sharply.

Marie shook her head and smiled in her bliss. "No, Fräulein Schneider, I could not have been hurt. The Lord Jesus wouldn't let anything happen to us."

Some of the other girls started to giggle and Fräulein Schneider shook Marie angrily.

"What are you talking about!"

"He spoke to me," Marie said. "First the blood fell from His wounds and then He spoke to me. His mouth was bandaged up but He said something to me."

The girls were giggling and nudging each other. Fräulein Schneider glared at them and they tried to stop but not all of them could.

"I said a prayer right under Him," Marie said. "And then His blood dripped in front of me and when I was leaving He said something to me. I don't know exactly what He said but I knew He had heard my prayer."

Fräulein Schneider, her face now turning scarlet with anger, shook Marie violently. "You gave me your word of honor you would stop telling lies!"

"I'm not telling a lie, Fräulein Schneider," Marie said tranquilly. In her state of grace the shaking didn't bother her.

"You miserable little creature!" Fräulein Schneider boxed Marie on the ear.

The child reeled back but even the blow did not bother her. "I am not telling a lie."

Fräulein Schneider boxed her other ear. "This is too much! I am going to have to report this to your father. He'll know how to deal with you."

Marie covered both her tingling ears with her hands and shook her head so that the tears fell this way and that. She did not know why she was crying. Nobody could hurt her in any way now. She was not even afraid of what Fräulein Schneider would say to her father.

"It was bad enough before," Fräulein Schneider said, her voice turning raspy in her fury. "Up to now you lied. But now you blaspheme!"

Marie shook her head wildly. "I saw Him and I saw His blood fall on the floor and then He said something to me."

"I have half a mind to take you inside that church and prove to everyone here you have blasphemed," Fräulein Schneider said distinctly.

Some of the other girls immediately pleaded with her to do that.

She shook her head. Herr Lenz might consider that was going too far. "No," she said, waving down the pleas. "No, the church is unsafe. I cannot take the risk."

She quieted all the children and said, "All right, girls, let us form two lines. Let us sing our school song as we march to the bus stop. Ready, now, we'll sing when I give the command, let us march, one, two, one, two."

The girl marching next to Marie hissed, "Liar."

Marie bit her lips and said nothing. Her good feeling was beginning to go away and she was beginning to wonder if she had really seen the Lord Jesus and whether He had really said something to her.

"Let us now sing," Fräulein Schneider, now in her place at the head of the line, called out. She opened her mouth and burst into music.

The formation passed the church and the lead element now was nearing the highway. The song, which consisted of only one stanza, composed by Fräulein Schneider, ended. Fräulein Schneider strode manfully, arms swinging, one flat-heeled thick-soled shoe placed purposefully in front of the other.

"Liar," the girl behind Marie sang out. "Liar. Marie is a liar."

The other girls around Marie took up the refrain. "Marie is a liar, Marie is a liar . . ."

Marie tried to explain but no one would bother to listen to her. She tried to contain the tears that again flooded her eyes but she could not. She fled back to the church.

The girls yelled, "Fräulein Schneider! Fräulein Schneider!"

Fräulein Schneider, caught in mid-breath, whipped round her head. She exhaled noisily, "Marie!" she roared. "Marie! You come back here!"

She ran after the child. "Marie! Don't you dare go back into that building! Marie!"

The other girls, chortling happily, broke formation and followed.

Marie disappeared into the church. A few moments later Fräulein Schneider entered the destroyed building. Streaming in behind her were all the girls.

Marie was kneeling under the cross. Her hands were clasped in prayer. "They said that I told a lie, Lord Jesus," she whispered. "No one would believe me."

"Marie!" Fräulein Schneider said.

One of the older girls screamed. Fräulein Schneider looked up at the cross and toppled in a dead faint.

31

✠ ✠ ✠

POLICE PRESIDENT ECKARDT HAD NOW ACQUIRED AN IMITATION cigarette that glowed at the end when he drew on it. He stood at the end of the hospital bed, gripping the white-painted iron footstead, and he pulled on the metal tube which lit up his face and then flickered out like the illuminated nose of a circus clown.

"You're fortunate they were content merely to tie you up there," he said, looking at Bauer with very little pleasure.

"Somebody just forgot to bring the hammer and nails," Bauer said.

"Very funny, Herr Bauer. I never realized you could be such a funny man. The question, Herr Bauer, is what do we do now?"

Bauer, his head bandaged and still in pain, could not follow Eckardt's restless movements. He contented himself with staring at the ceiling. "Is there a question, Herr Eckardt? I have given you the names and descriptions of at least five of them."

Eckardt paused and contemplated him sourly. "There is still what might be characterized as a question, Herr Bauer."

"Of course," Bauer said. "I almost forgot. We're in Germany." He closed his eyes and wished Eckardt would go.

"Let's sum up the situation," Eckardt said. "You were kidnapped by Werner Hausmann and some of his thugs."

"He denies they're thugs," Bauer said. "He is very clear about that."

"Yes, I know. The new style. In any case he sits in judgment on you, has you severely beaten, and then in the most execrable taste ties you onto a crucifix and leaves you there to die." He stood still and faced Bauer, blinking on and off like a tiny warning light. "Did he happen to mention to you why he did that—the cross, I mean?"

"If he did, Herr Police President, it escaped me."

"Have you formed your own opinion?"

"I suppose it was because the cross was there and I happened to be the only Jew around."

"Hmm," Eckardt said.

"How the hell would I know why Hausmann is crazy? Why don't you ask him?"

"Hmm," Eckardt said.

"I'm very tired, Herr Police President, could we continue this some other time?"

"No," Eckardt said.

"I could call the nurse."

"You pointed out yourself, Herr Bauer, that we are in Germany. And I am the head of the police." He resumed, "Now, according to the medical opinion here, if that child had not stumbled upon you, if you had remained where you were for another thirty-six hours, possibly less, you would have died. That was three weeks ago. You now are convalescing and the opinion here is that you will live. It is my duty to ask you officially whether you desire to press charges against your assailants. I could issue warrants for their arrest without your cooperation, but in that event the chances for conviction would be reduced considerably, if not eliminated altogether."

"I thought I made my position clear when I identified the men for you," Bauer said.

Eckardt shook his head patiently. "It's not quite so simple and there are certain things I must point out to you. I have watched Werner Hausmann and his followers for some little time now. I am quite certain in my own mind that they have committed several capital crimes here but I have never had the evidence to prove it."

"I would think not," Bauer said. "Not a man with his talents."

Eckardt ignored that. "He does not in the least fool me with his modern dress and modern words and those elegant manners. He is just as much a thug as any Brownshirt who dirtied the streets in the '20s and '30s. He's just cut his sail to the new wind. But he still appeals to the basest instincts in Germans. I don't consider this a uniquely German phenomenon. There are Hausmanns of one kind or another in every country of the world, including the one you have adopted for your own. There is however one thing that makes Werner Hausmann different from anyone else anywhere—it did happen here. And that hangs over all of us, a dangling sword, and I am sworn to see it does not happen again."

"Would you mind removing that thing from your mouth," Bauer said wearily. "Then perhaps I could take you more seriously."

Eckardt said in a flat, even voice, "Herr Bauer, it doesn't make the slightest difference how you take me or if you take me at all. You have been a God damned nuisance since you arrived here. You brought about the deaths of two Germans. I'm convinced of that. Now the only thing I can salvage out of this is to nail down Hausmann and some of those other pricks who think he's God. I want that even more than I want to see the last of you."

Eckardt, whose face had flushed slightly, was about to continue when the door opened and a sister entered the room. She took Bauer's temperature and pulse and marked it down on a chart and left the room without saying a word. Eckardt gazed out of the window and when he heard the door close he turned back to Bauer.

"You must know what you face," he said as though there

had been no interruption. "Werner Hausmann is a well-known, popular young man and a rising political leader with some devoted adherents."

"And I am a runaway Jew," Bauer said.

"For Christ sake get off that!" Eckardt said. He pulled the toy out of his mouth and jammed it into his pocket. When he spoke again it was calmly. "That is only the least of your sins, Herr Bauer. Although with some of our judges, who are the same judges who were judges then, that might be quite enough. But there is on your record something even more damaging."

"The fire raid."

"Yes, Herr Bauer, the fire raid. It would undoubtedly be brought out in court that you were involved in that bombing. Your life would be even more endangered. And that danger would come from a great many more people, people who don't give a damn one way or another about Werner Hausmann."

"Is my involvement in the raid still secret?" Bauer asked in surprise.

"To the general public, yes."

"You mean nobody around here is interested in the fact that a man was half beaten to death and was then left to die?" Bauer asked harshly. "And why it was done?"

"Nobody knows."

"The newspapers didn't bother to print anything? Not even with the business on the cross? This kind of fun and games is that ordinary in Germany?"

"Everything has been kept out of the papers."

"By whom? By Hausmann? He has that influence?"

"By me."

Bauer struggled to raise himself a little so he could see Eckardt better. The police official made no move to help him.

"You are registered here under a false name," Eckardt said. "Your luggage has been collected from the hotel. As far as anybody is concerned you've just left town. Even Hausmann doesn't know what has happened to you."

"Herr Eckardt, I didn't at all appreciate what was done

to me and I have an inborn dislike of any newspaper publicity. But as a point of interest, why did you keep this whole affair a secret?" He eyed Eckardt bitterly and fell back on the pillow. "I know. You're afraid of Hausmann. Jesus, the old stink. And were you also thinking about your precious tourists?"

Eckardt took a real pack of cigarettes from a pocket. He put one between his lips. He did not light it.

"It may come as a surprise to you, but in keeping what happened to you secret I had not Werner Hausmann's interest in mind, but yours."

"I'm touched, Herr Police President."

"Your interest alone."

"I'm deeply touched, Herr Police President."

"God damn it, Herr Bauer!"

"Yes, God damn it!" Again Bauer labored to lift himself. His head was ringing. "I gave you the information almost a week ago. You acted very excited, I remember. And here you are today, still debating whether to take action, sounding as pious as a saint about keeping this damned country clean, and at the same time scaring the hell out of me about the risks I'd be taking, and also managing to see to it that the good name of Werner Hausmann is in no way contaminated —and finally wrapping up the whole fucking lie as a favor you're doing for me. You're full of shit, Herr Police President, you're all full of shit, and the shit stinks worse now than it did when your sainted Adolf was hand-feeding it to all of you and you were swallowing it and asking for more. Now, just go away. Just leave me in peace. As soon as they discharge me I'll go, really go this time, and then your problems with me will be over, once and for all."

"Herr Bauer," Eckardt said.

Bauer fell back. "Just go."

"Herr Bauer."

"Just go, Herr Police President, you make me sick."

"Are you quite finished?"

"In the name of God, go."

Eckardt took the cigarette out of his mouth and studied it.

He dropped it on the floor and ground it carefully under his heel.

"It was my duty to inform you of the risk you will be taking, Herr Bauer," he said tonelessly. "I will give you all the protection I can. There is a police officer on duty around the clock outside your room now. But you still will be in jeopardy. It is my duty to so inform you and it it is my duty to ask you whether you are prepared to testify personally against these men."

Eckardt placed his big hands around the iron end of the bed again. He slowly, gently, closed his fingers.

"I might add, Herr Bauer, that I urge you to do so. I might add also that if I had to accept in advance the loss of your life as the price of putting Hausmann and his gang out of business I would pay that price."

32

✠ ✠ ✠

THE PRESENT DISTRICT ATTORNEY FOR THE AREA WAS A TALL, imposing man with a fine mane of white hair. Old friends could recall when the hair was cropped close, but *Staatsanwalt* Hans-Gunther Uhlig was an intelligent and adaptable man.

He sat now in his deep, padded swivel chair, turned away from his leather-covered desk, his plump, pink face distressed, his handsome, manicured hands making a small, unhappy arch. Looking at the wall, covered with framed proofs of the honors bestowed upon him in his brilliant career, certificates, degrees, diplomas, photographs of famous men, all attestations to indefatigable and incorruptible service to the state, to law, and to the people, he mulled over the unwanted information which had just been presented to him.

He found no answer on the wall. He said, "This is highly irregular, Herr Police President."

Eckardt, perched on the edge of the desk, was not astounded. "Delicate perhaps, Herr Uhlig. I will grant you delicate. But in what way irregular?"

Herr Uhlig swung around slowly. He surveyed his desk,

sprinkled with mementoes, but he received no guidance from them either. "Why must we bother with this, Herr Eckardt? Who is this man, Bauer? He's not a citizen of this city. We owe him no responsibility for more reasons than one. When he recovers he will leave, we will continue to keep the whole affair quiet, and that will be the end of it."

"He was at the point of making that very decision," Eckardt said.

Uhlig held up his hands and smiled in relief. "Then there is after all no problem."

"That's not quite true, Herr District Attorney."

"Oh, I'm sure you could persuade him. I'm absolutely positive of it."

"I'm afraid that would be difficult."

"In what way? Herr Eckardt, you are a most convincing man."

"I'm aware of that. It was I who urged him to bring charges against these criminals."

Herr Uhlig was too experienced a solicitor to disclose the incredulity and downright disgust that he felt. He reached over to a large silver cigar box which had been given him to celebrate something, opened it, read the encomium on the inside of the lid, found that clueless as well. He selected a small cigar, taking a great deal of time about it although all the cigars in the box were identical.

When he had it burning to his satisfaction, he asked, "And why did you do that, Herr Eckardt?"

"A man was assaulted and but for chance would have died. That is a crime. We are sworn to uphold the law."

"You state the obvious, Herr Police President. We both know what our duties are."

"Good," Eckardt said heartily, sliding off the desk. "Then I will issue a warrant for the arrest of the men immediately."

"Please, please, don't be so precipitous!" Uhlig said. He coughed. "Let us try to examine the entire situation intelligently."

Eckardt sat down again, on a chair now, sufficiently removed from Uhlig so that he would not be agonized by the smell of cigar smoke.

The district attorney stood up and began to wander slowly around the room, pausing now and then to straighten something hanging crooked on a wall. He had presence and dignity and he spoke in a quiet, authoritative voice, reviewing the events from their beginning. Eckardt listened patiently.

In finishing, Herr Uhlig said, in a kind of peroration, "It might actually be argued that, in refusing to allow this Peter Bauer to prefer his charges, we are in fact protecting him against further injury, possibly death."

"That is an excellent reason not to proceed," Eckardt said.

Herr Uhlig paused in his ambling around the countryside of his vocation and turned to Eckardt with his famous broad, dazzling smile. "I am delighted to find you in agreement, Herr Police President." He had had faith in himself in his ability to change Eckardt's mind, but had not dared to hope it would be this simple.

"Men commit the crime of attempted homicide and the district attorney argues that they should be permitted to remain free lest they or their friends commit a further crime on the victim," Eckardt said. "Your reasoning, Herr District Attorney, is unassailable."

Uhlig looked pained, then angry, and then full of business. "I did not realize you were being sarcastic, Herr Eckardt," he said curtly. "All right, let's have a practical look at this. What evidence do you have against Hausmann and the others?"

"Peter Bauer."

"I don't deny he was beaten," Uhlig said. "What evidence do you have that it was Hausmann and his friends?"

"We both know it was, Herr Uhlig," Eckardt said. "You know Hausmann and you know how he behaves as well as I do."

"What legal evidence do you have?"

"Bauer's testimony, for a start."

"Do you have witnesses?" Uhlig snapped.

"I'm not prepared to say."

"Ah!" Uhlig slapped his hand on the desk. "You have no witnesses. What do you have? You have the word of an enemy Jew, a man who by his own admission helped destroy this city and kill thousands of people, little children, you have only the word of this despicable traitor to pit against the word and the reputation of one of the most important citizens in Würzburg. How far do you think that would get you in any court of law?"

"I'm a policeman, not a lawyer."

"You certainly are not, Herr Eckardt," Uhlig assured him, "or else you would not have dared to come to me with something as ridiculous as this. Whatever lawyer Hausmann would hire would blow the case out the window in the first ten minutes—that is if I were so stupid as to listen to you and agree to allow the matter to get into the courtroom in the first place."

Herr Uhlig sucked in the smoke from his cigar as though it were a reward.

"You speak of witnesses, Herr District Attorney," Eckardt started.

"I most certainly do!"

"A capital offense is rarely committed in public. It is the nature of the crime to be perpetrated in private. We would not expect Werner Hausmann and his chums to beat up Bauer in front of the Residenz at high noon and then hang him from a lamppost."

"You do not amuse me," Herr Uhlig said stiffly. He studied the star sapphire on his finger.

"It is not my intention to do so, Herr Uhlig, I assure you," Eckardt said. He stood up and walked to one of the walls and peered at a photograph showing Herr Uhlig surrounded by admiring politicians. "It goes a little beyond the fact that Hausmann almost murdered Bauer."

"Are you still harping on the deaths of those other two men?"

"Yes. And possibly others."

Uhlig waved the ringed hand impatiently. "Herr Eckardt, you have developed a positive fixation about that. And you have supplied no motive whatsoever. Whatever you think of Werner Hausmann surely you do not believe him to be insane. Why would he want to kill Axmann and Reinhard? Because they had some little to do with Peter Bauer? In that case why didn't Hausmann just proceed and kill Bauer in the first place? In the end, so you say, that is what he tried to do? Why did he bother with the others?"

Eckardt studied a photograph of Herr Uhlig delivering a speech. "In the beginning it was only that Hausmann was trying to protect his father. From disgrace, surely, possibly from arrest and trial for positive cooperation with the Gestapo, possibly even for embezzlement."

"All legally arguable," Uhlig conceded. "But even if I do admit your hypothesis—to kill two innocent Germans?"

"They were not so innocent, not in Hausmann's book," Eckardt said, turning to face the state solicitor. "Axmann was an old SS man, yes, but he also was known to have smuggled dozens of Jews out of Germany, including Peter Bauer. Despite his old connections Axmann was opposed to everything Hausmann stands for—but more than that, much more than that, if it were not for Erwin Axmann there most certainly would not be a Peter Bauer here today, poking around the dirt of the past. Reinhard? Major Reinhard was a former officer in the *Wehrmacht* who brought charges against a homosexual SS *Standartenführer* who molested a young man in his command and threatened him with arrest as a spy of the underground if the boy didn't do his filthy business. Major Reinhard made his charges stick. The officer was court-martialed and cashiered. His name is Hausmann. He lives in Mainz. He is Werner Hausmann's uncle."

"Herr Eckardt," Uhlig said, "even if all this is true—"

"It is true."

"Even so, what would Hausmann's purpose be in killing those two men? At this precise time, I mean."

Eckardt walked over to the desk. "First of all, Herr District Attorney, you are judging homicide for what it is—the supreme affront of one man upon another. Werner Hausmann does not look at it that way at all. Werner Hausmann is not the modern young man he pretends to be. Werner Hausmann's code of conduct goes back twenty-five or thirty years. Murder to him is very little more than an exercise in tactics."

Uhlig looked at his polished fingernails. "That is your statement, Herr Eckardt. Nothing has as yet been proved."

"But Werner Hausmann had a purpose in killing those two men now, just now," Eckardt said. "He had a very understandable purpose. And he almost succeeded. His purpose was to get Bauer out of town before Bauer discovered who it was who had taken a priceless painting from his mother and had then called in the Gestapo to put her into a concentration camp. It would not have been very good publicity for a man with Hausmann's political ambitions—even a man with Hausmann's ideas. Especially a man with Hausmann's ideas. He has to bend over backward to sugarcoat his new Nazi philosophy. The new Nazis, Herr Uhlig, can have no personal involvement with the old Nazis. They can admire—up to a limited point—but always from a distance. What Peter Bauer could turn up would have been the kiss of death. No, Hausmann had a purpose all right. And it almost worked. I virtually ordered Bauer out of Würzburg and he was on his way out and Hausmann would have got exactly what he wanted—when that letter, that posthumous letter from Axmann arrived."

"I wish to God Axmann had never written that letter!" Herr Uhlig said fervently.

Eckardt exhaled and nodded. "Yes, Herr District Attorney, it would have made things more comfortable all around."

Uhlig stared at his desk and then his brow furrowed with a new thought and he raised his head abruptly. "Herr Eckardt, Hausmann's father—"

"Yes, Herr District Attorney."

286

"Arthur Hausmann is one of the most respected elder citizens in Würzburg."

"Yes, he is."

"He has many friends."

"In high places," Eckardt said.

"If this affair with Bauer were to come to court it is possible that Arthur Hausmann might become involved."

"It is possible."

"He is a very old man, Herr Police President."

"Yes, he's been lucky that way." The police official picked up his hat. "As is required, I have apprised you of the facts as I know them, Herr District Attorney."

Uhlig nodded glumly. "And it is my prerogative to decide whether or not to act upon them." He looked up at Eckardt as though challenging him to deny that.

"Exactly," Eckardt said. "If you make the decision not to prosecute, then I will advise Peter Bauer of his rights under present German law."

The district attorney held up his hands. "Eckardt, we have known each other a long time—"

"I will inform Bauer he has the right under the law to appeal next to the chief prosecutor in the state."

"Johannes," Uhlig said. "We have worked together so well—"

"I also will instruct Bauer that if the chief prosecutor takes the same position you do, that he has the further right under the law to present his charges before the High Court of Appeals."

Herr Uhlig lowered his hands slowly and rested them on the desk. "What makes you so determined to bring this mess into a court of law, Johannes?" he asked almost inaudibly. "And please do not speak to me about duties and responsibilities." He waited and then looked up. "You do not answer me, my old friend."

"Would the word 'honor' surprise you, Hans?" Eckardt asked.

"Honor? Not at all. We are honorable men."

"Honor, Hans, not just the word. The meaning of the word. Honor." Eckardt looked down at the unhappy face of the man he had known and had been associated with professionally for many years. "Not your honor, Hans, and not my honor. The honor of the community in which we live. Perhaps more than that. Perhaps the honor of Germany."

33

✠ ✠ ✠

THE LANDGERICHT IN WÜRZBURG IS LOCATED AT THE INTERSEC-
tion of the Sanderring and Ottostrasse just off one side of the
elaborate, sculptured garden of the Residenz.

The Sanderring here begins its short course through the
city, terminating at the Ludwigsbrücke over the Main, and
it crosses Ottostrasse at a narrow angle and the courthouse,
fitted into this pinched corner, is shaped like the head of an
arrow.

An arrow, some now say with pride, aimed at justice and
truth. An arrow, others whispered at another time, directed
aimlessly at the long and lovely park that borders the Sanderring.

The interior of the building was gutted in the fire raid,
Police President Eckardt informed Bauer as they proceeded
there in an official car, but the exterior had managed to sur-
vive the holocaust and during the reconstruction of the city
the stone and masonry were found to be sound so that all
that had to be done to bring a judicatory back to Würzburg
was to clear out the debris and build new chambers inside
the old shell. The venerable old gray building thus presented

289

to the street the same venerable old gray face it had for many decades, including the years of the Third Reich.

There was a small crowd held back by policemen outside the *Landgericht* when Bauer and Eckardt arrived. This did not surprise Bauer as he had been warned by the police president that the lawyer for Hausmann and the other defendants had spoken freely to reporters, seeking to win the earliest possible sympathy for his clients.

A policeman opened the door and helped Bauer, carrying a cane, out of the car. There was murmuring from the crowd. The remarks were all hostile and all low key. Policemen cleared the way and Bauer, with Eckardt at his side, limped toward the steps leading up to the entrance.

Bauer glanced up at the building, trying not to hear the rancorous comments; he was not that sure of himself and he could not forget where he was. He remembered the *Landgericht* vaguely from his childhood. How was he to look upon it now? As the same old place with a new set of parts? Or as new parts just making use of the old body? The old Germany or the new Germany. Or, being German, did it matter?

He climbed the stone steps painfully, still hearing the voices behind him. He had in his slow progress from the automobile heard himself referred to as a murderer, a traitor, a child-killer, and a few other things. He had not heard the word "Jew." He had heard it said by someone, somewhere, that the Jew was the most protected creature in Germany today. He could not certify that himself from his own experience as true. But, he had to admit, no one in the crowd had raised his voice. They had berated him with reserve and no one had attempted any physical violence. In this backwater of Germany, Bauer thought, the old German constriction of being disorderly in an orderly manner still obtained.

He walked through the new, bare, unadorned corridors and into the courtroom, which was new and bare and unadorned and as aseptic as the operating theater of a hospital.

The courtroom was already filled. The people outside apparently were those who had come to attend and who could not get in. Bauer walked down the center aisle to the benches before the rostrum on which the judges and jury would sit.

He sat down and rubbed the side of his leg. This was the first time he had been out of the hospital. This was the longest walking he had done.

He heard low-pitched conversation behind him. Eckardt had told him to expect a full house. The law stated now that in trials of this kind the public had to be admitted, that a higher court might declare a mistrial if the public were denied admittance. All of this, Bauer understood as he listened to Eckardt, was to get away as far as possible from the secret tribunals of Hitler's Reich, and he was quite sure that the German citizens took full advantage of this freedom. It would be to them more than a privilege. It would be a solemn duty. Freedom being legal, it would be illegal not to be free.

There was a stir in the room and Bauer turned his head and saw that Hausmann, Ullrich, and the others were entering the chamber from a side door, led by armed bailiffs. At the same time other armed officers of the court took positions in different parts of the room, two of them standing guard at the main door.

Hausmann, dressed faultlessly as always, his face calm, almost indifferent, selected a seat and took it with an air of negligence, not bothering to look across the short distance at Bauer. He might have been seating himself at his club or at a restaurant, and once seated he waited as serenely as he might have waited for a waiter to come and take his order.

The other defendants sat down on either side of Hausmann. Several had not his control. They stole glances at Bauer and then quickly averted their eyes. Ullrich fixed him with the longest eye of all.

Hausmann had style, Bauer thought, a little enviously. Hausmann had a manner he had never quite been able to achieve for himself. He tipped his hat. Hausmann had managed that old Hemingway dictum. He had his own grace under pressure.

He heard a shuffling of feet and looked up again to see the three judges and six jurors, together with the district attorney who had interrogated him in the hospital and whom he did not trust, now were entering the chamber from a door behind the rostrum and were taking their places and that the spectators in the room were standing up. Bauer got to his feet and rested on his stick. He was somewhat surprised by the casual entrance of the officials. There had been no announcement, nothing. They just walked in and sat down. When Germans disavowed ceremony, he thought as he resumed his seat, they did it as they did everything else, thoroughly.

Although the three judges in their black robes and round, flat, black hats and the three jurors who flanked them on either side all sat on the same level, it seemed to Bauer as he looked up that this was some kind of optical illusion, that actually the nine men formed a pyramid, with the senior judge, the *Vorsitzender* as the apex.

The senior judge, Franz Josef Ganzenmüller, was an elderly man, with a small, threadlike face, white brows over watery eyes, and cramped, rheumatic hands. Bauer had been informed by Eckardt that *Vorsitzender* Ganzenmüller had been a judge for more than forty years, which meant he had been a judge for the Weimar Republic and then for the Third Reich and now for the Federal Republic and had presumably found himself elastic enough to serve all three faithfully and with the fullest expression of his highest intelligence.

The junior judges were younger, the one on the left, fat, with the soft, smooth, glabrous face of a eunuch, although, as Bauer had seen, habitual beer drinking did that to a certain type of German face; the other, not so fat, and with a glacial, premature judicial stoniness.

The six jurors, all in dark suits, white shirts and dark, middle-width ties, were by definition six of Würzburg's sturdiest pillars, rational, wealthy, and stable enough to have their names included on the city council's master venire.

Chairman Ganzenmüller, having competed the initial rite

of moving papers to and then fro and then to again, surveyed
the courtroom, saw the plaintiff and the defendants all were
there, that the defense attorney was seated where he should
be seated, that spectator seats were filled with civic-minded
ladies and gentlemen as the law prescribed; he looked to his
left and saw that the district attorney was seated at his place
on the rostrum, just round the corner from the last juror;
content at last that all was in order he bade the plaintiff,
Peter Bauer, rise and tell his story.

With the necessary assistance of his cane, Bauer brought
himself to his feet. His body ached in a number of places.
He had a small patch of adhesive plaster on one side of his
head. His left instep, which had been gouged with cleated,
leather heels, was thickly bandaged. He had been guaranteed
at the hospital that all of his injuries would heal and would
leave behind no permanent damage.

He saw that Police President Eckardt had taken a seat
farther down the bench and that his face was professionally
inanimate. Eckardt made no response to his glance. He might
never have seen Bauer before. Bauer limped his way to the
rostrum directly below *Vorsitzender* Ganzenmüller.

The chairman peered down at him from moist, myopic
eyes. "Are you able to stand, Herr Bauer?" he asked in a
reedy voice.

"Yes, Herr Chairman," Bauer said. He had been briefed
by District Attorney Uhlig to address the senior judge in
this manner, that expressions such as "Your Honor" were not
used in German courts. Knowing the inordinate German affection for flowery titles Bauer knew he should have been
encouraged by this new turn, but for some perverse reason
he was not.

He noticed that the defense attorney, Herr Konrad Rudmann, was looking up at the rostrum with an expression of
skepticism. Herr Rudmann was a stout man with high color-
ing, a monk's horseshoe of hair around a bald skull that
gleamed in the strong courtroom lights, bushy eyebrows that
appeared to have been nurtured and combed. He seemed to
Bauer to be something who belonged more to the pages of

Dickens than to a German courtroom as he sat now at a small table near his clients, fiddling with a pencil, trying to communicate his disbelief in anything Bauer said or would say to the men who would make the decision.

"You may testify sitting down if you prefer, Herr Bauer," Ganzenmüller said.

"It will not be necessary, Herr Chairman," Bauer said. At this time, in this German courtroom, surrounded by his enemies, official and unofficial, he felt he needed a little grace of his own.

Chairman Ganzenmüller sat back and Bauer began his account of what had happened to him at the hands of Hausmann and his henchmen. He had been informed, again by Herr Uhlig, that the oath in a German court was taken, if at all, after the conclusion of the testimony and not at the start, and that even if a witness for whatever reason declined the oath, he was as liable to charges of perjury as though he had. Although all this had been made clear to him, the absence of the more familiar routine put him off. It was as though his words would not be taken seriously. It seemed to confirm his stubborn sense that the entire procedure was a farce, a meaningless formality, that would prove nothing and punish no one.

He was not interrupted as he spoke. The court and the jurors listened attentively. The district attorney from time to time admired his ring and managed to look fierce and apologetic at the same time. Hausmann might have been attending a play that bored him. The others were almost equally placid. The spectators did not utter a sound. The freedom did not extend that far.

When he was finished, Herr Uhlig asked permission of the chairman to put a few questions to his client. The permission was granted and Herr Uhlig hastily asked him one or two things to illuminate further a few of the points he had made. The district attorney was finished in less than thirty seconds and then Herr Rudmann stood up and asked Chairman Ganzenmüller if he might query the plaintiff.

Although Bauer had been informed earlier by Uhlig that

there was no such thing as formal examination and cross-examination in the new German legal system, the absence of these procedures increased even more his sense of disbelief in the validity of what was going on.

Herr Rudmann walked closer to Bauer and inspected him. Then, with his thumbs in the pockets of his beige vest, he said, "What you tell us, Herr Bauer, is an extraordinary story, something beyond the realm of imagination."

"Possibly that is why I did not bother to imagine it," Bauer said. His leg was hurting very badly now and he would have given a great deal to sit down.

"Abduction from a street in this law-abiding German city, a kangaroo court, a judgment, physical assault and then the blasphemy of a hanging on a cross?" Herr Rudmann spoke as though he were reciting the litany of an outlandish religion. "And even if all these weird events took place, to accuse one such as Werner Hausmann of being responsible?"

Bauer wondered why Herr Uhlig did not object to this impugning of his client. Perhaps that also was not the way things were done in German courts.

Herr Rudmann, his thumbs firmly locked by his belly pressing against his vest, rocked back and forth on his heels. "For the sake of argument, let us suppose this bizarre chain of events did in fact occur."

Herr Uhlig, despite his personal feelings, could not now allow himself to appear professionally incompetent before the public. He obtained the permission of the senior judge and then said to Herr Rudmann, "It is improper to denigrate Herr Bauer on those matters which can be verified, and will be verified, by other witnesses. Herr Bauer was in fact discovered in a burned-out church hanging from a cross, and was in fact cut down by the police from that cross. That will in due time be substantiated."

The district attorney made his statement in a bold and forthright manner, with all the strength and positiveness of his personality and of his office, and Bauer thought he was quite good. Then another thought occurred to him. Perhaps he again was being overly suspicious but why had Uhlig made such a careful point of limiting his objection to Rudmann's challenging Bauer's veracity only on those facts *which could be verified*? There were many matters, all the matters, in fact, except his ultimate discovery, which could not be verified. It could be said, he thought, that the district attorney, for all his seeming zeal, was actually making a point for the defense.

Herr Rudmann bowed courteously to the district attorney, who, being seated on the rostrum, was placed on a higher level than he was, and who had for that reason, a closer association with authority. "I have no such intention, Herr District Attorney," he said. "I know, as we all know, where and how Herr Bauer was found. That single point cannot in any way be questioned."

He turned his attention again to Bauer. "The people you say sat in judgment on you and then punished you—"

"Not the people," Bauer interrupted. "Hausmann and the others. Those people, sitting there. And I think the word punish is an odd word to use."

"The guilt of the defendants has not as yet been established, Herr Bauer," Chairman Ganzenmüller pointed out.

"It has been established quite satisfactorily to me, Herr Chairman," Bauer said. His leg felt as though it were on fire.

"But not legally," the senior judge reminded him in his spindly voice.

"Whoever it was," Rudmann resumed. "Did they give you a reason for committing this heinous crime of which you accuse them?"

Bauer had been warned it would have to come out, had been warned by Eckardt and even more strenuously by the district attorney who had urged him for this reason alone to drop the whole business and leave Würzburg. Some of it had appeared in the papers, leaked out by Rudmann, but because of legal restrictions on the printing in advance details of a case that was to go on trial, the accounts had been tantalizing but skimpy. Hence the crowd in the courtroom, hence the crowd outside.

But now it was going to come from him in full, from his

own mouth, and now that it was about to surface he felt the fear again. He felt overwhelmingly trapped, an alien in a hateful land, more than that, a Jew in Germany. He wished he had not been so insistent on bringing Hausmann and the others to trial, convinced as he was then and even more so now that he would gain nothing except the useless satisfaction of knowing he had not accepted the assault supinely.

"I was told that I was being tried by these men for my part in the fire bombing of this city," Bauer said.

There was a buzzing in the courtroom. Chairman Ganzenmüller did not have to quiet it. It died almost immediately of its own prudent volition.

"And did you in fact take an active part in the fire bombing and destruction of Würzburg?" Rudmann asked, looking more Pickwickian than ever.

"Yes."

Rudmann glanced up at the judge and jurors. He needed only a simple majority to win his case and one man could do it. Not that he had the slightest doubts about the outcome, but as an old legal warhorse he knew better than to take anything for granted.

"In what capacity, Herr Bauer?"

"As a member of the Royal Air Force."

"Of Great Britain?"

"Yes."

"As a refugee in Britain you were then required to enter the services of your host country," Rudmann said as though he were quite certain this was the fact.

"I was not," Bauer said. Why didn't Uhlig stop this line of questioning, he wondered, it was not he who was on trial here. He wondered why he had wondered.

"Then you volunteered?" Rudmann asked, in open surprise.

"I did."

"May I ask why, Herr Bauer, you did that dangerous thing?"

"I wanted to fight against a regime which all of you now

disavow," Bauer said. He could no longer feel his leg. He felt he was being held up by one leg and a cane.

"You were born in Würzburg, were you not?"

"Yes."

"How could you involve yourself in the bombing of your birthplace?"

"The people of my birthplace had murdered every member of my family and if I had not been smuggled out of Germany would undoubtedly have also murdered me."

There were again low sounds in the courtroom and the district attorney again asked the chairman's sanction to speak.

"May I suggest," Uhlig said, "that it is not Herr Bauer who is on trial, and may I also suggest that we are not trying the former government. And also that the war is a long time ended and is not in any way a factor in this proceeding."

Herr Rudmann bowed to Uhlig once more. "I accept the demurral of my colleague. I did not mean to discuss the war and the destruction of this city. It was just that something struck very close to home for me and, I am sure, for every German in this courtroom. I apologize for succumbing to understandable emotions."

Bullshit, of course, Bauer thought. But intelligent bullshit. Reminding all and sundry that whoever had done to him what had been done could also be said to have succumbed to understandable emotions.

He looked up at the court. The jurors were soberly shocked. The senior judge was shifting papers. The fat judge was shaking his head, causing tremors in his face. The not so fat junior judge had long ago exiled reactions.

"What perhaps is pertinent in my opinion, Herr Bauer," Rudmann said diffidently, "is how you felt on this bombing mission."

Chairman Ganzenmüller leaned forward and asked, "How does this relate to the case, Herr Rudmann?"

"Someone was very violent with the plaintiff, Herr Chairman. While there is no question in my mind that the court will find for the innocence of my clients, since they had nothing to do with this, still, there is no doubt that someone inflicted grievous bodily harm on Herr Bauer. This is a public matter now and will appear in print in this country and because of Herr Bauer's official status and the grotesquery of the circumstances quite possibly abroad as well. What I am attempting, for the sake of the reputation of this country and this city, is to show that this was not capricious cruelty, but that whoever committed this crime felt they had a sound moral reason—rightly or wrongly—for doing what they did. We do not want the world again to accuse Germans of senseless brutality."

Bauer could not quite follow the reasoning of the defense counsel but he granted it sounded nice and patriotic. Of course it would also have no harmful effect on any of the judges or jurors who might secretly believe Hausmann and the others were guilty.

Chairman Ganzenmüller whispered to the junior judge at his right and to the junior judge on his left and then informed Rudmann that his line of questioning was in order.

The defense, Bauer knew, had scored an important little victory. Not so important perhaps. The case had been lost before it began.

"Now, Herr Bauer," Rudmann said in a most reasonable voice. "May I repeat the question. Would you please describe the things you felt when you took part in the almost total destruction of the city that gave you your birth?"

"How did I feel?" Bauer asked. He thought he had never felt as tired as he felt now. "I don't remember how I felt. It was a long time ago."

How often had he been asked this question, by others and by himself?

Rudmann pursed his lips. "It was indeed a long time ago, Herr Bauer, and I can well understand how things tend to fade with the passing years—especially those terrible things of which one perhaps is ashamed and which one wants to put out of one's mind. But, surely, that night must have been an unusual night and one that left an imprint on your mind that you cannot have entirely forgotten."

It was, Bauer realized, a kind of opportunity. He could make a great show of conscience now, the thing the Germans did so well themselves, and which they always recognized and empathized with in others.

"How did I feel? What did I feel?"

Rudmann, in the manner of a kindly professor trying to help along a somewhat slow-minded pupil, leaned forward and asked, "Did you for instance feel like a god of vengeance? The avenging, eye for an eye, tooth for a tooth God of your Old Testament?"

That was clever too, Bauer thought. Hitting way below the belt but clever and if Rudmann could get away with it, a brilliant tactic. He waited for his attorney, Herr Uhlig, to say something. He waited for the senior judge to make some remonstrance. He heard nothing.

"No I did not, Herr Rudmann," he said.

"What did you see when you were in that airplane performing your duties?"

"Flames. I did not know there would be flames like that, that there could be flames like that."

"It was a hell," Rudmann suggested.

"It was a hell."

"Brought about, to the best of your ability, with your help?"

The growing sense that it was he who was on trial reached full flower. But for what? Because he had taken part in the raid? Because he was a native Jew? Because of both of those facts?

"The bombing of Würzburg was scheduled by the RAF and the United States Eighth Air Force. The bombing would have taken place with or without me."

"But it did take place with you."

"Yes."

"The destruction by fire of the city in which you were born, where your family had been born, where you had friends."

Bauer looked at Herr Uhlig, waiting for him to make some philosophical comment on the defense attorney's repetitive-

300

ness. The district attorney appeared to be totally absorbed in the questioning.

"There were no members of my family left alive in Würzburg, Herr Rudmann," Bauer said. "There were no friends. By that time in history they had all been dispatched to their own personal hell."

Rudmann nodded gravely. "Yes, the excesses of the previous government. And so you felt called upon to have blood for blood. Entirely understandable, Herr Bauer."

"I had a duty to perform. I was in the RAF. I have told you that."

"You must have been very young then."

The same trap, Bauer thought. Known now, but still unavoidable. "I was."

"Perhaps even below military age."

"Yes."

"Then you must have lied about that."

"I did."

Rudmann allowed time for that to sink in everywhere in the room. "You were too young, but you lied and persevered until you got into a uniform and in a branch of the enemy service that was inflicting the greatest outrage on your native land."

"My native land had denied in an explicit and particularly unpleasant way that it was my native land," Bauer said. How adroitly the tables had been turned to make him the defendant this day.

"I can understand, Herr Bauer, I can well understand how you must have felt," Rudmann said sympathetically. "The bitterness you must have felt! And one does things when one is in the grip of bitterness that one later always regrets. That applies to everyone."

When Bauer did not express his regrets the defense attorney continued.

"Still and all, still and all, the old buildings, the churches, the landmarks hundreds and hundreds of years old, the pride of this city for so many generations, the places familiar to you, places where you had been happy as a child, your school,

301

your playing fields, your synagogue." Rudmann dropped the last word almost by itself. "All of these you were quite anxious to wipe from the face of the earth, so anxious, in fact, that you scrabbled and lied to get into the British military service that would permit you to do it."

Bauer rested both hands on the handle of the cane. His body now felt it was made of lead. "I joined the RAF and I lied about my age because I wanted to fight against an evil. It was an evil, as I have already said, that you and almost everybody else in Germany now vehemently condemns. Let us name the name of this evil. Hitler. Adolf Hitler. National Socialism. All of you if asked now will say that he was a monster, that you knew nothing of the horrors that he perpetrated at that time. All of you, that is, except, as I am told, a few who would bring back those times in another form. Well, it was against that monster, against those horrors, that I chose to fight. I did not enlist in the RAF to bomb Würzburg. The question of bombing this city was not even under consideration when I first put on my uniform."

"When the decision to do so was made you were given certain orders," Rudmann said.

"Yes," Bauer said, knowing perfectly well where this route was leading.

"And you obeyed those orders."

"Of course."

"Is that your excuse now, Herr Bauer, that you were just obeying orders?"

"I was not aware that I had to make excuses to you or to anyone else in this courtroom, Herr Rudmann," Bauer said. "It was not my understanding that it is I who am on trial."

Rudmann was appalled at the thought. "Surely not!" he said, throwing up his hands.

"Is that what you are saying now, Herr Bauer, that you were obeying orders?" The question came from the junior judge with the face of poured concrete.

"I obeyed orders," Bauer said, sensing what had to come next, feeling the hatred like a miasma around him.

The other junior judge, speaking for the first time, seized

the flaming torch. "But by the judgment of the victors in Nuremberg and in all of the war trials since then that is not a justification for committing an immoral act." His voice was unexpectedly deep and resonant. "One should have a sense of morality, we are told. One should refuse to obey orders one considers immoral."

A juror with a small, square black moustache asked authorization of the chairman to speak and then said, "Perhaps Herr Bauer does not consider the burning to the ground of his native city and the killing of thousands of persons with whom he grew up and lived an immoral act."

Rudmann, quite happy to allow the court to serve as surrogate for him, stepped back and took on the air of an interested bystander.

Bauer looked across the room at Herr Uhlig. The district attorney looked back through him. He not only was the defendant now but he also was without a lawyer.

"I consider war to be immoral," he said in a low voice. He was very tired and in a great deal of pain. "I consider the Hitler regime to have been immoral. I consider the persecution and the slaying of Jews as well as anybody else who disagreed with Hitler to have been immoral. On a very small, personal basis, I consider the murder in a concentration camp of my mother and my father and my sister and my two brothers and all of their children and all the rest of my family here in Würzburg to have been immoral."

Rudmann brushed his shaggy brows upward with his fingers as though he were trying to push tears up his forehead and he nodded as dolefully as a funeral director consoling a bereaved. "Yes, of course, Herr Bauer, we all understand and sympathize."

He would have said more, to cut off Bauer's line of defense, but Bauer spoke before he could.

"How did I feel?" Bauer asked loudly. He did not know where it came from or why it came but he felt a new surge of strength. He straightened from his cane and lifted his head. "How did I feel, Herr Rudmann. How did I feel when I was in the belly of that airplane and saw Würzburg become

303

an inferno beneath me? What was I thinking? I don't see how that is your concern or the concern of anybody in this courtroom, but I'll tell you. I did think of my parents and my relatives and what had been done to them in one way or another by every soul who was below me."

There was a sibilant hiss in the room from the spectators behind him, a concerted exhalation of air, as though all of them had been holding their breaths until he had said what he had said.

Herr Rudmann saw an opportunity. "And that hatred, Herr Bauer, did that sustain you?" he asked in sudden feint.

"It did."

There was another long sound in the room. The defense attorney smiled. He had struck home.

"And then it ran out," Bauer said.

"What do you mean by that?" Rudmann asked.

"I mean they all merged, the dead you people killed and the dead I helped kill, they all merged into one, sharing the horror, all paying for something only God could explain." He was silent for a moment. He felt there was a halter around his neck pulling it down but he would not lower his head. "What was most painful, after the first hatred vanished, was that that which had destroyed all of us, and which I now was succeeding in destroying, now was part of me. It was something from which one could extricate himself mentally, perhaps, through rationalization, but emotionally there was no escape from it, no escape at all."

He was saying the things he had resolved never to say. He was saying the things he had tried for years to freeze out of his own mind.

Rudmann juggled the statement as though it were a hot potato and as though a potato was something he had never before seen. He asked, finally, "You were conscious then, even then, even at that moment when you were helping to burn this city off the earth, you were conscious of the monstrous crime you were committing?"

Bauer went on as though he had not heard, as though Rudmann had not spoken, not to him, "You could cry out inside yourself that you were not German but a Jew. You could remind yourself again and again that the Germans said you were not German. You could insist to yourself you could hate them, had every right to hate them, had a responsibility to hate them, a duty to hate them. But this was more rationale and it didn't work. Because I was German, as German as any German, perhaps more so because it had been taken away from me."

He stopped and Rudmann immediately opened his mouth to speak and closed it without speaking.

"And when that became inescapable," Bauer said, speaking over himself as though it were an advertence to the dead and he was the dead, "when I could no longer deny to myself that I was German—totally, completely, wholly German, every drop of blood in me German blood—then I had to accept the fact that what I was trying to destroy, to burn out as one would cauterize flesh to prevent the spreading of a malignancy, that what I was hating at that moment was myself."

The courtroom was silent. Chairman Ganzenmüller leaned forward. "Hated yourself, Herr Bauer, because of what you were doing then?"

The senior judge, Bauer saw, had not quite understood what he had said, at least had not understood it as he had meant it to be understood, and perhaps nobody had. He was by that accident then being presented with a final out, the ultimate opportunity to exculpate himself. Because what Hausmann and the others had done to him was now of no importance. He was the one being judged and that was as it should be because his had been the greater sin and he knew now that he had known that one day he would have to face Germans, here in Würzburg, where the act had been done, and he would have to tell them what part of that act he had done and why he had done it. And now that he had at last purged himself it was necessary only to reply to the judge's question with a yes, and everyone in the chamber, everyone in Germany who would read of it, would understand.

"That is not what I meant, Herr Chairman," he said.

305

Rudmann, who for a few moments had frowned in worriment, now was relieved, although still puzzled. "Explain yourself, Herr Bauer, if you please."

Bauer turned slightly and looked full at Hausmann.

"What I meant," Bauer said, "was that even though I was discarded by the Germans I was not at the same time given the privilege to be free. To be free of Germany, to be free of my own Germanhood, to be free of all the things that were in me, that are in all Germans. What I knew as I watched the fire was that I was cursed with being part of Germany, that it was a curse that was eternal, that although I had been denied, had been caused to run for my life, that none the less everything in my life that I loved and hated was in that blaze below me. What I meant when I said I hated myself then was that I hated myself for being a German."

The murmuring rose again in the room and Hausmann did not look away and Bauer felt that he must now sit down or else he would fall.

Rudmann cleared his throat. "Just a few final questions, Herr Bauer. When last were you in Würzburg?"

"When I was a child. When I was smuggled across the border into Switzerland."

"You have not been back here since the war?"

"No."

"To any part of Germany?"

"No."

"Then, Herr Bauer, may one ask what brought you back here after a quarter of a century. Surely you must have known, or heard, that we had managed to rebuild our city. Surely you did not at this late date hope to see any of the results of your work."

District Attorney Uhlig applied for permission to interrupt. "I consider the remark by Herr Rudmann to be inappropriate."

Rudmann bowed instantly. "I withdraw the statement. It was irrelevant and in bad taste." Of Bauer he asked, "Why did you return?"

306

"For personal reasons."

"I beg your pardon?"

"Personal reasons having nothing to do with this case."

Chairman Ganzenmüller spoke. "Herr Bauer, you have made serious accusations against Herr Werner Hausmann and against these other gentlemen, persons who have been considered examples of probity and value. The assault that was made upon you was a particularly ghastly one, one that would appear to go even beyond retribution for the role you played in the holocaust that was visited upon this city. Could you suggest to this court any other reason Herr Hausmann might have had for doing what you charge him with doing? Any reason of a more personal nature, perhaps?"

Bauer did not now bother to look at Hausmann. "There could be no personal reason. Until I returned to Würzburg I did not know Werner Hausmann."

Chairman Ganzenmüller then asked Herr Rudmann and Herr Uhlig whether either of the lawyers had any additional questions to put to Bauer. Neither lawyer had. The senior judge then turned to Hausmann.

"Herr Hausmann, it is my duty to inform you that under the German law you, as a defendant in this case, now have the privilege of addressing any question you please to your accuser, to challenge any statement he has made, in short, to ask or say anything that may help your defense."

Hausmann rose languidly to his feet. "I have nothing to say to that person." He sat down.

The man had, Bauer admitted ruefully to himself, the grand manner. There was something finished, polished, rubbed smooth about him. Nothing could touch him. Everything just slid off that elegant surface as though it were ice.

Chairman Ganzenmüller then polled all of the other defendants to determine whether anyone wanted to avail himself of his constitutional right to interrogate the witness or to take exception to anything he had said. Each man in his turn followed Hausmann's lead and declined to say anything.

"Herr Bauer," Chairman Ganzenmüller said now, "before

you sit down you may take an oath with relation to your testimony, or you may refuse. In either event your testimony has exactly the same value."

"I will take the oath, Herr Chairman," Bauer said. The oath for what? For the charges he had made against Hausmann and the lot? Or in a far more profound sense as the affirmation of his own long-delayed catharsis?

A bailiff handed him a laminated card and he read aloud to the court what was printed on it:

"I hereby swear by God Almighty that I have told the whole truth and that I have omitted nothing. May God bear me witness."

It was not quite true, of course. He had omitted reference to Arthur Hausmann.

He returned the card to the bailiff and started at last to his sanctuary on the bench. He felt a thousand years old. He thought he detected something new on Eckardt's face and he wondered whether it was because he had refrained from dragging the elder Hausmann into the case even though by doing so he would have established a more intimate motive for Werner Hausmann to have done what he had done, and might have thus strengthened his case.

Why had he left the old man out of it? He could not have answered that just then.

He did not think much on it because as he made his way back to the bench he saw Marliese. She was among the other spectators, sitting three or four rows back. He had missed her when he entered the courtroom.

She did not look at him. She was not looking at her brother or at anything else. She was staring straight ahead into space with the dead eyes of the blind.

34

✠ ✠ ✠

THE GERMANS WERE A DURABLE PEOPLE, BAUER HAD TO ADMIT, and even old men had stalwart bladders. Chairman Ganzenmüller called no recess and from what Bauer could detect behind his back nobody left the courtroom.

Witnesses now were produced from some hideaway, the first being Fräulein Wilhelmina Gerda Schneider, who, for the occasion, was dressed in a flouncy print on which grew a luxuriant tropical garden of outsized red and yellow and orange flowers surrounded by ferns large as palm trees, and a white hat with a brim the dimensions of a small umbrella on the front of which was affixed a very red artificial rose. Fräulein Schneider also carried a small, pink silk parasol.

Facing the court she described with more or less accuracy the circumstances of the finding of Peter Bauer on the crucifix of the abandoned church. Her testimony was by mutual stipulation of the attorneys held to include that of all the little girls in her class since they were deemed to be of too tender an age to be incorporated into a legal proceeding of a criminal nature. Fräulein Schneider, upon concluding her narrative and upon inspiring no queries from either lawyers or defendants, departed, after having opted not to take the oath, possibly because she had neglected to report the fact that she had delayed notification of the crime to the police for at least ten minutes during which time she was indulging herself in the outmoded gratification of a swoon.

After Fräulein Schneider there were brought forth a number of doctors from the hospital where Bauer was officially still a patient. These experts testified as to the number and extent of Bauer's injuries and to a man expressed the opinion that had he not been found and given immediate medical attention he would have survived no more than another day or two, if for that long.

Although Bauer had been informed of this before he could not escape a chill as he listened to these professionals testifying dispassionately, as though citing statistics, how close he had been to death.

Herr Rudmann questioned the doctors in an attempt to make them admit their prognosis was little more than an educated guess but the doctors would not retreat an inch and then, having second thoughts, the defense counsel dropped that line of questioning when he realized belatedly that it might create the impression he believed his clients had actually been involved in the attack on Bauer and that he was trying to minimize the seriousness of their offense.

After the initial shock of hearing himself soberly presented as a candidate for a coffin, Bauer found the proceedings increasingly without meaning. The trial, if Bauer *vs.* Hausmann could in earnest so be described, had the programming and the strict, limited mime of a minuet, with about as much punitive validity. He knew that by German law and probably by the law of any land he had no case against Werner Hausmann and the others, that his charges were entirely uncorroborated, and, more, he was convinced that even if he had a case, in that courtroom he would have none.

Was that why he had not exposed Arthur Hausmann? Because even that revelation would in the end have succeeded in accomplishing nothing but damage to an old man? Or was it because at one time Arthur Hausmann had loved his mother and she had a feeling of tenderness for him? Or was it more truly because he and Arthur Hausmann had worked out their own mutual quittance and that anything beyond that would be nothing but intrusion?

He wondered in passing how much Marliese knew of those old and forgotten days.

The next and final witness on the agenda was Police President Johannes Eckardt and as the brawny police chief took his stand before the court Bauer saw Ullrich and three or four of the other defendants sit up just a little straighter. Even Hausmann, who had never abandoned his attitude of total disinterest, seemed to Bauer now to be a shade more alert.

In short, flat, unemotional sentences, as though reading from a police report, Eckardt told the court his office had been notified of the discovery of a man on a cross, that he had gone to the church, that he had found the plaintiff, Peter Bauer, tied to a crucifix and almost unconscious, that he had had Bauer cut down and he had summoned an ambulance, that Bauer had been given emergency treatment in the church and then had been removed to the hospital, and that as soon as the doctors had permitted he had questioned Bauer and had elicited from him the names of his assailants.

Herr Rudmann leaped out of his chair and appealed to the senior judge for permission to intercept the police president's testimony. "May I for the record clarify the statement made by Herr Eckardt?"

Chairman Ganzenmüller granting him liberty, the defense counsel said, "It is more accurate to put it that the plaintiff gave the police president the names of the men he *said* were the assailants. It has not yet been the judgment of this court that the men here on trial were in fact those assailants."

"I stand corrected," Eckardt said.

"As a matter of fact," Rudmann went on, having waited for just the right moment to make this point, "there is absolutely no substantiation from any source whatsoever that any of these gentlemen, whose public and private lives have been without blemish, had anything to do with the heinous assault on the plaintiff."

"Defense counsel is entirely correct in his objection," Chairman Ganzenmüller ruled. "Until the judgment of this court is handed down the defendants are presumed to be innocent."

Herr Rudmann bowed to the court and sat down.

"Acting upon the information given to me by Herr Bauer, I presented the facts to the district attorney. He agreed to accept the charges and prosecute the case."

District Attorney Uhlig managed to look virtuous and unhappy at the same time.

Chairman Ganzenmüller asked whether anyone wanted to interrogate or contravene the police president, and upon receiving no response he thanked Eckardt and indicated he might sit down.

"Before I do, Herr Chairman," Eckardt said, "there is one more point I would like to make."

Herr Rudmann rose to his feet but when the senior judge nodded to the police official he sat down.

"The hospital doctors have testified that Peter Bauer, if he had not been found, would have died within forty-eight hours or less," Eckardt said evenly. "Immediately after he was found and I was informed of the degree of his injuries, I posted a policeman in front of the church to ascertain just how many persons visited there. The church obviously is not in use but I assumed there would be curiosity-seekers who would go there for one reason or another. It now has been just over a month since Peter Bauer was tied to that cross to die. In that time there has been a total of two visitors to the church. The first, an old lady who told the policeman on duty she had at one time been a communicant, came two weeks and three days after Peter Bauer was carried out. The second, a young, amateur photographer, went there the day before yesterday. But for little Marie Lenz, Peter Bauer would have remained on that cross for exactly seventeen days. I might add that the elderly lady was almost blind and in my opinion would never have noticed what would have been a carcass hanging from that symbol of our Lord, Jesus Christ."

Police President Eckardt walked back to his seat in a courtroom otherwise empty of sound. His footsteps made a slow, even tattoo. He did not glance at Bauer as he passed him.

Bauer looked at him astounded. He had had no conception of the thoroughness and perseverance with which Eckardt had investigated the case and he wished that it could have been put to better use.

Herr Rudmann took the floor. His face was at its gravest. "All of this is very disturbing indeed," he said, his thumbs slipping automatically into their tight little vest pocket niches. "Very disturbing indeed. It is unsettling to know that we have in our city unlawful elements who endanger the life of a visitor. Although it cannot be said with exactitude that Herr Bauer is a visitor." It was unnecessary for him to look at the court to make certain they had taken his meaning.

"Nonetheless, Herr Bauer has the right to expect the same protection by the law as anyone else here, German or visitor," he continued, speaking on the side of angels. "Personally, as a law-abiding German, I deplore the unfortunate attack on Herr Bauer, and I would expend every effort to bring the miscreants to heel. But it is my duty under the constitution of the Federal Republic, in my position as attorney for these defendants, to point out that apart from the statement made by the plaintiff, there is nothing, absolutely nothing, to link the defendants, singly or as a group, to this crime. I make this statement for two reasons, first, to underline the truth in this matter, and, secondly, as a preliminary to informing the court that none of the defendants desires to speak in his own behalf. All of them are innocent. All of them submit their names, their careers, their families, in fact every part of their existences, to speak for them. They are prepared to remain silent and to wait to hear the decision of the court, confident that they will be, on the basis of the unconfirmed facts presented, exonerated."

Herr Rudmann ended his summing up soberly, all of him oozing the reasonableness and justness of what he had said. He turned to look at his colleague, the district attorney, to see whether Herr Uhlig had any wish to call up any of the defendants for questioning, as was his privilege. It was a purely formal gesture, he felt, having certain knowledge about how Herr Uhlig felt about the whole affair. What he saw astonished him.

Police President Eckardt was standing at the rostrum directly below the district attorney and he was talking to him and the police official's manner was tough and hard and he was making no effort to disguise it. It was almost as though he were talking to a prisoner. That shocked Herr Rudmann, but what shocked him much more was the district attorney.

Herr Uhlig was stunned. His face was dead white and his hand, gripping a ball-point pen, trembled. He was shaking his head slowly, not in denial, not in refusal, as Herr Rudmann could see, but in shattering incredulity.

Eckardt backed away and sat down and after Herr Uhlig looked down at him as though begging a last-minute boon, receiving none, the district attorney wet his lips and said to Chairman Ganzenmüller, who was regarding him with no less surprise than the defense counsel, "Herr Chairman, I realize this is somewhat irregular, but with your permission, I would like at this time to bring forth another witness."

Whispering riffled through the courtroom. The defendants, with the exception of Hausmann, glanced curiously at each other. Bauer looked at Eckardt. The police president might not have been there. He was sealed off in a privacy of his own.

Chairman Ganzenmüller considered the district attorney's request, and said, "You may call your witness, Herr Uhlig."

The district attorney, his last hope gone, opened his mouth and then closed it and then opened it again. He seemed not to be able to summon the breath to project his voice. When he finally got out the words they were mumbled and faint as though he still hoped that somehow they might be unheard or at least misunderstood.

"I would like to call before the court one of the defendants, Kurt Hassler," he said.

The other defendants looked up in astonishment as Kurt Hassler, his blond hair falling across his forehead, stood up and walked to the rostrum. Hausmann frowned slightly as Hassler walked past him but he did not look up.

Kurt Hassler paused before his leader. His eyes were more troubled than ever. His face was wasted and suddenly old. "It was not to have been that way, Werner," he said almost under his breath. "We were just to frighten him and maul him a little. It was not to have been that way at all."

Hausmann still would not look at him and the young man continued to the rostrum. He raised his head. "As God is my witness, everything that Peter Bauer has accused us of is true."

The three judges and six jurors remained in their consultation chamber scarcely more than five minutes and when they returned to the rostrum in their black robes and dark suits like a phalanx of ravens the courtroom quieted immediately.

Upon Kurt Hassler's confession there had erupted in the chamber a most un-German uproar and since this rarely happens in German courts and German judges are not equipped with gavels as are judges in less well-behaved countries, Chairman Ganzenmüller had extreme difficulty in restoring decorum.

Throughout the clamor Bauer had sat stupefied.

The defendants were dazed and reeling by what Kurt Hassler had made public. Hausmann alone maintained his composure. There even appeared upon his face a setting of fatalism, as though he had had a dim sense that this disclosure was inevitable, or perhaps, if it were not that, that it was simply that he was already adjusted to accepting the consequences of his action.

Herr Rudmann, when he recovered, instantly mounted an onslaught on Hassler's credibility, switching thereby from defense counsel to prosecutor, demanding to know finally whether the state had promised the young man a reduced sentence for betraying his comrades.

"I am not an attorney, Herr Rudmann," Hassler had replied quietly. "But even I know that without my confession there would have been no sentences at all."

Bauer remained bemused. At one point he looked down the long bench at Eckardt. The police president's eyes were closed and there was a small smile on his lips as though he were asleep and dreaming innocent dreams.

For no reason it occurred to Bauer that he had been in the presence of the police official for more than three hours and he had not once seen him resort to any contrivance to fend off the exactions of nicotine.

Chairman Ganzenmüller now ordered the bailiffs to bring the defendants before him. The men, with the exception of Kurt Hassler, were lined up, Hausmann in their center, armed officers of the court standing vigilantly behind them. Hassler was kept off to one side with his own bailiff to guard him. Once again Hausmann managed to create the impression that he was in no manner involved, that it was he who was removed from the rest of them, and from everything else.

Chairman Ganzenmüller adjusted a pair of narrow, oblong, steel-rimmed spectacles on his nose with his stiffened fingers, his face immediately assuming the look of a medieval alchemist. He peered over the spectacles at the men below him, studying each face separately, his blurred eyes remaining the longest on Werner Hausmann.

The onlookers in the courtroom, having not as yet rallied fully from their own shock, looked in silence at the judges and jurors, at the backs of the defendants, and most specially at the backs of the armed officers, subdued altogether by the new and menacing atmosphere in the room.

Chairman Ganzenmüller cleared his throat once or twice. "You have individually and collectively committed a crime, not only against your accuser, Peter Bauer, but against the Federal Republic."

His voice was as thin as it had been during the session, but from somewhere it had mustered a lean resonance.

"We are an unfortunate country in world view," he continued. "I believe that we are not alone in this time and in this world in demonstrations of cruelty and brutality. I am

316

quite certain Herr Bauer, who now resides in the United States, reads there in his daily paper of acts of violence no less severe that that which he experienced here—on Negroes, on students, on protestors, on ordinary people whose only offense perhaps is to disagree with their immediate authority. That, however, is no consolation for us in Germany. We have as a nation visited unparalleled horrors on millions of persons. We have a requirement now to be better than anyone else, to have more dignity, more decency, more self-control than anyone else. We are still after a quarter of a century being judged by the rest of the human race and will be for years to come."

The senior judge's voice, as though being honed by use, was now sharp and clear.

Bauer listened, transfixed.

"That is why I say that your crime of attempted murder against Peter Bauer was only one of your crimes, and perhaps the lesser one at that. In a very real sense you have all been traitors to your country. The quiet things, the good things, the becoming things that are done all over Germany every hour of the day will not get one millionth of the attention the world press will give to your hideous act. All over the world people will read and hear on radio and see on television what you have done and will say this is typically German, that the German always has and always will be a beast, a beast that should forever be chained, caged, kept in a pit, locked away from decent human beings.

"It is solely for the crime you committed against Peter Bauer that I am authorized to pass sentence upon you. The powers invested in me by the constitution do not permit me to punish you for the greater crime you committed against Germany."

The frail, elderly judge paused for a moment and Bauer contemplated him almost with awe. In the jurist's fragility, in the meager timbre of his speech, in the power of his thinking, Bauer realized he was viewing a man. And how had this man shaped himself to so many masters? Perhaps, Bauer thought, it was the concept of the law itself that had given him sustenance, as though, debased as it had been during the day of the terror, debased and ignored and flouted and revised to fit the will and the mood and the capriciousness of the Leader, it still had in some way to be maintained, held close, adhered to, never, never abandoned. Perhaps Judge Franz Josef Ganzenmüller had through those years held on to that more important thing, the idea of the law, until that day when it could again be presented untainted.

Vorsitzender Ganzenmüller again inspected the face of each defendant. He returned in the end to Hausmann.

"For conceiving, for instigating, for directing this criminal act, an act which in addition to all else is offensive to all Christians in its impiety, I sentence you, Werner Hausmann, to ten years in prison."

Hausmann drew in his breath. There was an echoing gasp from the assemblage in the courtroom.

Bauer, still in a state of disbelief, looked again at Eckardt. The police president appeared not at all impressed.

"To each of the other defendants, with the single exception of Kurt Hassler," Chairman Ganzenmüller continued, "I hand down sentences of five years in prison."

Several of the young men sagged. One began to weep. Ullrich might have been receiving directions on how not to lose his way in a strange city.

The senior judge now turned his eyes to Hassler. "To Kurt Hassler, who made possible the confirmation of the charges made by the plaintiff, who did so without any thought of reward but solely from a revulsion of conscience, I hand down a sentence of three years in prison."

Hassler received the judgment impassively.

Bauer heard a scurrying of feet behind him and the opening and closing of a door, a newspaperman on his course.

"The prisoners will be removed to cells here," the senior judge said, "until that time when they will be transferred to a federal prison. Kurt Hassler will be segregated from the others, both here and in prison. The trial in this courtroom now is officially concluded."

The bailiff began to herd the condemned men out of the

courtroom. The citizens of Würzburg watched them go, still calcified.

One by one the men stepped silently and docilely out of the courtroom as though the mantle of convict was already on them.

At the door, Hausmann stopped and pushed a bailiff violently to one side. He turned back to the courtroom and thrust out his right hand in the old salute. He shouted, "What I did I did for the honor of Germany! Heil Hitler!"

35

✠ ✠ ✠

HAVING NOTHING NOW WITH WHICH TO OCCUPY HIS ACTIVE mind, Police President Eckardt again pulled on the little mechanical cigarette with the lighted tip. "I think this is the best of the lot," he said. "Except that the battery doesn't last very long."

"I would never have believed it," Bauer said. He realized he had already said that four or five times.

"No, I didn't think you would," Eckardt said.

Bauer smiled tightly. "But Herr Hausmann had himself the last word."

"I imagine they will take a little of that starch out of him where he is going." Eckardt leaned forward in the chair in the small hospital room. "It seems to me that I'm hearing an old broken record, but may one ask when you have the intention of going?"

"From here or Würzburg?"

"First the one and then the other."

"They want to take a few X-rays and make certain my head is in one piece again. They're very big on X-rays here, naturally. After that, I'm off."

Eckardt tapped the metal tube against his teeth. "How often have I heard that, Herr Bauer?"

Bauer said soberly, "I take your advice, Herr Police President. I should have taken it sooner. I'm sorry for the trouble I've caused you and I thank you for everything you've done."

"It was worth it to me. I'm sorry you had to be the guinea pig but the episode was of value. Something filthy was unearthed and held up to the light and then put where it could infect no one else."

Bauer gave a short laugh. "For how long, Herr Police President? Will they ever actually serve time at all? They have an appeal."

"They do."

"And the sentences will be lowered or perhaps reversed altogether. Let's not discount Werner Hausmann and the friends he has."

"Is that how things work out in America, Herr Bauer?"

"That's how they work out everywhere. Especially, I would say, Herr Police President, here."

Eckardt looked at him with interest. "Do you still believe that?"

"I guess I do."

"Even after what transpired in court?"

"That bowled me over. I admit that. But I'll still wait to see how it all ends."

Eckardt stood up and began to pace the room. It was not a very large room and he had to make frequent turns. "I can't say for sure, my friend, but I'd bet against it. The testimony of that young man will make a reversal quite difficult, if not impossible. And there obviously has been a great deal of publicity in connection with this trial, here and abroad, and too many people will be watching to see if there is a whitewash. No, I think your friends will take advantage of every legal instrument available to them, but I believe that in the end the judgment and the sentences will stand. Does that make you happy?"

Bauer lay flat on the bed and looked at the ceiling. The cracks there had long since formed patterns for him. "I'd be less than human if I didn't want to see those bastards punished," he said. "But perhaps it's a little more than just that."

Eckardt faced him with an amused smile. "You would then have greater optimism for the future of Germany."

One of the series of fissures had in some manner formed themselves into the head of a basset hound. "I think that moment arrived for me before the judge said what he did. I think the moment for me was when that young man stood up and spoke." He was silent for a moment, and then said in a low voice, "No, Herr Police President, perhaps I don't need to know the conclusion after all. Even if these men manage to get themselves off, something still will have changed in me."

"Hassler is brave," Eckardt said after a little while. "Misguided, but quite brave. I think he may have found his way now."

"His spontaneous confession came as no surprise to you, Herr Police President."

Eckardt grinned. "You noticed that? You were clever enough to have a quick look at me at that moment?"

"How did you persuade him?"

"I'm a policeman."

"I see."

"I can assure you there was nothing of what you in the United States call the third degree."

"Of course not."

"You were the one who started me on the track," Eckardt said. "You have an uncommonly observant eye and a very good memory. To have remembered the slight hesitation of Hassler in the church would have been observation enough, under the circumstances. But to also remember his name and to provide a description and to remember other names . . . You would have made a good policeman, Herr Bauer."

"I'm honored." Bauer wished that he were standing so that he could make a suitably modest bow. Instead he pushed himself up on his elbows. "But you said nothing about Hassler to the district attorney until the last minute. He was flabbergasted."

322

"You noticed that too. No, after Kurt Hassler agreed to corroborate your story in court I kept the information to myself. I was afraid he might meet with an accident."

Eckardt glanced at his watch and then walked over to the bed.

"I might not have the pleasure of seeing you again, Herr Bauer," he said. "It may come as a shock to you but I have duties other than to shepherd you. I shall continue to leave a police guard outside the door. And when the time comes, and I hope with all my heart it's soon, I'll provide you with an escort to the train. As I think about it, as a matter of fact, I'll have someone accompany you until you cross the border."

After Eckardt left Bauer dozed off and was wakened by the arrival of Joachim Remers and his plump, pouter pigeon of a wife. Frau Remers brought with her a Thermos jug filled with lentil soup.

"Not chicken soup?" Bauer asked.

"Would you have preferred chicken soup?" All of Frau Remers' collops drooped in her disappointment. "Joachim told me this was your favorite, with the frankfurters cut up in it." She turned on her husband. "Why did you tell me that?"

Bauer took her soft hand and held it tightly. "It's my little joke, Tilly. Honestly, this is my favorite."

Frau Remers looked suspicious. "You are not just saying that to protect your old friend?"

"I swear it," Bauer said. "It was just my little American joke."

Frau Remers inspected him for a moment and then broke into a smile that was like the sun coming through a lowering sky and then the three of them talked about how dreadful all of it had been and how marvelous it was that the guilty men had been caught and would be punished and who could have imagined that someone as well known as Werner Hausmann could be such a lunatic, Tilly and Joachim remembered when he was a boy growing up in Würzburg, so quiet, so polite, so intelligent, one never knew, and after a while, during which

323

time Bauer sampled the soup and pronounced it fabulous, the Remerses left.

Bauer walked with them down the hospital corridor, followed by the policeman, and he bade them farewell at the door and promised to call them before he left Würzburg, and then he went out into the courtyard. The doctors had told him to exercise a little each day. It was an agreeable afternoon and some of the patients were sunning themselves. Bauer thought he could hear some music in the distance but he was not sure.

He walked around for a little while in the gentle peace of the courtyard, conscious of the uniformed man who trailed him at a discreet distance. He saw people look at him and then whisper. He sat down on an empty bench. His police escort took his post not too far away. Now the courtyard with its trees and grass and flowers was perfectly still.

Bauer thought how enjoyable a cigarette would taste. He wondered whether there would ever come a time when he would not think how much he would enjoy a cigarette. And what purpose had been served in his having freed himself from cigarettes? But for the faith of a small child it would not have made the slightest difference to his health whether he was a smoker or not.

At least he had been able to do without those gadgets, especially the ones that lit up. That Eckardt was something. Stationing a man outside the church to tally visitors. Probably only a German would have thought of that. Only a German would have seen to it that it was done.

That little child, Marie. He had never been able to meet her. He had wanted to see her and to thank her but her parents decided it would be better for the little girl if she never saw him again, not after having seen him as she had. He had found out about the doll house and had persuaded her parents to let him send it to her.

He thought he heard the music again, trumpets and drumbeats. The sounds were faint and far away. Maybe more leavings from the past, to be heard when one cocked one's head a certain way.

He was feeling a little tired now and he raised his head and started to get up to go back to his room. He saw Marliese walking toward him. She was wearing the boots and the short skirt he had first seen her in and she had a leather bag looped around her shoulder. She looked magnificent. She also was a stranger.

"Please don't get up," she said. "How are you, Peter? The sister told me you might be here."

"Oh, I'm fine," he said.

She sat down next to him. She looked extraordinarily attractive. He wondered why.

She opened her bag. "Do you mind if I smoke, Peter?"

"I never have."

"I know, but this is a hospital. Not that that should make any difference."

He took the Zippo from her and lit her cigarette. She took in a long, slow pull and breathed out the smoke. He thought it smelled wonderful. He thought she looked absolutely stunning. Why was that? Was it because he didn't know her and it was like having a great-looking woman walk up to you and say hello and sit down and ask you if she might have a cigarette?

She took another puff and he thought her hand was handsome and he tried to bring to mind what that hand had done for him at one time. He could not.

She seemed nervous. He wondered what had brought her. What had happened between them had been eliminated. He could not now remember they had spent a day wandering together, drinking wine, eating, and for that day they had been chums, that afterward they had put aside the glass wall and had as friends given themselves to each other, that they had listened to the lost sounds each of them had made, that they had got to that place together, that rare place, had got there and had held on, held on to each other, in that overwhelming and almost unbearable fear that they might fall away and fall away alone.

They had at that moment saved each other's lives and now it was as though it never happened.

"I had to see you before you left," she said at last. She looked away.

Why? He said nothing.

"I couldn't let you go without seeing you."

What was she saying? Beyond marking time? And why? Anyway she was good to look at and she made him feel good and she made him feel the summer was still around.

He would like to go to bed with this woman, he thought, as though he had not been to bed with her once before.

It took a little while more and a few more drags on her cigarette and a few more turnings away so he had the profile to admire as well.

"I was the one who told my brother about you," she said. "About your having been in the raid."

Now he had the reason. Again the tidy German need to be honest in the small details.

She was facing him now, fairly and squarely, forswearing all evasion, taking it on the chin, straight on. He felt tired again.

"I had to tell you, Peter," she said.

Of course she did. Good German *Hausfrauen* don't leave dirt around anywhere, not in the darkest corner.

"The information came in a cable from Washington to Captain Atkins in response to a query he sent there about you. A normal checkup. The answer was in praise of you. But he wasn't the one who told Werner. I did."

Guilt was an indulgence, like eating strudel. And the very last of the pastry had to be licked from the fingers. What was it Hans Frank had said at the Nuremberg trials? "A thousand years shall pass and this guilt of Germany will not have been erased." Only this wasn't even that kind of guilt. This was an earlier guilt, older than the Nazis. Only time was as old.

"All right," he said, because he didn't know anything else to say.

"I didn't want you to go away thinking it was Captain Atkins who was responsible," she said.

"Thank you." Was that the right reply? Had he ever entered this woman's body? Had she ever cried out to him in her bright, open, free, unhindered, limitless sensuality? Had he

326

ever held her so tightly she wept in pleasure as he spent himself in her?

And had he ever felt what he had felt with her? Had he felt it then, or ever?

"One more thing, Peter," she said, resting her elbow in her other hand, holding the cigarette to her lips, her face raised, her wide mouth and her full lips still turned to him. "I never wanted anything like that to happen to you. I suppose I wanted something to happen to you else I wouldn't have gone to Werner."

She was being forthright and he knew that that nurtured her.

"But nothing like that, Peter. And I never knew what happened. Werner never would say."

He nodded, not believing, and what did that matter? Had they ever slept together, exhausted, smelling the sweet, warm sweat of their labors?

She stood up and put a hand on his shoulder to keep him from rising. She might have been knighting him.

"I had to tell you," she said. Having got rid of it she now was full of strength. It blazed out of her. She could have led an army.

"Yes," he said. He could see the shield and the spear.

"I shan't see you again."

"No." They seemed to tell him that as though it were a diploma they had won.

"*Auf Wiedersehen*, Peter."

"*Auf Wiedersehen*, Marliese."

She put out the stub of the cigarette in the little metal container on the end of the bench. She smiled politely. She seemed to have nothing more to say and yet she did not leave.

How could there be nothing, he asked himself. He knew that it had not been that much, but how could it be nothing?

"One thing more, Peter."

"Yes." And what was that one thing more? He looked up at her. She loomed over him like a statue.

"I've broken off with Roy Atkins. I've quit my job at the base."

327

"Should that be of interest to me?"

"No, of course not. But it means something. I haven't worked it out yet but it means something."

She bit her lip and she seemed a little bewildered and he wanted to do something but he didn't know what to do.

"It was not that easy," she said. She appeared even more bewildered but now she did not need help. "And I've missed him. My God, I've missed him. But I've done it and perhaps it means something."

She strode across the courtyard to the doors leading to the street, her leather bag swinging from her shoulder, and he watched the splendid figure go, and the beautiful, beautiful legs in their leather boots and he tried to remember that he had made love to her and again he could not.

He sat on the bench for a little while longer in the gentle, lingering sun of the afternoon and he let the peace rest on his face and his hands and he thought about Father Stolz and Sister Angelica and he wondered if they were enjoying the late sun where they were and then he got up and with the policeman trooping silently behind him he went back to his room.

He felt very tired now and sad, and he knew that had to do with her, and he fell asleep and he woke to the sound of the door being opened and he sat up and knew he was still asleep, that this was another kind of dream. He saw something being dragged into the room by a donkey and a bear and he saw the door being shut and when he opened his mouth in this dream to make some kind of sound, the bear clapped a paw over his face and pressed something hard against his side and then something was pulled over his head but it had eyeholes and he could see through it and then something was pulled up over his legs and tightened and the muzzle of the gun was pushed into his side again and he was lifted out of the bed and hustled out of the room. As he left he looked down and he saw the policeman on the floor, a trickle of blood from a gash in his head spreading out and soaking into the green carpet.

36

✠ ✠ ✠

IN THE HOSPITAL CORRIDOR THE WALKING BEAR BEGAN TO CAPER, kicking out his feet in a kind of clumsy dance and a sister bearing a tray came round the corner and saw the three of them. The donkey brayed and she began to laugh and Bauer opened his mouth behind whatever it was that had been pulled over his head and he felt the pressure in his side again and he said nothing.

He was in the middle. He could see the bear shuffling his feet and he could see the donkey holding his tail in his hand and waving the bushy end of it. Everyone who saw the three of them burst into laughter.

They turned a corner. A man and a little boy were coming down the hallway. The bear growled menacingly and the little boy cried out and grabbed the man's hand. The bear patted the little boy on the head and told him not to be afraid of bears, that bears loved little children and all they ever ate was honey. The donkey brayed to show he agreed and he tickled the little boy's face with the end of his tail.

The man laughed and the little boy laughed and then Bauer felt himself being moved along down the corridor again and now the bear was doing his little dance again and was singing a Franconian folk song in a funny way so that two nurses coming down the hall started to giggle.

"Do something funny," the bear said to Bauer.

It seemed to Bauer to be a youngish voice and an educated voice and at that moment a very exhilarated voice. He looked around for some way to escape, for someone to help him, and he felt the hard gun point in his side again.

"Do something funny," the bear said again.

The donkey said, "Hee haw!"

They came to a glass door that divided the hallway and in the reflection from the glass Bauer saw that between the walking bear and the walking donkey there was a clown with a pointed hat, a white clown's suit with black buttons, and a mask with a sad, broad clown's grin and on the cheeks of the mask were two red spots and under each of the eyes a long, painted teardrop.

"Do something funny," the bear said for the third time in his happy, spirited voice.

He waved his arms and a nurse at a desk smiled.

"Say something," the bear said.

"Hee haw," the donkey said.

"How are you?" Bauer asked the nurse and he did not know his own voice but it must have been a funny voice because the nurse shrieked with laughter.

Now he felt the bear's arm and the donkey's arm slip under his arms and the bear and the donkey began a skip and a jump and at first he was dragged along the corridor and then he felt the pressure again and he began to skip and jump with them so the three of them hopped down the hall and everyone who saw them, nurses, doctors, visitors, patients, all burst into laughter at the funny sight.

He wondered why nobody seemed surprised, why everybody considered the sight of a bear and a donkey and a clown ordinary, and then he remembered the music he had heard earlier in the courtyard, the trumpets and the drums, and at the same time he remembered the last time he had seen the carnival from the balcony overlooking Barbarossaplatz and

Marta putting a pillow under his arms so the iron railing wouldn't cut into him and holding him so he wouldn't fall over.

They reached the entrance to the hospital and a lady coming in held the door open for them and as had all the others started to laugh at the sight of the bear and the donkey and the clown, and the bear gave a happy grunt and rubbed his nose on the lady's cheek and the donkey brayed and then the three of them went out into the street.

They walked up the block making everybody laugh, and Bauer heard the sounds again, louder now, and the other sounds with them, fifes and the tinkling of bells and people laughing and clapping hands, and he thought how cleverly it had been planned, and he thought how naïve they all had been to have believed that with Werner Hausmann behind bars that was the end of it, that his young followers who were not behind bars would do nothing, would accept the defeat and incarceration of their leader with no protest, that Bauer, brought back to health, would be permitted to leave the city unmolested.

The bear and the donkey joined voices in another Franconian folk song he had not heard since he was a child and he felt an elbow jab into him and he joined in the song about the little boy who fell asleep in a meadow and woke up to find himself changed into a goat and the song was very funny coming from a walking bear and a walking donkey to say nothing of the clown, and the three of them waved their arms and sang and hopped and skipped their way down the street.

At the corner they turned into Juliuspromenade and now Bauer saw, and remembered, they were in the direct route of the parade. The sidewalks on both sides were packed with people, waving flags and pennants, shouting, cheering, lifting up small children to see, the ecstatic youngsters gripping the ends of the long strings of huge balloons in all colors. The music and the noise were deafening.

The sun, almost gone now, glinted on the shining armor of knights carrying banners bearing the Maltese cross and the insignes of Franconia and Bavaria; on crusaders, long, double-handled broadswords dangling at their sides, the iron hooves of their giant caparisoned horses clattering on pavement, making sparks, echoing off the sides of the buildings. There were medieval soldiers in reds and yellows with long, streaming lances, and there were monks and priests and abbots and jesters and there were men pounding drums and men blowing trumpets and men playing on flutes and fifes. There were clowns and lions and tigers and a long serpent and there were walking trees with branches that flapped. And among the marching and riding men there were great floats with lovely ladies from the Middle Ages in long, pointed hats and veils, and floats with angels and fairies waving wands.

Then the bear and the clown and the donkey were in the parade themselves and for a little while the line they found themselves in joined hands and moved one way and another on the thoroughfare. Bauer's hands were held very tightly by the donkey and the bear.

He saw a mounted policeman stationed at a corner, surveying the parade and the joyous people. He cried out to the policeman for help. He believed he cried out. He opened his mouth and cried out. But he heard nothing. He heard nothing from himself, nothing except the singing and the shouting and the drums and the trumpets and the fifes and the flutes. The policeman did not hear him either. He leaned on the pommel of his saddle and gazed benignly at the festivities.

Bauer cried out again and tried to pull away. He was gripped harder. His voice, whatever sound he made, was drowned, blotted, absorbed.

The bear saw the policeman. He put his mouth to Bauer's ear. "Don't be a fool, Bauer. He'll never hear you."

The donkey put his mouth to Bauer's other ear. "And don't try to make a run for it. This would be the most perfect place in the world to kill you."

"Sing," the bear said.

"Sing," the donkey said.

"Be thankful for your disguise, Bauer," the bear said. "If the people here knew who you were they would tear you apart."

They now were passing across Barbarossaplatz and by looking up Bauer could see the balcony, the duplicate of the balcony, from which he had looked down, Marta holding on to his belt, and that balcony was filled with people now, including a small boy, and all the other balconies were filled as they always were during the carnival parade.

"Sing," the bear said as they started up Theaterstrasse.

"Sing," the donkey said.

Bauer felt the pressure again and he realized his hands were free and he knocked the gun away with his elbow and at the same time drove his foot down hard on the bear's shin and he stopped dead so that the bear and the donkey went on ahead of him, the bear hopping in pain and the children shrieking at the bear dancing in that funny way and Bauer ducked and stood still so that the line behind what had been his line passed by him and now he was separated from the bear and the donkey and he let another line pass so that now there were two lines between them and he started to edge toward one side to get out of the parade.

He found himself seized on either side by a marching shield-bearer and a knight on foot and he saw the entire line was linked arm in arm, moving right and then left, and he tried to call out and he tried to pull away and the shield-bearer and the knight laughed at his good fun and his boisterous participation in the carnival and then they started to sing a rousing marching song and he felt himself getting weak.

He looked for the donkey and the bear but he could not see them. He tried to free himself but the knight and the shield-bearer laughed and held him more tightly. He felt himself getting weaker and then for no reason the shield-bearer released him and he managed to get his hand away from the knight and he dropped back another line in the parade and was welcomed by a jester and a bearded monk.

He tried again to make his way laterally between the lines, to get to the curb, and another line passed by him and his legs were almost gone now and as he stumbled to the side he heard children screaming at the antics of the comical clown and his legs went altogether and he fell against a float.

He felt hands grab him and pull him up to the float. He sat on the edge, resting on his hands, his legs dangling. He tried to catch his breath. He had to collect himself. He was on exhibition there for the donkey and the bear to see. He had to drop off the float and get away.

Now it was getting dark and some of the marchers lit torches and flambeaux and he was suddenly surrounded by lights and he saw that half a dozen torches on the float had been lit and he felt he was at the footlights of a stage, exposed on all sides.

He needed just a little time. His breathing was coming easier now. He needed a little time and a little more strength. He needed wind and a little strength and then he would be able to slip off the float and get away.

He waved his arms now and again as a good clown should and he listened to the drumbeats and the music and the laughter and he looked around in the darkening twilight and he could not see the bear and the donkey. He thanked God for that and he willed himself to stillness in the blare and the tramping of feet and the creaking of wheels and the clacking of the horses' hooves and finally he felt himself strong enough and he dropped off the edge of the float not forgetting, for his audience, to wave his hands and bob his head.

Ahead of him he saw what he thought was another mounted policeman, although he could not be sure in the uncertain light and the flickering candles and the yellow torches. He guided himself sideways as the float passed him by and he saw that he was only a few feet now from the sidewalk and his legs were holding up well and his arms were seized again.

"Did you have a nice ride on the float?" the bear asked.

37

✠ ✠ ✠

THE AUTOMOBILE WAS PARKED IN THE AREA IN FRONT OF THE
Residenz and Bauer was shoved into it. They had passed the
mounted policeman and it was a mounted policeman and
Bauer had tried to attract his attention but the bear and the
donkey waved their arms too and made sounds and the policeman had laughed in his good nature.

Now Bauer was jammed against one side of the rear seat
of the car and the bear got in next to him and the donkey got
behind the wheel. They drove away from the parade and the
people and the noise and after that it was very quiet. There
was only the sound of the tires, on cobbles, on pavement, and
then on a road leading out of the city.

"Haven't you all had enough?" Bauer asked.

Neither the bear nor the donkey answered.

"How many more of you want to land in jail?" Bauer asked,
knowing what a feeble question that was.

The bear took out a pack of cigarettes and lit one. It was
funny, Bauer thought. It was funny even then to see a bear
smoking. It was very funny and he wanted to laugh and he
wished he could. Bears are always so worried about smokers

335

starting forest fires, he wanted to say. There was a whole American folklore about that, he wanted to say.

They were on the outskirts of the city now and the night was full on them and the headlights of the car now were picking up only scattered buildings.

"For God's sake," Bauer said. "Haven't you done enough?"

They rode on in silence and now Bauer felt no fear, he was beyond fear; an apathy had taken over. He was tired and he was weak and he was in Germany.

There was only one question. How were they going to do it this time? And this time they would see to it that they did it properly.

He saw a collection of cars and then the outlines of the ruined church.

"Again?" Bauer asked. And that too was funny in a way and he wished again he could think of it as being funny.

The donkey turned from the wheel. "It was the way he intended it," he said reasonably. "You know that. It's what he wanted."

The bear spoke, also for the first time in the car. "And it has to be exactly as he intended it to be. You can understand that as well."

"And don't you think anybody will be able to figure it out afterward?" Bauer asked. "Don't you think about that?"

The donkey was paying attention to his driving again but the bear shrugged. "It could be anybody. They won't be able to prove anything. There are more than just a few of us and they won't be able to prove anything and they won't want to prove anything. It was bad enough, what went on in the court, and they won't want any more of that."

"But the important thing is that this is what he wanted," the donkey said, his eyes on the road. "This is the way it has to be."

The donkey pulled the car up to the curb. The bear started to open the door but the donkey put up his hand in warning and at the same time leaned toward the windshield. The bear leaned forward too to see what the donkey was seeing and

336

Bauer tried to make out what it was that had alarmed the donkey.

All he could see were automobiles, some large and some small, and behind them the jagged wreckage of the church. He felt the gun in his side again.

"What is it?" the bear asked.

"Wait here," the donkey said.

He snapped off the lights of the car and now the street was illuminated only by its own pale lights and he got out of the front of the car and moved forward cautiously. Bauer and the bear strained to see what he had seen and they saw him stop at a little clump of trees with low branches and under the branches almost hidden was an automobile.

The donkey, Bauer thought, had crazy eyes all right. He would never have seen that car.

He watched as the donkey moved slowly up to the car and then walked around it and then he opened the door and put his head inside.

The bear leaned forward farther over the front seat and turned his head away from Bauer to watch the donkey and Bauer felt the insistency of the gun relax and he saw it was his chance, the only chance he would get, and if he failed at least it would happen quick and he prayed that he could summon enough strength and he moved slightly to one side and drove his elbow with every ounce of power he had into the bear's belly and he heard the bear gasp and saw him double over and he held his two hands together, fingers entwined, and brought them down as a cudgel on the back of the bear's head. He heard the bear gasp again. He grabbed the bear by the ears and bashed his head down on the wooden frame around the front seat and he pulled his head up and slammed it down again. He let go and the bear slid down to the floor and the bear's snout made a gurgling sound.

Bauer felt around until he found the small automatic and then he looked through the windshield. The donkey's head was emerging from the car under the trees but he appeared not yet satisfied and he walked to the front of the car again.

The bear groaned and Bauer reversed the gun and hit the bear on the head and when the bear groaned again and thrashed out with an arm Bauer hit him again and the bear made another choking sound and was silent.

Bauer looked through the windshield again. He could not see the donkey. He opened the door and got out of the car. He pushed the door almost shut. He did not want the donkey to hear the sound of a door slamming nor did he want him to see an open door.

He backed away from the car. He found himself on the edge of a pine thicket. He turned and ran into it. Once under cover he moved more slowly. He had to parcel out his strength thriftily. The gun felt very good in his hand. He had never used a gun except in training during the war but it felt very good.

In the silence there was only the muffled, cottony sounds of his footfalls on the soft earth, on the pine needles. He stepped into a small hole. He pitched forward. He would have fallen on his face. He managed to break the fall by thrusting his hand against the trunk of a nearby tree.

He remained there, his foot in the hole, supporting himself against the tree, and he breathed hard as though he had been running and for a long time. He felt the first new wave of weakness on him and he knew the false vigor the little piece of steel in his free hand was giving him was running out.

Then he heard a shout and he knew the donkey had discovered he had escaped and then he heard other voices. He thought he heard a car. He thought he could see through the branches of the grove the lights of a car, broken by the tree trunks as though by unevenly spaced posts of a fence.

He wondered whether he should turn to where he had seen the lights, to the road. He might be able to get a lift. But who would stop in the night and give him a lift. And how would he know if a car did stop that is was a passing motorist and not one of them?

It was better to stay in the shelter of the trees. He would keep going until he could go no longer and then he would stop and sit down and wait until daylight and ask God that they would not find him.

He stepped out of the hole and rested against the tree for another short moment and then he moved on, slowly, husbanding himself, and presently he heard the sounds of voices behind him and the sounds of feet, many feet, tramping in the pine copse.

He tried to move faster but he was draining. He felt his way from tree to tree with his left hand. His right hand held on to the gun. He must not lose the gun.

The sounds of the voices grew closer and he believed he heard his name being called. He pushed himself harder, using each tree to help him on. He felt sweat pouring down his body and his breath came harder and he felt a pain in his chest and he knew he was emptying fast and there wasn't very much more left.

He pushed on, his breath whistling, his lungs burning, and he clawed the trees and held the gun, his talisman, and he stumbled into a tree and he twisted and slid slowly down and he felt the rough bark on his back and then he was on the ground, trying to find air, tasting bile. He could hear the voices and the footsteps getting close.

He had a small choice. He had a small, terminal choice. He could shoot himself now or he could wait and fire a few bullets into them before he fired a bullet into himself.

He wondered if he could do either.

He heard the donkey call out his name again, he was positive it was the donkey, and he thought perhaps he could shoot him. He might be able to manage that because of what the donkey had done to him and because the donkey was a German donkey and had been brought up to believe Jews died like sheep and had absolutely no talent for killing.

He pushed himself up higher against the tree trunk to improve his position and he heard the feet coming nearer and he held the gun out and put his finger on the trigger and held his right wrist with his other hand.

He prayed that the donkey would come through first, that

339

he would see the donkey first, the bear wasn't going to be able to be around just then, and he wanted the donkey now, and he held the automatic straight out and he asked that he have enough strength, he felt he was draining dry, he asked that he last long enough and that the donkey come first, and then a light blinded him so suddenly he almost fell over and he heard a voice he knew very well say, "Put down that silly gun, Bauer, you might hurt someone."

He knew the voice but he also knew that could not be, it was part of being drained dry, the weakness, the fantasies taking over again. His mind was going, he knew that, and he didn't trust it, he didn't trust anything and he kept the gun up. Then the light left him and swung around to light up the face of the bearer and he saw Eckardt, it was no mistake, it had been his voice, and he opened his hand and the gun fell to the earth.

The light was on him again and he tried to get to his feet. He heard someone rushing through the brush and a light was turned on her. She stopped and stared at him as he got himself up and she started to laugh. She looked at the clown in front of the tree and she laughed. She put her knuckle into her mouth and she slipped down to her knees, laughing, laughing, her face covered with tears.

38

✠ ✠ ✠

THE HAUPTBAHNHOF IN FRANKFURT IS A MAJOR GERMAN RAIL-
road terminus and it is always very crowded and there are
several restaurants under the one roof, including three, scattered among the bookstalls and other shops on the main
level, which sell many different kinds of sausages and several
varieties of beer.

They however were in one of the better eating places, one
that had a bar that sold more than beer, and a bartender
who was not daunted by requests for dry martinis.

She chuckled suddenly with no provocation. It seemed
she had done that quite often since that night.

"Stop that," Bauer said, feeling himself about to laugh
and considering that was no way to make solemn farewell to
Germany.

"But you were so funny," she said. "A clown in the middle
of a forest. I never saw a clown in a forest before."

"No, very few of us have," Eckardt said. "And we
wouldn't have seen this clown. That could not have been
easy for you, Frau Neubert."

The laughter fled from her. "I would have done it any-

341

way." The laugher was gone now, from her eyes, from every-where. She drank a little of her martini. "As soon as they telephoned and told me about it, I would have told you, Herr Eckardt."

"Yes, I'm certain you would."

"But when they asked me to be there, to sit where my brother had sat, to watch as he would have watched, and then to tell him." She shuddered. "They're crazy. They're just crazy." She paused. "And Werner, he must be crazy too. Why is there always that kind of craziness in Germany?"

"It's not only Germany, Liesl," Bauer said.

Eckardt, making his little light go on and off like a blinker, looked at him curiously.

"And they wouldn't even have told me," she said. "If they hadn't known I was the one who had told Werner about Peter the first time, they wouldn't have told me."

"It won't be too pleasant for you there now," Bauer said.

"I'm going to go away. I've wanted to go away for a long time and now I have the reasons."

"Where will you go?" Bauer asked.

She shrugged. "I don't know. Somewhere."

Eckardt looked at his watch. "Drink up, Bauer. I don't under any circumstance want you to miss your train. No, the drinks are on me."

Bauer picked up his valise and they left the restaurant and went down to the main level. The sign was posted for the Paris train. They walked toward the gate, past men and women eating frankfurters and drinking beer at stands outside the restaurants.

When they reached the gate, Eckardt said, "I'll wait for you here, Frau Neubert."

Bauer shook his hand. "Thank you again."

"A man in plainclothes will be with you on the train. You will not know him."

"I'm damned sick and tired of having to thank you," Bauer said.

"Thank me by staying out of Germany, at least Würzburg."

"Perhaps not," Bauer said.

"No," Eckardt said. "Perhaps not."

Marliese walked with him down the platform until he reached his car. "You must win back the money you owe your wife from that stupid card game," she said. "A man should never be in debt to a woman."

"When did you decide that?"

"I have believed it always. It is undignified for a man."

"I am in your debt."

"That's different."

"Why?"

"I've never been to Paris. How long will you be in Paris?"

"I don't know. Why is it different?"

"It was my duty. I brought about what happened to you the first time."

So she thought it was only because of the air raid. She didn't know anything about her father.

The conductor blew his whistle. Bauer took her hand.

"Call me when you get to Paris," she said. "Could you do that?"

"Yes."

"Let me know what it's like in Paris. Tell me whether I would like Paris."

She looked lost. He didn't know why he thought that but she looked lost.

"I will," he said.

She looked at him and he knew that if he asked her to go with him she would step into the train and then his life would take a new turning. He got onto the train. He walked into the car and looked out the window. She raised her hand.

The train moved out of the station in the way good European trains start, unsuddenly, unnervously, with no jerking, and he watched her standing on the station, her hand raised, not waving, just raised.

343

She looked marvelous and he knew that when he got to Paris he probably would call her. And why should he not?

He looked out the window again. She was still standing on the platform. She was still holding up her hand. Or was she holding it out?